RADIANT
SHIMMERING
LIGHT

RADIANT
SHIMMERING
LIGHT

Sarah Selecky

HARPER
AVENUE

Radiant Shimmering Light

Published by Harper Avenue, an imprint of
HarperCollins Publishers Ltd

First edition

HarperCollins books may be purchased for educational,
business, or sales promotional use through our
Special Markets Department.

HarperCollins Publishers Ltd
Bay Adelaide Centre, East Tower
22 Adelaide Street West, 41st Floor
Toronto, Ontario, Canada
M5H 4E3

www.harpercollins.ca

Cover and interior design by Lola Landekic

Library and Archives Canada Cataloguing in Publication
information is available upon request.

ISBN 978-1-44345-567-1

Printed and bound in the United States
LSC/H 9 8 7 6 5 4 3 2 1

RADIANT
SHIMMERING
LIGHT

For Molly Blyth

*Out beyond ideas of wrongdoing and rightdoing, there
is a field. I'll meet you there.*
—Rumi

*Being good in business is the most fascinating
kind of art.*
—Andy Warhol

January 2016

My dearest Lilian,

Hello, gorgeous. I'm writing you from Venice, California.

I love the weird, brave, you-can-do-anything energy of
Los Angeles.

This morning, I found white feathers and rhinestones scattered
on the sidewalk as I walked to the beach.

I met a wise seagull at the shore. We danced in the surf
together as a silver balloon, untethered, floated away in the
sky above me.

Gratitude and respect to the incredible women who attended
the spectacular Express Your Enlightenment (EYELos Angeles)
last night. It was an honor to meet them, and to witness their
transformation begin.

The EYE tour is a gathering of souls. Like-minded women who
are quenching their thirst for life and love. Women just like you,
who know deep in their hearts that they're meant to live a life
they love, doing something beautiful and real. Women who
understand that they are meant to help the world transform as
they evolve into their highest, most inspired selves.

I'm sending you this special note because I know you live in the
Ontario area. It's not too late for you to get tickets to Express
Your Enlightenment Toronto, Lilian! I'm only coming to your city
for one night: Saturday, January 9th.

As you know, early enrollment for the Ascendency Program is open.
But you don't need to be an Ascendant to come to any of my EYE
events! These are open to all women. And we have a few spots left.
But just a few. You still have time to decide, but don't take too long.

Lilian, are we holding your seat? I want to see you there.

This Saturday night could be the turning point you've been waiting for.

Express Your Enlightenment events happen every year in different cities around the world. I don't know the next time I'll be in Toronto. This is your chance. You don't want to miss it.

Click here to register now.

Love,
Eleven

I AM TEMPTED to check Instagram, but it's still early morning. I haven't even had a cup of tea yet. Morning is sacred creative time. As an artist, I must fight the urge to look at what other people are making before I make something myself. *Create before you consume.* How will I use my creativity this morning?

I put the kettle on for tea. My phone makes a tinkling sound.

Define yourself. Declare your intention.
#depthcharge

I open a coconut, apricot, and chia granola bar. It's small and sticky, and I eat it in two bites. It's delicious. Why did I eat that sugary thing for breakfast? Organic cane sugar is the second ingredient. I should have made myself a slice of gluten-free toast with tahini. Now I have chia seeds stuck in my teeth.

My newsletter is scheduled for 11:45, just in time for people's lunch breaks. I let my client list know that I have new blank cards ready in my Etsy shop. It's a dachshund set, four watercolour portraits of Millie, a dog with a blue aura and a goofy smile. I usually get a couple of orders when I send out a newsletter.

This apartment is a sublet. I have it until the summer, when the tenant returns from Thailand. Then I have to find a new place. Even as a sublet, the rent here is steep, and every little bit from my Etsy shop helps. I'm not sure where I'll live this summer, but I'm trying not to worry. Things have a way of coming exactly when we need them. It just takes faith and trust.

My kettle whistles. I open a brand-new box of ginger green tea and select one of the individually wrapped tea packets. I tear the top, but the paper of the tea bag is caught in the seal of the packet. I manage to rip the tea bag itself, and scatter tea leaves all over the floor. What's the matter with me?

I stop and breathe. I have a problem with negative self-talk.

Joy does not exist without gratitude.

The wind blows outside, but the plastic sheeting on the living room window stays tight. The ice has formed feathery patterns on the window. I am grateful for the pretty ice, but I haven't been able to see outside since December. It's been a cold winter. My fingers are cracking, and I have red, sore, chapped lips from the dehydration.

I pick another packet from the box. When I open this one, the string is long and knotted, with three tags stapled to it. The bag itself is empty. I pause to text Juliette.

> **Me**
> **Going to meet
> Nana Boondahl and Sophia now!**

> **Juliette**
> **Ooh good have fun**

> **Me**
> **Thank you SO MUCH!!**

What will I say when I meet Nana Boondahl in person? I open a third packet of tea. This one looks normal, so I put it in my white-and-silver Live What You Love mug. I douse the bag with cold water first, to protect the flavonoids of the green tea leaves, and then pour over the hot water.

> **Juliette**
> **You're welcome**

> **Me**
> **Things have a way of
> coming exactly when we need them!**

Out of curiosity, I carefully open another packet from the box. This one contains a completely unsealed tea bag, with no string or staple. Half the loose tea is out of the bag, and this spills onto the counter when I open the packet. Why is this happening? What does it mean? There's a new moon tonight. Maybe it's in a weird planet? I look it up on my Astrofy app. Capricorn? That makes no sense at all. I check

www.ismercuryinretrograde.com and the answer is yes. It doesn't go
direct until January 25. Oh, great.

I place the latest staple-free, string-free tea bag on the counter on
top of the spilled leaves. I arrange the knotted stringy one next to it,
looping the strings and tags into an S-shape. I raise my phone over the
arrangement and take a pic.

@LilianQuick> What the?! Help me, @EssenceTea!
#teafail #mercuryinretrograde

I pull on leggings and a long grey sweater that covers my butt
and thighs. It's comfy and warm. I hope it doesn't look sloppy. I stop
myself. *Live the way you love to feel.* I want to feel comfortable in my
own skin. I feel warm. I feel warm and comfortable as myself today.
One of the best things about turning forty? I don't care what other
people think. Finally, I can just be myself.

Juliette
xo

Me
I need new clothes!
Me
can you go shopping with me next week?!

Nana Boondahl is Canada's second most famous writer, after
Margaret Atwood. Her poems are on every high school and college
curriculum in the country. She's also the creator of Luze. This is
why I love her so much: she's a successful artist, and she's a successful businesswoman. She's actually one of the only women bil-
lionaires in the world who earned her fortune without a husband
or an inheritance.

Luze is a skin-correcting balm that blends with every skin tone,
reduces pore size, and smooths uneven colouration. It's still an iconic
beauty item after twenty years on the market. Every woman keeps a
tube of Luze in her cosmetic case, guaranteed.

But truly, Nana Boondahl is a poet. I keep her most recent collection, *Trees, Where the Rain Left Off,* on my bedside table. Her work is so poignant and lyrical. "Your Nature" is the poem I'm always quoting, though. It's an old one, a classic. Everyone reads it in high school English class. I've almost memorized it.

Taste the V-shape of your life, it starts.

I love it. I mean, I don't know what she means by the V-shape, but I also *know* it, deep down inside myself. There's something in my gut that just *responds* when I read that. I know it intensely, in a way that can't be put into language. She uses such simple words to make that feeling happen—I mean, V-shape? What is that? Nana Boondahl has a rare and brilliant mind. She's a national treasure. She must be in her seventies by now, but you can't really tell how old she is by looking at her. Her skin is flawless and unwrinkled.

Nana Boondahl has commissioned me to paint a portrait of her greyhound.

Juliette made the connection for me. Juliette knows everyone. Her site, purejuliette.com, is one of the top lifestyle design blogs in the world. She just designed an exclusive line of dishware for the Hudson's Bay Company. Juliette showed Nana Boondahl my website and some of my pet aura portraits, and apparently, she was impressed by what she saw. I'll never forget the day my phone rang and the voice on the other line said, "Hello, this is Nana Boondahl." That's all she said, at first. Like she wanted to wait a beat to give her name time to land and settle in my ears. Who makes phone calls anymore without texting first?

Me

Thank you *again* so much
for connecting us! I am full of great fight!

Me

great fight

Me

I mean great fight

Me

omg autocorrect

Me

GRATITUDE

Me

ok wish me luck I'm
almost out the door!

Live the way you love to feel. I switch my phone camera to selfie mode and snap a picture. My forehead looks extra big. I delete the pic right away. I just wanted to see.

Me

Hi Yumi. Just confirming
that I'll be at the studio at 9. Thanks!

Yumi

🖤

I forgot to charge my phone last night, and now it only has 30 percent juice left. I plug it in to get some last-minute charge before I go. I pack a sixteen-by-twenty sketchbook and my tin of drawing pencils. I open the tin to see if my pencil sharpener is in there. It is not.

I usually work from home, but my sublet is far too small to have Nana Boondahl meet me here—it would look unprofessional. Yumi lets me use their studio when I have appointments, for a small rental fee. I can't afford to rent a studio of my own, obviously. I can hardly afford my sublet. So I have gratitude for this arrangement. Yumi's a night owl and usually sews past midnight, but the studio is empty in the morning.

I find my pencil sharpener in my desk drawer, along with a soft eraser I know I'll need. My phone blurts.

@EssenceTea> Oh no @LilianQuick! Our apologies.
We're sending you a complimentary tea sampler. DM us
for details.

This is why I love Twitter!

I pull on my Sorels, my heavy parka, and my red plaid earflap hat. I wrap an oversized buffalo plaid scarf around my neck three times. I am hoping for a *Twin Peaks* look: retro and lumberjane at the same time. I'm overheating. I feel dizzy, choked by my scarf. My stomach turns. I need fresh air. But as soon as I go outside, the cold air is going to hurt my face. I slather cocoa butter on my lips and hands to protect them, slip on fleece mittens, and brace myself. I hate winter. No! Replace that thought with something positive: I'm going to meet Nana Boondahl and her dog. On my way out, I take off a mitten and try a selfie again. My clothes look cute and hygge, but my face looks lopsided and I have bags under my eyes. I delete the pic.

The street outside is frozen and still, the light lemony white. It's so cold, it feels as though the air has had the wind knocked out of it. It's hard to breathe. My phone buzzes in my mitten.

> **Fleurje**
> Agh! Crap. Crazy day Lilian. So sorry I
> 4got our phone date yesterday. Can u try
> me tonight or tomorrow early aft?

> **Fleurje**
> It's been crazy busy. Weekdays are still flex – or
> there's next Monday. Would love 2 see u

> **Fleurje**
> ps sorry my messages r so long! I'm on
> my iPad and the screen is bigger

> **Me**
> It's ok! Yes try me tonight!

> **Me**
> no wait I forgot it's Eleven tonight! Can you come?

> **Fleurje**
> Maybe! What's at 11?

Me
Eleven Novak

Fleurje
is she self-help?

Me
no! feminine leadership
Me
www.elevennovak.com

Fleurje
(...)

Me
lmk if you can come

Fleurje
(...)

Yumi stands at the door to the studio, their face red and cold. A delicate light-brown stubble sparkles over their cheeks in the morning light. How do they have such perfect, poreless skin, when they stay up so late every night, drinking nothing but alcohol and caffeine? It must be good genes. Or maybe Luze. Though I doubt it, because they are such a natural beauty they don't have to wear any makeup. Today they wear a black motorcycle jacket zipped all the way to the neck, with a grey cashmere scarf stuffed in. They clutch a paper cup of coffee from Rupert's Roastery. I don't drink coffee—it raises the body's pH, and I try to keep mine neutral. The steam swirls up and out of the cup in a gorgeous twist. There's nothing like the look of a hot cup of coffee on a cold day.

"Nana Boondahl is coming today with her greyhound," I say. "Wish me luck. I'm a nervous wreck."

"You don't need luck," they say. "You're a genius."

I let out an awkward laugh. Yumi says these things to me, and I never know how to respond. "Where are you coming from?"

"Long night," they say. "There was a thing in the Distillery, and then I worked here all night. I'm going home to sleep now."

"What's the dog's name?" Yumi asks.

"Sophia," I say.

"I love greyhounds," they say. "So calm."

Yumi isn't wearing any gloves, and their fingers look white. It's so cold, it hurts my eyes to see the exposed skin. Yumi is a study in contrasts: that soft cashmere scarf wrapped around their neck, those tough bare hands gripping the paper cup.

"Your poor hands!" I say. I take the key. "Why don't you make yourself a pair of mittens?"

"It was a sake tasting event last night," Yumi says. Their breath is a white puff. They have such a nice mouth shape, with a defined cupid's bow on their top lip. Even with lip liner, I couldn't make that happen to my mouth. "I think I love sake. Does that make me a cliché?"

"Sake is objectively delicious," I say. "I think you're safe."

They hand me a brown paper shopping bag. "This is for you."

I open the handles with my mittened hands and peer in. Pale-blue cashmere.

"I found it in the pile, and it's perfect as is. It would be a shame to cut it. I thought the blue would look nice with your eyes."

I met Yumi at one of Fleurje's real estate client-appreciation events. It took me some time to get used to the pronoun—the stubborn habit of language. But Yumi was patient with me whenever I messed up. I am grateful to them for showing me that reality is not what I think. Everything is not black and white. Yumi simply being Yumi is a gift, and it doesn't have to be gender-specific. I'm always inspired when I see them. They're truly living Eleven Novak's Sacred Ascendency Prayer: *Let yourself want what you want.* I wish I was more like them.

We're so different from each other. For instance, they work best at night, I work best in the morning. They drink coffee and alcohol, and I avoid all acidifying food and drink. I hate the cold, and they complain about the heat in summer. There I go, trying to make my reality binary again! I always want things to be one way or the other. I have to keep working on this.

What would Yumi think about the Ascendency Prayer? Should I invite them to come with me to see Eleven tonight? Probably not, because it's about feminine empowerment. This makes me sad: Yumi is excluded from men's groups and women's groups. I almost ask them how they feel about this, but when I look into their eyes, my words waver, and I have to look away. Why do I feel so flustered around them? I thank them for the gift, push the key into the lock, and open the door.

"You'll need the space heater today," they say before they leave. "Last night was freezing, and it isn't much better this morning. Stay warm." Yumi is so nice to me!

It's cold inside the studio. Piles of merino and cashmere slouch around the floor, organized roughly by colour. Yumi is a talented picker—they go to warehouses every week to buy used sweaters by the pound, and Yumi has a knack for finding gems. Then they come back to their studio and sort these used sweaters into piles according to usability. They cut and discard any stained, pilled, or moth-eaten parts. Then they re-sort according to colour. Yumi designs new sweaters with these old materials, and measures, cuts, and serges together the old knits into new pieces. Since they were featured on the Arts and Makers Network, Yumi and their designs are famous now. Every sweater is one of a kind, and runs from three hundred to nine hundred dollars, depending on the design and the quality of the used wool. I could never afford to buy one of Yumi's pieces. One sweater basically equals a month of my rent.

I pull my mittens off, check my phone battery (22 percent), and hang my parka on the coat rack by the door. I move Yumi's serger, a block of plastic and chrome threaded with four tall spools of black thread, to make space on the wooden table for my sketchbook. The piles of wool will just have to stay where they are for now. Maybe they'll insulate the place against the draft.

My upholstered dog-model cushion is right where I left it on the floor, with three throw pillows. I plump up the pillows and arrange them in an inviting triangle on top of the cushion, and set a heart-shaped peanut butter cookie in the centre, freshly baked by the Caninery.

There's a note tucked in the bag, written in sepia ink in Yumi's beautiful block lettering: FOR LILIAN, FROM YUMI. They drew a handful of six-pointed asterisks all around the letters.

The sweater Yumi gave me is a V-neck, and it's a pretty blue shade. It's a generous medium, so it looks like it will fit me. I arrange it nicely on top of the brown paper shopping bag to show off the V-neck and I place one sleeve carefully askew. I snap a pic. The folds create curvy shadows. I use the Clarendon filter to amp up the blue.

> @LilianQuick> @ReKnits thank you Yumi! Love my
> new cashmere!

A small black cube—the space heater—squats under the table. I move it next to the chaise lounge and plug it into a bare, scary-looking outlet that's missing a cover, and I turn it on. It whirrs with a fierce sound. I rest my hand on the radiator just to see. It's warm. The radiator looks old and is probably original to the building. It's covered in thick coats of white paint, chipped and uneven in places. I snap a pic, and try to focus and go macro to get the texture. There are years in those layers. If paint could talk!

I check my Instagram feed quickly. Seven people liked the pic of my tea bag fiasco from earlier this morning (I double-posted it on both Twitter and Instagram), and one person just liked the sweater pic. I don't recognize the handles of the likers. I take a studio selfie, angling the camera so the warehouse windows show behind me. My cheeks are red from the cold. I look bohemian and cute. I take a minute to update my profile pic. I don't want to seem narcissistic, but it's important to stay current.

I slide my phone into the drawer of the table, to keep myself away from distraction once Nana Boondahl and Sophia arrive.

It costs fifty dollars to go to Eleven's EYEToronto event. But when Nana Boondahl gives me her deposit today, I'll have enough to pay for a ticket. I hope they haven't sold out already!

◊ ◊ ◊

Eleven Novak is my cousin. Her given name is Florence, and I haven't seen her in twenty years. When I was a kid, I spent every July and August visiting her—and her parents, Aunt Rosie and Uncle Jimmy—in Evansville, Indiana. Our mothers are sisters. When I was a baby, my family lived in Indiana too. My memories of Fort Wayne are filmy, but I can remember a few things: yellow-green light coming through tree branches, a brown rug with long tufts that I liked to comb with my fingers. When I was three years old, my father became a PhD candidate in philosophy at the University of Toronto, and my parents moved us to Ontario.

We spent our summers in Evansville. Aunt Rosie and Uncle Jimmy lived in a three-storey blue-and-white house with balconies on every floor. A large pot of red geraniums stood next to the mailbox at the end of the driveway, and two flags hung from angled poles on either side of the front porch. I loved the way the bright white stars popped against the navy blue. I grew up thinking that because I was half American, I had an advantage over everyone at home.

Sometimes Aunt Rosie would drive Florence and me to the store for candy, barrettes, and Vanilla Coke. We practised our made-up dance routines on the shiny floors, leaping up and down the aisles to Cyndi Lauper. The store would be full of fourth of July paraphernalia, and I wanted to buy it all: the window banners and swags, starred toothpicks, and red-white-and-blue flip-flops. I liked to think that America was mine too, even though I was only there a couple of months out of the year. I bought stars-and-stripes stickers and brought them home. I stuck them on my school notebooks to keep the summer alive as long as I could. The flags said, You are fun, exciting, and powerful!

This was back in the eighties, obviously. Canada has Drake and Bieber now, but back then, we only had Céline Dion and Corey Hart.

Dear FIRST NAME,

Happy New Year! I know, it's been a long time since I've written.
I'm sorry! Life has been VERY busy here at Quick+Friday.
I've been working on several special commissions for the
holidays, including this portrait of Maya, an Aussie shepherd
from Colorado. And look at these two calico cats (they're
twin sisters)! I also had a great time making this note card
package—a set of four different designs, each featuring this
very cute dachshund named Millie!

Please click here to see my full gallery, finally updated with my
recent work! Whew!

The holiday rush has calmed down, so I have two or three
sittings available this month for your fur baby.

Make your appointment now! Don't miss out!

Best wishes,
Lilian

NANA BOONDAHL HAS amazing wavy white hair that's dyed a deep turquoise at the ends and fades up gradually to mint green, and eventually natural white at the roots. She wears the waves swept up and pinned to the top of her head, where they sit like swirls of cake frosting. She also wears a long, baggy, camel-coloured coat with many pockets. It's belted, which makes it look bathrobish. If you're Nana Boondahl, you can wear whatever you want.

"Welcome to my studio," I say. "I share it with the designer Yumi Senza, who is mid-process right now. Please excuse the woollens you see."

Nana Boondahl steps into the studio and makes it her own, just by standing in it. Her energy courses around her in waves. I step back to give her more space. She has a very strong presence. Her eyes go to the wooden table where I've set up my sketch pad and pencils.

"I am curious to see what colour you will use to capture the light around her," she tells me. "What do you think?"

The elegant greyhound stands patiently in the doorway. One-quarter of Sophia's tan body is neck. She wears a white fleece coat—more of a cape, really—with a woolly, knitted, tube-like extension that covers her throat and most of her head. Her ears are tucked neatly away under this hood. She is wide-eyed and humble, but looks at me with dignity. I take her in, and feel the hot pink-purple light around her.

"Magenta," I say. "It's so pretty. Can you see it, too?" I've never met anyone else who can see animal auras.

Nana Boondahl shakes her head. "I once knew a woman who could see auras. It was when I lived in Greece. She saw them everywhere. It made her dizzy, and sometimes sick. She would faint if she was with more than six people at once."

"I can only see animal auras," I say.

"What a shame," she says. "Apparently, human auras can be very interesting. Unstable, but dynamic."

Juliette told me that Nana Boondahl was eccentric. "Thank you for coming in person," I say.

"We are very interested in your work," Nana Boondahl says. "Say hello, Sophia." She nods to the dog. "Polite."

Sophia sits on her narrow hindquarters and balances there.

"This must be so cold for her," I say.

"She was rescued from Florida." Nana bends down and pushes down the fleece tube, releasing the dog's ears and face, and leaves the fabric ruched around her neck. "She was a racer. Quite successful, actually. Oh, look at her face!" She makes her voice go small. "*This is so unfair*, she's saying. *I wasn't built for winter.*"

"I know how she feels," I say.

I make Nana Boondahl a cup of coconut-almond tea and let her get settled on the chaise lounge under the window, by the space heater. I unclip Sophia's leash and invite her to my drawing area.

Listen to the messages from your body. My body tells me about colour. When I see colour, I feel it. It's a sensation, like hot or cold. Every colour feels a bit different to me. It's hard to explain. It's kind of like synesthesia. But then, of course, I'm seeing and feeling colour around animals that other people can't see. I know, it sounds complicated. It's not, really.

I first learned that I could see and feel coloured light around Kitty—a grey tabby cat, my first pet. In the second grade, I earnestly described her emerald glow in a mortifying show-and-tell presentation. Immediately I realized my mistake. Children can be cruel. But things got better as I grew up and learned to be more careful about what I share with others. I never stopped seeing the auras—coloured light radiates around dogs, goldfish, hamsters, even pigeons—but I kept it to myself for years.

Now, as an adult, I don't feel the need to hide it anymore. I include auras in my pet portraits because they're part of the animal's being. I feel them together, the colour and the animal. They're inseparable.

Sophia sniffs around the upholstered floor cushion, finds the cookie, and eats it: two small crunches and an inhale. She licks her chops delicately. When she does finally lie down, her thin body looks like a bundle of branches. The angles of her limbs collect in triangles. She exhales and shows me the grate of her ribs. Greyhounds are so thin! I begin to sketch.

Nana Boondahl sets her cup of tea down on top of the space heater, which is probably an electrical hazard. She opens a silver case that came out of one of her deep coat pockets. It's the size of a pack of gum, and engraved with a filigree design. She opens it and looks inside—there must be a mirror set into it—staring intensely into the silver lid. Her turquoise-and-cream hair frames her face and brings out the blue of her deep-set eyes.

"You've got quite a draft in here," she says to the mirror.

I move from pencilling Sophia's ribcage to her front legs. When I'm drawing the lines of a dog's body, like the sweep of spine from neck to tail, it helps if I forget that I'm drawing and become the line itself. This requires deep concentration. The first few lines can be rough and sketchy, but generally I can lose myself in the drawing fairly quickly, and get to the right place. But it's hard to focus with Nana Boondahl in the room, watching me.

My phone buzzes in the drawer.

I prefer it when owners leave the dog with me for the sitting. When they have errands to do, or at least, emails to answer. They can be in the room, but when they're on their phone, it's as if they aren't even here. Nana Boondahl doesn't appear to have a phone.

"There's a café right around the corner," I tell her. I focus on Sophia's delicate, bumpy spine, trace it with my eyes as I move my pencil across the page. There: a few inches of line that feel accurate and honest. Then I lose it again, because I've started to think too much about what I'm drawing. The line turns false and self-conscious as I try to draw her tail. My phone buzzes again. I back up to the last detail that still feels alive on the page.

"Feel free to wait down there. I can call you when we're finished."

An e-cigarette materializes between Nana Boondahl's fingers, and she inserts it into her mouth and works it with her lips.

"Oh, no," she says. "I enjoy watching you work."

I feel a little thrill when she says this, but I want her to leave so I can focus. Having her energy in the room is intimidating. Can I use the energy? How can I work with it? I take a deep breath, look back at the page, exhale. *Remind yourself, "I'm here."*

I find the line of Sophia's tail again. I stare at the dog, soften my focus, and let her in. My peripheral vision opens up. There it is—the real line of tail. What I see with my eyes and what my pencil traces on the page become one. For a little while, I almost forget that Nana Boondahl is in the room with me.

I finish when I have five solid sketches, most of them with true lines. I remember Sophia's magenta light with my mind and body. Auras never leave me—I remember the way they feel the way I remember places I've visited. I slide the sketches into a portfolio case to take home with me, where I'll start work on the painting. "Sophia is a beautifully still dog," I say. "She made the session so easy! I wish all my clients would pose so quietly."

I open the drawer of the table, take out my phone, and activate my MoneyJack credit card reader.

> @ElevenNovak> @LilianQuick So nice to hear from you.
> I've comped two tickets for you. Come see me tonight!
> Bring a girlfriend. Xx

It's a private message on Instagram. I read it again, because my brain can't make sense of it. Years before Grandma Bertolucci died, my mom and Aunt Rosie had a big fight and stopped talking to each other. The fight was about Uncle Jimmy. When we were in Evansville for summer vacation, my mom told Aunt Rosie she should get a divorce. Aunt Rosie got angry, said that my mom was jealous, and then kicked us all out of the house. Our families grew apart after that.

The Novaks are famous Evansville lawyers, and they have a lot of money. Uncle Jimmy's father and brothers were lawyers too. Literally, the firm is called Novak, Novak & Novak. My dad couldn't work, because he had to write his never-to-be-completed philosophy dissertation. He received many extensions for his PhD, and at some point the department told him to finish it whenever he could. My mom supported us by working at Red Lobster. When I was a kid, we ate a lot of cheese buns from the restaurant, with cucumber, mustard, and slices of mortadella. My dad died before he finished his thesis.

Aunt Rosie and my mom have very different personalities. My mother's bohemian lifestyle never appealed to Aunt Rosie, who was the more traditional one. Uncle Jimmy and my father were opposites: my father had a quiet, absentminded way of speaking, and would look at your forehead while talking, while Uncle Jimmy spoke as though performing on a stage. He could direct the energy of an entire room.

I haven't heard from Florence since Grandma's funeral. We were twenty when she died. A few years after that, my dad died of a heart attack. The Novaks sent flowers, but they didn't come up for his funeral. As far as I know, my mom and her sister still barely talk to each other.

Last year, I saw Florence in *O Magazine*, in a group portrait of awakened leaders, all committed to elevating the state of humanity in their own ways. I recognized her right away—her wide and lopsided smile, dainty heart-shaped face, and outrageous curly blond hair. The name listed under the photograph read Eleven Novak. But this was my cousin Florence, definitely. With a new name.

I looked her up online to learn more about her story. I couldn't find anything about her childhood. Instead, I found YouTube videos of Eleven speaking to large audiences about her struggle with drugs, alcohol, and manic depression as an adult. One day, she said, she woke up outside, at dawn, by a riverbed. She was barefoot, her legs ached, and she was wearing a black dress with a man's grey hoodie over it. For a few moments, she didn't know her name or where she lived. It was on this morning, she said, that she felt peace for the first time in her life. It was a profound experience. She felt so deeply connected to the trees and river and sky, she felt that she wasn't separate from them. And she knew that she had been called to teach other people how to find this deep connection.

Poor Florence! I knew she had suffered living with Uncle Jimmy, who had such a scary temper, but I had no idea she'd been struggling so much for the past twenty years.

I got in touch with Aunt Rosie right away to find out where Florence was living, but Aunt Rosie would only give me a P.O. box in New York.

I sent a card to that P.O. box—a painting of a sweet papillon with a fizzy green aura I thought Florence would like—and included a short hand-written note. I tried to be excited and gracious without sounding like a stalker, because she's famous now. I didn't want her to think that was the reason I was getting in touch. Her Ascendency Program changes people's lives, and I'm sure everyone wants to be her best friend now.

My note read, *I'm so glad I found you—congratulations on all your success! You're such an inspiration, and I am so grateful that we're family!*

I started tagging her and sharing her Sacred Ascendency Prayer on social media after that, with no response. Until this message, today.

Nana Boondahl looks at me smoothly. "Sophia is my teacher," she says. Then, in a small squeaky voice, she says, *"I don't know why people work so hard at yoga when they could just lie down and relax instead."*

Using the MoneyJack app, I type in the deposit amount that Nana Boondahl owes me. Does Eleven write her own social media? Would she have sent me the message herself, or had an assistant do it for her?

"I'll get to work and call you when the painting is ready," I say. "Would you like to leave me a deposit or pay in full today?"

"Thank you, she says."

I smile at Sophia. "You're welcome," I say. I hold my phone in the palm of my hand and look back at Nana Boondahl.

"I'm sorry," she says. "What did you say before?"

"A deposit," I say. "Will you be paying by credit card?"

"I will pay in cash," she says, "when the painting is complete."

I hadn't expected this. I need her deposit money to pay my January rent, which is already late.

"If you have a credit card, it's very convenient to leave a deposit this way," I say, and I show her my phone. "We can just swipe it right here."

"No thank you," she says. "I prefer to pay with cash. Just send me a bill when you're done."

I place my phone face down on the table and feel swimmy. Do I have to *tell* her that I need the money? She's a poet. She should know! But she's a billionaire poet. Maybe she's forgotten what it's like to be an emerging artist.

"I'll need more than a week to finish," I say.

"Yes, of course. Take your time. You'll have it by next month? Whatever time you need, that's fine."

I can't let her leave without giving me a deposit. What if I rushed the painting? I could work on it at night, and try to finish it in half the time. "Can you come to the studio to pick it up next week?"

"Really, there's no hurry," Nana Boondahl says. "I leave for New York next week and will be there until the end of January. February is fine." She stands up and ties the belt of her coat into a knot. Sophia looks up, and the tag on her collar clinks with the movement.

I know what Fleurje would do right now. She negotiates million-dollar real estate deals every day—she knows how to direct conversations about money. She'd simply say, "I need a deposit in order to finish the work. Thank you."

Why can't I just say that?

"Okay then," I say. My lungs shrink and my chest feels tight. "I'll just send you an invoice when I'm finished. Can I call you in February?"

Nana Boondahl makes her voice go high. "*I look forward to seeing my portrait.*"

I can't breathe. "I really admire your work," I say to Nana Boondahl. "Also the way you've made your career as an artist and as an entrepreneur."

"Oh?" she says, without looking at me. "Well, you know what that's like."

I laugh and look down. My arms are crossed. Oh no! Closed-off body language! I drop my arms and let them hang by my sides. Nana Boondahl stands in front of me, statuesque and calm. Her arms, covered by caramel woollen sleeves, are like two elegant cedar trunks.

"Was your family in business?" I ask her.

"My father was an architect. My mother died when I was young."

"I'm sorry," I say. "I meant, did you have any business training?"

"No," she says. "I wanted something, it didn't exist yet, and so I made it. It's a lot of work, as you know."

"Yes," I say. "It isn't easy, making a living, making art. I don't know that I'm doing it in a balanced way."

My phone buzzes on the table. Eleven?

The greyhound lies down on the floor in front of the door and sighs, waiting. Her magenta light is fluttery and warm. It really is beautiful.

"You have talent, that's inarguable," she says. She looks at me and tilts her head. "But your skin is losing elasticity."

Nana Boondahl thinks I have talent! She said "inarguable talent"! I'm shocked. It's not that I don't think I'm talented. It's just that—this is *Nana Boondahl*.

"I'm always dry in winter," I say. I can't afford Luze, but I moisturize with coconut oil, which is more natural anyway. "Can we make a date for the portrait pickup now?"

"Of course." She pulls a small brown notebook out of her coat pocket and feels around for a pencil.

"Here," she says, and hands me a container of Luze in the brand's iconic silver-lidded, dark-green glass jar. This is probably about eighty dollars' worth of cream!

"Thank you!" I say.

"I have nothing to write with," she answers.

There are ballpoint pens in the Mason jar on Yumi's table. Stuffed in the jar with the pens are orange-handled scissors, a pencil with a neon-pink troll topper, and a pair of armless magnifying glasses copper-wired to a chopstick. My phone buzzes on the table again. I reach for the jar and look at my phone at the same time. My hand collides with something sharp. I gasp from the slice, which is more shocking than painful.

I yank my hand back, and this action pulls the X-acto knife that is embedded in the palm of my hand right out of the jar. It clatters to the floor. My hand drips blood.

"Oh no," I say. "Oh God. I'm bleeding."

Sophia stands up slowly and sniffs the air in my direction.

"Let me see," says Nana Boondahl.

I show her my hand and feel weak. It looks less and less like my own hand the more I stare at it.

"That's not good," she says. "That's going to require stitches."

The floor beneath me is covered in bright red drops in a swirly pattern. The contrast is so pretty, and with my boots in the picture, it would make an edgy toe selfie. But my hand is covered in blood. I have to stop the bleeding. More important to stop the bleeding!

I grab the blue sweater that Yumi gave me and wrap it around my hand. I use my wrist to help me wrap it around and around. My hand is now starting to throb.

"Can you tie this for me, please?" I ask Nana Boondahl. "I'm so sorry about this. Oh God, I'm very sorry." Nana Boondahl ties the sleeves in a knot around my hand.

"This is cashmere," she says.

"I have a great wool wash," I tell her, fully delirious now. "Do you know Plunge products? It's a small company from Nova Scotia. They make a delicate wash that you don't need to rinse out. I use it for cashmere."

"Can I call you a driver?" asks Nana Boondahl. "I'd like to get you to an emergency room."

"A driver," I say. "A driver." I say the word a couple of times in the hopes of understanding it. The word is a sound with no apparent meaning. It feels like the word "driver" is meant to signify something useful. Something that would fix all problems. Yes, I need a driver.

"Can you tell me the number?" she's asking me.

"I'd like a taxi, please," I say calmly. "Use PickUp. It's cheaper."

"The number?" she says.

I use my left hand to pick up my phone. On the screen a notification lights up from Ticketz.

**Emmylou Harris is coming to Massey Hall in April!
Tickets on sale now.**

I press the purple PickUp logo and a map opens up on the screen, with a marker for where I am, at the studio, and a cluster of yellow taxi icons around the nearest intersection. A badge pops up.

There is a problem with the credit card on file.
Click here to fix it.

"I'm so sorry for this inconvenience," I say. My voice sounds prerecorded. "The app isn't working. This is terrible. This is embarrassing. I'm so sorry."

"Stop," Nana Boondahl says. "Please. You need to put your coat on." She turns to the door. "I'll hail a taxi for you outside. Come, Sophia."

Nana Boondahl and her dog leave the studio. The sun comes up over the buildings across the street, and narrow strips of light lick the floor of the studio. I pull my coat on, but my right hand won't fit inside the sleeve because the sweater is balled over it. I use the left sleeve and drape the right side of the coat over my shoulder like a cape.

Nana Boondahl opens the taxi door for me and closes it when I fall inside. The seats are cracked pleather and the heat is on. I close my eyes. The car drives away from the studio. I didn't schedule a pickup date for the portrait, and I didn't get a deposit. And how will I paint Sophia's portrait without my right hand?

Namaste, Lilian,

As I write this, two blue whales are swimming in formation right outside the window above my desk. Their tails reach up and out of the water and then slide back in again, like they're waving.

It is with a wide-open heart that I wave to you, as well. Greetings from Oahu, Hawaii, where I am blessed to be teaching a silent Active Meditation Retreat for three hundred souls this week.

In Hawaii, rainbows are a simple daily reminder of the prismatic nature of our atmosphere and spirit. As we surf our consciousness during Active Meditation, I am aware of the warmth that suffuses our bodies and the sound of the ocean behind me, relentless in its consistency and commitment to reach the shore, wave upon wave.

This January, I wish you the same consistency and commitment. Know that when you show up again and again to your meditation—be it on zafu and zabuton, surfboard or snowboard—you are also joining us in this retreat. Listen to your breath, hear the way it is like the ocean, and drop into the present moment with us.

Know that wherever you are, we are connected through our breath and the mystery of consciousness.

Blessings,
Jonathan

I DON'T HAVE any cash on me, and there's a problem with my credit card. The taxi driver feels sorry for me. When we get to St. Joe's, the nurse at the hospital takes my health card number and I feel grateful to live in Canada, where I can get access to safe medical care even though I'm a completely broke, people-pleasing self-saboteur who would rather injure herself than ask a client for money.

Negative self-talk! I should give myself more kindness. I plug my earbuds into my phone and scroll through Jonathan Rasmussen's meditation app. I'll be waiting here for at least two hours.

"Welcome to Making Space for Bliss." His voice is dark and delicious. I love his New Zealand accent, the way he lingers on some of his vowels.

"Find a quiet place. Prepare yourself by placing your two feet squarely on the ground. Balance the weight of your head on top of your spine. That's it. Take a dip bridth.

"Good. Now take another dip bridth."

I breathe. I should have asked her for a deposit. I should have demanded it. I have so much work to do on money. This is happening because I didn't ask for what I am worth. But I *did* get free tickets to see Eleven tonight. That was a totally unexpected gift from the Universe. That's worth a hundred dollars! I just have to think about money differently. Allow the money to come to me, in whatever form it comes.

"When you are ready, close your eyes."

I do as he says, and the emergency room disappears. Jonathan Rasmussen stretches out his esses softly. This makes his words hiss in an ambient way, like a waterfall.

"This meditation is all about bliss. As you breathe, access your deep reserves of peace. You are heppy. You are joyful. You feel calm. Picture an ocean of light above you. Inhale, and breathe in light. Exhale, and know that right now, you are safe, and surrounded by love." My phone vibrates.

Fleurje
can't come 2night sorry

No! She took so much time to think about it that I thought there was a real chance I'd get to see her tonight. Oh Mercury in retrograde, screwing with our plans. I haven't seen Fleurje in forever. She's showing houses constantly—evenings and weekends especially, because that's when her clients are off work. Well, she was *close* to saying yes. Maybe she *wishes* she could come? This is what I mean about Fleurje's boundaries. She just says no.

It's rare that Juliette can do anything spontaneously because of her girls, but I try anyway.

Me

Come to Eleven with me tonight!

Me

Guess what? I got us tickets!

It doesn't show that it's been delivered yet. She's offline? But Juliette is rarely offline. Maybe she's in a subway tunnel.

I check my Instagram feed for something to take my mind off my throbbing hand. There's a short video from @tunameltsmyheart of Tuna playing with a green dog toy, growling a snotty-sounding growl. A sun-drenched shot of @JuVsJu drinking a bottle of PureSilver water in her rumpled, rustic-looking camper-van bed. She quit her corporate job last year and is making her living on Instagram now, with product sponsorship. Her photos are pretty, even if they're staged. Ooh, Eleven's posted a selfie! She's in the window seat of an airplane, wearing mirrored aviator lenses. Her curly gold hair takes up most of the frame.

@ElevenNovak> En route. NYC to YYZ.
#Ascendency #EYEToronto

She's going to be in Toronto tonight, and I'm actually going to see her. I double-tap the pic to like it.

Even when our families were in touch, we were always the ones who would drive down to Evansville. They never came to Canada. Okay, they came once. But Uncle Jimmy and Aunt Rosie's house was so big it could fit all of us, and our tiny house had only two bed-rooms, so it was cramped. Florence and I had to sleep in one room. I gave her my bed, and I slept on the floor in my sleeping bag. The Novaks had five bedrooms and five bathrooms. It was much nicer to stay there—I got my own room, which was done in kelly green. Florence's bedroom was done in lavender.

They had a big backyard with thick green grass that sloped down to the river. The Ohio River always looked brown, like chocolate milk. We weren't allowed to go near it. Near the back fence was a large wooden doghouse for Charlie, their black Lab, painted blue and white to match their house. Charlie had a dark-purple aura, a heavy colour that draped around him like a cloak.

Florence was an only child, like me. We were born only one month apart, to the day: she was born November 19, I was born December 19. Uncle Jimmy and Aunt Rosie's first child, a boy called JJ, drowned in the river before I was born. Nobody ever talked about him. I don't remember how I learned about JJ—I grew up with that information stored in my body, the way I grew up knowing that I don't make friends easily, or that Uncle Jimmy was rich.

I adored Florence, who was confident, fearless, beautiful, and athletic. She was smart, and she had a great imagination. She made up most of the games we played, which often involved complicated rules, long-term plans, and strategies. And even though I was a shy kid, she always thought up a role for me to play.

My hand throbs. Should I tell Yumi about the accident? Warn her about the blood on the floor? I mean, them? I should go back and clean up the blood on the floor. I feel hot. My face feels sweaty. Am I hungry?

I should call someone. I scroll through my contacts with the thumb of my left hand. Everyone I know either has a normal job and can't talk until after work hours, or they're obscenely busy with their unconventional and successful careers and never check voicemail.

There's April Rosenblum. I know April from the One of a Kind Show. Her booth was beside mine in the Rising Stars section last Christmas. She makes tiny white porcelain sculptures that look like alien creatures with pointy ears, metallic eyes, and eerie, multi-limbed bodies. It's not like we're real friends. I mean, I like her, and I watched her booth for her when she took breaks. I think we got along well for those ten days. But I couldn't really call her now, from the hospital. *Hi April! I cut my hand on an X-acto knife after a sitting with Nana Boondahl's dog! I think I blew it, and totally repulsed her by standing in a pool of my own blood! I'm at the hospital now, waiting to get stitches! I had to stiff the taxi driver because I'm so broke! How are you? How's business?*

There is nobody for me to call.

I hold my phone over my fat, blue-cashmere-wrapped hand and turn my palm over, so the knot shows. I take a pic. Too grotesque? What if Yumi sees what I've done to their sweater? I delete the pic and post a note to Twitter instead.

@**LilianQuick**> Ouch! Pls send healing thoughts. Had a run-in with an X-acto this morning.
Too sharp.

@**DogGone**> Oh no! Feel better

@**TruGirl**> Oh no! What happened?

@**MarieReal**> Ouch! Sending love + light.

The notifications float up on my screen and collect in a list. I watch them come in, and it makes me feel a little better. I love my digital community. I have so much support from friends and colleagues and clients from all over the world. Marie Real is a pet portrait artist from Mexico City. We haven't met in person, but we connected on Pinterest. I know from her feed that she lives a bright and colourful life, she has so many beautiful friends, and she's always laughing. She's a light, an inspiration.

@MattTwoforone> Caution: blades may be sharper than they appear!

@TigerPaws> Meow! I'm so sorry!

I'm not sure who those last two tweets are from, but isn't that nice of them?

With the local anesthetic, I don't even feel the stitches. The doctor is efficient, and I thank her for doing such a good job with the sewing. *Joy does not exist without gratitude.* She tells me that there will be a scar, to keep the wound clean and dry, and that I can go.

In the elevator, my phone pings.

Juliette
what time?

> **Me**
> **starts at 7!**

Juliette
maybe yes

I try PickUp again, just to see what the credit card issue is. The Universe is taking care of me: my call is answered, and a taxi arrives on the screen. Computer chip technology is based on liquid crystals, and the electrical charge from computers is very similar to human electrical charge. After the trauma of the accident, my energy probably interfered with my phone energy. Or wait, no, it's Mercury in retrograde.

I watch the car icon with joy. It moves slowly and directly toward my blue pin. There is so much beauty and magic in this simple event.

Juliette is coming tonight! Her response was so quick. One of the things I don't love about texting is that all texts feel exactly the same to me. I get a text from my cell phone company and it looks just like one that comes from a friend. Except with me and Juliette—I can always tell when a text is from her, and I mean just by seeing it (not because I've chosen Circles for her text sound). When her texts appear on my screen, they feel more bright and sparkly than other people's texts. It's because we're connected. Some people don't like Juliette because she's so perfect. But I truly think she's a beacon, and people who resist her perfection are threatened by her light. Everything is beautified by Juliette's presence. Even the simple words she texts are radiant and full of positivity.

Wait, am I just trying to make things binary again, so I feel the comfort of certainty? I'm tired. I want to curl up on the couch and stop thinking about binaries. But that's the essence of privilege, isn't it? If you fit into the dominant culture, you get to stop thinking about disrupting it whenever you need a break. Does Yumi ever take a break?

I have so much to work on. Eleven couldn't be coming at a better time.

My dearest Lilian,

My heart is full of admiration for the supercharged women I am meeting in cities all over North America. I hope you can attend <u>one of our events on this tour</u>, but even if you can't, I want to share some of this inspiration with you.

Today I'm sharing Charlene's story. I received this letter from her last night. This is a story about what happens when a woman knows her own worth and expresses her enlightenment. Enjoy.

With love,
Eleven

P.S. If you want last-minute tickets for an upcoming EYE event happening in a city near you, you might be in luck. <u>Click here</u> for tour dates and venues. I'm off to Toronto, Canada, tonight!

◊ ◊ ◊

Dear Eleven,

Thank you for the life-changing experience I had at the Ascendency last year. It was scary for me to register for the program, because I had to put it on my credit card, which was already close to maxed. I had to borrow money from my parents to make the trip to New York for the first weekend. I own a small business: I make hand-dyed silk scarves that are printed with botanicals using solar printing techniques. But my business has been struggling. I'm also being treated for clinical depression. I registered for the Ascendency because when I read your letters, I feel like you're talking directly to ME. Your video class on how to live a day like it's the Two of Cups made me cry. I felt called to work with you, no matter what. Money couldn't be an obstacle.

But going into debt to come to your event was a risk. When I arrived in New York I was full of doubt. What had I done? How stupid and irresponsible was it for me to spend money I didn't have on another self-help workshop?

That first weekend, surrounded by so many energized souls, feeling your energy from the stage—something inside of me shifted. It was as though a hand from the sky came down and swept away a gray cloud that had been covering my eyes and heart. As the work continued, I felt myself expanding as an Ascendant: I opened myself to accepting more love, generosity, and success in my life.

Now for the incredible part of my story. Three months after that first weekend in New York, on the flight back home from the Ascendency graduation ceremony in Oahu, I sat next to a woman who was wearing shoes made from textiles a friend of mine designs. I recognized the shoes and complimented her, and discovered that she's a buyer from Volym Studio in Sweden. She was in the U.S. on her annual buying trip.

Eleven, she ordered a thousand of my hand-printed scarves! She said it's just the first order, and that they'll be featured in Volym Studio stores all across Sweden. The income from that order was so large, I paid off all my debts and still have enough to hire an assistant in the studio.

My whole life has changed.

I am certain that it was the energy shift of the Ascendency that allowed me to notice the possibility for wealth all around me. I am so grateful to you and your team for transforming my life.

Love and light,
Charlene

THE TAXI DRIVER arrives at my house and I give him five stars on PickUp, because when you're feeling a lack of abundance, it helps to be generous.

"Can you give me a good PickUp review?" I ask him. He nods.

I feel cleansed and forgiven. The sunlight is gleaming on the rough ice-crusted sidewalks, making them glow in a dusty way, like Herkimer diamonds.

I eat another one of those granola candy bars to give myself energy, knowing that it's just going to make my blood sugar spike and crash. Why didn't I have an apple and some nice raw almonds instead?

I want to give myself a manicure and dress up a bit for EYEToronto. I choose silver polish. I can hold the brush in my right hand without feeling any pain, just some discomfort. I don't have great control so the results are a little messy, but the silver doesn't show the bumps. Painting my right hand is awkward as usual, but manageable. The polish looks like liquid metal, and it's captivating to watch it dry. I take a picture of my hand, with my palm wrapped in gauze, and post it.

@LilianQuick> Bandaged paw!

I check Facebook while my nails dry. There's a new Funddit campaign to start an ethical hotel chain, where everything is made locally and profits are shared with charities. If I had money, I'd contribute to that. A tattoo artist from Bulgaria posted a time-lapse video of a flower gradually appearing on someone's arm. Niley Barque, the graphic novelist, posted an update on her breast cancer: no chemo needed, just radiation. She doesn't know who I am, but I like her post to show my support.

My hand is giving off heat. It's gotten cloudy outside, and the light in my apartment feels murky. I turn on a lamp. The texture of the upholstery is embossed into my nail polish. How did I do that? My cuticles are coated in polish. I totally messed up this manicure. The couch cushion has smears of silver on it too. The tenant has a grey couch, so maybe it doesn't show too much. I pour myself a glass of tap water and break into a bag of lightly salted avocado oil–popped pop-corn. My phone has a bunch of banner notifications from Instagram likes and comments. Somehow I missed three texts from Juliette.

> Juliette
>
> **just saw your hand on IG why don't you come over tonight**

> Juliette
>
> **it's an off day house a mess but would be nice to see you**

> Juliette
>
> **are you okay**

So nice! I'd love to spend some quality time together before we go to the EYE event. I am so grateful for my friendship with Juliette. We met at U of T when we were both fresh out of high school. I grew up in a small northern town, surrounded by lakes and forests. When I got to the city, I was eighteen years old, excited to ride the subway. Juliette had gone to an all-girls' private school in Toronto, and knew all the best places to go downtown. We took Italian 102 together and became friends in the Tick Tock Tea Room, where we drank cappuccinos with extra cinnamon after our early-morning language lab classes. She's always been the Juliette she is now: an excellent lis-tener, total support and encouragement, a friend who makes time for me no matter what's going on in her life. Female friendships are so important! Where would I be without my girlfriends?

Dear Lilian,

Happy New Year! I love January, don't you? I know it's our darkest season, and the cold (for those of us in the northern hemisphere) can get quite fierce when there isn't the anticipation of the holidays to warm us anymore. But there's a stillness to this month that fills me with peace. When the trees are dormant and our family calendar gets quiet again, it's a great excuse for me to linger and practise the art of hygge with Knigel and the girls.

Hibernation can be luxurious. Today's post is chock-full of cozy options that will make your January deep and delicious.

Here's a sampling:
We made these homemade beeswax candles with a pine cone motif to light up dinner time, bath time, and our grown-up downtime. They're surprisingly easy to make using a variety of silhouettes—click here to watch my video tutorial and download this PDF of different wintry shapes to use for the appliqué.

January is all about white beans at our house! Here's my recipe for fire-roasted white beans with garlic, sage, and pine nuts. Who said you can't barbeque in January? I've included some shots of Knigel by the fire in our snowy backyard, to inspire you as you stir cannellini over the grill (don't worry, I'll show you how).

Finally, you can download my easy and pretty cabled leg warmers pattern. Mabel and Siebel both have a pair, as you can see here! Siebel wanted pink ones (as usual) but to make it more interesting to knit, I chose three different shades of raspberry and created an ombré effect. Mabel wanted classic ivory ones, and I think she's rocking the winter-white look in her matching coat and hat.

Happy hibernation to you and your family,
xoxo, Juliette

JULIETTE'S HOUSE IS done white on white, with white-painted wood floors and white curtains in every room. The upstairs hallway and bedrooms are carpeted in white. Her white sofa hangs back in the living room, beckoning everyone with its velvety, come-hither frame. Juliette stacks it with shaggy white mohair pillows and layers of white and ivory blankets. It looks like a dessert: layered crepes and dollops of whipped cream. I step into her house and feel as if I've entered heaven.

She hugs me, and there's a sour, metallic scent on her neck, like tinned salsa.

"Do you have nail polish remover?" I ask her.

Her younger daughter comes to the door dressed in woolly pink leggings and a pink knitted tunic.

"Lily," she says, and clutches her mother's shins.

"Hi, sweetie," I say. I can't remember her name. I always remember Juliette's firstborn, Siebel, but the name of her younger child escapes me. It rhymes with Siebel. It's old-fashioned. I need a mnemonic for it, clearly. I can't believe I keep forgetting it.

"Mabel, go ask Sieb for nail polish remover please. Tell her it's for Auntie Lily!"

Mabel (*Mabel!*) goes nowhere. Siebel arrives at the door on her own, holding a bottle of pink nail polish remover. "Here," she says, and thrusts it toward me.

"Wow! How did you know I needed that?" I ask. Siebel stares at my knees and remains silent.

"She must have heard us," I say.

"Probably," says Juliette. "Come on in. House is a mess. I'm sorry I don't have anything to offer you . . ." She turns around and walks toward her kitchen, with Mabel (*Mabel—like a fable—got it*) and Siebel trailing behind. Mabel does a jumpy slide move along the white hardwood floors in her sock feet, dancing an awkward kid-Charleston.

In the kitchen, Juliette pulls out a box of flatbread and a store-bought plastic tub of green puree.

"Guacamole," she says. "Have you had dinner?" She hands me a plate with scalloped edges and a heavy spoon with an abalone handle. "Okay," she says. "Okay. Are you okay? What happened?"

"I was wrapping up with Nana Boondahl this morning, and—"

"I want to talk about *that*, by the way. Bookmark that."

"—and I cut myself on one of Yumi's X-acto knives."

Siebel stands up on tiptoes so her nose and fingers are at counter level. She tips over the box of flatbread and slides her hand into the box. "I want a Babybel with my crackers," she says.

Mabel climbs up the footstool so she's right next to her big sister. "Me too!" she says.

"Girls, it's just about bedtime. No snacks. This is special for Auntie Lily."

"No, I *want* some." Siebel reaches for the spoon beside me and dips it into the guacamole, pulling up a big glob. "Here," she says, and heaves the spoonful toward me. Most of it lands on the plate.

"Thank you," I say.

Juliette takes the spoon out of Siebel's hand and gives it to me. "Let's get you a Babybel then," she says. "Sorry, Lily. You were saying Yumi was using your X-acto knife for something?"

"No, I cut my hand on one of hers—I mean, theirs." I eat some of the stale flatbread. The guacamole tastes like sulphites, or some other preservative. Whatever the flavour is, it is not actual lime juice. I'm surprised, because this is *Juliette*. Then again, it's great to see that she's become more relaxed about stuff like this. Serving store-bought snacks shouldn't have to be a big deal. Juliette is successfully running her empire as a lifestyle entrepreneur, mothering her two little girls, and being a five-star friend all at the same time. She's amazing! I love that she gives herself permission to buy pre-made food at the corner store. She's an inspiration. I can't wait to introduce Juliette and Eleven. Eleven will *totally* connect with Juliette. They're both at that similar level of success, they're both so empowered, they both have so much business acumen.

"How was Nana Boondahl?" Juliette asks. "Did you get along as much as I'd hoped?"

Both girls are now manipulating the red wax with their fingers, trying to get at the balls of cheese in their own ways. Mabel bites directly into the wax and looks up to watch her sister. Siebel peels it away deftly with her small fingers. Mabel looks back at her cheese, sees the teeth marks in the wax, and starts to cry. "NO!" she says, and reaches for Siebel's cheese.

"NO, MABEL!" Siebel screams at her.

"Sorry, Lily," says Juliette. "*How* did you cut yourself?"

"It's okay," I say. "I'm great. No biggie. I got stitches and it's all fixed. I'm fine. I'm excited about tonight. Will Knigel watch the girls while we're out?"

Juliette looks at me, and her bright face appears to drop a few pins. "Oh," she says. "I'm sorry, Lily. I can't come tonight. I totally forgot about that."

"Where's Knigel?"

"He's here," she said. "He has a game tonight. He'll be at it until late."

Knigel plays video games with other people online. He designs games for work—the one he's working on now involves zombies. The game tonight might be for his work. Knigel and I aren't close—he doesn't make eye contact, and I don't know how to talk to him. He might be somewhere on the spectrum, actually. Or just uninterested in me. Anyway, he's online most of the day and night, but I never know for sure if it's for work or leisure. *Rest until you want to play; play until you want to rest.*

"Don't touch that!" Juliette says to Siebel, who is now inspecting the contents of the refrigerator. A large cake on a jadeite pedestal stands prominently on the centre shelf. It's covered in smooth, pale-blue fondant. Sugared flowers cascade over the top of the cake and spill down the side. There's a sparkle inside the flowers—are the stamens coated in sanding sugar? Glitter? Tiny Swarovski crystals?

"I want milk," says Mabel, and she drops her ball of cheese on the floor.

"Can I have a piece?" Siebel twists and pivots, both hands on the fridge door. She looks back at us and grins at her mother. "I want a piece of cake."

"No. That's for the shoot tomorrow," says Juliette.

"What's tomorrow?" I ask.

"A writer from *Lovely* is coming. They're going to do a story about my kitchen, and she's doing the photos. I said no, Siebel! Close the door."

"ONE PIECE." Siebel keeps her eyes on her mother, a hard and taut gaze.

"Milk!" screams Mabel.

"This cake is too fancy for *Lovely*," Juliette says. "They're going to hate it. I shouldn't have made such a fussy cake. Honestly, my stomach falls every time I look at it—it's so stiff and over the top."

"Mommy," calls Mabel. "Mommy!"

"You're going to be in *Lovely*?" I ask. "That's amazing! Congratulations!"

"Girls, time for bed."

I pick up my phone and take a second to check my mail. "Do you use PickUp?" I say. "If you don't have it yet, sign up for it with my code, and I think we both get a free ride."

"I have Uber—love it," Juliette says. "Girls, it's time for bed. Mabel, you can pick two books you'd like me to read."

"Uber is misogynistic, though," I say. "It's a sexist company. PickUp is feminist."

"Get *The Seven Swans*," Siebel tells Mabel. Mabel crouches on the kitchen floor, picks up the sticky ball of cheese she dropped earlier, pinches a piece off, and puts it in her mouth.

"Should I go?" I ask. "It's bedtime, I should go."

"She only says *Seven Swans* because it's the longest book we have." Juliette takes Mabel's cheese and throws it in the trash. Mabel starts to cry and runs out of the kitchen. "Get dressed for bed," Juliette says to Siebel, and closes the refrigerator door. "Lily, please stay. I *want* you to stay. Relax. Have a bite to eat"—she gestures at my plate of guacamole—"and enjoy some quiet time. I'll be back down in a minute and you can tell me all about your day with Nana Boondahl."

The palm of my hand aches. I've had all the quiet time I need today. "Thank you for sending her to me," I say. "Again. Really, thank you."

"Of course," Juliette says. "You're the best at what you do. And you see things other people don't see. You have that in common. I knew she'd love working with you."

Her hair is pulled off her face and fastened with a red velvet bow that just pokes through her dark curls. It looks like a perfectly knotted ribbon, but it's an elastic. The red is a shade that matches her lips exactly. She's not wearing lipstick—that's just her natural colouring. When I see her red hair tie poking through her relaxed, messy bun—Juliette calls it a *chignon négligé*—I know there's not really much hope for me. I mean, the colour of her hair tie is the same colour as her lips.

What have I been doing with my life, while Juliette has built her empire? I spent my twenties temping at a design firm that made ugly corporate logos, drinking too much Pinot Grigio, trying to sell nutrition products on weekends. I'm selling my art now, I guess. But basically, I'm a forty-year-old blogger. I can barely even keep my tax receipts organized properly. Juliette and I are the same age, but I'm still living like I'm twenty-four years old.

"I should get going," I say. "But thank you for dinner! I'm going to try to get to the box office a bit early, see if I can give your extra ticket to someone."

Juliette looks pained. "Wait," she says. She leaves the kitchen. Siebel watches me. I smile at her, but she doesn't smile back. She just stares at me. I raise my eyebrows and wiggle them. Siebel remains still, a statue of a child. "It was so nice to visit with you girls tonight," I try. She just stands there. I pick up my phone to check email again, and she cringes and covers her face with her hands.

"I'm not going to take a picture of you, Sieb." I say. "Relax."

I pull my thumb down the screen to refresh, and a new email from Eleven drops into my inbox.

Juliette comes back with a fifty-dollar bill. Mabel toddles along behind her. "Here," she says. "In case you can't sell my ticket. I'm sorry I can't go tonight."

"No," I push the bill away.

"Please take it," Juliette says.

"Our tickets were comped by Eleven," I tell her. "They're free."

"Well, take it anyway. I feel terrible that I said I could go when I can't."

It's a slick new bill, not even creased or folded. "Thank you for offering," I say, "but it's really okay."

"Are you planning to sign up for her—thing?" Juliette scoops up Mabel and fits her on one hip.

"It's not anything like selling Go-Manchura," I say.

"Or BioChronos," she says.

"This is just a seminar. I'm not going to start selling anything."

"I don't like seeing you in pyramid schemes," she says. "They're cults."

"Go-Manchura was an MLM," I explain, "but the products were high quality and not available in stores. And no matter what you say about the scent, all of BioChronos's ingredients are one hundred percent natural."

Siebel pulls on her mother's free arm, stretching out the sleeve of her sweater, holding the wrist end scrunched in her little fist. "Come *on*," she says. "Mama, come *on*."

"Well, have a great night." Juliette sighs. "Sorry I stood you up."

Just as I'm leaving, I remember what I wanted to ask her. "Nana Boondahl was pay-averse," I say. "She didn't give me a deposit. That's weird, right? She'll pay me eventually, right?"

"Strange," says Juliette. "Why didn't she pay you?"

"She said she'd rather do it in full, when I'm finished. I think it was about the MoneyJack. I think she's not into credit card payments."

"She might be paranoid about digital," Juliette says. "She *is* a senior citizen."

"She's a million-dollar brand," I say. "She has to do digital."

"She pays people to do digital for her."

"Right," I say. "Of course she does." I wave goodnight to Mabel and Siebel. They stare at me with sleepy, remorseful eyes.

"Nana Boondahl will pay you when you finish. Don't worry," Juliette says, and closes the door.

The tall brick houses on Juliette's street stand close together, and warm yellow light glows in their narrow windows. All along the street, large, all-terrain strollers are padlocked to the shared front porches.

Juliette is a good friend. Even though our thirty-minute visit was disjointed and unsatisfying, I still feel more in touch with who I am after seeing her. I'm lucky to have a real friend in my life, someone who's known me for so long. I should see Juliette in person more often. The next time I feel lonely, instead of streaming old episodes of *Sex and the City* on my laptop, I'm going to make the effort to come across town and see Juliette.

I walk unevenly over ice and concrete until I get to the end of the street, where I can catch a streetcar.

Hello Lilian,
I'm in Toronto—you're here, right? You're coming to EYE? Would you like to meet tonight? Come to Mutable Dragon PH 9 p.m.
xo E

Sent from space with love

Hi!!
Yes I'm here! Guess what? I'm coming to EYE tonight! So excited! On my way there now! See you after the event—yay!
xoxo, Lilian

I remember one of the first secret summer missions that Florence organized. We went across the street, to the golf course behind the neighbour's house. We hopped the little wooden fence that separated the golf green from the neighbour's yard. It was after dinner. The sun was going down, and the light was turning from orange to blue. The golfers had gone home, and we were alone on the course. We were ten years old.

"Follow me," she said, "and I'll show you where to find them." She walked a few steps ahead of me, and then slowed down. Her eyes were closed and her hands were up, as though she was touching something in the air I couldn't see. "Here," she said. "I can sense them. They're very close to us."

I closed my eyes to see what she meant. Could I feel them? Maybe! What were they?

"Yes!" she said, and opened her eyes. "Go there." She turned around and pointed to a hedge a few feet behind her. "Go through the passage."

There was a gap in the hedge—not big, but I could squeeze through the branches. On the other side, the lawn turned to scrubby grass and dirt. We'd hit the end of the golf course and the edge of the woods. The air smelled like barbecued chicken from a backyard nearby.

"Do you see the path?" Florence asked me, through the branches.

I looked ahead. There was a path that led into the woods!

"Yes," I said.

"Follow the path," Florence said, "and look for the trail."

I walked along the path, and she stayed behind. It was darker in the woods, and the fireflies were blinking on and off. The dry sticks cracked under my feet. A bright-pink bone caught my eye: a golf tee. About a foot away, another golf tee, this one white. I followed the line of tees off the path and into the trees. The trail went on for some time. A light wind blew through the trees, and the leaves above bristled. A piece of red-and-white cloth lay on the ground ahead of me—Aunt Rosie's tea towel. I bent down and lifted the edge of it.

"You found them!" Florence said. She'd been following me all along.

She told me that she'd found this strange hole in the ground, full of leaves and litter. She cleared it out in the spring, and then started collecting balls. She'd almost filled the hole—there were probably a hundred golf balls already in there.

This was our summer mission. There were years of lost golf balls in these woods. We were going to find them all.

"Then we'll sell them to golfers," she said. "We're going to be *rich*."

When I think about it now, finding discarded golf balls in the woods doesn't feel exciting at all. But Florence could turn anything into the best game. We spent that summer in the woods, finding golf balls like Easter eggs, and hoarding them. We needed to build another hiding place for some of them, because we couldn't fit them all in the hollow anymore. We hid the overflow in a cardboard box, under a pile of leaves and branches. I turned out to be a good hunter—I found about two hundred of them that summer.

"What will you buy with your money?" Florence asked me.

"Who are we going to sell them to?"

"I have a connection," she said.

I wanted a Cabbage Patch Kid. Florence had three of them. She wouldn't tell me what she wanted to buy. We never got to cash in our treasure, anyway. After hunting with Florence all summer, it was time for the long drive back north with my parents. She promised to send me a letter with a cheque in it. The cheque never came. The next summer, I asked her.

"Stolen," she said, and shook her head. "We were robbed. Someone found our stash and took it before I could sell it."

It seemed unlikely, but then again, they probably weren't hidden very well. It's not as if she would have sold them without telling me.

I thought I'd be early, but there's already a line of women wearing black coats and tall boots standing in front of the Sony Centre. Eleven's signature lime-green carpet is unrolled outside the glass doors. I join the line of women who are standing on it. A young man inside the building lifts his hand at me. Do I know him? He has a narrow face and a coffeeshop beard. I wave back. He searches my face. He wasn't waving at me. He's cleaning the glass doors with a cloth.

The city feels iced down, the January air whittled to its cracking point. Crowds of after-work overcoats hustle past me and I hold my breath to avoid inhaling smoke. Who still smokes, anyway?

The box office opens and the line starts moving. Women are inside, holding lime-green tickets in their gloved hands, their faces shining under the warm lights.

"Have you read Jonathan Rasmussen's new book?" says a woman behind me. "Apparently, he looks at the spectrum between schizophrenia and autism, and shows how anxiety and depression are on the same spectrum. We all live somewhere on that line, between those two states."

"From what I've heard," says her friend, "he would know."

"Is he autistic?"

"No, but he's divorced."

The crowd of women moves ahead. Puffs of exhaled breath punctuate the slinking line. Eventually I get to the entrance, pull on the door's brass chevron handle, greasy with the fingerprints of multitudes, and make it to the box office. It's warmer here in the foyer, where people are neither inside nor outside.

"Lilian Quick," I say. "There should be two tickets for me?" The girl at the box office flips through a black plastic box filled with index cards and alphabetical tabs. My tickets will be the only ones filed under *Q*, as usual. But she doesn't find any.

"Would there be another name?" she asks.

"I'm Eleven's cousin," I try. "Is there a guest list?"

She smiles. "That's probably why," she says, and looks in an envelope on her desk. "Lilian, right?" She passes the two green tickets under the acrylic arch onto a concave steel plate and says, "Enjoy your night." I feel like a VIP!

Outside, women gather in small groups on the green carpet, their hair gleaming under the lights of the marquee. I go back out, because that's where a ticket hopeful will be waiting. Tonight will be a gift for a stranger! Someone has ventured all the way downtown, hoping that there will be a last-minute ticket waiting for her. She doesn't know why she even came, because she knows that it's sold out. She just felt inexplicably pulled to the Sony Centre. And then I'll give her a ticket for free, and she'll feel the Universe taking care of her, and we'll both feel like it's our luckiest day!

"One last ticket!" I call out to the sidewalk. "Does anyone need a ticket for tonight?" The women in line watch me sympathetically.

"My friend couldn't come," I explain to someone behind me. "Last minute."

"Oh, too bad," she says. She moves forward in line.

I close my eyes and imagine warm light radiating out of me. I picture the woman this ticket belongs to. It helps to be specific: she is wearing a black coat, a wool scarf, and velvet gloves. I send out my light and connect to the morphogenetic field using my heart energy. I picture her walking to meet me halfway. She is thrilled. This is a wish come true for her.

I open my eyes to greet her.

An icy slice of wind cuts across the concrete and slams into the crowd. It makes a vicious sound as it sears past the tall buildings of downtown. Minuscule bullets of snow and city grit scrape my face and feel like a rash.

"Does anyone want a free ticket for tonight?" I call. The wind takes my voice away. I go back inside.

Inside, the lobby is buzzing with anticipation and possible success. The merch booth is stocked with T-shirts, sweatshirts, galaxy-print leggings, and coffee mugs, all with Eleven's tagline, Want What You Want, printed in gold script. In a big square bin, there are gold-and-silver framed prints of her Sacred Ascendency Prayer for sale, wrapped in plastic with cardboard corner protectors.

Last fall I rented a booth at the convention centre for the Dogapalooza show. I had a pipe-and-drape booth for my pet portraits, while the other business owners sold dog coats and sweaters, combs and brushes, vitamins and supplements, kibble, training books and DVDs. There were presentations by famous trainers and dog fashion shows. The halls hummed: participants were frisky, optimistic, slightly panicked. Not the dogs—the people! It's all that buying and selling at once that does it. Dogs don't care about money, and I love that about them. The Sony Centre has a similar buzz tonight, even though it's a seminar, not a trade show. I wish there were some dogs here tonight, to balance the energy.

A woman with long brown curls walks toward me, still in her winter coat. She wears heels and leggings. A quarter inch of bare ankle peeks out between the top of her shoe and the cuff.

"Hi!" I smile brightly. "Do you need an extra ticket for tonight?"

"No thanks, honey," she says, and strides past. Her heels click on the polished floor. A heavy scent—patchouli, or vetiver?—trails behind her.

"Were you at the Portland event last summer?" I turn around. The voice belongs to a woman in a body-conscious ivory dress, moss-green pumps, and opaque yellow-green tights. Her hair is short and clipped close to her head, and she wears big gold hoop earrings. My eyes drink in the intense colours she's wearing—the spring green shouts against the darker green. It's electric.

She's not talking to me; she's talking to a girl wearing a head-band. "You look familiar," she says to her.

"You've probably seen me on Eleven's site," the girl says. "I'm a case study. I give a lot of testimonials. My picture is out there."

"Are you an Ascendency grad?"

"Not yet," the girl says. "But the work has already helped me so much. I'm totally saving up for Ascendency."

"Excuse me," I interrupt. "I mean, hi!" They both look at me. The woman with the brightly coloured tights is wearing a necklace with a gold *E* pendant.

"Do you know where the auditorium is?" I know how to get to the auditorium, but asking strangers for help can be a nice way to make a connection when you're alone in a crowd.

The younger of the two smiles at me. She wears the headband around her head like a flapper, and her eyeshadow is magnificent: three shades of violet, with a streak of the darkest colour just under her eyebrows and the lightest, a silvery dust, in a halo around her lids and under her eyes. It gives her a mystical, owlish look.

"Your eyeshadow is stunning," I tell her. The best way to calm your nerves when you're around people is to give honest compliments. It takes courage at first, but it's just like a gratitude practice: soon enough, giving compliments becomes a healthy habit of joy. *Courage is action in the presence of fear.*

"Thank you!" she says. "It's from Glimyr. It's made with rose quartz and amethyst." She's about my height. Her cheekbones will really come out in about ten years.

"The auditorium is there," the woman with the moss-green shoes says. "We're in line for the bathroom."

"I'll wait with you," I say. "If that's okay."

"The men's is open too, if you want." She points across the hall, where another crowd of women gather. "Not that the line is any shorter over there!" She laughs. Her teeth are gorgeously white.

The centre is full of women. So many women are wearing black leggings with sweaters overtop. Leather lace-up boots and black ankle booties with heels. Tall boots that go up to their knees. Leggings and boots: it's a thing!

I pull out my phone just to see and there are several more condolences for my posting about my hand. Emojis sprinkled throughout: happy faces with tears, prayer hands, a tiny ambulance with a red cross. People are so nice. I feel warm and surrounded by care.

"How did you hear about this event?" the girl asks me. "I'm trying to place you. Do we know each other online? Have you done Ascendency?"

"No," I say. "I'm here because I grew up with Eleven." The girl's eyes widen.

"Wow," she says. "Really?"

"Wait, you what?" says the woman in green shoes. "What's your name?"

"Lilian," I say.

"Lilian," she says. "Lilian who? I'm an Ascendency grad! We should know each other!"

"My name is Lilian Quick," I say. "But I haven't done her program. I'm Eleven's cousin."

"I'm Violet," she says. "It's an honor to meet you." I like Eleven's followers already. They're humble and respectful.

"Ohmigod, it's hitting me," says the girl with the purple eyeshadow. "Eleven is your cousin? She's *amazing*." She holds her hands out in front of her like the air is heavy. "I *love* your cousin. She literally changed my life."

"I know," I say. "She's always been this way, even when we were kids. I knew she'd grow up to do something significant."

"Can you tell us her real name?"

Listen to the messages from your body. I almost say her name but my throat feels heavy. Does she want people to know about her childhood?

"I don't feel right talking about that without her here," I say.

Violet nods. "Say no more."

"We haven't seen each other for a long time."

"I'm catching what you're putting on."

"What a funny turn of phrase!" I say. "Where are you from?" Oh no! Why did I say that? It sounded like criticism!

"California," Violet says carefully.

"Sorry, I don't mean *funny*. I've just never heard that before, 'catching what you're putting on.'"

"How many of Eleven's events have you gone to?" interrupts the girl.

I shake my head. "I haven't even seen her onstage before."

"Oh, wow!" she trills, purple eyes blinking. "Okay, I haven't seen her in person before either, this is my first time, but I *have* been in her live tele-classes before. I've been following her for a year and a half now. She's *real*."

The bathroom lineup moves infinitesimally and a woman with long red braids squeezes past us and the rest of our cluster. Her boots click as she walks out. So much good hair tonight!

"Do you read her newsletters? Do you get her Daily Depth Charges? Have you seen her YouTube channel? Did you know she was part of the Oprah conference this year?"

"Are you an Ascendency grad, too?" I forget if she told me that already.

"No," she says. "Violet and I just met tonight. But I'd *love* to go to Ascendency. It's on my vision board. Does that sound ridiculous? Did I just say that out loud?"

A mechanical hiss. Three toilets flush almost in unison. Our line moves up a chunk.

"I'm Kim," the girl says. She offers me her hand. "It sounds silly, but I'm just starting to realize that I'm spiritual. I never admitted it—or recognized it—before."

"I love the way Eleven creates such a safe place for women to connect like this," says Violet.

"It's a wonderful community," I say. "I'd love to stay in touch. Here's my card." I open my wallet and find two clean cards. They both showcase a painting of Bruno, a yellow Lab with an olive-green aura.

"Can I take a picture of us together?" Kim asks, phone in hand. "This is just so cool, meeting Eleven's cousin."

"Sure!" I say. "Tag me in it!" She steps close and puts her face beside mine. Her phone flashes when it takes the pic, and I know it will make my face look big and doughy.

"Can you do it again without flash?" I ask. "I know that sounds weird and vain." *Let yourself want what you want.*

"Let me do it," says Violet. She steps back, taps Kim's phone a few times with her index finger, and then snaps us. She hands the phone back. "Gorgeous," she says.

We are now standing at the threshold of the women's bathroom. We focus on the double lines of steel doors quietly. Women are talking to each other over and under the stalls.

"Have you read Jonathan Rasmussen's new book?"

"I've read *about* it, but I don't have it yet."

"I heard it's transformative."

"Honestly, I don't understand most of it. It gets too theoretical."

"I don't know if I'm going to get the book yet. I want him to come to Toronto."

"He lives here now."

"He lives in California."

"He was just divorced."

"I thought he lived in Stockholm!"

"No, he lives in Toronto. He's not divorced. He bought a house in High Park."

A bathroom stall opens, and I go in.

"How does Eleven know him?"

"From Bali, I think."

"Eleven never lived in Bali. Are you thinking Hawaii? She lives in Maui."

"She used to live with a woman from Maui. Now she lives in Kauai."

These people know more about Eleven than I do. I didn't know that she knew Jonathan Rasmussen. It makes sense though—they vibrate at the same frequency. I flush the toilet and watch the tissue seat cover twist into the plumbing and go. I release the metal rod that locks my stall and go out again, and another woman takes my place. These women are Jonathan Rasmussen groupies.

I've been following him for about two years now. Longer than I've followed Eleven. He started Active Meditation, a program in New Zealand that incorporates surfing and yoga with mindfulness study. I've never taken any of his workshops, but I love his app and his newsletters. He's written four books, and all of them have been on the *New York Times* bestseller list. Since Active Meditation, he's expanded his offerings and launched two new programs on his website. Active Meditation, the in-person program, is exclusive now. You have to be on a list for over a year before you can register, and getting on the list is only by invitation—you have to know a graduate of the program to get an invite. This year, his new big product is an online program called Your Money Your Life, a course on wealth intimacy.

I wish I could do a workshop with Jonathan Rasmussen. When I read his emails, I feel warmth and light, as if his energy is radiating out from wherever he is. His words are powerful and clear. I haven't read his books yet, but his emails are smart, honest, and personal.

I touch my lime-green tickets. Seats F12 and F13. Okay, it's time to go.

The woman in seat F11 has a hoarse party voice like a football coach. Her eyebrows are plucked into two sperm-shaped arcs, and she wears bright-orange lip gloss that's a bit too warm for her cool, pale skin.

"I'm in seat *eleven*!" she calls to the women beside her, all down the row. "What does that *mean*?" Her smile is so wide. I'm charmed by her positive personality. Thick brows are back in style, I want to tell her. You're young! It might not be too late to grow yours back! And if she wore a bright-pink gloss, she could highlight her natural beauty. I'm so judge-y! Why do I feel the need to be critical right now?

"It's a sign," I tell her. "This is going to be a good night for you!"

She turns to face me and I am pinned by her dark eyes. They aren't unfriendly, they're just jarring, because her pupils are large and intensely shiny. "I know, right?" she rasps.

I take seat F12 and put my purse on the empty seat beside me. I'm sad that Juliette can't be here. The stage floor is dark grey, and Eleven's chartreuse signature is splashed on a big screen behind the stage. A clear acrylic podium stands stage left, with a skinny white microphone bent over it. A white cord runs down the side of the podium, along the floor, and offstage, behind folds of black curtains.

I take a pic of the stage and Eleven's huge signature. Some of the crowd gets in the shot. The signature turns out blurry because it's dim in the room. I put a filter on it to make it more colour-saturated and hope the blur looks atmospheric.

@LilianQuick> Crowd is pumped for @ElevenNovak tonight! #EYEToronto #limegreen

Soft music plays: trumpets and bass. An Auto-Tuned ocean wave. The murmur of a female voice saying something in Spanish. The women in the theatre thrum with the beat. A petite woman wearing black-framed glasses walks onstage and looks out at us, taking in the crowd. Her face is projected on the screen behind her. Her thick hair is styled in short, natural twists, parted impeccably on one side. She looks at us as though she is about to introduce something we have all our lives wished to see, but don't believe exists, like a talking dragon, or Santa Claus. The voices in the theatre hush, intensify with an increase of whispering, and then go quiet again.

"Good evening," the woman says. The mic is too high for her. She pulls it down, but it won't go all the way down, so she lets it hover over her eyes and nose as she speaks to us. The white mic stands out against her dark-brown skin. She's wearing a tailored black dress, opaque black tights, and tall black boots with heels. Her matte lipstick glows red. "My name," she says, "is Yolanda."

When we hear her name, we all applaud and cheer. It's exciting to see Yolanda in person! This is Eleven's right-hand woman! I know from reading Eleven's newsletters that Yolanda runs the show. She's very organized.

"We love you, Yolanda!" shouts the raspy woman beside me.

Yolanda smiles and inhales deeply. When she exhales, the crowd goes quiet. It's as if she's just calibrated the energy of the whole crowd to match the energy of her own body. Yolanda has an intimidating presence. I can feel it from here.

"Before we start tonight, we want to ask you to turn off your cell phones. Please do this now." The woman next to me slips her phone out of her back pocket. Mine is already in my hand, and I click the tiny lever that turns the volume off. The screen shows an image of a bell with a line through it to confirm that my phone is indeed on silent. I turn it on and off again just to make sure. It's so hard to trust it.

The woman beside me powers her phone right off. So do the women all along the row. Their faces glow in the light of their small screens, and one by one each goes dark. Do I have to turn my phone *off*-off? Isn't silent okay?

I check my inbox one more time. Refresh. *Updating. Downloading 1 of 1.*

Automated E-Payment
Lilian, Julio Guthrie sent you $75.00!
Click here to deposit.

This is the remaining payment from the schnauzer portrait I did last month! Wow! What are the chances of it coming *right now*, right at the exact moment I'm powering down my phone and getting ready to watch Eleven? It's a wink from the Universe—it's so obvious. I'm in the right place at the right time. The lesson for me here is to relax and trust. Money will come to me when I need it. I made seventy-five dollars today, not counting this free ticket, which is almost like making fifty dollars. Plus what Nana Boondahl owes me. I'm going to assume that she *will* pay me, of course. If I can use my hand to paint, I'll be okay for rent this month. Money comes to me when I need it.

I power my phone down and slip it in my purse's phone pocket. There's a floating moment, not unpleasant, where I feel the freedom of not having it in my hand, but this quickly turns into blankness that I fill with thoughts. What am I missing? Should I have deposited the money right away? What if people are commenting on my feed? I won't get my texts, but anyone who sends me a text won't know where I am, or why I can't answer. Unless they see my feed, because I just posted a pic of where I am right now, so they can see that. Oh, my active mind! Thinking is taking me out of the present moment. I try to focus on something that is happening right here, right now. Something I can notice but not think about. Yolanda smiles and walks off the stage. Whatever it was that she just said, I missed it.

The lights dim. The music rises. The crowd hoots and woos and then holds its breath.

Eleven appears. She comes on the stage in vanilla sequins, sparkling like a unicorn, walking in shiny champagne stilettos. Her hair is a long, glistening mane of gold, yellow, and platinum streaks. It moves around her head with a power all its own and settles over her shoulders like a royal creature.

The woman on the stage is older than the girl I remember. Obviously. I should have expected that—I've seen her in photos. But it's still a shock to see it in person. Eleven is Florence, but twenty years later. The air lights up around her.

The crowd screams and applauds, and Eleven bows to us, palms together. Her sequined dress makes a spectacle of itself: the stage lights reflect and shoot silver pellets of light into the air. She beams at us. The arm of a tiny headset mic extends along her jawline, matched to the colour of her skin so it is almost invisible.

She's always been dazzling. Even as a kid, Florence had something that nobody else had. She had height, strength, and oh!—she had that big head of gold hair. How I wished for her hair! Florence taught me how to dance. She taught me how to talk to other people. She taught me how to tell jokes. She taught me how to do a lot of things.

"Welcome to Express Your Enlightenment, gorgeous women! I haven't been to your city for many, many years. It's a bit surreal to be here right now, I have to tell you. I don't remember much about this city except a trip I once took to the zoo. And that tower. The tower is still here, I see!"

I don't remember going to the zoo with her. Did we go to the zoo together? But we didn't live in Toronto by the time she visited. We lived farther north, in Sudbury. Maybe Uncle Jimmy and Aunt Rosie brought her to the zoo on their way up to visit us. Or maybe it happened and I was there, and I just forgot.

"It's wonderful to be here. I want to thank you for coming tonight, for putting your minds and bodies and spirits together in one place, for one powerful evening, with all these like-minded souls. This is a rare occasion, to be together like this, in real time.

"I want to honor this choice that you have made. I want to acknowledge your presence and your power. And I want to tell you with deep sincerity, thank you.

"I know there are some of you in the audience tonight who have been to Express Your Enlightenment before. Hello, friends!"

Applause sprinkles throughout the theatre, and someone calls out from behind me: "Hi, Eleven!"

"And there are many of you here for the first time, people who are new to me and my work. Welcome!"

We clap again.

"As a way to feel grounded and connected to each other, let's start the evening with some Active Meditation." A purr of recognition and approval spreads through the crowd. "I have a surprise guest tonight," Eleven says. She looks over her shoulder and off-stage, smiling to someone behind the black curtains. Then she looks back at us.

"Jonathan," she says. "Sweetheart, can you come out here and take us through?"

I blink. My heart jumps up in my chest. Jonathan Rasmussen is here? Tonight? This was not on the ticket! Around me, women are whistling and heaving their arms into the air like wings, clapping together in slow, whopping percussion, as their hands meet above their heads in namaste.

He's more delicate than I imagined he would be. He wears a wine-coloured button-down shirt, untucked, with dark jeans and black Converse sneakers. His legs are nicely shaped, but they look disproportionately short. Maybe because Eleven is standing beside him, the height contrast appears unfair. His shirt sleeves are rolled back several times, revealing wrists that are covered in whorls of dark hair. I stare and stare at him. I want so much to take a picture so I can save this moment. He's smiling and hugging Eleven now. His hair is wavy and thick, just like his website head shot. He looks just like himself! Except for his size.

The screen behind the stage goes black, and the entire room darkens.

Then the sound of ocean waves. The screen lights up again. Turquoise waves crashing into white froth on a sandy shore. "Stand up, please," says Jonathan Rasmussen. We stand up, hundreds of us, and make a theatre-wide rustle.

"You're at the beach," says Jonathan. "Can you feel it? Keep your eyes open. Always keep your eyes open when you meditate. You don't want to shut down. You want to be open to the world around you.

"Lit your ears be microphones. Your eyes are a camera. Your skin feels the salt spray. You breathe in, and you breathe out. Your skin is so very . . . *sinsitive.*"

He says the word softly, and the mic picks up every nuance of his esses. The waves on the screen rise and fall, and I feel my mind and body become one thing. For a few seconds. I slip out of it again and see that it's a projection on a screen and I'm standing in a theatre. But for a few seconds, I was there! I try to focus again.

"This is your spirit," Jonathan whispers. "This is your centre. Feel it in your body. Now I'd like you to start moving a little. Just start with your fingers. Your wrists."

I wiggle my fingers. My hand doesn't hurt at all anymore, but the bandage and the gauze feel tight, and my injury makes that hand feel heavier than the other one. I make circles with my wrists.

"You are the ocean. Fill the way the waves crash and pull up, crash and pull up . . ."

He says "crash" like "crèche." I lose any sense of the meaning of the word "crash," and instead I only hear *crèche, crèche, crèche.* It is the sound of the waves themselves. *Crèche, crèche.* Jonathan Rasmussen is just a silhouette on the stage. He is dwarfed by the waves above him.

"Move from side to side now," he says. "Begin your sway. Feel that you are the ocean. You carry the ocean inside your belly. Your spine is seaweed. Move with the water. Move with the water. Feel your skin, the way it interacts with the air in the room. See that it is also touching water. The water is in, the water is out. You are in the wave. You are the wave. This is your centre. There is no centre. You are right here, and you are there."

I sway with his words.

"You are everywhere," Jonathan Rasmussen says.

The row in front of me moves like an underwater forest. We are all strands of kelp moving in the water. We move ourselves like waves until we become water.

My hand. Something is dripping out of the palm of my hand. I can feel warm blood on my fingers, seeping and pulsing out. My hand is bleeding! Is my hand bleeding? The theatre is too dark. I can't see what's happening. I hold my hand up to my face to see if I'm imagining the wetness. Could it be the Active Meditation? Am I in a trance? The bandage is intact. I feel it, and I think I feel wet. My stitches must have broken. I must be bleeding through the bandage. I have no idea how gory it looks. In the dark, my fingers feel monstrous, my palm feels big and fat. I can't see the edges of my hand. Are the drips as bad as they feel? How much am I dripping on the floor? I wish I'd brought an extra piece of paper towel from the bathroom.

I reach down beside me to touch my purse. Both hands feel sticky now from the blood. I'm making a mess of everything. When I turn around, I am faced by a row of swaying women. The light from the ocean on the screen makes their faces glow. They stare and move like they're slow-dancing. They look like beautiful zombies. I raise my right hand above my head to slow the blood, and with my other hand, I feel around my purse for a soft pile of wool. My gloves. I raise my other hand to meet the first, both hands in the air now, and wipe my fingers and my wrists with my gloves. The gloves are made out of thin wool—they're not even absorbent! My Active Meditation is ruined.

The stage lights rise slightly, and the ocean fades from the screen. I'm the only one with her hands up. I lower my arms and hold the gloves to my hand, apply pressure so the bleeding will stop. Eleven hugs Jonathan Rasmussen and sends him out through the curtains and offstage. She stands in the centre of the stage, very still. She holds her arms out at her sides, both hands cupped up slightly. The sequins on her sleeves sparkle and give off light. It's a pose I recognize from a picture of Jesus that used to be on the wall in our grandma's bedroom.

Without any preamble or introduction, Eleven begins to call out her Sacred Ascendency Prayer. It's familiar to everyone, because we've all downloaded the desktop wallpaper. Eleven's Ascendency Prayer is the long form of her tagline, *Want what you want*. She's had the prayer printed on mugs, embossed onto notebook covers, and embroidered on pillows. You can buy phone cases and prints in her online shop. Many of the women in the audience recite it with her.

I have it memorized, too—I try to make a point of doing one of each of the prayers every day—but I'm so floored by Eleven's presence on the stage, I can't find my voice. My body tingles as she says the words. I can feel my own heart beating. That's Florence! My cousin Florence!

Create before you consume.
Listen to the messages from your body.
Remind yourself, "I'm here."
Do no more than three things a day.
Love is a verb, not a noun.
Dance about it.
Joy does not exist without gratitude.
Courage is action in the presence of fear.
Rest until you want to play; play until you want to rest.

Let yourself want what you want.
Live the way you love to feel.

I sit in my seat with my hands in my lap and watch Eleven's mouth as she speaks. She sways from stage left to stage right, her blond hair glinting under the gel lights, her shoulders shining.

I almost booked the painting pickup date with Nana Boondahl. Why would I stab myself just before making that date? Why do I keep sabotaging myself like this? Do I have some issue with my own worth? Some fear of entitlement? Or is it fear of success? Regardless, even with the surprise money from the Christmas schnauzer piece, I need to finish Sophia before next month. Maybe I don't charge enough for my work. But my clients couldn't afford my work if I charged what I should. What's wrong with me? This isn't how you're supposed to run a business. This isn't a successful life. I'm too old for this.

"Do you love who you are?" Eleven asks us. "Do you love where you are going?"

The audience murmurs, a sound like wings ruffling. Nana Boondahl isn't my usual type of client. But maybe she is, now. Maybe things are shifting. Maybe I'm attracting a new kind of client. I *have* been working on wooing. One of the bravest things I've ever done was go to Sarah Polley's housewarming party with Fleurje to woo Parker Posey. Fleurje was invited because she sold Sarah the house. I knew Parker Posey was going to be there, and she has a dog she loves so much he has his own Twitter feed: Udo. Not surprisingly, he has a purple aura! I did a drawing of Udo and I brought it to the party.

That move really opened it all up for me and my business. It was my first shot at the art of wooing, so it was a bit awkward, true. I had hoped to meet Udo in person, but she said that he doesn't like crowds, so she had to leave him at home. I gave her the portrait— nothing too large, just a five by seven in a simple wood frame. She's ecologically minded, so I knew she'd appreciate not having plastic. She placed it in her purse, a canvas bag that read VOTE. She was really very grateful. I think she *loved* it. I used archival paper and UV protection glass.

I waited to see if she'd tag me on Twitter. But—nothing. She's pretty busy, I guess, with promoting her new book on green living and eco-friendly transportation. So I eventually tweeted Udo directly.

@LilianQuick> @Udodog! Do you like your portrait? xoxo Lilian

@Udodog> @LilianQuick YEAH THANKS!

Once Udo tweeted me (!) I got *hundreds* of new followers. Right away I posted some new pics of pet aura portraits, to show what kind of work I can do for commissions. It was a good business strategy: I leveraged! This was over a year ago now. Maybe I need to pull another stunt like that—more wooing. I'm not great with people, but I can do it when I have to.

"I love you all so much," she calls out over our heads. Her voice is deep and she speaks slowly and I can hear her breathing. "You are perfect and you are beautiful. Do you know your own beauty? Do you know your own worth?"

We nod yes.

"Show me! I want you to show me that you know your own per-fection. Will you show me?"

"Yes," we say.

"Say it!" Her hair quivers under the stage lights. "Say it with me! *I am perfect as I am!*" I see Florence up there, in flashes—like a ghost of young Florence is living right underneath Eleven's features. Twenty years is a long time. But Eleven looks so different, and it's not just age. There's a sheen to Eleven that I didn't see on Florence. It's not that Florence didn't have brightness—she did. Seeing Eleven onstage, so shiny, reminds me how beautiful Florence was as a girl, even without the shine.

"I am perfect as I am!" we yell.

"Louder!"

"I am perfect as I am!" I yell it as loud as I can. Fleurje has a thing about not screaming more than once at a concert, whenever a star makes a demand for screams. She says it's unreasonable, and besides, since she's the one who paid to be at the event, she's the one who wants to be dazzled—she doesn't think she should have to push herself to dazzle the star of the show. I think she's afraid to lose control. I shout, "I am perfect as I am!" again. Seat eleven beside me is in her element. Screaming is in her Genius Zone. She rasps and coughs out her promise with dry, passionate enthusiasm, and laughs as she claps. Her laughter is so dry, it sounds like she needs a glass of water. But she's a sweet person, you can tell.

"Can I have a mic, Yolanda?" Yolanda steps out from the curtains and hands Eleven a cordless microphone. Eleven takes the stairs beside the stage, steps down, and walks through the aisles, scanning the audience.

"Why did you come here tonight, Toronto?" she says. "Why are you here?" The house lights go all the way up, so we are all exposed. My hand is dry. There's no blood! My mind totally made that up. I totally overreacted when I was encased in darkness. Isn't that funny, how the mind can take over like that and make something out of absolutely nothing? It felt so real. This is a good self-learning moment. What else have I been telling myself is real, when it's only been an illusion?

Eleven stops in front of someone sitting by the aisle near the front. "Hello," she says, and gives the mic to her.

The woman has salt-and-pepper hair and wears purple glasses. She holds the mic in one hand. "Hello," the woman says.

"Why did you come here?" Eleven asks.

The woman looks at the microphone, and then looks up at Eleven. "I came to be inspired," she says.

"You came to be inspired! And how do you feel so far? What's your name?"

"I'm Linda," she says. "I feel like it's . . . time for me."

"Time! It's time, Linda! Good! I'm glad to hear it. I'm so glad you know it's time. Time for what?"

"Time to listen to my intuition?"

"And do you know how to hear your intuition? Do you know how it feels when you are listening to it? Do you know where your intuition comes from?"

"From . . . my heart?"

"Yes," Eleven says. "Yes, your heart. But also your second brain. The one in your belly. The one your body knows. The one you activate by . . . wait. Do you know how to activate it, Linda?"

Linda looks at Eleven and says, "Sex?"

We all laugh. It's kind, though, and it relieves tension. We are laughing with Linda, because any one of us could have said the same thing! It's tough to be put on the spot like that, in front of everyone. And the way Eleven was asking, it *sounded* like she was talking about sex. It totally did.

"Yes!" Eleven laughs too. "Sex is a fantastic way to activate your intuition. But sometimes, you know, we're just not *in the mood*, are we, Linda? Sometimes we're feeling a bit . . . stuck. Not so sensual, actually. Not so *into it*. Hard to go from zero to ten just like that. You have to invigorate yourself with love, even before that. You have to activate the part of yourself that *feels desire* before you can feel desire! And I don't just mean *sex*. Although, that's part of it, isn't it?"

The crowd cheers. I have a feeling every single person in this room has more sexual experience than I have. I'm okay with that, though. I'm comfortable being a loner.

"There's another way you can activate your body, Linda. There's something you're going to learn here tonight. Something so easy you can do it anywhere. Something that your body recognizes right away as deliciousness. We're all going to do it together. Right now. Can you guess what that is?"

"Um," Linda says into the mic. "Is it dancing?"

"Yes!" says Eleven. "Dancing!" She takes the mic back and walks to the front of the stage. "Whenever there is a question, whenever you feel a block in your divine center, whenever you feel that your body isn't picking up the clues, what are you going to do about it?"

"Dance about it!" we shout.

"Heart first, darlings. You dance, heart first. Get up! Stand up!"

We all stand up and reposition our smushed coats over the chair backs behind us.

"Dim the lights, Monicke love." The house lights go dark.

Eleven looks out at the crowd. "Can we have something that rumbles, Monicke? Can you introduce us to our hips, please?"

Aretha Franklin bounces out of the speakers. The women around me swivel their hips and swing their hands in the air. I bend my knees and bounce that way until I catch the beat. I can't remember the last time I danced! That can't be good. I'm going to schedule regular dance breaks at least once a day. I will set an alarm on my phone to remind me. The woman beside me swings her head side to side. Her hair whips across her face, and her arm mirrors the movement. She's syncopated! I'm moving my hips, doing the best dance that I can in this row of theatre chairs, but my body is a flag shaking in the wind compared to the woman in seat F11. She moves with confidence. She's smiling as she shimmies, and sees me watching her. She grins, full of joy. I wish I could do what she's doing. Her dance moves look professional. Maybe she's actually a dancer. Maybe she teaches dance classes, and has already performed on a stage. *R-E-S-P-E-C-T*, sings Aretha. I close my eyes so I don't start copying F11's moves and look like I don't know how to find my own dance moves. When I close my eyes, I can feel the music better.

The song is over. We're in our seats. "A consciousness shift is happening *right now*," says Eleven. "Never before in history have we had this opportunity. The digital impact holds unprecedented power for our world. We can connect to each other in ways we've never connected.

"This is about true, loving power, gorgeous women. I'm talking about your worthiness. Your presence. The magic you hold in your core. Every single one of you is incendiary. I'm talking about your willingness to rise."

The room is charged. It hums with heart energy. My own heart feels so open, and I can feel everyone's open heart around me. This is what connection feels like.

"Are you here with the rest of us? Do you want this awareness to catch fire? Do you want to join a community of women who empower by pure presence?"

We all cheer and shout, *Yes!*

"Are you going to RISE?"

I'm moved. My cousin has a way with words. She's an orator! It comes more easily to her because she's American. True public speakers aren't afraid to be seen as impolite, like Canadians are. Yes, I'm ready to rise! Yes, I'm ready to feel creative and empowered and connected! Yes, I'm ready to be alive in my own life!

"Say it with me three times, and we will turn it into an incantation. Yes?"

"We are going to rise," we call. "We are going to rise. We are going to rise."

"This is what the Ascendency Program is all about, my darlings. In Ascendency, you learn how to harness your own creative energy— the source that is life itself—and you bring it to fruition.

"I would like to call some of last year's Ascendency graduates to the stage. Come up, my darlings. Come up, come up, come up."

Throughout the theatre, women stand up and make their way to the front. They walk up the steps to the stage one at a time and arrange themselves in a semicircle. They are all dressed up: they wear pencil skirts, sleek sheath dresses, and heels, and each of their outfits features Eleven's colour palette: white, green, and gold. Violet is up there, in her lime-green tights. The big screen lights up so we can see their faces. Violet's *E* necklace is a shiny spot of gold. The same pendant hangs around the necks of the other Ascendency grads, too. Oh! They all have the same necklace!

"My name is Jess," says the red-haired woman at the left end of the arc. "When I started Ascendency, I had one hundred dollars in my bank account." She wears a white dress with a green silk scarf. The green of the scarf looks lovely with her hair. Redheads are so lucky.

"I put the program on my credit card and hoped for a miracle," she says, and looks over at the other women on the stage with her. They nod and smile. "The thing is? What I didn't realize at the time? That I *am* the miracle."

The women on stage clap and murmur their agreement to encourage her. "That's right," says Violet. "Say it."

"Eleven showed me how to find the power that I already had. She showed me how to get out of my own way and *be* the energy that is already there. Now it's one year later, and I've launched my own business as an EYE Life Coach. And this year, I can't even believe I'm standing here telling this to you . . . this year, my income hit six figures!"

We all cheer at that. I want to clap, but my hand. Instead, I whop my knee with my good hand. How amazing. Could she be for real? The crowd pulses with excitement. She's for real!

Violet holds the mic next. "When I signed up for Ascendency," she says, "I was doing really well as a spa owner in Monterey. But I was so stressed out. I was overworked, unhappy, stretched too thin. I asked myself, How can you promise to give people the gift of serenity and relaxation when you're running around like a chicken with its head knocked up?

"After Ascendency, I took an honest look at my life dream. Of course, I still want to give people the gifts of peace and serenity. But I don't want to manage a spa. Being a spa manager was never my dream! So after learning what I learned in Ascendency, I became an EYE Life Coach, and now I have the freedom I've always wanted. I work from my laptop twice a week, giving Skype sessions to people who are in the midst of difficult life transitions, like divorce, illness, having children. I feel like I'm helping people, because I learned how to take care of myself first. And here's the strange thing: now I'm making even more money than before, when I was a burnt-up spa owner."

I love Violet's story. She is so honest. I can relate: I always catch myself thinking that money will make my problems go away.

The mic is passed to the third woman in the row. She wears a stretchy white dress. She's the shortest one in the group by at least a foot, even in those tall caramel high-heeled boots. "I'm Whitney," she says. "When I signed up for Ascendency, I weighed two hundred and eighty-six pounds. I felt ashamed about my size. I felt ashamed when I went shopping for clothes. I felt ashamed when I was in the grocery store. I felt ashamed to just *be*."

The theatre is very quiet.

"I was thirty-eight years old. My husband was stationed in Afghanistan. I wanted to have children. My doctor told me that she was concerned about my health, and said it would be difficult to conceive. I felt ashamed when I was at the doctor. So, I started dieting. I counted out five walnut halves every morning. I snacked on romaine lettuce and pretended it was chips. My weight didn't change, but I felt even worse. I hated myself.

"A friend from work sent me one of Eleven's emails. It was a poem Eleven had written about comfort. Some of you might even know it." A few of the women onstage nodded. "There was this line, 'I look for comfort in the high place and the low place / But I find true comfort in my own face.' When I read that line, I just started bawling. It was exactly what I needed to hear—it came at the exact right time for me to see it. I enrolled in Ascendency that day. I hadn't even read any of Eleven's other work—I just took it as a sign from God.

"In the first year of Ascendency, I stopped dieting and started to love myself. And I lost thirty-five pounds, *without even trying*. It's been two years since then, and I've lost sixty-six pounds. My husband is back in the States now." She smiles and looks shyly at the women who stand on either side of her. "And I've recently found out that I'm pregnant with my first child!"

Everybody cheers. The women on stage all hug each other. A wave of joy spreads through the theatre. Most of the women in this audience must already be mothers themselves or want to have children. Everyone seems genuinely happy for her. I've never felt a maternal instinct or a biological clock, so I don't really get it, but it's nice to feel the surge of pleasure around me.

One by one, the other women share their stories too. One woman quit her corporate job and formed a band, another told her whole family she was a lesbian, and another found her soulmate and moved to a horse ranch. I feel so inspired. I love painting, but my business isn't supporting me financially. I know I'm missing something. This experience might actually be the thing I need the most. This might be what takes my business to a new level. Can I afford to do this? These women are so smart and connected and successful. Can I afford to *not* do this? I wish Fleurje were here. She'd just tell me to do it and write it off as a business expense. It's clearly professional development. I could do that. I have some room on my business credit card. Maybe I can do Ascendency. If Eleven has a payment plan.

Eleven is the glowing centre of the stage. The grads stand behind her in white and green, flanking her on both sides like wings. "The Ascendency Program attracts women from around the world," Eleven says. "Now, I wish I could take all of you this year, but I can't." She sweeps her hand slowly across the audience. "Part of what makes the program so powerful is that it's such an intimate group." She stares up toward the back of the theatre. "Only about one-tenth of you would fit into Ascendency." How many of us are here? Two thousand?

"Some of you don't know how Ascendency works, so let me just tell you a little bit about it. Ascendants travel to meet each other for three in-person retreats. The first retreat is in New York City, the first weekend of March. The second retreat is in Portland, Oregon, the first weekend in April. The third and final retreat—and the graduation ceremony—is in Oahu, at the start of May. We also meet for two Telerituals during the program. Every week of the entire program, students get live calls with the women in their hand-picked Potency Circles.

"Ascendency can trigger some big life changes, so participants will always have the opportunity to receive support from expert EYE Life Coaches, at any time. We record all the calls, of course, so if you have to miss a Teleritual, or even one of the in-person retreats, you can experience them later, on your own schedule."

A cold breeze hits the back of my neck. A door must be open somewhere, letting in a draft of outside air. I use my good hand to wrap my scarf around my shoulders.

"I want to thank all of you for coming tonight. I am grateful that you are here, sharing your divine light." She smiles, and the air around her dazzles. That's my cousin. I'm so lucky: she's my *family*!

"If you pay in installments, the tuition for Ascendency is nine thousand, eight hundred and ninety-five dollars," Eleven says. "If you pay all at once, it's nine thousand, five hundred and seventy-five dollars." She smiles. "But just for tonight, because the energy in this room is so magical, I've decided that anyone who enrolls in Ascendency with a payment plan can do it for seven thousand, nine hundred, and ninety-five dollars. And if you enroll tonight and pay all at once, it's seven thousand, five hundred and seventy-five dollars. That's *two thousand dollars less than the price of regular tuition!*"

Cheers of excitement through the theatre. The numbers are all mixed in my head—wait. Is it seven thousand dollars or eight? If I pay on a payment plan, is it still two thousand dollars off?

"If you want to sign up for Ascendency, you just have to go out those doors at the back—we have a table set up in the lobby. Anna-Mackenzie is sitting there now, waiting for you!"

A woman a few rows ahead of me stands up. "Eleven!" she shouts. "I'm going to do Ascendency this year!"

The women on stage jump up and down, and the theatre applauds and screams happily. Seat F11 jumps out of her seat and shouts in her scratchy voice, "Me too! I'm going to do Ascendency this year! *Yeah!*" People are stomping their feet, standing and cheering. I'm trying to do the math in my head. What would the deposit be for an eight-thousand-dollar program? I want to be up there, on stage with my cousin and that arc of shining women.

"Look around, my sweethearts, look around! I have a special treat for you tonight—here they come, right now!" Several women carrying big trays come out of the black curtains. They wear giant white ostrich feathers in their hair. They take the stage steps one by one and wander up the aisles, their feathers twitching in the air like cats' tails, so we can see them in the crowd. The trays are stacked with white cupcakes in gold paper liners. The women distribute themselves through the theatre evenly. One tray is coming closer and closer to row F. Tiny chartreuse toothpick flags are stuck in the top of each cupcake. A gold *E* is embossed on each flag.

"These are special cupcakes, my loves," she says. "These came all the way from a bakery in Portland, Oregon. Yes! That's right. We flew them in just for you tonight. These are from the Conscious Cupcakery. This bakery is owned by an Ascendency grad named

Winnie Prudhomme. Winnie stores her special gluten-free flour blend in a sacred room, where it is infused with the positive intentions of meditating monks. She bakes the cupcakes to the sounds of daily prayer chants from a Tibetan monastery. These cupcakes are no ordinary treat. They're dairy-free, naturally sweetened without sugar, and made with pure, unprocessed oils. When you eat them, you restore your own peaceful energy. Enjoy!"

People peel off the cupcake wrappers slowly and take their first bites. They look so good. I'm hungry. All I've had to eat today is two granola bars and that weird guacamole at Juliette's house. The polar opposite of these little cakes, which are made with love and intention. How will it feel to eat one? Will I be able to feel the energy? I eye the feather that looks like it's closest to our row. There aren't that many cakes on each tray, once the rows start getting to them. Do they have enough? Are there enough to go around, really?

"Before I leave you tonight, we are going to dance together one more time!" Eleven cries. "Monicke! Set us on fire!"

Eleven is laughing now, and I recognize that big grin. It's Florence, through and through. The music starts up again—Alicia Keys. Eleven's headset mic must be turned off now, because I can see her mouth moving as she laughs and dances, but there's no sound. She looks like Aunt Rosie when she laughs, her mouth wide in a way that would be ugly if you tried to describe it to somebody, but when you see it on her face, you're stunned because it's so beautiful.

I dance, and close my eyes and tell myself to trust that there are enough cupcakes for everyone. The air smells like vanilla and cardamom. My hand doesn't even hurt anymore. I zig-zag my feet in the little space I have in front of my theatre seat, jumping side to side, not a real dance move really, but who cares, it feels so good to jump like this. I haven't checked my phone for more than an hour, and I don't even care what I've missed. I'm going to put Ascendency on my business credit card and I'm going to trust that there will be enough work to pay for it. Sophia's portrait is just the beginning of a rainstorm of portraits coming my way. I can launch a winter campaign, and once people see that I'm working with Nana Boondahl I'll have so many more appointments, and they'll be the kind of client I really *want* to attract. I will use the power of attraction to find the very best subjects. No more poverty mindset!

The cupcakes reach our row, and F11 passes me one. "I'm going to do Ascendency!" I shout so she can hear me over Alicia Keys. "I'll see you in Oahu!" I cry.

"YEAH!" she shouts back to me and jumps up and down. She raises her gold-and-white cupcake with the tiny green flag up above her head. "Awesome!" she says. "I'll see you there!"

"My name is Lilian!" I shout, and take a bite of my cupcake. It tastes like sweet, spiced clouds from heaven.

"NO WAY!" F11 cries. *"My name is Lillian, too!"*

And just like that, the magic sets and freezes into glittering place, like a crystal, and I see how things will be from now on. There are no coincidences.

Anna-Mackenzie's name is written on a name tag that's stuck on her wool sweater: ♥ Anna-Mackenzie ♥. Golden freckles cover her forehead, nose, and cheeks.

"Oops!" she says. "You must have tapped the wrong number by mistake." She shows me the MoneyJack screen on her tablet: *Declined*.

"This is for the payment plan, right?" I ask. "Just a deposit? I can't put the whole amount on my credit card today."

"Just a deposit." Anna-Mackenzie smiles. "Here, try again," she says. Her hair is the same colour as her freckles. She has the colouring of a red fox.

I wipe the stripe of my Quick+Friday business credit card on my thigh and slide it through the reader again. I tap OK, and then tap my four-digit PIN (my childhood phone number, 7896), and then tap OK once more. *Processing* . . .

"What happened to your hand?" she asks. Her earrings are crystal-studded triangles.

"I did something stupid," I say. "Oh, I love your earrings!"

"Thank you!" she smiles. "Wait, do I know you?" she asks. "You look familiar. Have you been to another EYE event?"

"Nope," I say. "This is my first one."

She looks puzzled. "Hmm," she says, and shows me the tablet screen. *Declined*.

The deposit is too much. I can't book Ascendency. What was I thinking? I can't even pay my rent.

"It's okay," I tell Anna-Mackenzie. "There must be something up with my balance. I didn't expect to enrol today. I'll have to go home and check my account. I'm sorry."

"Listen," she says. "We can try a lower amount, if you want. To see if a deposit will go through. Then when you get home you can pay the rest of your installment online. That will secure your spot in Ascendency, at least. And we can make sure you get the special rate. Don't worry."

"Thanks," I tell her. "I'll figure something out later."

"You'll figure something out," she says. "Just call this number when you're ready. We'd love to have you in our community, Lilian."

I button up my coat and get ready to leave the Sony Centre. Behind me, I hear a high voice say, "I thought the Ascendency was a woman-only space."

"Sometimes she invites him as a balance, because his energy is the divine masculine," someone answers.

"They used to date each other, though," the high voice says.

A third voice, low like a purr: "It helps with sales. Some women aren't used to so much feminine power."

I feel barely there. I have a vague feeling of myself, a thin presence. I'm not distracted, exactly, but I can't find traction on anything either. It's like a part of me wants to observe what I'm experiencing, so I'm here, but not really here. I turn on my phone, and it buzzes and beeps in my hand. This is a relief, and I feel a warm current of clarity when I see a rush of texts and IG notifications pile up on the screen.

Fleurje

How was it? Sorry again I couldn't go w u 2night.
Life is so crazy! Had a client call in the middle
of dinner—house closing now! Still waiting by phone

@**SweetPurr** likes your photo

@**Oceaneyes** likes your photo

@**Dolcedolce** likes your photo

@**UnderDog27>** @KellyViolet Check out @**LilianQuick!**
Pet portraits for Gus!

@**terrificpaws** likes your photo

@**Momtogranada** is now following your posts

Fleurje
DONE! Owners happy buyers happy I'm happy!
I live 4 nights like this!

@**JiffyUp>** Poor you! Feel better

When Florence and I were really little, like six years old, Uncle Jimmy let us ride on his back. He'd get down on all fours and we'd cinch our legs around his waist and hold on to his neck, and he'd romp around the backyard until he threw us off. Getting thrown off was part of the fun. One time, he threw me off and I tumbled onto the lawn sprinkler and cut my foot. I cried pretty hard, and Uncle Jimmy looked stricken. He picked me up in his arms, carried me to the porch swing, and set me down carefully, like I was a fragile ornament. When she saw the blood, Florence started to cry too, so then he picked her up and sat her carefully right next to me. Aunt Rosie said she couldn't look, so she hid in the kitchen while my mom cleaned up my foot and put a few Band-Aids on the cut. Uncle Jimmy gave Florence money and told her to get me an ice cream from the truck. She ran down the street and brought me back a Drumstick, and one for herself, and we ate them together on the swing. I still have a scar on the top of my foot from that fall—a pale line, like a brushstroke.

The sounds in the auditorium aren't as harsh. People have started to go home. I've lost track of my new friend Lilian, and I follow the pack of women out of the theatre, keeping an eye out for her. I can't find her anywhere. What if she spells her name Lillian? I didn't even get her last name, so I can't find her on Facebook. I bundle up before I go out, wrapping my scarf around as much of my face as possible. The cold ices my eyes instantly, and makes me blink. A jewelled chain of taxis waits in front of the doors. The marquee lights are dimmed now, or at least they appear to be less bright than they did before the show.

◊ ◊ ◊

At the Mutable Dragon the halls are papered with warm grey damask. A woody, resinous scent emanates from a low table in front of the ground floor elevator, where long thin sticks stand in an inch of oil in a glass jar. The central staircase curls up the inside of the hotel like a large tail. The chandeliers are crystal, the air spiked with light. Before I get in the elevator, I check myself in the mirror. My hair looks flat and lifeless. Should I really be doing this? Is Eleven actually expecting me to show up? I run my fingers through my hair to fluff it, take a deep breath, and press PH.

The penthouse is a large suite with multiple rooms and a panoramic view of the city. I spot Yolanda right away, dressed in her sheath of black, standing by the candlelit juice bar, looking sleek as a knife. A group of the graduates who'd been onstage are dancing together. One woman seems to be leading them in the dance: her thick hair is pulled up into a high, thrashing ponytail, and she's highlighted her copper-brown skin with purple sparkles. I bet that's Monicke. Drum and bass undulates from invisible speakers all around, and the entranceway is strewn with a variety of heeled boots and shoes.

"We're waiting for the light shew," announces Jonathan Rasmussen, from the corner. He's standing alone in front of a large sheet of window, wearing that same wine-coloured shirt and those Converse sneakers, even though everyone else appears to be shoeless.

"What *is* it, though?" Anna-Mackenzie asks. "Is it a cell tower, or what?"

"It looks like Seattle," Yolanda says.

Eleven has changed into jeans and a lemon T-shirt. Her feet are bare. She sees me at the door and her face brightens when she recognizes me. She spreads her arms apart and comes over, one hand carefully balancing a wine glass full of green liquid. She wraps one arm around my shoulders, keeping the other hand extended so she doesn't spill. Her hair is all over my face. She smells sweet, like cake and flowers. I have to stop smiling to keep her hair from slipping into my mouth.

"I've missed you so much," she says quietly in my ear. "Thank you for coming."

Her shoulders are strong. Even though she's only hugging me with one arm, half a hug basically, I can tell she's still athletic. I've always loved Florence's arms and shoulders. When we were little, we used to match our arms up to compare suntans. Both of us were blessed with the Bertolucci olive skin, so it was a fair contest. She's so close, I can see she's used a pencil on her brows. I've never pencilled my brows. Mine are dark naturally, so it's a beauty step I rarely think about. Eleven is blond, and her pale eyebrows could make her look washed-out on stage if she didn't enhance them. Her skin has a nice colour tonight—even though it's January! Would she get a spray tan? Well, she was just in L.A.

"You look beautiful, Florence," I say. "Even more than I remember." I sound so stupid! That was such a soap opera thing to say.

She lets go and steps back. "Call me Eleven, sweetie," she says, and smiles. Then she turns around. "Lilian is here!" she announces to the room. "This is my Canadian cousin!" She puts her hand around my waist.

As she speaks, all the faces in the room turn from Jonathan Rasmussen to me. They stare at me, their eyes moving down to my bandaged hand. Whitney, the pregnant Ascendency guard, waves.

"Leave your boots here," Eleven tells me.

I unzip them as instructed and stuff my coat into the packed hall closet. It stays up without a hanger, sandwiched between the others. I tiptoe around the salty boots and enter the room. Someone at the bar hands me a glass of foamy red wine. When I sniff it, it's pomegranate juice.

Jonathan Rasmussen glances at me. His eyes are dark brown, and his eyelashes are startlingly long and full-fringed. Abruptly he turns around and redirects his attention to the city outside. The cranes on top of the condo buildings are lit with coloured lights, lines of bright candy over the horizon.

Eleven glimmers in the dim hotel room. I lift my pomegranate juice to her green juice. "I loved your show," I tell her. "Is it a show? Do you call it a show?"

She grins. Her mouth moves sideways when she smiles, just like it used to. "You can call it a show. I like to call it an experience."

"You looked amazing onstage. Can I just say I am so proud to be your cousin right now?"

"Thank you," she says. "Yolanda was giving me grief because I went off-script at the end. But I felt the crowd and I thought they needed to hear the numbers."

"I'm so glad you got in touch. I mean, I was coming anyway. But thank you for inviting me. I was just about to get my ticket, and then you messaged me."

"What happened to your hand?"

"That's actually why your message was so special. I had this accident in my studio, and I was having kind of a rough day, and then I heard from you! Your timing is perfect. But I'm not surprised. You're connected."

She nods and then shrugs her shoulders. "I try," she says.

"It's been so cool to watch you become—famous. Can I say famous? You inspire so many people. I've been reading all your interviews and articles. I love that you came to Toronto."

"I couldn't miss Toronto," she says.

"You did come to stay with us one summer, though," I say. "Remember?"

"It's been so long," Eleven says, and sips her green juice. Her white nails stand out against the green. "I don't remember much from when we were kids."

"I remember *everything*," I say.

"Memory is fascinating, isn't it?" she says. "The way it's connected to the imagination."

"You know what's interesting?" My juice is pleasantly tangy and bitter, but it makes my teeth feel fuzzy. "We've been out of touch for so long, but we have been doing such similar things in life all this time! We're still kind of on the same path, even though we got there separately. I also went through a rough patch, like you. And I have an online business now, too. Everything you talk about in Ascendency makes so much sense to me."

"I've seen your site," Eleven says. "You've made animal auras into your career. That's so smart. And it's risky." She sips. "You're leveraging your superpower. I respect that."

"You've seen my work?" I ask.

"I have," she says. "You should meet our Temple dog, Portia. She's here tonight."

"I love the lime green you're using," I say. "I love your whole colour palette! It's so refreshing."

I used to be a drinker. I could drink a bottle every night. I mean, I was on the verge of becoming an alcoholic. I don't drink anymore. Drinking kept me from being present. That was the point of drinking, of course! I used to have social anxiety, and the wine made things feel better. A few years ago, I found a website for people like me. Not actual alcoholics, just people who used drinking to avoid real life.

The website suggested that I start journalling. It said that I should write something down in my journal every time I wanted to pour myself a drink. After a little while, I discovered that I was drinking because there was something I didn't want to feel. It sounds so obvious, I know. But this truly was a breakthrough.

That was when everything really changed for me. I quit drinking wine, built my own website, stopped journalling, and started blogging instead. You know, it's true: when you are committed to walking the right path, the Universe really does conspire to help you.

I started painting dog auras, which was just something I felt like doing for no reason I understood. That's when I met Yumi and began renting space in her studio. I mean, *their* studio. I started my pet portrait business, and named my company after my first dog, Friday. I did my first Dogapalooza show. That was the start of my career.

Yolanda and Whitney look over at me. I guess I've been staring at them. I raise a hand and smile. What were they talking about? Eleven gestures for Yolanda to come over.

"Lilian," says Eleven. "I have a proposal."

Yolanda has her own green drink. There's a layer of sea-green foam on top and a circle of lemon affixed to the side of the glass. She sips from a thin straw so it doesn't disturb her glowing, matte red lipstick. Her necklace is a gold pyramid.

"We're at forty-five percent," she says to Eleven. "So that went well." She looks at me. "How did you enjoy tonight's experience, Lilian?"

Yolanda stands majestically. She has energetic height—some people do. Even though I am physically taller than she is, I can feel that her energy rises about a foot over mine.

"Everyone was inspiring," I say. "I especially connected with Whitney's story."

"The women we showcased this evening are just a few out of thousands," Yolanda says. "Our numbers keep growing."

"That's part of why I invited you," says Eleven. "I know this is informal and unexpected. It's not usually how we do things."

"Oh yes it is," says Yolanda. "It's always how we do things."

Eleven waves her hand. "Well, I go by instinct. My actions might not seem rational at first, but they're always for a *reason*."

"What actions?" I ask. "What happened?"

"Anna-Mackenzie found you on Instagram first," says Yolanda.

"Get out," I say. What a negative phrase! I should stop saying that. "I mean, she did?"

"She's been following your work all year. She loves your paintings."

Anna-Mackenzie follows my Instagram account? So that's why she recognized me, at the desk!

"But did she know I was Florence's cousin? I mean Eleven! Eleven's cousin?"

Yolanda shakes her head. "She saw your Udo portrait," she says. "She showed all of us at the Temple. It went around. We all loved it."

"You showed it to your church?"

"The Temple is where we work," Eleven says.

"I knew that." What's wrong with me?

"I grew up with two Chihuahuas," says Yolanda. "Taco and Tequila."

"I'd love to paint them," I say. "We can book a sitting through Skype. I know you're in New York—I can do it with photos too, but I prefer a live sitting."

"Oh, they're long gone," Yolanda says.

I can't believe I just did that. "I'm sorry for your loss," I say.

"But now we have Portia. Have you met her yet? She's here tonight."

Eleven interrupts. "Actually, Lilian, we would like to bring you to New York."

"For a sitting? For Portia?"

"When Anna-Mack started talking about you at the Temple," says Eleven, "I didn't pay attention at first. I don't have a pet of my own."

"Anna-Mackenzie is Portia's primary caregiver," says Yolanda.

"But one day," Eleven says, "she showed me your Twitter feed, and I saw your picture. I recognized you."

"It was a surprise," Yolanda says.

"I was stunned, honey," Eleven says. "I couldn't speak for the rest of the afternoon."

"You had some feelings," Yolanda tells her. "You needed to ride those waves."

"I believe things happen for a reason," Eleven says. "We've been looking for someone with art and design experience to work with us in-house, at the Temple. Yolanda, Anna-Mack, and Monicke are the architects of the Ascendency—they direct all the marketing, communications, and production."

"Plus all our event volunteers," Yolanda adds.

"I write all my own posts, of course, but Anna-Mack formats them as newsletters and helps me with content. It's time for us to up-level our daily visual content with a devoted director of art and design. Our team is very special. It would have to be a very significant person who would be joining us. I was waiting for the right person."

"Wait," I say. I do have lots of digital design experience. "You want me to come to New York?"

"You don't have to come right away," says Yolanda. "Not until February. Monicke and Anna-Mackenzie will show you around the Temple. You'd catch on very quickly. We use the same mailing software you use for Quick+Friday."

"You want me to work for *you*?"

"When I saw your paintings, my whole body responded," Eleven says. "I had a physiological reaction. I meditated on it all afternoon. I kept seeing you in my mind. Was I responding because of our history? Or was it because of our future?"

Yolanda nods. "You took your time," she says.

"And then I remembered: time isn't linear. It's a spiral, or a wave. And so my mind-body reaction to your Twitter account wasn't because of the past or because of the future."

"Because *Remind yourself, 'I'm here'*?" I say.

She touches my arm. "Sweetheart, exactly! The past and the future are just stories that we tell ourselves. What matters most is *now*, obviously. I wanted to get closer to what I was feeling about seeing you, *right at that moment.* So I went to your site to see what I could learn about you right away."

Yolanda checks her phone, lights up the screen, and thumbs a message back to someone.

"I worked for a design firm for five years," I say. I was a temp, but still.

"When I saw your online aesthetic, my mind-body felt aligned and peaceful. It was a really solid intuitive hit. I always make decisions based on how my nervous system reacts. It has never led me astray."

"I'm sorry to interrupt," Yolanda says. "But we are now at fifty-five percent."

"That's the afterglow!" says Eleven. She raises her glass. "You do beautiful work, Yolanda."

"I still don't like you talking about tuition," Yolanda says. "It's too much for them to take in."

"I wanted to shock," Eleven says. "The more I say the numbers, the more attuned they become to the amount."

"We talk to them about it when they come to the enrollment desk."

"They need to picture the money itself to make it part of their mind-body. Then it becomes a possibility." Eleven turns abruptly to me. "Just come with us."

"Wow," I say. I can't tell if she's for real or not. Why does she want me? Did she really think this through?

"Ascendency is from March to May," she continues. "That's the hustle. The rest of the year won't be as busy. Come in February. How long will it take you to pack?" My God, she sounds just like Uncle Jimmy.

"The lights are on!" announces Jonathan Rasmussen, who has been standing in front of the window all this time. "The light shew has begun!"

"How's your mom?" I ask her. Aunt Rosie is a mystery to me. Way back when Facebook started, my mom found her sister there, but as soon as she started commenting on her posts, Rosie blocked her. "She must be proud of you right now."

"I'm grateful for her health," Eleven says.

I pause. She waits for me. I don't know how to ask about Uncle Jimmy. "And your dad?" I say.

"He golfs," she says. "And he goes to church."

"They're still together, then," I say.

"Yes."

"Do your parents fly out to Kauai to see you?"

"No."

"So do you ever see them?"

"Not often."

There are so many people listening to us in this room. I wish I could talk to Florence privately.

"Look!" Jonathan Rasmussen says. We all look out the window. It's the CN Tower light display: purple and red light moves up the building like fluid up a needle, and then spins around the bead on top with flicks and flashes, turning yellow and green and blue. "Every hour," he says. "It does this every hour on the hour, did you know?"

As I look at my cousin's wide-featured face, my mind bobs and floats. I feel wobbly. There's so much that I want to talk to her about.

"My mom moved to Florida after my dad died," I say. "Did you know? I don't know how much you know."

"I don't know anything," she says. She looks into my eyes. "Tell me."

"She sold our house," I say. "She moved back to the States after the crash, and bought a little trailer home on Amelia Island. It's nice for her. There's a community there, and she can walk to the beach."

"Is she retired now?"

"Before she sold the house, she made a vision board with everything she wanted: pictures of the beach, sunsets, palm trees. She totally manifested it."

Eleven raises her glass to this. It's half-full, with a green residue. Behind her, through the window, purple light flashes. It's pretty. I don't get to see this view of the city very often.

"She still waits tables, but only part-time. And she's making crafts with beach glass and driftwood," I say. "Mobiles, jewellery. Things for tourists. She's part of a co-op. There's a cute little store."

Yolanda floats over to the bar to return her empty glass. The bartender wipes the juicer with a cloth and snugs the snout of it, cleaning the fibrous remains of the last carrot-pom juice. "One more Green Pasture please," Yolanda says, looking down at her phone. I don't know Florence anymore. Why would I even consider her offer? And why would she trust me to do this job? Something just doesn't make *sense*.

"Thank you for the invitation," I say, "but I can't afford to move to New York."

Yolanda slips her phone back into her dress pocket. "New York has galleries," she says to me.

"I paint people's pets," I say. "My work isn't in galleries."

"New York has dogs."

"It's more that I'd have to sublet my sublet," I say. "I really don't know how I could do it."

"Let it be easy," Eleven says. "Just come for a few months and see what happens."

"I've been trying to visualize abundance. I really have. But I'm in a bind at the moment, Florence," I say. Did she flinch when I said that? "I mean Eleven, sorry." The juicer engine squeals when the kale is pressed through.

"How do you visualize it?" she asks. "Walk me through it."

"I have a cash flow problem," I say. The cucumber makes a softer sound in the juicer. The kale smells sulphurous. "Also I have credit card debt."

"Here's what we're going to do," Eleven says. "You're going to come work for me, you're going to stay in our Temple guest suite for no cost, and we're going to pay that debt of yours off in two weeks or less."

Yolanda picks her glass of green juice off the bar, and then Anna-Mackenzie is there, asking for a carrot-pom. She holds a small golden dog in her arms. The skin inside the dog's pointed ears is delicate and pink. She has a delicious tangerine light around her. The dog is relaxed but aware, watching the action behind the bar with interest. Her little nose sniffs the air. This must be Portia!

The woman with purple glitter on her cheeks stops dancing and joins the others at the bar. She rubs Portia's head, massages her ears. The dog closes her eyes in bliss. It *is* Monicke.

Eleven sees me looking at the dog. "What color do you see?" she asks me, and I'm eight years old, sitting on a rock with Florence, the one time she came to visit us in Sudbury. I'm describing the pink aura of the chipmunk that flitted up the trunk of a pine tree. I'm telling her about Kitty's green light, describing the purple around Charlie, describing the auras of all the animals we see together. She's listening with wide eyes. Florence has always believed in me.

"Light orange," I say.

"Come to New York."

"You sure you don't know someone else who can do this?" I say.

Eleven's face clouds over. She fixes her eyes on mine. She points at me, but not unkindly. "I'm going to give you some unsolicited advice." Her signature white fingernails are smooth and shiny, like they're made out of Bakelite. "Don't sabotage your own happiness. This is a choice. You can choose to say yes to this. Life does not have to be a struggle. Life can be easy and you can be happy."

Her expression is pure Florence: her eyes are big, hard, and candied-over with passion. Yolanda, Monicke, and Anna-Mackenzie stand quietly at the bar, pretending not to listen. Eleven's eye contact is intense and I want to look away, but I can't. I'm still captivated by her, even after all these years.

"What if you believed that you deserved this?" Eleven says to me.

Red flashes up the tower, and then down again. A helicopter flies above the two new condo buildings that are connected by a bridge of purple light. I feel the height of the sixteen floors we are standing on and something in my chest flaps its wings. I feel dizzy and sick. I want to believe her.

"You don't know how much my rent costs," I say.

"You have a story about scarcity, sweetheart," says Eleven. "I understand that. I've known you all your life, remember. I've seen where you grew up." She grabs my hand and holds it tight. "I'm telling you now that your story is *not the truth*. It's a story. Just a story you've been telling yourself for a long, long time."

Anna-Mackenzie steps toward me. "You can tap on that, you know," she says. With the index and middle fingers of one hand, she touches her forehead four or five times, like a stalled sign of the cross. Portia, still in her arms, looks up to watch her hand as it moves. Anna-Mackenzie brings her hand back down and pats Portia's head, smoothing her ears down. "With practice, you can correct old stories."

"Don't worry about money," Eleven says to me, still holding my hand. "You will learn this in Ascendency. Money is neutral. Money can be love."

"Yes," says Jonathan Rasmussen. Has he been listening to us, too? He puts his hands together in namaste, but with a clear drink between his palms. Eleven lets go of me and mirrors the gesture back to him. The tattoos on her inner wrists almost touch each other. In navy blue script, the left wrist reads: *this too*. The right wrist reads: *shall pass*.

My heart flicks its tail and turns around.

"Okay," I say. "I'll think about it."

"Wonderful!" Eleven cries. "Good. I knew that it was meant to be, the day I saw your face on Anna-Mack's phone. The Universe works in mysterious ways, and I pay attention when it points something out to me like this."

Maybe she's right. I don't want to say no to this because of fear. My discomfort is just a sign that I'm approaching change. Magic only happens when you leave your comfort zone. Obviously, she has some kind of plan.

Maybe this is why I had to come alone tonight: the Universe wanted us to be together again.

"Put Lilian in the Ascendency," Eleven tells Yolanda. "I want my cousin to be an Ascendant."

"Of course," Yolanda says. I'm bursting with happiness, but Yolanda's expression is cool and unreadable.

◊ ◊ ◊

It's two o'clock in the morning by the time I get home. I brush my teeth and do my two-step facial ritual: I remove my makeup with soap and water, and then splash my face with cold water to close my pores. I crawl into bed and check my phone. Facebook is all about a big Internet crash. I didn't even know it had happened, but Etsy, Spotify, Netflix, Airbnb, and a whole list of other websites were hacked tonight. Or their servers were hacked. So they crashed or something. But MailFix wasn't part of that list—it is still safe. So my newsletter went out as scheduled today, but all the links were broken because of this security breach. All my shop links! All that marketing, useless.

The wind sounds like an animal outside, pacing, circling my apartment, roaring at the windows. I breathe deeply. Even though this hacking crisis has happened, my chest feels quiet and expansive, with no fluttering birds. I breathe in slowly and fill my belly with air. I exhale. My work with Eleven must already be having an effect on me. Because I know that I am going to be okay, even though none of my newsletter links worked. It's so cold outside, and I'm grateful to be safe and warm. I am so fortunate. I have so much. Where are the homeless people of Toronto sleeping tonight? I do Tonglen: I breathe in, feeling how cold and uncomfortable they must be, and I breathe out, sending them warmth and comfort.

Then I take out my laptop and quickly write another newsletter that will fix the problem.

It isn't until I'm falling asleep that I realize that newsletter was from my past life, and is already outdated. I won't be needing Etsy anymore. I won't be booking any new sittings with pets for a while. My future is in New York City, and the Ascendency.

February 2016

Dearest Goddess Lilian,

It can feel very dark for many of us this time of year. Winter is not about striving and surging forward—it is about stillness. Stillness is difficult for us.

Winter is the out breath of the year, and February is the end of that long exhale. We are almost finished. Our breath is almost . . . gone.

This reminds us that the only thing that is meaningful to us, in the end, is connection.

What do we really have? What's left?

We have love.

Our love is not sun-dependent. My dearest petal, love is real. Even when we are shivering and taking vitamin D supplements. February shows us how warm we really are. Because when we yearn for the vitality of life, we feel so alive. When there is yearning for love, there is the promise of love.

The truth of February is that the darkness of winter has started to lift. Slowly but surely, the days are getting brighter. The angle of the sun has changed, and there is hope. We needed this winter so we could reflect on what we want out of living. When the sun shines again, we will be prepared for it. When we are out of breath, we will know who we are. And we will know what we are breathing for.

The Ascendency Program happens in the spring. It runs from the beginning of March to the beginning of May. This is the perfect time to reflect on your past year. Be kind to your wintry self—know that you have rested for a reason. Set your intentions for the spring.

It starts in two weeks, Lilian. <u>Will you join us?</u>

The Ascendency is intense and immersive. It is an initiation to the spiritual path of the divine feminine.

Do you have the energy for this journey?

Do you have the desire to immerse yourself in the profound joy of your spirit, and feel yourself finally take flight in your life?

The Ascendency might be spiritually right for you at this time.

We still have a small number of spaces available for last-minute enrollments. If you would like to find out more about the program, <u>make an appointment </u>with one of our talented EYE Life Coaches, <u>read about the experiences of past graduates</u>, or <u>check out our FAQ page</u>.

I hope I see you at Ascendency this year, Lilian—if it feels right for you.

<u>Click here to enroll now.</u>

Note: All this month, whenever you see a red paper heart, a long-stemmed rose, or any other Valentine's Day symbol, my wish for you is that it becomes a reminder of the love you have and the aliveness you feel.

Love,
Eleven

Portia comes to meet me at my desk in a little white sweatshirt with red hearts. Her tangerine aura is bright and energizing. Her tail twitches happily and her ears go back when I reach down to pet her. Once I've been properly greeted, she trots back to her bed under Anna-Mackenzie's desk.

"I like it," Yolanda is looking at Anna-Mackenzie's laptop screen. "It's simple enough for everyone to learn, but it will look great when they're all moving together."

"Can Lilian just send them this link?" Anna-Mackenzie says. "Do you think we should password-protect it?"

"Use a password that feels special," Yolanda says. "Protect it, but make it feel like a gift."

"Like a gift. How about live what you love?"

"Not quite right."

"Delight?"

"Something else."

"Something else," Anna-Mackenzie says. "Oh! Dance about it!"

Yolanda nods. "Correct," she says.

I check my mail pocket to see if anything has come through since yesterday. The sculptor Liu-Ng designed our mail system. It's a piece of art: three rows of white porcelain envelopes attached to the wall, three in each row, making a square of nine. Next to it, a floating acrylic shelf holds a collection of postcards: black-and-white photos of Virginia Woolf, Edna St. Vincent Millay, and Francesca Woodman; images of elaborate dresses and shoes left over from the Met's Alexander McQueen exhibit, drawings from old botanical guides. We use this retro system instead of email whenever possible. Of course, we use Røle to transfer digital documents and graphics and to communicate about event production. It tracks and manages our staff calendar, Eleven's editorial calendar, affiliate promotions, and scheduled communications for the Ascendency and EYE Life Coach launches.

The Temple is more efficient and life-affirming than any other office I've worked in! Of course, it's been a long time since I've temped in a corporate office. There's a note from Monicke in my envelope, on the back of a Georgia O'Keefe:

Your bell arrived today! Pick it up at my desk when you're ready.
—*M*

I look for Monicke at the front desk, near the elevator. I can't find her right away—then I look down. She's on a yoga mat, lying flat on her back with her legs stretched up against the wall. Her laptop is open on the floor beside her. She's wearing her purple headset with iridescent crystals over the earpieces and talking to someone through it. She smiles at me and raises one finger, so I wait.

THE TEMPLE is mounted high on the wall behind her, in large, brass block letters. Her desk, like mine, is a slab of white marble fixed to thin steel legs. But hers has two levels: half is raised so she can stand behind it and the other half is at regular sitting height. Monicke believes in Rich Movement: the goal, she says, is to move your body in all kinds of different ways as much as possible each day.

"We need three cars for Saturday night," she says to the ceiling. "The fifth. March fifth. Do you have white?" She listens to the caller, lowers her legs, turns over onto her belly, and types something in her laptop. "Sedans are just fine," she says. "Are they white? Get me white!" Monicke always sounds like she's softly laughing, even when she's making demands. She's a real New Yorker: her parents immigrated from India, and Monicke grew up in Queens. One thing I love about New Yorkers is how they get stuff done. People just ask for what they want all the time—guilt-free! Monicke isn't impolite, she's just *direct*. She asks for what she wants, and more often than not, she gets it. Of course, it helps that her voice sounds like the furry side of microsuede. You wouldn't *want* to say no to that voice.

She smiles, moves into goddess pose, and raises her fist in the air. "Perfection! You did it! Let's book those on our account. Eleven Novak. Thank you, Ray-Ray." She jumps up from her squat and claps her hands. I wish I could move like Monicke.

"Here you go, Canada!" She hands me a cardboard box the size of a brick. A white label on the top reads, *Harmonix Earth*. "Did you see the note about the venue change on Saturday night?"

"I did," I say. "I'm updating all our Ascendency New York communication today."

"Did you see the Valentine's Day enrollment email?"

"It looks good! It went out to everyone on the list who hasn't already enrolled."

The box is lighter than it looks. I take it back to my desk and open it right away. Inside, there's a bamboo box and a small mallet, both wrapped in tissue paper. Engraved into the top of the bamboo is *Remind yourself, "I'm here."* I open the hinged lid, and a long steel bar is suspended inside, held up by black threads. I hit the bar with the little mallet and a bell sounds.

Everyone in the office stands in mountain pose, eyes closed, and takes a deep, contemplative breath.

"Sorry!" I say. "I was just testing my new bell."

These moments we take to contemplate our breath are short pauses in the day that make all the difference to our rhythm and energy. Ringing the bell is a chance for all of us to get out of our heads, to feel what it means to be alive, and to remember that we are all connected. It's a great practice for an office. This should be in all offices. Banks should have breath breaks. Governments should have breath breaks.

"You're testing your new bell!" Portia's collar jingles whenever Anna-Mackenzie moves or speaks. They're like two parts of the same person. "It sounds amazing! What tone are you?"

"I'm A," I say. "What tone are you?" In my first week here, an Ascendency grad named Marie rang a series of Celestial Crystal singing bowls over my body. Then she read my energy levels after each one, to determine my tone. She's one of the world's only Celestial Crystal Astral Tone and Sound Therapy Master Practitioners, and she has clients all over the world.

"You're A! That's *so you*," says Anna-Mackenzie. "I'm F."

After our session, Marie said my A tone is for the sixth chakra: the third eye. The third eye chakra is all about vision, intuition, and mystical wisdom. Marie told me that I might even be clairvoyant or clairaudient. The bowl she used for my tone was made out of quartz crystal, which balances electromagnetic energy and holds the vibration of white light, which of course is what refracts into rainbows. The experience was incredible. I heard the sounds, but I also felt them in my body, like colour. My chest filled with the sound of the bowl and tears welled up in my eyes as I lay on her table. Our bodies are crystalline in structure, Marie said, so when the crystal bowls ring, the sound waves are synchronized in harmony with our bodies, and our cells understand the sound on a deep level. That's why they are so healing. Because all life forms have electromagnetic fields, the crystal tone has a balancing effect on my tissues, organs, and cells, as well as my metabolism and endocrine systems.

My new Temple phone buzzes. Like our Temple laptops, my phone has a brushed gold finish, like a foil-wrapped dinner mint. I grab my white earbuds and plug the jack in.

"The Ascendency, this is Lilian," I say. "How can I help you?"

"I forgot to tell you!" It's Monicke. "Record your bell on your Temple phone and set it as the ring tone. You should still keep it on vibrate when you're in the office, but let it ring when you're out in the wild."

I add this to my TewDew app. What's the most efficient way to organize my TewDew? Should I segregate my lists and create separate ones for design work and general admin work? I just put everything in one big list for now. It's totally manageable.

"Have you seen Eleven today?" I ask Anna-Mackenzie. She has a rough chunk of rose quartz on her desk, and a small tumbled crystal quartz next to it. An angel card is propped up between the two crystals: an image of a blue-eyed blond woman with tall, thin wings, draped in white sheets. Her arms are outstretched, palms open. *GRACE*, the card reads. *John 4:18*.

"It's Friday," she says. She's done her hair in a complicated set of interlocking French braids. "Didn't she tell you? Eleven has a four-day work week. She's not here on Fridays."

"Right! I forgot." All day I was looking forward to Eleven's sparkly, motivating entrance. The Temple feels empty without her here. Now I won't see her until Monday. Sunday is Valentine's Day. What will I do this weekend? I'm sure everyone else has big plans.

No! Change the negative thoughts. Replace them with love and generosity.

"Your hair is amazing," I tell Anna-Mackenzie. "Did you do it yourself?"

"Thank you!" she says. "I follow Kinsey McIntyre for braid tutorials. I can do yours one day, if you want."

I'm so lucky to be here! It doesn't matter that I'm spending the weekend alone. I can use the time to get ahead on my TewDew tasks.

Dear Lilian,

Happy Valentine's Day! I absolutely adore this holiday, even though I know it can make some people (okay, Knigel!) squeamish. But I can't help it. I'm a romantic, and Valentine's Day is my happy place.

I have sweet memories of making valentines as a child, in school. We would tape brown paper bags to the sides of our desks, and then go around delivering "mail" to each other. I want to give the same warm, magical feeling of valentine-making to my girls as they grow up, and teach them that it's not how much they have in life that matters, it's how much they love.

Today's post is bursting with love: I've put together an inspiring mix of fresh and delightful crafts, recipes, and activities for you and your family this February.

Make these dreamy floral valentine cards with your children in an easy afternoon—using watercolours and straws! On the site, I post a complete how-to, with clear pictures of all the steps. (Also, a darling picture of Siebel teaching Mabel how to fold a piece of paper in half, to make the cut-out heart symmetrical. I couldn't resist!)

Even Knigel loves these caramel-filled valentine chocolates. I use a heart-shaped silicone mould (supplier listed in the tutorial) that makes it easy for the chocolates to pop out once they've cooled. Easy-peasy! Best of all, my recipe uses dates in the filling, which are naturally sweet and sticky, like caramel—but without all the high-fructose corn syrup. If you use raw cacao instead of regular chocolate, the sweetness is even more mellow and delicious.

Surprise your little ones on Valentine's Day with this pretty candy necklace and bracelet set! The "beads" are made out of candied violet and rose petals, and they taste as beautiful as they look! Stringing the candied flowers can be a little fussy, but it's so worth it. You'll just need a sharp needle and silk thread. (Suppliers for the candies and the thread are listed in the tutorial—if you can't find them in your city, you can order them easily online.)

Happy Valentine's Day! All my <3,
xoxo, Juliette

EVERY MONDAY, ARMAN delivers a new bouquet of flowers into the ample lap of the gold Buddha statue that sits against the far wall of our office. Today he brings bubblegum-pink snapdragons. This marks my fourth Monday at the Temple. Arman removes the wilted white daisies and green spider mums that were there before and puts them in a plastic bucket. He passes my desk, the bucket swinging from his hand. He's an archive of strange and recently discovered facts.

"*Gracias*, Arman," I say. "What's the news this morning?"

"A museum in London is going to put on display the skull of Winnie-the-Pooh. Her teeth rotted from all the honey they fed her!" He winks to Monicke at the reception desk as he steps on the elevator and disappears. Where does he find out about this stuff?

My phone vibrates. A reminder from my calendar app: *Inquiry at 1 p.m.*

Registration for Ascendency is now closed. I can't tell by the energy in the office if we reached our goal or not. Everyone is working quietly. Eleven arrives after her lunch meeting, just in time for Inquiry. She sweeps past my desk, and the sweet, woody scent of amber trails behind her. "Virgo full moon!" she says. "Okay ladies, now let's get in formation!" She pulls off her long white coat as she walks, passing her handbag from one hand to the other so she can remove the coat and drape it over one arm. Two stacks of gold bangles clink on her wrists. "Sweetie, can you make us some of your special tea, please?"

"The water's already on," I say.

"You make the *best* tea. Canadians and Brits always make the best tea."

◊ ◊ ◊

We all sit around the marble-topped table in the meeting room. Even Portia, who radiates her tangerine light. One day, I want to capture her in watercolour. It would feel so satisfying to paint her little golden ears, get the line of her back and tail down, make a splashy cloud of light orange using a wet brush on wet paper. The desire to draw her comes over me like a craving. Then I remember the tea.

I set out a pitcher of almond milk from the bar fridge and a small bowl of coconut sugar. The kettle clicks and I pour boiling water into the teapot. Yolanda has already set five white mugs on the table.

"Let's start Inquiry," Eleven says. "Yolanda, you go first."

Yolanda always starts Inquiry. She just has that energy—she doesn't talk a lot during our meetings, but when she does, her words have freshness and power. I wonder if she's an Aries.

"I'm grateful for the people on this team," she says, and pushes up the sleeves of her charcoal sweater. "I'm proud of directing this year's enrollment. It was a success." She twirls a silver ring around her index finger. "I desire quiet time," she says, "to recover from the campaign."

"I'll go next." Monicke has taken her shoes off, and sits with her feet together on the seat of her chair, her legs in butterfly position. "I'm grateful for my healthy body," she says. "I'm proud because I DJ'd my nephew's wedding this weekend. I mixed old-school bhangra with Beyoncé and it *killed*." Monicke places her palms on the table. "And I desire a ticket to the Formation World Tour."

"Sold out?" I ask.

"Still want one," Monicke says.

"I am grateful for spirit." Anna-Mackenzie always thanks God in Inquiry. Anna-Mackenzie grew up evangelical Christian in a small town in Kentucky, not far from a museum that has life-size exhibits of Adam and Eve living with dinosaurs. Anna-Mackenzie believes in evolution, though. She says learning non-dual spiritual thinking helped heal her relationship with the church.

"I'm proud of our Ascendency registration," she says. She speaks with her eyes closed, and the orange from Portia's aura glows up the lower part of her face. "We have some special souls coming to this year's Ascendency." The dog's ears fold back as Anna-Mackenzie speaks. "And I desire a productive workday, one that feels calm, but energized."

I go next. "I'm so grateful for this work," I say. "Since I've started, I've paid all my credit card bills in full. I'm already out of debt!" I smile at Eleven. "I'm proud of figuring out the subway system," I add. The New York subway map is like a nest of snakes, but I figured out the green line, and that's the only one I've needed so far. "And I desire . . ." I pause.

Everyone at the table watches me. What do I *really* want? When you're in touch with desire, you're in touch with your life force. It's so important. I can't think of anything that I desire right now. Do I want friends? Do I want more money? Come on, Lilian. *Let yourself want what you want.*

Portia whines, and Anna-Mackenzie pats her head. Portia's ears stick out from her head like two handles. Her fur is the colour of taffy. I want to paint her. I'd use a thin brush and white gouache to get the lines of her whiskers right.

"I don't know what I desire," I say. "Honestly, I have everything I could ever want in my life, right now!" I uncross my legs to release the blood in my knees. My new Manifested Denim skinny jeans are so tight, they cut off my circulation.

"Thank you," says Eleven. "I am grateful for all of you. I watched you hustle during enrollment. You're stunning." The room is quiet. "I'm proud of what we've achieved," Eleven continues. "We stayed consistent throughout the campaign. The temptation was there, to use scarcity in our messaging. But we didn't, and we succeeded."

Anna-Mackenzie glances at Yolanda. Yolanda just barely nods her head.

"Gorgeous women," Eleven says, "registration for Ascendency is now closed. We have two hundred and thirty-three new Ascendants this year!"

Two hundred was the record from last year. We broke the record!

"However," says Yolanda, "you did trigger some fear in your messaging this year."

"There's always a moment of tension before growth," Eleven says. "You know there's tension before someone learns something, or buys something, or evolves in any way."

"In my opinion, you pushed it too far in the second half of EYE," Yolanda says.

"Noted," Eleven says. "Thank you."

"I still have to do the exact calculations with payment plan variables. But we brought in about two million in sales."

"Show me the numbers later this afternoon."

Eleven sips her tea, closes her eyes. When she opens her eyes, we are all staring at her. "We are shifting gears now," she says, "from enrollment to full-on Ascendency preparation. Before we move into that new grind, I want us to appreciate the feeling of our accomplishments."

Eleven passes each of us a pale-blue envelope. "Congra-tulations, team. Because you were able to align your energy with the women who need Ascendency, they heard the call. Your hustle, your prayer, your strategy—it all came through. More than two hundred women are going to find themselves cracking open and rising to their highest good, because of you. You invited them, made sure they felt safe, and let them know they were ready. They aren't in hiding anymore." She beams. "You should feel *amazing*," she says. "I've made each of you appointments for manicures and facials at Bliss."

"Thank you!" says Anna-Mackenzie.

Monicke pulls out her phone. "Oh," she says. "The fiber-optic daylight guy is at the front desk. I gotta meet him." She stands up. "I'll come back if there's time."

My phone vibrates. I've placed it on top of my notebook, face down. It's probably another social media notification. I've been PhotoCrafting the images and quotes for Eleven's Depth Charge posts, and today's is getting a lot of attention. It's a photo of Eleven on the beach in morning light, wearing a mocha dress that echoes the colour of the sand. Her feet are in the surf and her arms are out-stretched. In the space above her arms, written in the sky, I added one of her quotes: *Light is who you are.* At the bottom of each photo, a watermarked hashtag: *#depthcharge*.

Eleven posts her own Twitter and Instagram pics, for the obvious reason: authenticity. I schedule the uploads to Pinterest at seemingly random times according to the algorithms of our follower engage-ment each day of the week. That way, it looks as though she posts whenever she feels like it. My name is invisible, of course. It's not going to feel authentic if she's not doing her own posting on those accounts. People just want to feel close to Eleven, and it's my job to give them that feeling of closeness.

"Without meaning, life feels empty," Eleven says to us. Her face is iridescent and shiny: Glimyr on her cheekbones? Eyeshadow? Luze? "And so we grasp at things to fill the empty feeling. But here at the Temple we *create* meaning in the world. That's what makes this work feel so essential, and so honest." She takes a deep breath, closes her eyes, and exhales. "Thank you for everything you bring to this work. You are transforming lives, holding a sacred space for women to break open, enter the flow, and become their most empowered selves."

I close my eyes and breathe, to let that really sink in.

"Now let's look at our schedule for this week," Eleven says, "and get our tasks clear. The next two weeks will be intense. Yolanda, take us through the calendar. Lilian, can you make us more tea, please?"

"With pleasure," I say, and as I pour water into the kettle, my heart feels full of light and purpose.

Dear FIRST NAME,

Happy spring! Life has taken me on an unexpected but incredible adventure. I moved to New York City! I am still getting settled in my new place, but I wanted to let you know why it's been so quiet over here at Quick+Friday. More details will be coming soon, I promise.

My pet portrait sittings are on hiatus for now, but I still have lots of cards and prints available in my shop, if you'd like to place an order.

Meanwhile, stay in touch with me as I begin my new life as a New Yorker. Follow me on Instagram and Pinterest!
Now I'll leave you with these <u>portraits of puppies swimming underwater</u> by artist Seth Casteel.

Best wishes,
Lilian

"We might have married," Eleven tells me on the way to our coffee date, "if things were the way they are now." Eleven's driver, Abdul, is taking us to Benton & Glossary, the café-bookstore that's been featured in *Wild and Free* magazine. I haven't been there before—I can't wait to see it.

"I had no idea," I tell Eleven. "I thought you were in a band all that time."

"We were young," Eleven says. "We were both escaping our families, our upbringing. I was there for the spirit of the land. She was there to surf."

We're driving past Radio City Music Hall. Whenever I see that building I feel as if I'm in the cast of *Annie*. Not that I'm an orphan—I'm just an only child. Well, my father is gone, and I only see my mom once a year. So, sort of an orphan.

"My mom said you were singing with a band in Hawaii."

Eleven leans forward and speaks over the back seat. "I adore you, Abdul, but this leather isn't working for me," she says. She leans back. "When he renewed his lease, he got this one. I asked him to take it back. I offered to pay him, straight up, if he got a different model."

"It's luxury," Abdul says into the rear-view mirror. "I love it. I love the smell."

Eleven shakes her head. "It's not my business," she says. "I know it's not my car."

"Do you have a picture of Bea?" I ask. My phone vibrates in my purse. Oops—I forgot to turn the bell on!

I inhale and exhale, feeling the air fill my chest, and try to open up deeply so I can get a belly breath in. I am a shallow breather, unless I pay attention. The point of the bell is to pause and breathe during your day. Eleven has advised us that if you use your digital devices this way, as reminders, it can turn every moment of interruption into an opportunity for meditation. Eleven is brilliant. She guides us all through the wilderness of modern, disconnected life.

"I do." She draws her finger over the face of her phone. A woman in blue surf shorts appears, facing away from the camera, with a curve of coloured stripes over her bum. She's holding her sneakers in one hand, staring out at the waves.

"I can't see her face, though," I say. I want to know more. She fell in love with a woman! What else happened to Eleven during her missing years? Eleven puts her phone away. "I love that picture of her," she says. A deep crease develops between her brows, and her face looks tired. "I have other ones, but this has her spirit in it. I like to keep this one with me."

Tears come to my eyes. I touch Eleven's wrist. We don't say anything. What is there to say? Bea drowned in a surfing accident in Oahu.

Eleven stares ahead, past Abdul's shoulder, watching the road.

"Does Aunt Rosie know?" I ask.

"I don't talk about Bea with them." Eleven twists open the lid of one of the plastic water bottles Abdul has left for us. I'm surprised she'd drink from a plastic water bottle, but I don't mention it.

"You must have been devastated. I wish I'd known. I could have been there for you."

She takes a sip of water and screws the lid back on. "Thank you for listening. You're not like the rest of our family. You were always special."

The one time Florence and her parents visited us in Sudbury, it was early summer. My mother picked me up in the station wagon on the last day of school—she'd taken the afternoon off work, which was rare—and Florence was with her, a surprise for me. Florence was in the front seat, already dressed in her bathing suit—a blue-and-white polka-dotted bikini and silver glitter jelly sandals. She jumped out of the car and instantly we did the secret patty-cake handshake we'd made up the summer before: two claps, palm to palm and then hands back to back, shake right hands and then left hands across, link arms and spin. Our bodies remembered it like no time had passed at all. My mother didn't even say anything bad about two-piece bathing suits, and how inappropriate they are for girls under the age of seventeen. Almost all the space in the back of the car was taken up by two plastic orange lounge floaters, and I squished in with those. My mother had brought my red bathing suit, which I changed into in the back seat. There was a bag with beach towels, apples, Ritz crackers, a jar of peanut butter, and three spoons. She took us straight to Ramsey Lake. We were eight years old.

The sun was bright and the sky was clear blue, with puffy clouds that looked like animals. Florence and I played in the water until one of the clouds covered the sun too long and our teeth started chattering. Even with her lips blue from the cold, I wished I looked like Florence, lean and golden. I wrapped myself in a towel the way she did, tucking it under my arms instead of over my shoulders. I tried to let it drape over my body so that it hid my chubby belly. She laughed in an unhinged way I'd never heard before—crazed and high. Her laughing made me giddy. She laughed because we were using the spoons to spread peanut butter on crackers.

Sudbury was an ugly place—everyone knew that. They trained astronauts in parts of town where the landscape was all rocks, like the moon, the foliage wiped out by pollution from Inco. But Florence saw something else. "I love Canada," Florence announced, as if Ramsey Lake represented the whole country. "It's so nice here!"

The visit started off well. My mother and Aunt Rosie lounged in lawn chairs in our backyard, and Uncle Jimmy made them rye and Cokes with a big bottle of whisky he'd bought at the duty free. When he asked my father to drive with him to the grocery store to buy steaks for the grill, my father looked as if he'd been chosen for a starring role. The two of them came back with plastic bags full of meat and a case of beer, laughing like friends.

They were supposed to stay a whole week, but the visit was cut short after a couple days.

Uncle Jimmy shouted something at Aunt Rosie, and that started it. Most of the time, Uncle Jimmy was funny and charming, but once in a while, something set him off. When he yelled, my father left the room and went to his office in the basement, where he often spent his days and nights, working on his thesis.

My mother told me and Florence to go outside and pick some rhubarb in the backyard. But Florence wouldn't look at me. Uncle

Jimmy, his face red above his yellow shirt with an alligator on the chest, pointed at my mother.

"You shut the hell up," he said, "and don't tell my daughter what to do." Florence became very still. The air between her body and mine silently prickled.

"Go outside, girls," my mother said. "Now." She touched the back of my neck gently with her cool hand.

"You don't tell my daughter what to do and you don't tell my wife what to do." Uncle Jimmy turned to Florence and Aunt Rosie. "Get your things, we're leaving."

Florence looked at her mother.

Aunt Rosie had wilted into a smaller version of herself. "Go on," she whispered. "Get your things."

"Now," Uncle Jimmy said, and took a menacing step toward Florence.

Florence went pale and her eyes turned dark. "Yes, sir," she said.

She walked down the hall, went into my room and closed the door. My mother pushed me outside, but I could still hear the shouting that started again. My mother and Uncle Jimmy were yelling at each other, and Aunt Rosie made a shrill sound that went up like a question.

My mother's voice was stretched and frayed. "How can you let him speak to you that way?"

I walked to my hiding spot, a divot of rock at the top of the hill behind my house. It was cushioned with a dry bed of pine needles and protected by a cluster of white birch trees. From up here, I could see the rooftops of the houses on my street, and behind those, the smokestack at Inco. I could see everything from here, but the way the trees covered me, I was invisible.

Kitty, my grey tabby, prowled up the rock and found me. She could always tell when someone was upset. She rubbed the side of her face against my shin and then stretched out on her back so her whole body lay along my leg. Her aura was pure shamrock.

They left that afternoon. I cried and cried when Florence drove away. I couldn't eat. I went to my bed and lay on my stomach with my head on my arms and I couldn't stop crying. My mom came in, rubbed my back, and said I'd see Florence next summer but didn't say anything about Uncle Jimmy. That was the first and last time Florence ever came to Sudbury.

My phone buzzes again. I touch my purse with my hand as if to calm it. "I'm here any time you want to talk, Florence. Sorry. Eleven." She nods.

When will I get it? It's Eleven now. Eleven. *Eleven.* "The Universe has helped us find each other," I say. "To work together. Isn't that incredible? To have been disconnected for so long, and now to be here, doing this together?"

Abdul drives past Village East Cinema and Bar Veloce. Benton & Glossary is here? We're not far from the Temple guest suite, where I'm staying. I live above a sake bar on East Tenth—as soon as I saw it, I took a pic and texted Yumi. They said they already knew the place! It's famous.

"I'm not surprised at all," Eleven says. "When I think about it, it makes sense. It's the perfect geometry for our experience." She squeezes my hand, and we both smile.

We leave the East Village and drive further along the East River, past the dog park. I should go there and sketch sometime. We drive by it too quickly for me to see any colours, or anything more than a few wagging tails. Which reminds me—Sophia's portrait. A wash of guilt pools in my stomach. I emailed Nana Boondahl before I left Toronto, telling her I was moving to New York and the portrait would be delayed. I haven't worked on it since I got here.

My phone goes off again. It's more social media, I'm sure. But it could be Yolanda trying to reach me. Maybe she needs to tell Eleven something. It could be important. I pull my phone out of my purse.

Yolanda Clarke replied to a comment on
"Light is who you are."

You have 640 calories left today.

@kidandbeetle likes your photo

@TullyRamp likes your photo

Yolanda doesn't usually join in the conversation on Eleven's Facebook. I wonder what's happening in the comment field? I should be on top of that!

"Here," Abdul says. He stops the car in front of a pink-and-burgundy door.

"Benny and Gloss!" says Eleven.

"Something's happening on your Facebook page," I say. "Let me just look into it for you."

"I'll get us pillows," Eleven says. "And the cardamom coffee."

I stand outside the pink door and open Facebook. Yolanda just responded to a request about registration, and posted about how to get on the waiting list for next year. That technically should be my job, but Yolanda knows I'm out with Eleven, so she jumped in for me.

Me
Thx for being on top of it in FB!

Yolanda
np

Me
Why so many registrants asking now?

Yolanda
it's safe to try know, bc it's too late.

Me
Do they know it's too late?

Yolanda
they might Notting know they're dong what they're dong

Me
Thanks again!

Yolanda
have fun

We sit on salmon-pink velvet pillows, in macramé hammock swing chairs. A hanging table floats between us. Succulents pose in shallow dishes on the windowsills, and air plants hang from the ceiling in glass terrarium bulbs. The walls are covered with books. Benton & Glossary is a bookstore, and everything is for sale.

"Open it," Eleven says. The box is a pale-grey square tied with a dark grey ribbon. By its size, I guess that it's an Instagram photo book. Or coasters, but Eleven probably wouldn't get me coasters. Photo coasters maybe! The ribbon is tied in a knot under the bow, and I dig at it with my fingers to loosen it.

Inside the velvet-lined box, a beaded necklace rests in a coil. It's a mala from Lunar Devotional, one of the companies Eleven works with for her product line. Most of the beads look like tropical nuts or seeds, brown and pocked. Every five brown beads, there is a shiny pale-purple stone. I pull the necklace out of the box and hold it up in front of me. At the bottom hangs a large, faceted, teardrop-shaped stone. Light green, almost turquoise, with subtle feathery patterns running through it.

"It's amazonite, with amethyst," Eleven says. "Amazonite is a truth stone, for courage and integrity. And amethyst, for psychic protection, visions, and dreams. New York can be disturbing for creative and intuitive souls. You can wear this to protect your gifts, now that you're living here."

It's perfect! She knows me so well. I put it over my head and admire it. The stone is heavy, and I already feel it grounding me.

"Those are rudrakasha seeds. They bring abundance, and increase prosperity."

"I love it," I say. I'm humbled by her generosity. Eleven's line of malas from Lunar Devotional costs *hundreds* of dollars. "Thank you. I love it."

"I'm so glad you're here with me," Eleven says. She places her hand over her heart, and I do the same. We swing in our chairs, the energy from the plants humming all around us. The pink in the pillows and the green in the leaves play with each other in the light of the room. I feel enchanted, with the amethyst protecting me.

This would make such a lovely Instagram pic! But no. I will not interrupt this moment by taking a picture of it.

Dear Lilian,

I'm at home in Queenstown, New Zealand, as I write this, visiting my family. As some of you know, we lost one of our elders last month: my uncle Robert passed away on the eve of his seventieth birthday. The day after Uncle Robert's funeral, I spent the day tramping through the mountains. I paid attention to my thoughts as I walked. I breathed in the land and invited steadiness. I exhaled the sky and let go of my agitation. I danced to the music of wind moving over the rocks and touched my consciousness there. And yet, the restless feeling remained.

The mountain in front of me looked like the silhouette of a man sleeping. It made me think of how our own deaths live perfectly inside ourselves. We are not here forever.

In Maori tradition, there is a concept called *tūrangawaewae*. It means a place to stand. Like many immigrants, I have a complicated relationship to home. New Zealand is my home, but so is America. I'm getting ready for an intensive retreat tour this spring, and that too is my home. I travel because I find myself when I am in motion.

Finding a place to stand is a voyage of discovery for many of us. In Active Meditation, we teach our bodies how to help us find our ground. And through the earth, through time and space, we are connected to each other.

I've been moved by the outpouring of support I've received in emails and condolences on Facebook and Twitter. It means so much to know that you're sending me your thoughts and prayers. Thank you.

Wherever this month brings you, be it sunshine or snowfall, I hope you find your *tūrangawaewae*.

Namaste,
Jonathan

WE'RE IN COUNTDOWN mode now. Seven days until opening night of Ascendency. We're going to be on the ground, getting everything ready for those two hundred and thirty-three women to descend upon us. As soon as I get back from this walk with Anna-Mackenzie, which is a much-needed break, a chance to pause and breathe and restore, I'm going to sit down and make myself a new TewDew list for next week. I drink the rest of my almond milk macaccino. Maca root is an adaptogen that helps the body adapt to stress, and is good for hormone balance. It's full of calcium. I wish I had ordered the large instead of the medium.

"The end of February looks bleak, but it's so full of potential." Anna-Mackenzie pauses while Portia squats to pee on the dead grass.

"I love your coat," I say. It's bursting with colour. "That pink, against all this grey and brown." A jogger pounds past me. I didn't even hear her coming. Central Park is teeming with Lycra-clad runners at lunchtime.

"I can almost hear the buds in the trees," Anna-Mackenzie says. "At this stage, the branches look dead, but really they're at their most alive."

"You think we're going to be ready for next weekend?"

"Of course we will." She pulls Portia's leash gently to get her moving. "It always feels like this before Ascendency. It's never one hundred percent down pat before opening night. We're going to be fine. Everyone pulls together. Our volunteers are strong."

We meet a dark brown Australian cattle dog, easily four times the size of Portia. His owner stops to let the two dogs greet each other on the path. They touch noses, the cattle dog bending down to reach Portia. The dog has a gentle, peach-pink aura all around him.

"What's his name?" I ask the owner.

He looks up from his phone. "Doris," he says.

Portia barks once, sharply, and Doris lies down in front of her, wanting to play. Portia raises one paw, sniffs the air in front of her, and then turns around. She looks bored.

"Ooh," I say.

"Rejected," Anna-Mackenzie says.

We continue along the path, headed toward a stone arch. I think I recognize this bridge from *Elf*. Walking through New York is like walking through all the movies you've ever seen!

"You know, Portia really likes you," Anna-Mackenzie says. "She always raises her head when you come into work. She responds to your voice more than anyone else."

Portia sniffs the base of a lamppost, her ears splayed goofily.

"Oh, Portia! The feeling is mutual." I do love this dog. She's a bright orange light on an overcast day. "Can I walk her?" I ask.

Anna-Mackenzie gives me the leash. Portia feels like a fat hummingbird on a string—the leash is alive with her energy. I haven't actually walked a dog since my Friday.

Friday was a stray, a medium-sized black mutt with a bushy tail, a white mark on her throat, and a vibrant purple aura. She found me— one night, she walked into my mom's cottage timeshare, as though she lived there. I was up for the weekend. She was a gift from the Universe. I think a family had abandoned her in the forest. People do that! They drive their dogs into the woods and then leave them there. People can be cruel. But she must have lived in Toronto before, or a city of some kind. She was so street smart, she'd walk right beside me, stopping at the corners to wait for the lights to change. She didn't even need a leash.

"I'm glad you're working with us," Anna-Mackenzie says. "You being here has made my job so much better. Lighter. You're good at what you do. Eleven seems different with you here, too."

The wind picks up, but it feels warm, and smells like melting snow and willow buds. "Different how?" I ask.

Anna-Mackenzie thinks.

I take out my phone and aim at the branches above us. They're stark against the sky, vibrating with energy. I post the pic to Instagram with no comment. Words aren't always necessary.

"She seems more grounded with you here." Anna-Mackenzie finally says, flipping up the collar of her pink coat to block the wind. "Happier."

"Well, she just broke her record for Ascendency enrollment," I say. "That could be why she seems happy." I don't know why I just said that. We *are* growing close! I make Eleven a cup of tea every day now. I use the rose-petal green tea from a special tea shop in Toronto, because I know it's her favourite.

Anna-Mackenzie puts her hand on my shoulder. "No, it's because you're her family," she says.

"Did she tell you that?" I ask.

Anna-Mackenzie smiles and pats my shoulder. "She doesn't have to," she says. "You can see it. She's extra-protective of you."

"In my family, being related doesn't always make you happy," I say.

"Eleven is thrilled that you're here," Anna-Mackenzie says. "Trust me. And she has told us that you're special. She said you've always had magic powers." Her eyes twinkle.

"I see colours around animals," I admit.

She nods. "You see colors around animals."

"She was the first one who ever believed me."

"She told us that you were born with a gift," Anna-Mackenzie says.

My heart flushes at this. "Eleven and I *used* to be very close," I say. "When we were little, we were close."

We pause under the stone arch, and Portia squats. "The way you heal the world is that you start with your own family," Anna-Mackenzie says. She unfolds a plastic bag, slips her hand into it, and bends down to pick up Portia's poo. She ties the bag in a knot. "Mother Theresa said that."

We walk out from under the arch. The sky is solid grey-white, with no texture. If I painted it, I'd do it wet on wet, a simple wash of Payne's grey. I'd do Portia in raw sienna, obviously. It would feel so good to paint! "Can I take a selfie of us?" I ask. "Out there, with the buildings in the background."

I get into position, and Anna-Mackenzie puts her arm around me. We smile. I snap a few shots, and then we look at them. There's one where my eyes look squinty, and there's one where her face is blurry. The third one isn't exactly gorgeous, but we both look cute enough. My mouth is a bit crooked in it, but I post it anyway. It's not like I'm flawless! Imperfection is okay.

**Love this woman! Afternoon walk with
@AnnaMackPeace. #Ascendencyprep**

I scan the location options that Instagram lists: Strawberry Fields, the Dakota Apartments, Manhattan NY, Central Park. I choose Central Park.

Everything about this day is perfect. This is what work-life balance feels like! Everything is finally balanced in the proverbial pie chart of my life—work, family and friends, spirituality, money, health. I love being forty. I've never felt stronger, healthier, or more solvent.

◊ ◊ ◊

On Saturday, emboldened by the February sunshine and another pay-cheque from the Temple, I take myself on a date to the Guggenheim to see the Dahleria Prize portrait show. The Dahleria Prize show-cases contemporary portraiture from around the world. I've wanted to see this show forever, but it never comes to Toronto.

The whole show is beautiful, but I'm caught by one artist in particular.

He paints larger-than-life faces on huge pieces of mounted can-vas. A man's face, craggy and kind, with a white beard and hazel eyes, is about six feet by six feet square. I stand in front of the painting and go over the brushstrokes with my eyes. The oil paint is deeply textured, dry and cracked in some places, glossy and wet look-ing in others. The artist has chosen a limited palette—everything is made up of the same muted pinks and greens. The paint is put on in layers, and then peeled and scratched, and then painted again. It looks almost sculpted, marked with thumbprints and finger smears. When I step back from the wall, I see an old man looking at me with care.

My phone makes a hollow electronic tinkling sound that echoes through the gallery room. It's a reminder from my Astrofy app.

**Moon in Scorpio. Take care of your finances.
Attend to your intuition. Get rid of any unnecessary
things in your life. Transformation is highlighted today.
Meditate. Cleanse.**

I get a pretzel from a street vendor I pass on my way to the subway. I cover each bite with a squirt of yellow mustard. The dough is soft and warm and steamy in the chilled air. I lose myself in it: the crunch of the salt and the tang of the mustard. I know the gluten is inflammatory, and the white flour will make my blood sugar spike. All this salt will make me bloated. I know it, but I eat it anyway.

I've never tried to paint a human face before. I just play with watercolours and do pictures of people's dogs. I wouldn't know how to paint something as transcendent as the portrait I just saw. That's *real* art.

◊ ◊ ◊

Anna-Mackenzie's brother-in-law died on the weekend. The Temple is in shared mourning: we light candles and cover the fibre-optic daylight fixtures above our desks. We create time and space to hear Anna-Mackenzie's Compost Heave, to clear the way for new thoughts and energy. Portia hasn't left her side all day.

I honestly didn't understand what happened to him, at first. It's too simple, too terrible. Last year, Anna-Mackenzie's sister said Paul was complaining about a cough. The cough was so bad, it kept the whole family up at night. He was uninsured—he didn't go to the doctor because he didn't want to spend the money. Her sister said they couldn't afford medicine, anyway. Paul was doing contract work for a paving company that makes parking lots. He couldn't take time off without losing money, so kept going to work even though he was sick. His cough got worse and worse, until he couldn't breathe.

Who dies from a bronchial infection?

"I had no idea they were uninsured," Anna-Mackenzie says. "If she'd told me they were in trouble I would have sent them money."

She's lying down on Monicke's yoga mat, and we're all kneeling and sitting around her. "I would have paid for antibiotics. I would have paid for the doctor. But it's too late now. It's too late." She passes her phone up to Eleven. "Look at my nieces," she says. "What's going to happen to them?"

"Beautiful," Eleven says. "What else? What else do you want to say?"

Monicke has one hand over Anna-Mackenzie's forehead and one on her heart chakra. She's been giving her reiki throughout the Heave. "They're going to get through this," she says. "Your sister is a strong woman, and those girls have you in their life."

"I'm going to buy them the best insurance that exists," Anna-Mackenzie cries.

The phone is passed to me. Three little girls with strawberry-blond hair sit on a brown couch. They're all wearing matching pink sun-dresses. The one in the middle smiles directly at the camera with joy in her eyes: the quintessential Anna-Mackenzie smile.

"Honey," says Eleven, "we know this is hard. We are here for you. You've done an incredible job heaving this compost. You can let go of it now."

"I'm so sorry," Yolanda says.

"It's time for you to get up," says Eleven. "You've turned this."

Monicke plays Santigold on her phone. After a moment's delay, the Temple's built-in speakers catch the Bluetooth signal and the sound pours out all around us. Monicke claps and spins and gets everyone in a circle. We dance about it.

Eleven and I lock eyes and all of a sudden we're thirteen years old, and we're both doing Jennifer Beals's moves from *Flashdance*. We kick out and lift our arms and dance together, in sync. Florence is in her matching black leotard and black leggings and I'm in my red bathing suit, and we're in front of the mirror in her bedroom, jump-ing, spinning, and pointing. Incredibly, our bodies still remember the moves we taught ourselves almost thirty years ago.

We all dance together until the song is finished. But by the end of the song Anna-Mackenzie's face is pleasantly pink with sweat, and she's smiling gently.

"Anna-Mackenzie," I say, panting a little, "I can make some extra time this week. What do you need to do next?"

"Let's see," she says, and tucks her red hair behind her ear. "The How to Prepare email for Ascendants is ready—I updated it with the changes. Just make sure that the new version is the one that's scheduled, and that the old one is deleted. I think I deleted it. It could be sent manually, even. I've started to put together the sequence for both Telerituals, but we need to double-check the intro email and then schedule the whole sequence. The photographer for our glam sessions needs to be sent a reminder and a venue confirmation. We need to send all our Ascendant grads the reminder about the dance mob this weekend. Oh, and I have to reply to Dee Kay. She changed her airport arrival time."

"I can help," I say. Portia lies down over my feet. This little dog tries so hard to be of comfort to all of us! I'm already busy: I have to design and pre-schedule all the Daily Depth Charges for March, work on Ascendency NYC, and figure out what to do about my Toronto apartment. The man who sublet it to me is coming home early, so I have to clear out and put all my stuff in storage. And we have to start prepping for Ascendency Portland. There is no extra time, not really. But Anna-Mackenzie has to go see her sister right now. She's part of our Temple family, and as she herself would say, family is priority.

"What if I took care of the Ascendant grad emails?" I ask. "Would that lessen your load today?" Should be straightforward— the Ascendant grads are tagged in the system. I just have to write one email, and then send it out.

Anna-Mackenzie's eyes are red-rimmed, and her mascara is splodged from the Heaving. She looks at me gratefully.

Monicke puts her arm over my shoulders. "Canada's got those," she says. "And I'm taking care of Dee Kay and the photographer."

"You'll take care of Dee Kay and the photographer?" Anna-Mackenzie sniffs and smiles. "Thank you both!"

"Leave the Telerituals for now," Yolanda says. She collects her papers from the table and fastens the clip of her pen to the top corner. "There's lots of time for those."

"I love our team," says Eleven. "Lilian, can I just say, it's *wonderful* to have your lightness and energy here. Sometimes, and I know you know this, everybody, extra hard work is necessary. If you want to change the world, you have to hustle. So I appreciate the extra work you're taking on, and at this crunch time, too. Gratitude and respect." She smiles at me, and puts her palms together in namaste.

"We're a family," I say.

Florence's next-door neighbours had abandoned their house. They had four kids, Florence told me, and one was a baby who used to cry often during the days. Their house looked like Uncle Jimmy and Aunt Rosie's—three storeys high with big picture windows and a front porch. But it had a turret on the second floor, a round room with windows on all sides, which made it look like a castle. They'd left in a hurry, Florence said, and had been gone for almost a year. The newspaper and the mail didn't come anymore. Whoever had been mowing the lawn for them had stopped, and the grass was overgrown and weedy.

We were fourteen years old, it was a hot day, and we were bored. The Ohio River was brown and tepid. Barges of coal slowly floated up from Kentucky. Aunt Rosie had stopped speaking to my mother again—they argued a lot that summer, and while their silences were unpleasant to be around, they weren't treacherous, like the fights that involved Uncle Jimmy. My father had taken the station wagon to the University of Evansville library, and my uncle had the Buick. "Stop doing everything he wants," my mother said, which made my Aunt Rosie slam the door when she went out to fill old Charlie's bowl with fresh water.

Florence suggested we go into the house next door, through a bathroom window that had been left unlocked. There was no alarm system, she said. She'd done it before. It was easy to get in—so easy, I wasn't afraid of getting caught, at first.

The house was dark and silent. Their kitchen was almost as big as my whole house in Sudbury, and plastic toys took up about half of it. Barbies with designer dresses silently lined up on the kitchen counter, arms bent at the elbow, fingers pointing to the ceiling.

Their dresses gleamed iridescent peach and blue. A big Barbie mansion, with a pool and a slide, sat under the bay window. The living room contained several lumpy couches and chairs covered with crocheted blankets. We found hardened dog turds stuck to the carpet. Uncle Jimmy and Aunt Rosie had a clean, bright house with powder-pink walls and plush green carpet in the living room. Everything in their house was spotless, always. I thought that was because they were rich, but these people had money, too.

"All the clocks in the house stopped at the same time." Florence pointed to a grandfather clock by the stairs. The hands read 9:15. "See how the moon is showing? That means it was night."

We went upstairs. Florence wanted to show me the bedrooms first, but I was more interested in the turret room, which was stifling hot, bright with sunshine. I opened a window to let in some air. The floors were shining honey-coloured wood. The room was empty except for a big stereo console that was pushed awkwardly to one side, unable to fit against the rounded wall. I slid open the doors and found the cassette tape collection. They had some good albums: *The Joshua Tree* and *Document. The Joshua Tree* tape was brand new, still wrapped in cellophane. I pressed some buttons on the stereo, but the house had no electricity.

"Follow me," Florence said, and she disappeared into the bedroom. I put the tape back and went down the hall to find her. The bedroom was dim, and it smelled like herbal soap. There was a large abstract painting above the bed, the canvas swiped with strokes of pink, brown, and orange. A gold-faced clock in a glass dome sat on the night table, the hands in a straight line across: 9:15.

"What happened to them?" I asked. "Why did they leave everything like this?"

Florence stood in front of the armoire, one hand holding a dark wooden box. "Nobody knows," she said. "Maybe they moved to Europe."

I thought about it. "They could have been abducted by aliens."

She looked around and nodded. "That would explain the clocks."

She held out the box. "We pick the one that speaks to us the most," she said. "Just one."

Gold and silver jewellery lay in the square black velvet compartments. Florence closed her eyes and let her hand hover over everything for a few seconds. She lifted a sparkly bracelet and dangled it
in the air like a small snake, and put it back. She pinched a pair of
diamond studs from another square, rolled them in her palm, and
then put them back. Then she held up a pendant that had a big green
stone in a teardrop shape—an emerald—with small diamonds set all
around it.

Cold pebbles lined up along my spine. "I don't want to steal anything," I said.

My cousin's eyes were gentle. "We're not *stealing*," she said. A
sweet energy sparked off her like rays of light. "I promise, it's okay
to touch them."

Florence held the box of treasures out to me. The walls soft-
ened around us. I stared into the black velvet holes and felt tingling
behind my eyes. I selected a pretty gold brooch covered with gems.
It was the shape of a pear.

She clipped the necklace around her neck. I pinned the sparkly
pear to the strap of my tank top, and sucked in my tummy when
I looked down. We went back to the turret room, and Florence lay
down in the middle of the room, where a band of sunlight cut across
the floor, and stretched her arms and legs out like a star. The diamonds threw shattered sprays of rainbows on the walls.

I couldn't stop thinking about the family. "It probably wasn't an
alien abduction," I said, "because people don't actually disappear after
that." I wanted to suggest that they'd found a tesseract, which made
perfect sense, but I was afraid Florence would think I was immature.
It had been a long time since we'd read Madeleine L'Engle.

"I hate him," Florence said.

I lay down beside her on the floor, surprised that she'd brought
up Uncle Jimmy. We never talked about the way he treated her. The
flat breeze painted a glaze of sweat on my skin, and the brooch on
my chest reflected the sunshine like a disco ball, covering both of us
with specks of light.

"In a few years when you go to university you can leave," I said.

"He lies, and you can't tell," she said. "Everyone thinks he's so great. But your mom can see."

"What about your mom?"

"When your family leaves, things will get worse," she said. "They always do."

The emerald lay just below the divot of her throat, the size of a sunflower seed, with diamonds all around it.

"He locks me in the basement," Florence said.

My skin turned cold and sticky. "What?"

"Downstairs." In the sunbeam, her face toughened, and her eyes turned dull. "To punish me. He seriously *locks me in the basement.*"

I pictured Florence alone in the dark. "He can't do that," I said.

She laughed an ugly laugh. "See? I could tell you more, but you wouldn't believe me. That's how he does it."

"I do believe you. Always. You can tell me anything."

"My mom's even worse. She just lets him." The emerald around her neck was lit up from the sun, and glowed like a green light.

Underneath us, the living room pulled at my peripheral vision, like it wanted to suck us down into it. I reached out and took her hand and we lay there. I was scared, about everything else she wasn't saying. Eventually, Florence stood up and said we should go. I unpinned the pear on my tank top and gave it to her.

Without looking at me, she slowly removed the necklace. I watched as she put the two pieces in her pocket.

Did I try to stop her? I did not. At that moment, I only wanted to go back to Florence's air-conditioned house, to go into the vanilla-and-garlic-powder-scented pantry for the box of Oreos I knew was on the middle shelf, left corner.

Florence and I stayed quiet for a couple of days after that, and spent more time apart than usual. I felt nervous around Uncle Jimmy and Aunt Rosie, so I would bring my sketchbook out to the back-yard. I drew hallways and corridors lined with doors on either side and practised the lines of perspective with multiple vanishing points. Sitting at the table for dinner with my parents, Florence, and her parents, my skin felt rubbery and my stomach hurt. After dinner,

back in my bedroom, I ate candy. It was soothing to pick out different Jelly Belly flavours one by one, and follow the recipe suggestions
on the back of the bag.

I remembered this years later, when I was doing an intensive
weekend seminar with BioChronos Integrative. In the seminar, we
were asked to share something we'd never told anyone else—a secret
that we'd been carrying since childhood. We were supposed to write
it down and then give it to our sharing partner, and hear them read
it back to us. I brought the memory from where I'd hidden it in my
mind: lying next to Florence in that strange round turret room, the
sun hitting the emerald on her neck, the way it looked as if there
were a light inside the stone.

I couldn't do the exercise. After so many years, what I knew
about Uncle Jimmy felt like a veil that lined my body, inaccessible
in words.

Dearest Goddess Lilian,

It's here: the start of your awakening is upon us. Ascendency NYC is this weekend. Are you ready?

It's spring in New York. Can you feel the season shift where you live? If you live in the Southern hemisphere, you're moving into autumn now. If you live near the equator, you might be coming into typhoon season. Our earth is always changing, always moving. What does it feel like for you?

The air in Manhattan smells a bit more earthy and full of life today. I can feel the rush of life in the trees, a powerful energy that trembles from tiny green buds. I feel the new and ancient stirring in the earth, the fresh energy in the breezes from the south. The air is alive with feathers and birdsong. Crocuses gape open, their bright yellow insides hungry for the sun. They are like us. They are showing us our own true desires.

This changing time feels essential to our awakening. It's not an easy season—it's a confronting one. It asks so much from us. Spring is a season of transformation.

There's a reason we start the Ascendency at this time of year. I cannot wait to meet you at the brink of this change. May you feel the flicker of new life, the energy of renewal, and may it bring you the nectar of your own rising.

See you on Friday!

Love,
Eleven

March 2016

Dear Lilian,

I don't know what it is about March, but the very moment the calendar pushes past February, I'm in spring mode. Even though it won't look like spring here in Toronto for at least another month! We're still caked in ice and snow, and yet I'm spring cleaning and taking on all sorts of fresh projects that I can't wait to share with you on my blog today.

It's become more and more important for me to take time for myself this year. I know you can probably relate to this. As a wife and mother of two, the time I have for myself is extremely limited, and if I'm not careful, I'll fill the little time I do have with to-dos that keep me distracted and busy, with no time to reflect or rest. I share my photos and reflections from my Sacred Solitude project here. I encourage you to set up a Sacred Solitude project for yourself this spring, too. Feel free to use my ideas, and please let me know yours in the comments below the post. If you'd like to join me and my Pure Juliette family, tag your posts with #sacredsolitude so we can all see, and know that we're doing this together.

This spring has also been about experimentation, creativity, and learning. I bought this white ukulele at my local music store and I have been teaching myself the classics, like "Somewhere over the Rainbow" and "All I Have to Do Is Dream." I painted these tiny flowers on the face of my new uke with non-toxic enamels. It's such an easy and fun way to personalize the instrument. Here's a tutorial I made, so you can try it too! There are a few stencils you can print out, in case you don't want to go freehand.

To celebrate St. Patrick's Day, we are making our own Shamrock Shakes! The best thing is that these are healthy enough to have for breakfast! They're sweetened with banana and a little bit of coconut syrup (or stevia, if you prefer). And of course, spinach is invisible to children when it's in a milkshake!

My biggest project, and what I'm most excited about, is our coach house renovation. We have been converting our old bike shed into a studio space for Knigel. The exterior siding is barn board I sourced from a century-old barn in northern Ontario. We splurged on the kitchenette. I found this canary-yellow apron sink on my Homme app and had to have it! See the before and after pictures here. I'll keep that link updated with new photos as we continue the reno!

If you're reading this and you live in a part of the world that is flowering right now, send some of those blossoms this way, please! Meanwhile, I will keep dreaming of spring.

Till next month,
xoxo, Juliette

SOULCORE IS A holistic workout that combines ballet, belly dance, and kettle bells. Monicke and I go on Wednesday nights because Shawna is the instructor. The way she teaches is so motivating, I wouldn't miss it! I can't believe I'm even saying this, because I've always avoided exercise. I like to dance, but I've always stayed away from gyms. New York is changing me: SoulCore is the highlight of my week. I've lost a little weight, and I feel strong.

The ambient tribal beats are looping in and out from speakers all around the room, and I'm doing spinning jump squats with a twenty-pound kettle bell in my hands. Monicke is beside me doing the same thing, in her purple leggings with the cosmos printed on them. I feel our deep connection, as if we are two parts of the same whole. My quads are burning and I kind of want to throw up, but there's a force inside of me that tells me, *go, go, go, don't stop, don't stop, you're doing great, you're amazing, you're perfect!* Actually it's not a voice inside me—it's Shawna's voice! But it's coming from inside my own head because our boundaries have melted! And my vision fades, making the colour in the room go away a bit—that's how I know my heart rate is in the red zone—and Shawna is counting down now, *five more, four more, three more, two more . . .*

We stop jumping. "Put your kettle bells down," Shawna says. "Now stretch it out with me. Cool-down time." The music rumbles, fades, and then comes back in cool, calm notes. We're panting. We're sweating. I can't believe I'm doing this right now. My vision starts to feel tingly, like when I see auras around animals.

"Breathe," Shawna says. "Let your heart rate come down. Pay attention to your heartbeat."

She asks us to lie down on our mats and close our eyes. "Relax into this moment," she intones. "In this moment, you are perfectly safe."

I feel colours around me, a prism that curls up out of my peripheral vision and over my eyes. But there aren't any animals in here. Where is the beautiful coloured light coming from? I cry silently. My tears seep out of the corners of my eyes and drip down my cheeks. They spill into my ears. I look amazing, I feel amazing, I have an amazing job, and amazing friends. I'm going to meet Yolanda for dinner at Selasa, the best vegan Ethiopian restaurant in New York, right after this. I'm going to be an Ascendant. This is my life. I feel worthy of this. SoulCore is my church.

I wipe my eyes to mix my tears in with my sweat, and turn my head to the side. Monicke is watching me. Her face is slick with sweat, and her dark eyes are glowing.

"Canada, you have a *very* high vibration right now," she says. "I can feel it from here."

The colours recede and I feel clear again. "I don't know why I was crying," I say.

"You broke through the physical plane," she smiles. "Our bodies aren't separate from our minds and our spirits. And obviously, our emotions. You're in the emotional body now. I'll give you some Jin Shin Do to help balance your Qi, so you can integrate."

◊ ◊ ◊

Yolanda and I sit across from each other at a low table on the floor, sprawled on Selasa's orange and fuchsia cushions. Our boots are standing on a rubber tray beside us, next to Yolanda's New York Public Library tote bag. It's full of hardcover books. There are at least four or five books in there! Yolanda's so smart. I should read more.

"I've been single for years," Yolanda says. "I love being single. Besides, theoretically, our separateness from each other is an illusion, right?" She interlaces her fingers and rests her hands on the table. "At least, that's what physics tells us. So singleness—or solitude—is in fact only one facet of a life otherwise defined by interconnectedness." Yolanda orders the Spice Goddess combo platter for two. The waiter totally thinks we're a couple.

"Exactly!" The lantern on our table casts an elaborate shadow, a beautiful flickering fish-scale pattern. "As long as you know that everything is connected, then there's no such thing as loneliness. It's incredible to talk to you about this. My friends at home can't relate. They think I'm lonely."

"Why did you invite me here?" Yolanda asks.

"To dinner?"

"To an Ethiopian restaurant."

"Do you not like Ethiopian? I'm sorry!"

"I like it," she says. "I'm just curious why here."

"Because this is *Selasa*! Also, it's all vegan and gluten-free. I have this diet."

"Okay." She picks a fuzz of lint off her sleeve.

Then I see what she's asking. "No!" I laugh. "I mean, of course not."

"It's fine," she says calmly. "As I was saying, there's nothing inherently wrong with being single."

"I actually love being alone," I say. "I enjoy my own company."

"I never wanted to get married," says Yolanda. "I knew I'd never have kids. My sister's chosen that path, and when I look at her life now, well."

"Where is your sister?"

"She lives with my mom in Detroit."

"Your dad?"

"He left when we were kids. My mom raised us herself. She worked for the Marriott."

I nod. "My mom worked at Red Lobster. I remember her coming home every night in her uniform. The vest, the tie, the ugly black running shoes. I was so upset by those running shoes!"

"My sister works for the hotel now," Yolanda says. "But she doesn't make enough to buy my nephew new clothes."

Why did I have to say that about the shoes? I should just listen to her. It sounds like I'm trying to make Yolanda's experience all about me. "Yolanda," I say, "does your family have insurance?"

"They do."

I sigh. "Health care is different in Canada," I say. "How old is your nephew?"

"Six. His dad left him, too. I'm going to make sure he goes to college."

"You're paying for his tuition?" I say. "That's amazing."

"I'm the only one in my family who went," she says. "I'm a nerd. Scholarship. I graduated from Michigan."

"You run the show at the Temple, don't you?" I ask her.

Yolanda sighs and pushes her glasses up her nose. "Eleven and I have mutual respect for each other," she says. "But we have different strengths."

"How long have you been friends?"

She looks at me. "I wouldn't use that word." She sips her water. How does her red lipstick not come off on the glass? "She's my boss. I have a lot of expenses. I send money to my mom and my sister, too. And Eleven treats us well. I've had some terrible jobs. The Temple has an excellent benefits package. I get my glasses, dental, massage, everything."

"It pays well," I admit. I know I'm lucky: My rich white cousin gave me this job. I don't have to pay rent right now, and I don't have any dependents. And the exchange rate! When I turn my paycheques into Canadian dollars, I'm making thousands more.

"It's good I love being single," Yolanda says. "Because I wouldn't have time for a relationship, even if I wanted one."

"Marriage isn't necessary anymore," I say. "If you don't want to raise kids, then there's little reason for it."

"True. Do you know anyone who is married who is genuinely happy?"

"I don't think my friend Juliette has spent any real time with her husband since she had children."

"Children are statistically proven to be the fastest way to ruin a marriage."

"Dating looks fun, though," I say. "If you made time for Tinder."

"Well of course, but that's because dating has sex," says Yolanda.

"I wouldn't know," I say.

Yolanda laughs. "You don't date?" she asks.

"I haven't had sex," I say. "Other than with myself."

Our platter arrives at this moment. It's the size of a laundry basket, piled with arrangements of curries and stews in little silver compartments. Our server clearly heard what I just said. He sets the platter down in front of us and avoids making eye contact with me. He gives us each a side plate of rolled-up injera pieces and scurries off.

"You're not joking," Yolanda says, and adjusts her side plate. "How did you manage that?"

I tear a piece of injera off the roll and scoop up sweet potatoes with it. "I've always been an introvert," I say. "And I was overweight and awkward when I was young." The sweet potatoes are creamy and spicy, with a buttery flavour. But it can't be butter, because Selasa is a vegan restaurant!

Yolanda eats a minuscule portion of injera. "I've never met a virgin before," she says.

"Maybe you have," I say, "and just didn't know it."

"I lost my virginity when I was fifteen," she says. "That was too young."

"I'm forty," I say. "That's probably too old."

Yolanda drops her hands and stares at me. "Lilian, no!" she says. "No! You're not *forty*!" She gives me an appraisal. She scans the skin around my eyes, and goes up and down over my face. She considers my hair. "No way," she says. "You're thirty-six, max."

"Eleven and I are the same age," I tell her. "I look a lot younger than I am."

"White people always age faster," she says. "What's your secret?"

The sound of drums and thumb piano tinkles out of the speaker in the corner. "I splash my face with cold water every morning and night," I say. "Closes the pores."

A bell sounds, the ring coming from under our table. Yolanda looks at me, and then looks down at her lap. "Oh," she says. "That's me." She touches her phone. The bell stops ringing. I close my eyes and take a deep breath. Yolanda is a C tone. The sound is familiar and comforting. I wonder what chakra it's for. Yolanda is very matter-of-fact, very earthy. C is a good tone for her.

I forgot to Instagram our meal! I open my eyes and take out my phone. To get a good shot, I move the glass lantern so it's in the frame with our big plate, and I snap it.

Deliciousness at Selasa with @YolandaClarke.
#Ascendencyprep #vegan

I should slow down on the eating. I've already scarfed a quarter of our shared platter.

"What was it like growing up with Eleven?" Yolanda asks. "I heard her parents were strict."

"Aunt Rosie was always nice to me," I say, which is true. "I remember Florence had to call Uncle Jimmy 'sir.' But isn't that what some people call their father in the States?" I wait for her to agree, but Yolanda doesn't answer. "Their house was beautiful," I say. "I loved going to visit her every summer." It doesn't feel right to talk about my memories without Eleven here.

Yolanda is a slow, meticulous eater. I shouldn't be surprised—she's a detail-oriented person. Maybe she's a Virgo. The silver plate is a big circle. I work my way around the other side and scoop up the spicy lentils, trying to slow down so it's not obvious that I'm eating too fast. It was the SoulCore class that did this to me! That metabolic afterburn. These lentils are very good. I think they're made with cloves.

"So are you ready for the Ascendency?" Yolanda asks.

"Helping Anna-Mackenzie kept me late at the Temple, but I think I'm on track," I say. Opening night is in two days. My phone vibrates.

"I mean as an Ascendant," Yolanda says. "Are you ready for 'the rupture'?"

I check my phone.

@**JonRasmussen** likes your photo

That means he knows we're here! I wonder where he is right now. He's giving the opening meditation on Friday night, so he might be in the city already. He's staying at a hotel while he's here, I think. He *would* be staying at the Temple guest suite, but that's my apartment now.

"What was it like for you?" I ask Yolanda. "You're an Ascendency grad, right?"

"Oh no." Yolanda nibbles a piece of injera. "I admire some of Eleven's work. But she's not my teacher."

I have one more injera roll left on my side plate. I rip off half of it and mop up the rest of the sweet potatoes on my side of the platter. My shiny teal nails really confront the orange of the table-cloth. Did I pick the right colour? Maybe I should have gone for classic red.

"Who's your teacher?" I ask.

She shrugs. "I follow my own advice," she says. Yolanda is so self-possessed!

"When's your birthday?" I ask. "Just out of curiosity."

"September twelfth."

"I knew it!" I say. "I love Virgos. You always know the right way to do things. Perfection is just *innate* for you."

"What are you?"

"I'm a Sagittarius," I say. She takes another sip of water, and I have to ask. "What kind of lipstick do you use? How does it always look so elegant? Do you not lick your lips ever, even when you're eating?"

"I use a layer of pressed powder first," she says. "It's Kat Von D."

"Colour?"

"Santa Sangre. Everlasting."

I could never pull off red lipstick like that! "I thought every-one who worked at the Temple was an Ascendant," I say. "I mean, Eleven asked me to do the program. I thought it was a prerequisite for our job."

"Well, Eleven was very clear that you were to be our art and design lead this year," she says. "When she has an instinct, she fol-lows it. And she felt that you would benefit from Ascendency."

Another bell sounds—this time, it's an A tone. My own phone! It's the first time I've heard it in the wild. Yolanda pauses, and gives me time to inhale and exhale.

Jonathan

I need an assistant for Friday meditation. Can you do it?

"You don't take a breath at the tone?" I ask.

"It's technically not working hours," Yolanda says.

Jonathan Rasmussen wants me to be his assistant? What? How? "Look at my nails against this tablecloth," I say to Yolanda. "Doesn't the orange and blue make you feel a charge?"

She nods. "It's cool," she says. "Good color."

"It's not an easy contrast, like green and red," I continue. "Green and red have similar values. Orange and blue are too different— orange has a lighter value, even at its most pure." Jonathan Rasmussen wants me to be his *assistant*! "Think of purple and yellow—they really vibrate against each other. Their values are even more distinct. Pure yellow is even lighter than orange."

"You know a lot about color," Yolanda says.

"I love colour," I say. "I love, love, love, love, love it." I almost feel drunk! I'm so happy. I dig into the salad at the centre of our platter and fill the last half of my injera with the oily leaves. It's delicious.

When I come home from dinner with Yolanda, I check my phone— nothing but some more IG likes—and shuck off my ankle boots by the door. My clothes feel tight. I unhook my bra and unzip my jeans to release my body. I feel two sizes larger than I did this morning. How? After SoulCore and everything? I light my lemongrass-and-lavender soy candle.

I ate most of the food tonight. The lentils were heavy and saturated with oil. Yolanda only ate half of the fresh salad in the centre of the platter, and I ate everything else. The sweet potatoes, the curried root vegetables with raisins, the tomato and grease eggplant. Plus I ate all my injera. Does Yolanda like me? I can't tell what she thinks of me. She wouldn't call Eleven a friend. So what would that make me? I turn all the lights out, and except for the little candle on the shelf above my mattress, the room is dark. City light glows around the edges of the curtains—it's not even midnight yet, and the club downstairs serves sushi until dawn. Everybody out there is happy. Everyone out there has a normal, happy life. They're talking with friends, laughing about their jobs, planning their upcoming vacations. They belong here—this is their neighbourhood.

The candle casts a shadow overhead. I lie on the bed and feel it hanging over me. The flame licks the walls. I reach down and pick up my phone again.

Jonathan

I need an assistant for Friday meditation. Can you do it?

I didn't answer him at dinner. I didn't tell Yolanda that he asked me to do it, either. Honestly, I can't believe it. I didn't know that he even knew who I was until he liked my Instagram pic. Eleven must have arranged this. But why? And why would he want me to share the stage with him?

Laughter from the street below. I could go down to the sake bar and order a tea. I could just throw on a sweater over my leggings and go out.

Or I could take this quiet moment for myself and feel what it feels like to be present. I could take a deep breath and have a two-minute private retreat. I swipe the face of my phone with my teal thumb. Have I missed anything interesting on Instagram from earlier tonight? Juliette just posted a picture of the girls, asleep in matching polka-dot sleepers. @UnderOverWriter posted a picture of himself in Cambodia holding his latest book. He leans against a stone temple, his book held open so it covers his face. He never shows his face in his selfies. He's a travel hacker—his last book was on how to travel the world for free, on points. The new book is called *Find One Farthing*.

Oh! There's a video from @tunameltsmyheart! I love that little guy. The video is of him chewing a green stuffed toy—it looks like a pickle, but with a yellow face. He chews it and gives the camera a warning side glance and growls. It's hilarious!

I actually laugh out loud, and the serotonin floods my neurons, and I feel better. It's so important to watch your mind and ask yourself, what just happened, what just made you want to avoid stillness? Way better to watch positive videos of Tuna. I like the video and go back to my text feed.

Me

Hi Jonathan! Yes, I'd love to assist you on Friday
night! Thank you! Looking forward. xo

I put my phone in the charger and lie down, watching the candle flicker again.

Oh Goddess. I just wrote "xo" to Jonathan Rasmussen! Humiliating.

◊ ◊ ◊

Eleven gave me the afternoon off work to prepare for the first weekend of the Ascendency. When I told her I was going to be Jonathan Rasmussen's assistant for the Active Meditation session tonight, she said, "He knows where to find the gold, doesn't he?"

We were told to wear comfortable clothing tonight—Active Meditation is the opening event. I tried three different pairs of leggings before deciding on these black ones with the mesh stars on the ankles. I put on makeup and then I took it off, because who wears makeup to a meditation class? Then I reapplied it—just a little mascara, cheek stain, and lip gloss. Being well-groomed is a sign of self-worth!

"Try it with your eyes closed," Jonathan Rasmussen says in the class. "Now, open. See the difference? It's profound, isn't it? Remember: always keep your eyes open." The crowd moves back and forth in the darkened room.

Jonathan Rasmussen puts his hands on my shoulders and looks up into my eyes. He doesn't blink. His eyes are dark brown. The stage lights are intense, and his nose casts a big shadow over his face. We are face-to-face. I'm only a little bit taller than him. I can feel the warmth of his hands through my shirt.

"Listen to the music. See if you can play the music with your body. Like this," he says, and he moves my shoulders back and forth, one at a time, like I'm doing a slow salsa. I close my eyes to hear the music better. "Open your eyes," he says quietly. I open my eyes.

His face is very close to mine. The hair above his forehead is thick and shiny, and more sparse at his temples.

"This is *active* meditation, so your physical movement should connect to your breath." I breathe in and out more heavily, hoping that it's connecting to my shoulders. "Good," he says. "Now circle your hips." He moves his hands down my waist. "Like this," he says. "That's it. In circles. Can you sense how the music is circular?" I close my eyes to hear the circular music. "Eyes open," he reminds me. "Always eyes open." I open my eyes. "It's so good that you did that," he says. "I'm glad you closed your eyes. See what she did just there?" He looks at the crowd of women. "How many of you also closed your eyes to feel the music? Right. I know, it's the place we go by default. We go inside, we try to shut out the visual distraction. But I want you to feel connected to everything that is right now. Trust yourself. Trust that you can remain connected with your eyes open. Trust your four bodies—bring your mental body, emotional body, physical body, and spiritual body to the same place."

I keep circling my hips and moving my shoulders around. I feel wobbly and graceless. His hands leave my hips, and he watches me. Stay connected, he says with his eyes. Stay with me. You're right here. Feel it. Feel the circular drumbeats. You're here.

And I feel it! I feel what he says! I stop jerking around and I start to play the drums with my body. Every twist connects to a beat. It feels like dancing, but with more depth. I breathe in and out as I move, and my breathing breathes the music. I am part of the drums, I have become the drums. There are circles all around me, and inside me. I am made of the music, and I am making the music as I move in it.

Then, Jonathan Rasmussen begins to move. He turns his body to face the crowd, and he begins circling his hips and shoulders. He rolls his head. He lifts one leg, shakes it, and then does the same thing on the other side. The whole room is writhing together, just below us. The music is endless. The women of Ascendency are an ocean wave crashing to the shore of the stage. Jonathan Rasmussen and I are two fish roiling in the surf.

◊ ◊ ◊

On the other side of the pink silk room divider, a photographer calls and directs the women in front of her camera. She asks them each to smile, address a crowd, flirt with the man pouring their coffee, say yes to the job offer, accept an award. It sounds like acting. I've never heard a photographer ask for so many different poses. What a brilliant strategy: the prompts must bring out a different side to each of the women. I can see how imagining that you're accepting an award would change your posture, for instance, and thereby change your whole demeanour.

"Why not berry?" Gem twists the tube of lipstick to show me. "It's a shade darker than your actual lip color, so it will pop, but still look natural."

"I usually just wear pink gloss," I say.

"These are glam sessions, though!" says Shona from Seattle. She's sitting on the brown velvet bench in front of me, next in line for makeup. "I think the berry would look stunning on you."

Shona is so nice. I love women! I love how sweet and supportive women are when they get together and dress up. I've missed this. My girlfriends are always so busy. We never just hang out anymore, like girls.

"I'm going to finger-comb these curls in a minute," says Amira. "I'm just checking them." She lifts one of my new ringlets to inspect it, and gently touches the curls around my face. My scalp tingles with pleasure.

"I never curl my hair," I say. "Maybe I should start."

"You have a natural wave, though. Your hair *wants* to curl."

"Isn't she gorgeous?" Gem asks.

"Her hair shines like I've never seen before," says Amira. "It's so *healthy*."

"I'm using Vex on her eyes," Gem tells Amira. "Because the way the iridescent blue—look."

"Oh!" says Amira. "You *have* to use Vex."

"You have amazing eyes," says Shona.

"She really does," says Eleven, behind me.

How long has she been in here with us? Shona looks up over my shoulder, to where Eleven is standing, and her eyes light up with awe.

"Where are you?" I say. "I can't see you!"

Eleven moves closer, so I see her reflection in the mirror. "Lilian, you're not staff today, okay? You're participating as a full Ascendant." The breeze from the fans picks up one of her curls and waves it in the air. The amber and rose of her perfume waft over me. "I came in to tell you that Anna-Mack and Monicke have everything covered for this afternoon. So you can just let go of logistics and sink in."

"But I was supposed to meet Dee Kay," I say. "And make sure about her books." Dee Kay is arriving from California today, and she's couriered six cases of *Your Most Precious Asset* to give away to Ascendants tonight.

"I can't wait to see Dee Kay!" blurts Shona. "I can't believe she's going to be here."

"Done and done, sweetheart," Eleven says. She comes around to face me. She's wearing an off-the-shoulder cashmere dress in ivory, and her body floats like a cloud. Shona is openly gaping from where she sits on the bench. She's just staring up at Eleven's back, in adoration. Does she know that we're cousins? I wonder who knows.

"Thank you," I say. I try to sound professional, even though I'm not doing anything. I don't want to show off, but I *like* being an important part of this team. I'm so used to playing small. As if it's somehow better to be quiet and humble. Why have I done that for so long? It's so Canadian.

"What do you think, Eleven?" I ask. "Should I go berry? Gem, show her." Gem dabs it on my lips with a paintbrush. The lipstick smells like red fruit.

"Ooh, yes," says Gem. "See *that*."

Eleven smiles and holds her arms out to me. The script of her tattoos peeks out of her cashmere sleeves: *too* on one wrist and *pass* on the other. "Gorgeousness," she says. "Utter gorgeousness."

"Thank you for your reflection!" I say. Mirroring is an important Ascendency practice. When we witness each other, we are showing each other who we are. It's so important to be seen. It connects us.

I touch my mala and trace the facets cut into the amazonite. This is actually happening to me right now. I'm in New York City. I work with Eleven. I'm an Ascendant.

In front of the camera, I try to look the way Gem and Amira styled me. I pretend I'm accepting the Dahleria Prize for portraiture. The flash pops.

"You've learned so much this weekend, my darlings," Eleven says from the stage. "You've learned that when you feel adored, you become your highest self. You've seen what happens when we move together in dance."

We all cheer at this, because we were all part of an Ascendency dance mob in Times Square last night! I didn't have time to learn the steps before the dance like everyone else, but I was there. I *felt* it.

"You've invited the spirit of the divine feminine, and now you've experienced how it lights you up from the inside. You cannot un-know this feeling. It is yours. When you return to your life after this weekend, you will take this spirit with you. This isn't a hallucination; this is who you are."

My phone vibrates in my back pocket. My jeans feel tight again. It started after lunch. Maybe I should stop eating wheat entirely.

"Do you see the way it works?" Eleven walks to the other side of the stage. Dee Kay is on that side of the audience—she's sitting in the front row with Jonathan Rasmussen, Amira and Gem, and Ricki, the photographer. "Do you see that when you compliment the women around you, it takes you higher? When your girlfriend looks like a goddess, don't you feel the beauty inside yourself blossoming? We are built this way, women. We are built for beauty and pleasure. This is how our spirit renews itself. And we are not separate. We are so much more when we see how we are one."

My phone vibrates again, to remind me.

Jonathan
We're having dinner at Candle 79
tonight. Would you like to come?

Who is we? Does he mean Eleven? Or Dee Kay, who's sitting beside him?

But I've already made dinner plans with Shona from Seattle and the other two women in my Potency Circle: Anoosh from Illinois, and Matilde from France. They all fly home tomorrow morning. Oh! I will miss them.

As long as I remember that everything is connected, there is no such thing as loneliness.

"As little girls, we knew this instinctively. We knew how to play dress-up, and we knew that meant it was for ourselves. As we grew up, our culture began to tell us how to look. This happened for some of us earlier than others. For some women, there wasn't much time to play in our own beauty before we knew we were being watched. For some women, we were born into it. We learned early on that our beauty was for other viewers. That our beauty was for men. That we were meant to be *looked at*."

Jonathan Rasmussen looks completely at home in this room of women. He's so comfortable with his own sexuality, he can sit here with us without disturbing the energy or interfering in any way. Not many men could do that!

"And this is the tragedy, my angels! This exiled us from our home! Beauty is where we are all meant to live. It's where we are our truest selves. We are no different from the flowers, the waves, the dappled light in a forest that takes our breath away. Once you begin to understand your own beauty, you come back home to yourself."

Dee Kay nods as Eleven speaks. Her hair looks red-purple from the stage lights. Gem and Amira's glittering powdered faces are both raised to the stage. I'm wearing that same Glimyr powder on my face, tonight. Gem gave it to me yesterday, after my glam session, and told me that I needed it, because it made me look like I was "Aphrodite flying a tiger through heaven."

Me
I'm sorry I already have
dinner plans! Tomorrow?

I hope he's still here tomorrow. We all have the day off work, to recover from the weekend. Oh, I hope he doesn't have to leave tomorrow!

"I'm looking out at you here tonight, you beautiful women, and you simply take my breath away," says Eleven.

All around the room, the women move like flowers on stems. We are a garden of petals. We are alive in beauty. My phone buzzes.

Yumi
Okay I'll bite: what happened
at your first weekend?

I can't believe they remembered! I told them about the Ascendency weeks ago. Not even Juliette remembered what I was doing this weekend. I lift my phone, take a selfie, and send it.

Me
This!

Yumi
😍

Shona takes my hand and squeezes it. Anoosh, on the other side of me, puts her arm around my waist. I squeeze Shona's hand and slip my phone back in my pocket so I can hug Anoosh with my other arm. Matilde and I smile at each other. Leaving Toronto and moving to New York was the best decision I've ever made.

Dear Lilian,

That was it. That was Session One of the Ascendency. How are you, sweetheart?

So much happened to us last week in New York. So much.
Are you integrating? What does your old life feel like now?
Do you feel the divine feminine rising and radiating inside of you?

If you are having a difficult time adjusting now that you're back at home, please know that this is normal after an Ascendency weekend. This is transformation, and transformation can feel challenging. Expect some grit as you raise your consciousness. You will probably need more rest than usual. Give yourself salt baths to detox energetically. Let your nervous system acclimatize to the changes you are making within.

Remember your <u>Daily Practices</u>. Remember the rituals we learned: they connect you to your creative and spiritual self. Remember to pay attention to your intuition instead of cultural guidance. Now that you're on this path, you'll begin to see that your choices may not look "normal" to everyone. This is to be expected. This month, stay with your practice.

Remember to connect with the women in your <u>Potency Circle</u>. These women are your elemental support through Ascendency. Together, you represent earth, fire, air, and water. Remember your element and the qualities you bring to your group. For a reminder on ways to bring your element into your daily rituals, <u>click here</u>. Support each other.

This is only the start, my darling. Can you believe we've traversed so far already, and that this is only the beginning of the Ascendency? You are already so full and beautiful. You are divine. I KNOW YOU ARE. I saw you last weekend. I met your spirit!

Put this date in your calendar: our first Teleritual is on Saturday, March 26, at 8 p.m. ET.

With love,
Eleven

JONATHAN RASMUSSEN AND I watch a man in a straw hat play jazz on a grand piano in Washington Square. He's wearing fingerless gloves and a puffy vest over a sweater. The snow in New York is gone and the sunlight looks promising, but the air is still cold and biting. I'm wearing a slouchy wool hat to stay warm. Underdressed college students wrap their arms around themselves. Too soon for spring dresses and cute boots, girls! Too soon!

Jonathan has to leave tomorrow. We're spending a lot of time together, becoming closer and closer. I know it's only been a week since Ascendency, but it feels like we stretch time and space when we are together. Every day after work I meet him in the East Village, because that's where he's staying too, so it's "our" neighbourhood. We get our usual almond matcha lattes from Quintessence—they make their almond milk in-house—and then we go for a walk.

"Tell me more about your family," Jonathan says. "I love to hear you describe your childhood. I find it most interesting, your Canadian–American dichotomy. I'm from the Commonwealth, remember."

"It's like you having family in Australia," I say. "The New Zealand–Australia relationship is a lot like Canada and the U.S. A bit of sibling rivalry. But only from the smaller sibling—because the bigger sibling doesn't notice any differences."

"These days the difference is less apparent," Jonathan says. "We are living post-geography now." Sometimes he speaks as though he's reading from one of his own books. He's growing a beard and wears a gauzy navy blue scarf around his neck in a looped slipknot.

"You mean the Internet has screwed up our connection to geography?" I say.

He sips his latte carefully, to avoid getting foam on his moustache. "When we are living on the Internet," he says, "we are living in another space entirely. We are positioning ourselves outside real time. Our devices. The computer in your pocket. Facebook, for instance, is what we used to call a heterotopia."

I recognize this line from the back cover of his last book, although I haven't actually read it. I should read more books!

"*Exactly,*" I say. "You articulate that so well." I sound ridiculous.

"Do you use social media? And if so, how do you use it?"

"I use social media to connect to people," I say. "I have a blog, and a newsletter." A white dog walks past us, with pink balloons on her paws to protect her from the mud. She has a warm, flax-oil-yellow aura. "Of course, working with Eleven now, there's a big work component. I'm online all the time for work—I have to be."

"Isn't it interesting, how we justify things done for work."

"Well, you're online for your work," I say, and wish it didn't come out so pouty.

"I know," he says. It sounds like *ah noi*. "I am on my computer all the time. I live online."

"And is it satisfying to you?" The white dog stops in front of the piano player. She puts her ears back as he pounds the keys.

"I can't stand it," he says.

"It's how I stay connected to my friends," I say.

He looks up, as if checking the position of the sun. "You knew Eleven before she was Eleven," he says. "What was she like?"

"The same as she is now," I say. "Beautiful. Confident. Sophisticated. She always had a plan."

"She's a mysterious woman," he says. "I always thought there might be more to her story."

He looks at me intently. Why is he so interested in Eleven? "She's only a month older than me, but I always thought of her as my older cousin," I say. "Maybe because of her height."

"Were you close?"

"She was my best friend."

The piano player takes a break. He wanders around the fountain with his straw hat in his hand, collecting money from the crowd. I am sitting so close to Jonathan on this bench. Our legs are almost touching. My phone vibrates again.

"Sorry," I say. "I should check."

"For work," he says, and smiles. His eyes are kind. I think he's flirting with me. Is he flirting with me? Or is he just interested and present?

I let an Ascendant named Anastasia know that the glam shots will be sent out early next week and put my phone back in my coat pocket.

"I lost touch with her when we were still in high school," I say. He turns to give me his full attention, and his knees touch my thigh. "I saw her once after that, at our grandmother's funeral. By that time, our mothers were so angry with each other, they were barely managing to be civil. We didn't even talk to each other. I never saw her again."

"Did you ever try to find her?"

"I heard about her here and there through my mother. Florence quit college, bought a car, and is driving to Arizona. Florence is dealing blackjack on a cruise ship in Mexico. Florence is taking acting classes in L.A., doing theatre and commercials. Florence is living with some guy, picking fruit on a farm in Hawaii." Jonathan nods at this.

"For years, that was the last I heard about Florence. I pictured her on a tropical farm, picking bananas. I thought she must have met a sexy surfer."

Oh Goddess, did I just say that out loud? I'm talking to Jonathan Rasmussen! Okay, just own it. I smile at him knowingly.

"Hey, it heppens," he says.

His eyes are like raw cacao. His eyelashes are so full, they look like professional extensions. "I thought she'd be raising kids by now, in some bungalow with sand on the floor," I say.

"Why were they fighting?"

"Who?"

"At the funeral. Your mother and your aunt." A small cloud, his breath, rises between our faces.

"It was about my uncle," I say. "He was controlling. In a bad way." My words feel thin and needle-like. Jonathan Rasmussen sits very still, listening. It feels like something is pressing against my chest. "He was emotionally abusive to my aunt." I take a breath and whisper, "He used to lock Florence in the basement." As soon as I say it, my throat flushes. "I shouldn't have told you." I shake my head. "Please don't share that with anyone."

"Of course not," he says. He touches my hand, and I let him take it. His hand feels warm and reassuring. We sit quietly. A man throws breadcrumbs at the pigeons. A squirrel is in the flock, taking his share, and the man looks annoyed.

"She got away, though," I say. "She finally escaped."

"She's Eleven now," Jonathan says.

"She came back," I say. "For me, and for everyone." I sip my lukewarm latte.

A cold breeze moves through the park, and a cloud shifts over the sun briefly. The crowd looks dim and colourless for a moment, and then it all brightens again.

"Why did you ask me to be your assistant last weekend?" I ask.

He grins. "You seemed like you'd be up for it," he says.

"I am up for it," I say. "I'm up for anything." A child runs toward the clump of pigeons and they scatter, wings rustling. "If you ever had something else in mind, I mean."

When he looks at me, my heart jumps. Did I just say that? Am I doing this?

"Do you have anything in mind?" he asks.

"You're flying to Seattle tomorrow, right?" I say.

"Is it Friday already?" Jonathan says. The man feeding the pigeons dips his hand back into the plastic bag and throws a handful of breadcrumbs, and the birds walk back to him, their necks and breasts bobbing.

Let yourself want what you want.

"Do you have plans right now?" I ask. "Would you like to come over?"

Jonathan Rasmussen looks at me and smiles. I can't see his dimple clearly through his new beard, but I know it's there. A helicopter crosses the sky above us, and the man with the straw hat has seated himself at the piano. Noise rushes in my ears. I can't tell if it's music or engines or my own fear in my chest, pounding. The old Lilian would never have said that. This is me, rising. This is Ascendency! My phone buzzes.

"Okay," Jonathan Rasmussen says. "Should we get something to eat first?"

◊ ◊ ◊

I bring him to my apartment. He takes off his shoes and socks as soon as he gets here. We eat our collard green and nut meat tacos on my tiny couch and then we climb up to my bed. He sits with his legs tucked in lotus position. We spoon chia seed coconut pudding with strawberries out of plastic cups. Dark hair grows over the tops of his feet and covers his toes. The tough, calloused soles of his feet rest on his knees, open like leaves. I keep thinking, *Jonathan Rasmussen is in my bed*, which is very distracting. Jonathan Rasmussen is in my bed! To keep myself calm, I check my phone.

@PureJuliette> Healthy shamrock shakes, a new reno, and my #sacredsolitude project: new post is up! Link in bio.

You have 1,400 calories left today.

You have 14 tasks in TewDew that are overdue.

Raise your vibration. #depthcharge

"Come with me to Fidalgo Island this weekend," he says. I'm teaching a workshop at the Aerie Center."

"Where's Fidalgo Island?"

"It's an island on the west coast of Washington. Just north of Whidbey Island."

"I have too much work to do," I tell him. "I'm already going to Toronto this month. I have to pack and move my things."

He connects his phone to my portable speaker. "This is my spring equinox playlist," he says. Ocean waves, beats, and a woman's breath. "I could use your help on Fidalgo. We work well together."

"But I love working with Eleven at the Temple," I say. "I'm closing my studio in Toronto and moving my things here permanently."

He finishes his pudding and puts the plastic cup and spoon on the ledge above my pillow.

"Lilian Quick," he says. "I'm fascinated by you." He touches the sleeve of my T-shirt. Then he touches the seam of my jeans, on the inside of my knee. The music sounds blue-green, wavy, oceanic. Did he turn up the volume? It's getting louder, but in a good way. The woman's voice breathes, *The light is blue now, the light is blue.*

"I'm fascinated by you too," I say. I set my cup and spoon next to his. I reach out and touch his throat. His neck is a pelt of short dark hair. It didn't take him long to grow this beard. A week, maybe? I touch his throat in the place where his beard connects to his chest. "Jonathan Rasmussen," I say. My finger rests in the divot there. Am I really doing this?

I am touching Jonathan Rasmussen in my bed. *Raise your vibration.*

"That's only one of my names," he says. His hand is now on my thigh. "But what is my true name?"

Is that a Rumi reference? He uncrosses his legs and comes closer to me. He speaks softly. "I love your energy," he says, before I can think of an answer. "I can see the ways you are changing. You move like the spring equinox," he says. "It's incredible to watch you."

"You've been watching me?" His hand moves up my leg.

"I remember you from that hotel room," he says. "I remember your eyes." I touch my mala to feel the energy of the amazonite.

"Eleven's hotel room?" My mala beads are warm. My skin feels like silver, everywhere his hand touches. "In Toronto?"

His lips are on mine. His mouth is hot. His beard smells of garlic and strawberries. His nose presses into my face.

This is actually happening. Jonathan Rasmussen is kissing me. I can't wait to tell Eleven! Jonathan Rasmussen wants *me.* He's not just being clear and present and friendly: he really truly honestly deeply wants me. His kiss turns my whole body into a swirl, and I fall in.

Hello, FIRST NAME,

Introducing my new and improved online home:
www.lilianquick.com!

Working with Eleven Novak has been an eye-opening
experience. Her Ascendency Program has taught me how to
live life with confidence. I've learned how to still those anxious
voices in my head that always used to tell me I wasn't doing
enough, making enough, or being successful enough.

This site is not just about drawings and watercolours anymore. It's
about having the courage to choose the life you want to lead.
It's about knowing yourself, knowing what makes you happy—and
then going for it. It's about living the way you want to feel.

In my new blog, I'll be sharing what I've learned. I hope my
reflections inspire you. There will also be photo essays about
what to see and do in New York City, behind-the-scenes stories
about life working at the Temple, and notes about fashion and
style that I'm picking up here in NYC.

Remember when you used to have time to hang out with your
friends and share your favourite things with each other? That's
what I want for us on my new site.

This is me being Lilian Quick: the real Lilian Quick.

Special offer! Because you've been a loyal reader-friend
through this transition, all Quick+Friday's pet portrait prints and
art cards are 50 percent off today! This is not a public sale—
this is just for you. Note: I'm phasing out these products—once
they're gone, they're gone. So if you've been thinking about
getting one of my prints or a pack of my art cards, stock up on
them now while you still can.

Click here _to go to the secret sale page._

The password is: colour+light

Thank you so much for supporting Quick+Friday all these years. I'm really grateful for your friendship, and I can't wait for this new chapter to begin.

xo,
Lilian

SUNDAYS ARE MY Ascendency self-care days. I spend all day trying to connect creatively. I light the candle and call in the element that was given to me as an Ascendant—I'm earth—and surrender everything to the divine feminine. I read Dee Kay's chapter on the Impostor Syndrome and listen to her interview on the *Art of Love* podcast. She talks about how belief is stronger than reality, and how to set your intentions and rewire your brain so you believe what you visualize. It all makes SO MUCH SENSE.

Then why can't I paint? Why?

My colours are muddy. I'm trying to do Sophia, but the magenta looks like borscht. I can't paint anymore. Something happened when I cut my hand. The stitches healed and there's just a little scar like a smiley face now, but the energy changed. I can't find the truth in the colours at all. I can still feel her aura in my mind—dancing hot-pink happy flames—but when I try to make that colour with my paints, I just mess it up.

Maybe my earth element is interfering with the watercolours. I switch to coloured pencil. Most of them need sharpening, but the nub-ended pencils are buttery and the pigments melt onto the paper. I layer pink with red with pink. I need some blue in there to get the magenta right. I smudge the layers with my thumb to see how they settle with each other. I trace a cobalt-blue pencil in, very lightly. Too much. I wrecked it again. That's not the right colour at all.

I leave the sketch pad on the coffee table and get out a sleeve of gluten-free graham crackers and a container of vegan cream cheese. I bring it over to my bed, which I haven't made since Jonathan Rasmussen was here. I can still smell him on my pillow. I put on the Active Meditation spring equinox mix again, to hear that song he played. When I dip the cracker into the tub of cream cheese, it snaps. He hasn't texted me since Thursday. That's been the whole entire weekend. I know he's on the west coast, but he should be in touch, right? After we did what we did, he should email me or something. Do I email him?

I go through the sleeve of crackers one by one. When I slip one out, the one behind it lines up perfectly and slants just so, ready for me to eat it next. I used to eat cookies like this when I was a kid. I could eat an entire *box* of Oreos. I used to eat so much sugar! This cream cheese is just made of coconut oil and tapioca starch. Tapioca is basically carbohydrates, so there's not a lot of nutritional value in it, but it's not *bad* for you, either. I spread the cream cheese on a cracker with my finger. I've already eaten half the sleeve, which is more than a portion size. One of the things we do as Ascendants is have a digital sabbatical on our self-care day. So I can't check my phone to keep track of my calories. I have to remember to input it all retroactively tomorrow.

I'm starting to feel better about the painting now. I just need more rest, because of Ascendency. I can't expect to jump into painting when I'm doing all this intense transformative work. And—hello— I just had a life-changing experience with Jonathan Rasmussen. I should give myself some time with that.

The most incredible thing is, I feel like *myself* when we are together. He listens to me. I can let my guard down around him. He's honestly interested in me! I never thought that this would be possible. That someone like Jonathan Rasmussen would be interested in me. But he is, he is, he is.

I need to stop forcing the drawing, and just let it all settle. Let myself rest and absorb how life is changing. I need to be gentle with myself. This is Self-Care Sunday. I put the lid back on the cream cheese and carefully fold the empty plastic sleeve in half so no crumbs escape.

I check my phone and see what's happening in my online store. There are two new orders for Quick+Friday art cards. Success!

Dear Lilian,

As I write this letter to you, I am sitting on the upper deck of a ferry that just left mainland Washington for Whidbey Island, a small island near Seattle, where I will be making another new home.

It feels appropriate that I write this letter while crossing a passage, moving over a body of water, leaving one land mass for another. This move marks an important new chapter in my life. It is a transformation, and as with all journeys, the change brings with it great excitement and uncertainty.

There are two things, however, of which I am certain. First, it is an honour to introduce you to my life partner, Fifi Torre. Fifi and I have known each other for many years. We are both originally from New Zealand and studied with the same mentor, Roshi Tanner, <u>whose work I've written about here</u>. Fifi is the creator of the groundbreaking <u>New Mind New Yoga</u>, an organization that works to reduce unhealthy striving, cultural appropriation, and patriarchal dominance in contemporary yoga communities.

Second, it is with great love and gratitude that Fifi and I announce the birth of our daughter, Espuma Torre-Rasmussen. Our hearts are full, and we feel privileged to share this fullness, and the adventure and honour that is mindful parenting, with you, Lilian, and the rest of our community.

I invite you to join me for one of my upcoming workshops, <u>Active Meditation for New Families</u>. In the next month, I will be leading workshops in New York City, Syracuse, Washington, D.C., Vancouver, Cortes Island, San Francisco, and Costa Rica. My <u>tour schedule</u> is right here.

I know this new chapter of my life will present me with many opportunities for growth. When I look into the face of my baby daughter, I see a portal of spirit—the spirit to which we all belong, the spirit that knows our true name and essence.

May you also meet this spirit, and recognise it when it calls your true name.

Much love,
Jonathan Rasmussen

MONDAY MORNING. The moon is still in Gemini. The time changed to Daylight Savings last night, and losing the hour has made me feel drained. It's raining. I know rain is seasonally appropriate and necessary for things that grow, but I still feel pressed down by it. The dampness comes through my window and doors, seeping through these old apartment walls. I haven't touched my phone since reading Jonathan's newsletter last night. I can't bear to get out of bed and see everyone at the Temple today. What do they know? Was I the only one who didn't know about Jonathan and Fifi Torre?

I follow Fifi Torre! I've done her yoga videos! I check her Instagram. Her whole feed is pink, tan, and forest green. She's so flawlessly branded, she curates all her pictures in a palette! Her most recent post is a shot of her altar: a wooden Kuan Yin statue lit by candlelight. Then a close-up selfie: that coy smile, those signature short dark bangs. And a foot selfie: her cute unpolished toes at the base of her pink yoga mat.

I don't feel well.

I choose clothes for the day that will make me feel better. I pull on my new heather-grey jersey midi skirt with the white racing stripes and my tall vegan boots with the moto buckles. They're a bit narrow for my feet but they look good. I button up the green blouse that makes my eyes look turquoise and half-tuck it. I put on mascara, scrunch up my hair with volumizer, and act the way I want to feel. The way I wish I could feel.

We have to use the regular electric house lights in the Temple today because the weather is so grim. Fibre-optic daylight doesn't work in the rain. I arrive just after Anna-Mackenzie, who opens her umbrella and leaves it to dry on the lobby floor, beside the elevator. As soon as I arrive, her hand goes to the rose quartz mala around her neck and immediately I know that she knows.

"Good morning," she says.

My feet hurt from walking from the subway in these boots, but the sound of my boots on the marble floors makes me feel more powerful. It's worth it, to be able to wear these boots with this skirt.

I hang my raincoat in the cloakroom and pull my phone out of the coat pocket. I still can't look at its face to see if I have any texts. I just can't.

Monicke comes to my desk. "Eleven put a note in your mailbox, but in case you don't check," she says, "we have Inquiry a bit early today. Eleven wants us all to meet at ten. All the Portland prep. She wants to make sure we have enough time to connect in the chaos." She looks me up and down. "You look hot," she says. "Love those boots."

"Thank you!" I haven't spoken to anyone since yesterday, and my voice sounds like a high-pitched chime. Yolanda comes out of Eleven's office and drops an envelope on Anna-Mackenzie's desk. "Courier will pick this up at nine-thirty." She's wearing big silver hoop earrings. "Lilian," she says. "How are *you*?"

The elevator bell rings and Arman steps into the Temple with a bucket of forsythia. It's so yellow it shakes the air.

"*Hola*, Arman!" I say loudly. "I'm fine," I say to Yolanda.

Arman says, "*Hola*, Lilian." Is he laughing at me?

"It was an intense weekend," Yolanda says. I try to read her expression.

"It was," I say. Does everyone here know?

"Even an hour time change can mess up your circadian rhythms for a few days," she says.

"Yeah, that must be it," I say. "So interesting to just notice how the time feels in your body." Why am I even talking? I sound like an idiot.

"I can lead us in a simple Rich Movement practice," says Monicke. "Let's do something in Inquiry. I'll set up the yoga mats."

Yolanda nods. "If there's time," she says. "Eleven wants us to talk about something first." She turns around and disappears into the meeting room.

Arman is at the base of the Buddha, arranging tall sticks of forsythia in the vase. The wilted pink roses and anemones from last week are slumped in his green bucket.

"*Gracias*, Arman," I say. "What's in the news?"

He laughs. The yellow flowers are the strongest light in the room. "They killed a mountain lion in Idaho," he says. "And found there were teeth growing in the back of its head!"

"Why do you speak to him in Spanish?" Monicke says quietly, after he leaves. "You know he's from Iran, right?"

I'm a hose of gushing failure and ineptitude! Must I get everything wrong?

I kick my boots off under my desk to give my feet a rest. I should never have bought these narrow, narrow boots. In my socks, I pad up to the mail wall and check my porcelain envelope. It's stuffed with notes.

On a white index card: *Inquiry at 10 a.m. today xo E*

On a piece of blank white paper torn from a notebook with a perforated edge: *LUNCH TODAY?* ♥ *Monicke*

On a lime-green Post-it note on the back of a purple Georgia O'Keefe: *I've been there. Talk to you more at Inquiry.* —*Y*

There's a second note from Eleven. This is on her personal stationery—a heavy cream notecard with *Eleven Novak* embossed in gold at the top: *I've got your back. See you at 10. xo E*

I use the thirty minutes before Inquiry to confirm the numbers in the hotel blocks for Ascendency Portland. I call each of the hotels we've booked for Ascendants—the luxe, mid-range, and budget options. It's amazing how efficient I can be when I don't want to think about my life. I still have fifteen minutes before Inquiry.

I open up tomorrow's Depth Charge: *Your life is your choice to make.* The words are layered over a portrait of Eleven dancing in a white shirt, her crystal mala around her neck, her face obscured by her blond hair because she's shaking her head. The photo is slightly out of focus, so the effect is dreamy. I should have chosen a different Depth Charge for this photo. I rushed all the Depth Charges last month. In this one, for example, the message has so much clarity, but the image is too diaphanous. I'm going to pick another photo.

Anna-Mackenzie rings her desk bell, and her heart-chakra F tone fills the Temple. I don't have time for this! But I stop what I'm doing and stand up with everyone else. I close my eyes and breathe in. I open my eyes and breathe out. Anna-Mackenzie thanks us, and we all sit down again.

I have time. Just two minutes and I can finish this Depth Charge and cross it off my list. I open my image file and locate one of Eleven's hand holding a red ranunculus. Red is too passionate. Can I make it white in Photoshop? Better idea—I turn the photo into black and white and dial up the contrast. It looks crisp and inspiring: the white of the background is now very white behind the deep dark flower. It's almost Mapplethorpey. I'm proud of it.

Another bell rings. It's time for Inquiry.

Monicke has set mugs on the table and pours tea. Yolanda sits with her iPad like a wise oracle at the foot of the table. Anna-Mackenzie looks down into her tea when I come in. I sit down and accept a mug from Monicke. The tea tastes different—too sweet.

Eleven sits at the head of the table in a white blouse and dark jeans. Her crystal mala peeks out from under her lifted shirt collar. Her eye shadow sparkles with subtle lustre, mint green and honeyed yellow. She sees me staring at her. I take a deep breath and try to smile. She holds my gaze. My chin wobbles. Oh Goddess, am I going to cry?

Yolanda leads us through the Inquiry ritual, and everyone checks in as usual. Yolanda is grateful for her position at the Temple, and wants to be easier on herself. Monicke is grateful for the flowers that Arman brought today, and wants to run five miles in her new barefoot shoes. Why are they all looking at me? Do they know about Jonathan? Did he tell Eleven? Does everyone know? My heart swims in pale water. I am here but not here.

Anna-Mackenzie goes next. "I am grateful to all of you for the light you bring to my life and work every day." She smiles at me. "This week, I want to feel more productive. My desire is to organize all the testimonials from Ascendency New York, upload them to the website, finish all the copy for the Ascendency graduation ceremony in Oahu and set up the sequences, including autoresponders for the reminders and debriefs, and all the follow-up emails." She puts her hands into namaste and bows her head.

Someone's phone vibrates. I feel it through the table. Is it mine? No, I left mine on my desk.

"I'll take it from here," Eleven says. Has she forgotten about me? Usually Eleven goes last.

"I'm grateful for all of you, my darlings. I'm grateful that out of all the places in this beautiful world, you chose to come here on this rainy Monday morning and do this work with me. I am so blessed to be at this table with you." She looks at me. Why, why, why is everyone looking at me? "This week, I desire courage," she says. She closes her eyes. Courage for what? Why must she always be so cryptic and mysterious?

"I guess I'll go next," I say.

Monicke looks at me with her dark eyes, which are lined with electric-purple eyeliner and tipped with purple mascara. Anna-Mackenzie's long fingers and graceful hands are wrapped around her mug of tea, and she stares into it. Yolanda is wiping her glasses with a cloth.

"I'm grateful to be here," I tell everyone. "I'm grateful for these new friendships I've made. I'm grateful to you, Eleven, for making this happen. My life has changed since I came here."

I remember Jonathan's lips on my neck, and his voice. *You're fascinating, Lilian Quick.* I remember the feeling of his thighs, and his strength, like he was levitating above me, and then pushing down, and the way my body made space for his. I remember thinking, *I can't believe I'm doing this!* And also thinking, *Is it okay that I'm doing this?* And the way I felt excited but kind of sick. He smelled like raw collard green tacos. I knew he didn't love me, he never said "love," that wasn't the thing that was happening. Should it have been?

I wanted something from him, too, and besides, I invited him to my apartment, there was an obviousness to that, and if I didn't want to have sex with him, why would I have done that? His eyes were closed, his whole body on me, his fringed eyelashes resting on his cheeks. The light in my apartment was clear and bright. I could feel the trees getting ready to blossom in Washington Square. We were in the park only thirty minutes before this, and now somehow his clothes are off and my clothes are off and his body looks like a *picture* of a man's body. Of course he's strong, he's a surfer! His arms feel like metal when I touch them. This is exactly what I wanted.

But he can't really want *me*. I know this isn't real. I'm curious though. Is that okay?

I pull the covers over us because I'm cold, and because I prefer that he feel my body, not see it. His beard is on my face. He kisses me slowly, moves very slowly down to my breasts, breathing heavily. He is breathing so heavily I think, *Asthma?* but then I remember, *Active Meditation*, and I try to match his breathing so I feel more present and awakened. Jonathan Rasmussen is in my bed! I am having sex! I make a gasping sound. "Are you all right?" Jonathan asks me. "Yes," I say.

"What else about Jonathan Rasmussen?" asks Eleven. Everyone is listening. I'm talking out loud.

"I read his email last night," I say, "the same time everyone else got it, and I felt stupid. I feel—ashamed."

"Good," says Eleven. "What else?"

"I didn't know they were together!" My words feel hot and viscous. "I didn't know he was going to have a baby." I start to cry. "I didn't know he was going to be seeing *her* out west. He invited me to go there with him!"

Eleven nods. She sees me, sees the real me, my true core that's at the centre of everything. She's known me longer than anyone. Oh, it is so good to be known by this one person who has always been there for me!

"Was he lying?" I cry. "I feel like he lied to me. I don't know what to think."

"Great," says Eleven. "More."

My regular Inquiry check-in turns into a Compost Heave. Everyone is listening, and even though I'm not really looking at anyone else—only Eleven—I can feel how they are supporting my Heaving.

"That was the first time I had sex," I say. Eleven raises her eyebrows, and I see Florence's surprised face surrounded by a halo of curls. It's only for a second, and then she's Eleven again. I feel a spark of pride, just for surprising her, and then another surge of shame, because why am I so abnormal?

"Okay," she says. "And what else about Jonathan Rasmussen?"

"I probably shouldn't say this. But it was incredible. It *was*." My tears subside as I remember putting my key in the door and walking into my apartment with him. I did that. "Even though I was embarrassed to come to work this morning in case any of you found out that I had sex with him—well, *I had sex*! I finally did it. I probably shouldn't feel this way, but I'm glad I did it. Ugh! Is that awful?"

Portia blinks at me from where she sits on Anna-Mackenzie's lap. Anna-Mackenzie's expression is unreadable. Yolanda and Monicke both look like they want to say something, but the rules of Compost Heaving are that the speaker gets the floor until everything is Heaved and turned over and she feels satisfied and heard.

"Thank you, darling," Eleven says. "Is there any more?"

"Yes!" I say. "I'm angry." Red-orange heat spreads up from my lower belly and erupts from my throat. "He used me. He lied to me!"

"Good," says Eleven. "You have one more Heave left. What else needs to be said about Jonathan Rasmussen?"

The rain spatters on the Temple windows. It sounds like someone is shaking out a plastic tarp. It's coming down hard and fast and, from the sound of it, sideways. My tea is lukewarm. Eleven's eyes are cut and polished. She's here with me. We are doing this together.

"I wish he picked *me*," I say. My shoulders drop. My chest unfastens. "I wish I was Fifi Torre."

I make a rough inhale. I start to cry again.

Eleven nods. "Thank you for Compost Heaving about Jonathan Rasmussen with us."

It's quiet in the room as everyone lets it sink in. My feet are cramped, and my calves are prickly and itchy. Anna-Mackenzie passes me the tissue box. The rain beats against the windows outside.

"We need Beyoncé for this," says Monicke. She taps her phone. The speakers pick up the signal and we all stand up. I take off my boots and my socks, feel my feet on the floor, close my eyes, and dance about it.

Dear Lilian,
This is what you've been waiting for, my plum blossom.

Introducing . . .

My Conscious Chocolate Truffle Collection.

Sacred. Present. Powerful. Delicious.

A collaboration with Winnie Prudhomme and the Conscious Cupcakery in Portland, Oregon.

Because your body is a temple.

From origin to your two hands, these chocolates are pure love and intention, infused with my teachings.

The cacao is sourced from a small farm in Madagascar, where the trees have been cared for by one family for generations. Winnie then winnows the beans and turns the cacao into chocolate in her sacred Kitchen Temple.

While the chocolates in my truffle collection are made, my **Sacred Ascendency Prayer** is played over them again and again.

These are meditations in your mouth.

You are a goddess, Lilian. Present yourself with a gift that nourishes your gorgeous body, mind, and spirit. Feed your highest self.

Available in milk chocolate and dark chocolate. **Shop the collection here.**

Love,
Eleven

I sit across from Eleven at her glossy white desk with the gold-and-crystal hardware. Her desk is gleaming, even on this dreary day. The window beside her desk is taller than she is, and rainwater is beading up and streaming down the glass peacefully.

So it turns out that Monicke slept with Jonathan Rasmussen two Ascendencies ago, and the same year that happened, he slept with an Ascendant named Wendy, who lived in Dublin and flew to the States for the events. The following year, he slept with another Ascendant after he asked her to be his Active Meditation assistant. And—get this—Anna-Mackenzie had a fling with him, too. She didn't have *sex* with him, of course, because of her faith, but who knows how many other women he's slept with? There could be hundreds!

"You have a strong voice," Eleven says to me. "You always have. You were always different from anyone else."

"When?" I say. "Why was I different?"

"I looked up to you," she said.

"No, I looked up to *you*," I say.

I stare at her. Her face has fine lines all around the forehead. She looks forty years old. Because we're both forty years old now.

"Remember when you taught me how to draw?" she says. "Remember when we made comic books together?"

"I didn't teach you how to draw," I say. Every seven years, the whole body's cell structure changes, replenishes itself, and makes itself new. We've both made that complete cycle of cellular change many times over, now. Is this still my cousin? What do our memories even mean?

I remember the comic strip. She told me what stories to draw, and I drew them. We had two characters: Dog, who wore a pink cape that said "Anything cats can do dogs can do better" and Cat, who wore a red bow tie and said "mrow" to almost everything the dog did. Eleven made me pick aura colours for Dog and Cat. I gave Dog a green crayon aura and Cat a red one. The strip I remember had Dog trying to ride a unicycle—meant to impress Cat—and he landed face down, stars circling his head. "Mrow," said Cat, surrounded by red crayon flames. The End.

"I didn't teach you, but you were the one who pushed me to do it," I say. "I probably wouldn't have started *drawing* if you didn't have the idea to make comics."

She pulls her hair back, and her gold bangles clink down along her forearms. She uses a rubber band to fix her fistful of curls into a messy bun. "You're an artist. You've always been the most magical one in our family. You're the independent one."

"You shouldn't use rubber bands," I say. "They break your hair. Can't you get real hair elastics?"

"I don't know where to get them."

"The drugstore?"

"I don't have the time," she says.

"Have someone get them for you. *You're* Eleven Novak. *You're* the brave one. Never mind in our family, the whole world knows it."

"And you're *still* Lilian Quick," she says. "You've always *been* Lilian Quick. Do you get it?"

I look at her. The scent of amber and roses rises from her body and fills the space between us.

"Do you remember when we snuck into that house?" I ask. My palms prickle with sweat when I say this.

"What house?"

"The weird house next door. Remember finding the jewellery?"

Eleven presses her hands together in namaste. "I'm telling you that I admired you when you were young," she says. "Why are you changing the subject? Why don't you pause, and let yourself take in my reflection?"

"Thank you for your reflection," I say. "I'm sorry."

"Don't apologize, sweetie. Just be your brilliant self. You're an Ascendant now. You can't play small anymore." Eleven smiles. "You're not really that upset about Jonathan, are you?" she asks. She says it so kindly, it sounds like praise.

"I'm not all that surprised by what happened," I admit. "It's not a new story."

"I had a thing with him too once," she says. "Way back."

"Seriously?" I say. "Before Bea?" A bead of rainwater quivers down the window. When he asked me about her childhood,

I shouldn't have told him anything. Her story is not mine to tell.

"You know, if I wasn't so charmed by his accent," I say, "he would sound . . ." I make a face. *You move like the spring equinox.* Ugh.

"Kind of douchey?" she offers.

I laugh. "Some of the things he said to me! I'm cringing just thinking about it!"

Eleven smacks her hand down on her desk. "Honey, I *know*!" She laughs. "I've known him for a long time. I love his work. He's brilliant at what he does, he really is. Which is what makes this so difficult . . ."

The rain picks up and spatters against the window. Eleven checks her phone, and then sets it down on the table again.

"Are you going to say something?" My toes throb in these tight boots, and I'm hungry. Monicke has probably gone to lunch without me.

"I think *you* should say something," Eleven says. "I think you should share your story."

I swallow. "Why?"

"Because that's how we connect to each other. It is only when we make ourselves vulnerable that we can truly empathize with one another. By going into the fire, straight into the hottest part of the flame, you will either find comfort and meaning, or you will burn up your old life and begin a new one, transformed." Her eyes are bright and magnetic. "By sharing your own experience in the burning, you will illuminate the experiences of so many other women. Women who are feeling silenced right now."

"You think I should tell people about this?"

Eleven touches my hand. "Sweetheart, I know so. You must."

"But—what should I say?"

"Just write it. Write exactly what happened. Just be honest."

"Okay," I say. My heart starts to beat harder. The nerves in my belly shoot electric shocks of nausea. "And post it on my new blog?" *Courage is action in the presence of fear.*

Eleven nods. "Let me think on that a minute," she says. She stares into the air just beside my head.

"You can leverage this," she says after a moment. "Here's what you do. First, let's revamp your website a little. Use your glam session portraits."

"Put them on my site?" On my About page, I have a shoegazing pic of my toes in the grass. That's the only picture I have of me on my site.

"You want presence, presence, presence," Eleven says. "You want your face all over your site. People need to trust you. They have to feel that they know you, that you're open to being seen. You have to let yourself be seen—that's how you'll connect."

"But in the glam session pictures, I have that eye makeup on."

"You look *gorgeous* in those shots, Lilian! Remember, don't play small. Be yourself. Be your glorious, magnificent self. You're more powerful than you believe. Let it in. Let your followers see you at your best."

"Okay," I say. I can swap the About page pic easily enough, and find a plug-in that will put a picture on every page.

"Put your face on the banner," Eleven says. "At the very least, put it above the fold."

"Okay," I say. I open TewDew and start a new list. *Add picture to website.*

"Put it in a pop-up. Your picture should be on the pop-up, too."

"I don't know about pop-ups," I say. "They feel pushy."

"People have twenty tabs open on their screen. A pop-up is a kind way to help them focus. They don't want to be so distracted. They *want* to remember you."

"It still feels annoying."

"You're so Canadian," Eleven says. "What about an exit pop-up? It only comes up if people scroll up to change the address."

"What's that?"

"It's a WordPress plug-in developed by an Ascendant. And you can set it so it comes back only occasionally for individual users. You can set it to come every three weeks or so. More subtle."

I add *Set up exit pop-up* to TewDew. "Should it be the same picture?"

She thinks. "How many do you have from the glam session?"

"I have five," I say. "But they're not all good."

"Different tops?" she asks.

"I have three different ones."

"Great," she says. "Use them all, then. Pick your favorite and use it for the banner and the pop-up, and sprinkle the rest of them in wherever you can. Presence, presence, presence."

"Should I credit the photographer?"

"No need," Eleven says. "We worked that into our contract with Ricki. She knows."

"And then write a blog post?"

Eleven looks out the window at the rain. The cold light is stronger than it seems. It illuminates her skin where she faces the window, and her Bertolucci nose casts a slight shadow over her cheek. "I want you to send your story to *WhaleMind*," she says. "The editor is MaryLou Greenberg. I'll connect you by email. She's brilliant—she's a psychotherapist in Boulder. She's actually Maria Shriver's psychotherapist. We've done some work together. I know she'll love you. And *WhaleMind* will love to have your piece. They have a big team of interns, so they have flexible editorial calendars. It will go up on their site right away. You won't have to wait the way you would elsewhere."

She turns back to me now and presses the surface of her desk with her palms like she's preparing for downward dog. She's excited by the plan. "*WhaleMind* has a fantastic readership, and they'll be very interested in this story. So then all *that* traffic will be directed to your site. You know you need to do some guest blogging anyway, to build the Lilian Quick brand and get more exposure. This is the perfect way to start."

I add *Send story to WhaleMind* to TewDew. "My story isn't really that interesting," I say. "It was consensual. Semi-consensual? He was just cheating on his girlfriend. Maybe. I don't even know if he was cheating! They could have an open relationship."

"Oh, darling," says Eleven. "That doesn't matter."

I try to get my head around what she's saying. If I could just understand the perspective shift she's inviting me to experience, I would see it all clearly.

"I'm just a baby Ascendant!" I say. "I'm still new at this work! Isn't there anything in the Ascendency Prayer to help me get this?"

"*Pay attention to the messages from your body,*" Eleven says. "Pay attention to the brain in your belly. How did it *feel* when you found out he left New York to be with Fifi?"

"It felt awful."

"In your body. How did it feel in your body?"

"I felt sick."

"And when you thought about the child they're having together?"

"I felt stupid," I say. "I felt ashamed."

Eleven reaches for my hand. "And in your body?" she asks gently. "Without having language to name the feeling, what does your body tell you?"

I close my eyes and remember lying in bed with him, his hand tucking my hair behind my ear. I picture Fifi Torre with a big pregnant belly. I picture him caressing that belly with both hands.

"I feel wobbly. Unclear. Confused," I say. My stomach is tight. "There's an orange hardness in my chest," I say, "and my skin feels heavy."

She holds my hand with both of hers. "There's your answer, sweetheart."

"But it's just a feeling," I say.

"There's no reason for you to feel ashamed. He was in a position of power. He was your teacher." Eleven's phone, face down, vibrates on her desk.

"Right, but—not really my teacher," I say. "I worked with him in Ascendency, that's all."

"You need to acknowledge the power of your own voice, Lilian. Own it. Be strong. And remember, people love it when you tell your personal story." Her phone vibrates again. "That's how they connect to you. Just tell the story as you know it happened. You don't have to spin anything. Think about it this way: you're starting a conversation."

When she puts it that way, it makes sense. "I think I can do that," I say.

"Your experience is not an isolated incident. The conversation needs to happen." Eleven squeezes my hand. "Just write, and be yourself."

◊ ◊ ◊

I do what she says. I don't even think—I just write. I let myself say the things I want to say. It doesn't feel like a blog post, it feels like something else. I'm starting a conversation. I listen to my body: It hums. It feels like green electricity. I feel the way I do when I'm painting, when I'm drawing a line that I know is true. I write down my story, I listen to my body, and everything feels honest.

Before I let myself reread it or think about it too much, I email it to MaryLou Greenberg. I can't trust myself to read it and start fixing it up for other people to see. I'll only try to hide myself again. I have to honour my own voice, like Eleven says. This is my chance to go into the heart of the fire, like I did in the Compost Heave, and access my core of peace. By burning through my fear and pain, I am connecting to all the other women who have also felt fear and pain. I feel as if I'm being completely honest for the first time in my life. The honesty feels white-hot. I feel like a warrior. My blood moves through my veins like molten lava.

This is my first test as an Ascendant. This is what our practice is for! The Universe gave me this opportunity, and I will not squander it.

I wish I could see Juliette tonight. I miss her. It would be so nice to sit in her clean white kitchen and have a cup of tea and tell her everything that's been happening. I've been so out of touch.

                                                            Me
                                        Hi! Thinking of you!

Juliette
Hi!

                                                            Me
                                            How are you?

Juliette
(...)

Me
I'm coming to Toronto next Friday.
Time for a visit?

Juliette
Just putting the girls to bed! Yes come see me!

I wish I could just call her. Before she had the girls, we used to call each other and talk all the time. Didn't we? Before there was texting?

I Lost My Virginity to My Meditation Instructor
By **Lilian Quick**

When I first told my story to my closest friends, I felt ashamed and I didn't know why. Even now, as I write about what happened, I feel compelled to protect the name of a certain well-respected meditation instructor. I wish I didn't. His behaviour wasn't right. And yet, I'm still afraid to be writing these words right now, afraid to tell the truth about what happened. He's supposed to be a teacher of integrity, guiding us to be honest with ourselves.

I feel stupid. I feel like a cliché. I feel as if the whole situation was my fault to begin with. I feel as if, in the greater scheme of things, what happened to me isn't really that bad. I feel afraid to say anything negative about a spiritual teacher whom everyone loves so much. And I feel embarrassed, obviously.

When he put his hands on my hips, I thought I was special. As it turns out, I wasn't.

My story is simple: a certain teacher made me feel that I was special to him. He's handsome and smart, and I appreciated his attention. He asked me to work more closely with him during his classes. I happily did so. He flirted with me, and I liked it. I'm forty years old, single, and I was a virgin (yes, it's true). I felt as if he'd chosen me for a reason, that I was spiritually significant.

It sounds ridiculous now. I believed him when he told me that I was fascinating. I didn't know about his life partner, and the child they were about to have together. He didn't tell me about the other female students who had also invited him into their beds. I was not the chosen one after all. I am one of many!

I thought I was expressing my sexual freedom. But now I see it wasn't actually mine. It was his all along.

I know this is not a new story. There are other men: men who are our teachers, our trainers, our mentors, our employers. Men who feel entitled to us, as though we're here for their pleasure and amusement. In one way or another, they use us, lie to us, manipulate us, violate our trust. And guess what? They're allowed. It's working for them. Those men are respected by their peers, publicly appreciated for their work.

We don't talk about what they're doing, because it doesn't feel like we're allowed to talk about it. What would we say? Society tells men that they're entitled to women and tells women that we should feel lucky when we are found desirable. Like that's the biggest prize we can win.

How do we speak out against the system, when the system can choose to disregard our voice without any consequence?

I want that to change. I want to dissolve my humiliation. I want us all to use our voices. To recognize that if our silence comes from shame, we must disown the shame that was never ours to begin with.

I want to be clear: I wasn't traumatized by this, like other women I know. I'm lucky to have an incredible group of women in my life, and they're helping me rise out of my shame. But even with all that support, I'm afraid, as I write this. I'm afraid his other students will hate me for telling this story. I'm afraid that his partner—a woman I admire, actually—will hate me. I'm afraid he'll read this article. I'm afraid of what will happen next.

My fear wants me to stop rocking the boat. But this is my one wild and precious life, as Mary Oliver says. I want to live it honestly. And besides, this boat needs sinking.

Lilian Quick is a writer and an artist from Toronto, Canada. You can read more of her writing at www.lilianquick.com.

MaryLou loved my article for *WhaleMind*, and the piece is going live this afternoon. They're in Colorado, so the time difference means I won't see it until around dinner. I put all my nerves into work. There are days at the Temple when I can barely focus on finishing three projects a day, max. But today was hyper-charged. Time is elastic! We literally make time what it is, through our *experience* of it.

Today I designed the Portland walking maps, showing our main hotels and Ascendency event locations all around the city. I researched all the vegan restaurants on both sides of the river so Anna-Mackenzie can write our restaurant guide. I designed the event schedule for print: we're doing a Forest Sanctuary ceremony on the Saturday, then having a Sound Bath with Marie and the Celestial Crystal bowls, and Sacred Eating with Winnie Prudhomme on the Sunday.

I created the Ascendency Portland Resources web page, and designed a new banner for Ascendency Oahu: a photo of Eleven in a white linen jumpsuit, her generous blond hair gathered in a loose side braid, balanced on a stand-up paddleboard in tree pose, against the backdrop of the Pacific Ocean. I also ordered the Live What You Love notebooks and tote bags, the Let Yourself Want What You Want Post-its, lime-green highlighters, and Dance About It tank tops for all the grads.

I should walk part of the way home. I could use the exercise—I missed SoulCore on Wednesday. I should never have missed SoulCore! I need it more than ever right now. My nerves make my body feel as if my skin is lined with kiwi fur. When I leave the Temple, it's cold and damp outside, but I walk fast and swing my arms to get the energy out. My phone vibrates in my pocket, and then again, but I resist checking it. I've been on the screen all day long. I need to look at something else, something that is real: a sign for hot donuts, the chipped grey cornerstone of the deli, the grey tabby sitting on the steps with a mint-green aura, the jagged edges that the buildings make against the grey sky.

I walk and walk, all the way down to Columbus Circle. There must be something wrong with my phone—it's vibrating way too much. I put my hand in my pocket, flick the silent switch up and down to reset it. I accidentally pushed it off my desk this afternoon when I was scooping up some papers. Would that make it go weird like this?

A girl in a white crocheted beret and matching fingerless gloves leans against the lamppost at the subway entrance. She looks up at me and taps her phone with her thumb. My phone immediately rings in A tone, as if she made it happen. I breathe in and reach for it at the same time. I know, I should stop and just breathe! I got out of that habit recently, and now I can't seem to wait for my out breath before answering anymore. I'll practise the next time it rings.

Jonathan Rasmussen's face fills the screen. This is a picture I took of him last week, right before we got lattes. He's smiling at me, and my stomach curdles. I didn't name him in the article, but what if people figure out that he's the teacher I wrote about? I tap the red Decline button and quickly push my phone back in my pocket, my heart beating fast.

The girl in the white beret angles her phone toward me. She could be taking a picture. I'm wearing my goldenrod cashmere poncho: maybe she has a blog, and is taking a street style shot? Still, she should ask my permission. I am pretty sure she's staring at me. Is she taking a video? I skip down the stairs to the subway platform. My phone vibrates all the way down. As I hit the last step, I pull out my phone to check it—what is wrong with my phone?

Yikes, I have notifications. I scroll:

@WhaleMind just mentioned you in a Tweet
@ElevenNovak just mentioned you in a Tweet
@YolandaClarke just mentioned you in a Tweet
@AnnaMackPeace just mentioned you in a Tweet
@MonickePacheco just mentioned you in a Tweet
@restorativeyogagirl just mentioned you in a Tweet
@Priyalive1001 just mentioned you in a Tweet
@deidrewicks just mentioned you in a Tweet
@_livegreen_ just mentioned you in a Tweet
@bookishowl just mentioned you in a Tweet

@RaviMenner just mentioned you in a Tweet

@MrsRabbity21 just mentioned you in a Tweet

@mamatojustin just mentioned you in a Tweet

@Feminista_Vida just mentioned you in a Tweet

@PureRawOpen just mentioned you in a Tweet

@freemarie_ just mentioned you in a Tweet

@WillaUnst just mentioned you in a Tweet

@Caramella322 just mentioned you in a Tweet

@luckymakeup just mentioned you in a Tweet

@AnneEightyFour just mentioned you in a Tweet

@Xaviera89 just mentioned you in a Tweet

@eyesontheskies just mentioned you in a Tweet

@KatyLove just mentioned you in a Tweet

@CrystalYam just mentioned you in a Tweet

@CarmenSpagnola just mentioned you in a Tweet

@swedensweden just mentioned you in a Tweet

@theshannonwinter just mentioned you in a Tweet

@RafaellaBernini just mentioned you in a Tweet

@DocByrne just mentioned you in a Tweet

@AnnaLovind just mentioned you in a Tweet

@_WendyJupe_ just mentioned you in a Tweet

@EnidBorski91 just mentioned you in a Tweet

@saveourturtles just mentioned you in a Tweet

@EnidGlick just mentioned you in a Tweet

@Hotrunnercafe just mentioned you in a Tweet

@movebreathesitbreathe just mentioned you in a Tweet

@JesseRochester just mentioned you in a Tweet

@LoveMagick just mentioned you in a Tweet

@MadridGirl84 just mentioned you in a Tweet

@Dandantheman just mentioned you in a Tweet

@Miss_Stacey333 just mentioned you in a Tweet

@StashLocal just mentioned you in a Tweet

@AnneKathleenWu just mentioned you in a Tweet

@woman_and_sun just mentioned you in a Tweet

@thebossofme just mentioned you in a Tweet

@goldenharpsichord just mentioned you in a Tweet
@RachelHaddock just mentioned you in a Tweet
@thetarotlady just mentioned you in a Tweet
@3catsandadog just mentioned you in a Tweet
@MandyMcnaughton just mentioned you in a Tweet
@Forest_and_Tea just mentioned you in a Tweet
@U_N_I_C_O_R_N just mentioned you in a Tweet
@BigSister234 just mentioned you in a Tweet
@OneMoreBreath just mentioned you in a Tweet
@funkandfaster just mentioned you in a Tweet

I turn my phone to silent. I try to breathe. I step on the train. The doors close and we start moving. The ghostly faces of commuters hover in the windows of the train that runs parallel to ours. For a time, we swim beside each other like fish in a fast stream. My train speeds up, but the other train has momentum and leaves mine behind.

◊ ◊ ◊

My phone can't handle all these notifications. I mean, my phone can handle it, but I can't handle it. I was held hostage by push notifications all weekend. It's Monday morning, and I now have 15K new followers on Twitter. In the Temple, Monicke takes my phone and scrolls back and back on my screen to find out what did this. "It's not just from *WhaleMind*," she says. "I have a feeling there's something big in here."

"Why are you still getting push notifications?" Yolanda asks.

"She shouldn't be getting notifications," says Eleven. "She won't be able to breathe. Anna-Mack, show Lilian how to turn off notifications on her phone, please."

"I like to know when people mention me," I say.

"Canada! You're so polite," says Monicke.

"You can't read all of them. Your story is too big now. That would eat all your time. You have more important things to do, and you can't afford the distraction," Eleven says.

"But they're asking me questions, some of them," I say. "Personal questions. I can't ignore them."

"Boom," says Monicke, and she hands me my phone. "Found it."

"Why don't you connect with your followers in another way?" Yolanda takes my phone from me. "Aha," she says when she sees it.

@BreneBrown just mentioned you in a Tweet

"Who was it?" says Anna-Mackenzie.

"Brené," Yolanda says.

"Also Liz Gilbert," Monicke says. "She's in there too."

"Keep the conversation going on your blog," says Yolanda. "Then they can hear from you and feel in touch, but you don't have to respond individually." She straightens her glasses and hands my phone to Anna-Mackenzie.

Anna-Mackenzie swipes the screen with her thumb, scrolls, and taps three or four times. Then she gives it back to me. "There," she says. "Notifications for Twitter, Facebook, Instagram, and email are off. Now you can check when you want to check."

My phone looks the same as it always has. I press the home button. Just my lock screen image—CREATE BEFORE YOU CONSUME, a reminder I thought would help me not check my phone before work—and the time and date. Nothing else is different.

"You've got real traffic now," says Eleven. "What's your conversion rate?"

"I haven't set anything up," I say.

"Lilian!" Eleven laughs. "Sweetie, what are you doing? You've got all the clicks, but how can you expect to convert them to sales without affiliate codes?"

It dawns on me that this was her plan all along.

I remember going to a summer social with Florence and Aunt Rosie. It was an event organized by their church. We were all supposed to go together, but my mom stayed home with Uncle Jimmy and my dad that morning. She said Aunt Rosie needed a little break. When we got to the church, Aunt Rosie gave us ten dollars and told us to have fun. Florence put the money in her pocket and taught me how to play invisible. She told me, "If you believe you're invisible, they don't see you." And they didn't. She took a stack of *Archie* comics from the book table, a jar of strawberry jam and a stack of biscuits wrapped in waxed paper, both from the baking table, and two bottles of lemonade from a blue cooler that was under the hot dog table. It didn't feel like stealing, because we weren't being sneaky. At each table Florence picked things up politely, and smiled. She took everything, and nobody bothered her. We ate and drank under a big tree in the yard behind the church and lay on our stomachs reading the comics until Aunt Rosie came to find us. She held an umbrella for the shade. "All ready?" she said, as if we'd done nothing wrong. With Florence, I always felt protected, like I could make no mistakes.

"Is it too late now?" I ask.

"Lilian Quick," says Eleven, "You have the magic mojo people *dream* about having. It comes naturally to you. There's a learning curve, is all."

Monicke massages my shoulders. "It's never too late, Canada!"

"Ascendency is a large purchase," Anna-Mackenzie adds. "Unless you're actively campaigning, it's not going to be a big money-maker for you. The boutique products are useful to have up in your shop. They have smaller price tags, so people can practice buying from you."

I have a peculiar sensation. A swarm of bees, buzzing and alive, just out of range of my peripheral vision. I feel the buzzing without hearing it. Is this relief or anxiety?

"You'll get used to it," says Yolanda.

◊ ◊ ◊

It's Wednesday and the rain won't stop pouring. When I get home after SoulCore, I try to find a new meditation app. How do I get Jonathan Rasmussen's Active Meditation app off my phone? I want it gone. I try BeCalm. I get the premium version so I can access the specialized meditations for courage, creativity, and sleep. A woman's voice tells me to imagine I am covered in a fuzzy orange blanket.

The way she says "orange" is off-putting—a soft *o*, like *ah-range*. It reminds me of Jonathan Rasmussen's accent.

I download one called Whitespace, which starts with an animated video. A man explains the benefits of meditation in a voiceover. He has a British accent. "Start with five minutes," he advises. "As you continue your practice, the app will count your accumulated minutes and send you encouraging messages. Make sure you allow push notifications on your phone."

FindInsight is basic, with ambient sounds guiding the meditations, no voices at all. I set up my profile. A screen shows a map of the world, with little dots all over it: 2,771 people meditating right now.

---

1 sec left in Barcelona
Sean Turnham is meditating to Be Calm a Little Longer

3 sec left in West Lebanon, NH
Raquel Olivier is meditating to
A Conversation with Tara Brach
Your confusion will give way to wonder.

6 sec left in Edmonton
Randi is meditating for 46 minutes
Transcending past. Living in present. Creating future.

10 sec left in Trinidad and Tobago
Mike is meditating to Life is Kind

I can download different bells for $3.99 each. The standard bell that comes with the free version is okay, but I love the sound of Satya and Shenzhen. The Shenzhen one goes on and on—it's full and lingers in my ears in a beautiful way. I feel calmer just listening to the bell.

I check my website analytics. Most of my clicks are from California and New York, but I also have a solid clutch of Australians and New Zealanders. Canada is well represented—mostly Ontario and British Columbia. There are 373 people reading my website right this very second.

I check out www.anooshakhtar.com to see how my Potency Circle friend invites her followers to click on Eleven's affiliate links. Anoosh's home page shows her at a small wooden writing desk, sitting outside at the end of a dock, on a lake. A Mason jar full of white daisies is set on the corner of the desktop, next to a white mug, a black Moleskine, a fountain pen, and a jar of ink. At the top of the page, it reads: *Anoosh Akhtar, Memoir, Story & Archetype Coach.*

"Learn about your archetype, and the strengths and pitfalls that will affect you as you navigate the mythic journey that is your life. Learn why you surround yourself with the people you do, what you can learn from other archetypes, and how you can write your own epic story."

I click on a bright-yellow button: Shop.

"These are some of my favorite things. They are not my own creations, but I have experienced every one of them, and I recommend them highly. These are potent tools that can help you connect to your true self. Note: I may receive a small percentage for any orders you place through me. These modest affiliate payments, as well as my coaching income, are the way I make my living and put food on the table for my small family. My daughter and I are grateful for the conscious shopping that you choose to do here."

All of Eleven's products are listed here, including the crystal malas, her signature rose-amber face cream and body oil, a formaldehyde-free nail polish from Finch UK (in Eleven's sheer ivory shade), notecards and posters printed with the Sacred Ascendency Prayer, and an exclusive line of Manifested Denim in pure white.

It doesn't take me long to build a shopping page on my site. I install the basic template for e-commerce and link my affiliate codes into each product. I've forgotten my password to the Ascendency Affiliate Center, so I reset it to FridaY!123. All my passwords are still Friday-related.

Once I'm in there tweaking things, I take time to look over all the copy on www.lilianquick.com.

By the time I finish, it's late and I haven't eaten dinner. The sake bar is still open downstairs. I throw on a hoodie, dig my feet into my running shoes, and grab my key, phone, and wallet. I am so lucky to live in a place where there is late-night sushi!

"We only have noodles," the bartender tells me. His eyes are dark and cave-like. "Chef had to leave early, but there's still noodles if you want."

The walls of the bar are painted tomato red, and there are strings of white Christmas lights draped around and above the tables. Two men sit in the back corner, sipping tiny cups of sake and talking quietly over the tiny flame of a tea light on their table.

My noodles arrive, thick udon in steaming broth, and I struggle to eat them with the supplied pair of red plastic chopsticks. I'm going to feel bloated tomorrow. The restaurant is lit up and gleaming with red and orange, and the windows sparkle with rain. I should write a newsletter to my list, let them know how my life has changed. Eleven says to write your newsletters as though they are to one specific person—the more specific you are in your intention, the more you will connect to your whole audience. Think about who you most want to connect to, she says. Call them to you with the specificity of your language.

The soup is salty and delicious. I bring the bowl up to my mouth to slurp it, abandoning the chopsticks entirely. Yumi would love this place, and the East Village in general. I take a picture of my table, with the lights glowing in front of me, and send them a text.

Me
My downstairs sake bar! Thinking of you.

Yumi
💥 Love it! XO

They responded so quickly, it was like they were expecting my text! I love technology, and the way it connects us to each other.

The "XO" lingers in my mind even after I set my phone down. XO? In capital letters? I typed "xo" to Jonathan Rasmussen without meaning to, but it wasn't in *capital letters*. Doesn't capitalization require more forethought? It depends on what your phone remembers about your previous texts. It could be an autofill. Does Yumi type "XO" to people often? It's out of character for them. Or at least, they've never XOed me before. Did they read my *WhaleMind* piece? Am I overthinking this? I wonder if I'll see them in Toronto this weekend.

Dear FIRST NAME,

Expansion is the law of the Universe, right?

I've learned so much from <u>Ascendency</u>—self-care, how to be honest with myself, and that I have to make time and space in my life, so I can hear my essential voice. There's a lot of noise blocking that subtle sound, and that noise comes from both the inside and the outside. I'm also learning how to be vulnerable. Recently, I've learned that I have to be careful about who I trust with my vulnerability.

My work as an Ascendant has taught me to be more courageous and open, and to speak with integrity, even when it's unpopular. Sharing my story recently on <u>*WhaleMind*</u> took a lot of courage. It has changed my life in ways I didn't expect—even just a few weeks ago, making this website and being this transparent wouldn't have seemed possible for me. But I'm starting to understand that I have to grow when I'm called to grow—and this community, and the tools I'm learning in Ascendency, help me feel strong enough to do just that!

I hope my website will inspire you to do the same, however that looks for you—to answer the call of personal growth, to find your courage and your power, and to live in integrity.

Announcing my brand-new <u>Heart Shop</u>—this is my new online store, stocked with things I love, like <u>amethyst and amazonite malas from Lunar Devotions</u> and <u>Love Is a Verb, Not a Noun T-shirts</u>. These special products are hand-picked by me, and I promise they will make you feel connected and happy. You radiate when you feel good about yourself.

If you're interested in becoming an Ascendant next year, <u>let me know</u>. I'd love to tell you more about Eleven Novak's amazing program.

Warmly,
Lilian

TORONTO IN MARCH is cold, slick, and grey. the snow has turned into icy rain, and puddles of slush hunker down along the edges of the sidewalk. Cars splash along. Those of us who are walking outside lift our collars up and shield our faces from the sleet.

I've decided to do a social media mini-detox to clear my mind for the first Ascendency Teleritual tonight. I won't check Instagram/ Twitter, or Facebook all day. I can still check my email, just not social.

I'm staying in Fleurje's spare room this weekend, way out in the east end of the city. She is so nice to let me stay at her place, even when she's so busy. Everyone in the city puts their house on the market in the spring, so she's out working. She'd already left to meet a client before I woke up, so I went to Lady Marmalade on my own this morning, for chia pudding and a turmeric latte. I broke my mini-detox briefly, just to take a pic of my latte. Thirty-five people liked it right away. I'm getting thirty-five likes per second now! I kept refreshing the screen to see who else would comment. The likes kept on coming. It's pretty thrilling. But they weren't from anybody I knew, and nobody famous.

The mini-detox is an experiment. I'm not *quitting* social media, I'm just taking a break for one day. I want to save my attention for the live call with Eleven tonight.

When I arrive at my old apartment, it smells familiar: the air is sweet and cardboardy. I'm here to make sure it's clean and ready for the tenant when he comes back from Thailand. I already sold my furniture on Kijiji, thanks to Yumi, who made all the arrangements for me while I was away. The only things left in the apartment are the things that were there when I moved in. The table, the grey love seat with the nail polish stain, the bookshelf. The brown, tattered rug. Everything looks grubby to me now. I lived here?

The pocked floors have been mopped and the stained counters have been wiped. The bathroom faucet is shiny. The whole apartment has been cleaned already. Did Yumi do this for me, too? I close the door behind me, feeling sheepish. Why does Yumi always do so much for me? Am I a bad friend? Friendships aren't transactional. And yet. Something doesn't feel equal.

My old neighbourhood feels the same, but different. I've only been gone for a couple of months, but there's a new bar on the south side of Queen West where my coffee shop used to be. I didn't know it had closed. The old diner is gone, too, and now it's a dress shop. I walk east, heading to Yumi's studio. The slush licks my boots and seeps through the seams in my heels. The road salt will eat through this vegan leather if I don't thoroughly wipe it off later.

I let myself into the studio and stomp off the wet. It hasn't changed much since I left. Yumi has neatly arranged my things, and draped a thick sheet of plastic over my stack of canvases to keep them protected from dust and lint. That was nice of them.

The plastic covering Yumi left for me is useful. I use packing tape to seal the canvases inside the plastic, and make handles with two big long pieces of tape saddled around the whole bundle. I can use the large black portfolio to bring my drawings back to New York. The works on paper fit inside it easily. But my sketches—all those charcoal and Conté-crayoned paws, snouts, and tails—should I keep them? Store them somewhere? Or put them in the recycling bin? It's not as if I have a studio space anymore. One day I might, but keeping all this paper for "one day" is basically hoarding.

I can always make more sketches. I roll them all together in a scraggly tube and stick it in the blue bin.

I absolutely must make time in New York to finish the long-overdue Sophia portrait for Nana Boondahl. It's not about the money anymore—I don't need money like I used to. But it's unprofessional to leave the commission for so long. If I ground myself with a good meditation before trying to paint next time, I should be able to connect to the piece. I zip up my portfolio on all three sides and check the time. It's already three o'clock. I leave a gift for Yumi on their desk, with a note on one of my lime-green Temple Post-its:

Thank you! ♥ *Lilian*

I look at the heart. Maybe too much? I crumple that note and stick it in my pocket.

Thanks Yumi! Have a great season. —Lilian

My phone vibrates.

Yumi
You at the studio now? Meet me for 🍶 ?

Do I have time? I was planning to meet Juliette, but she hasn't answered any of my texts. And Fleurje is out with clients until way after dinner—I might not even see her while I'm here. Besides, I missed lunch. I crumple up my note. I'll give the mala to them in person.

◊ ◊ ◊

The sake bar is decorated like the inside of a wooden barrel or packing crate. Tin wall sconces cast dramatic and flickering lights on the walls. Our tabletop is black lacquer, set with a small oil flame in a glass votive and a white ceramic bud vase shaped like a fish. A single blooming branch sticks out of the mouth—a peachy-pink ruffled flower and three small buds that haven't opened yet. The warm light from the flame makes the flower look like it's glowing. It would make a beautiful Instagram, but it's my social media mini-detox day. Too bad!

Yumi's given me another woolly gift. "They cover your legs from the bottom of your parka to your knees," they say. These are repurposed cashmere and merino sweater arms, in royal blue and turquoise colour blocks.

"You've given me so many beautiful things!" I hold one up: it's a wide tube. "Wear them how?"

"On your thighs. Above your tall boots. They'll keep you warm."

"Amazing!" I say. "Thank you!" I roll the thigh warmers up together and stuff them in my tote. "I have a gift for you, too!"

I bought special malas from Lunar Devotional to give to everyone: Yumi's is made with hematite and quartz, for grounding and protection from negative energy. Fleurje's is malachite for prosperity and carnelian for strength. And for Juliette, I chose rose quartz and snowy howlite, because I know how much she loves pink and white.

I set the grey box on the table and slide it across to Yumi. It's so pretty! I mean, for a cardboard box. The swirly LD logo on the top is subtle, and the box is lined with grey velveteen. The beads are curled in a circle inside. When they open the box, the silver hematite glints in the candle flame.

Yumi picks it up. "Very cool," they say. They put it on over their fleece-lined plaid jacket. A burgundy silk tassel hangs from the centre. "I love hematite."

"It even matches your jacket," I say, pointing to the burgundy.

"I love it," Yumi says.

"I have one too," I say, and I pull the amazonite out of my shirt. The stone is warm from where it was tucked against my body. "But I thought hematite for you. It's a protection stone."

The waiter brings a small pitcher of sake for Yumi and a pot of green tea for me. I lift the lid of the teapot and poke the tea bag with my finger. It floats back up to the top.

"Hey," I say. "Did you clean my apartment for me?"

"Of course," they say.

"You didn't have to do that."

"I was there anyway," Yumi says. "Waiting for the guy to pick up your bed."

"Thank you again for everything," I say. I reach over the table and pick up their sake. "Aren't you supposed to let someone else pour this? Isn't that the rule of sake, to have someone else do it for you?"

Yumi shrugs. "It's not my rule," they say, "but do it anyway."

I pour a stream of hot clear liquid into the tiny cup.

"I love my apartment in New York," I say. "There's a sake bar downstairs. The one I texted you about! You'd like it."

Yumi picks up the cup. "How is your painting?"

"I haven't even had time to draw," I say. "The Temple has taken over my life! I'm so busy with the new website, and what's happening now with *WhaleMind* and everything." I pour my tea. It's pale yellow and smells like cut grass.

"The studio is not the same without you." Yumi looks at me intently.

"Thank you for saving my stuff for me. I was in a bad place this winter."

"I can keep the space for you. You don't have to leave it." They down the cup of sake quickly, in one swallow.

"I'm moving to New York, though."

Yumi pours the rest of the sake into the cup. "Not forever," they say. "Why don't you just keep the key."

The key is in a small zippered pocket in my tote bag. I reach around the back of my chair to get it. My hand brushes the thigh warmers as I feel around for the zipper pull.

"I'm in too deep at the Temple now," I say, and give Yumi the key. "I don't know when I'll be coming back. But thank you—again."

Yumi doesn't touch the key. "In too deep how?" they ask. "Did you meet someone?"

"No," I say. They obviously haven't read the *WhaleMind* piece. "I just mean that I moved to New York. I live there now."

Yumi drinks the last of the sake. The tin lanterns make long triangular lines of light on the wall behind their face. The sake cup is small in their hands.

"Cool," Yumi says, slides the key off the table, and pockets it. "Yeah, New York suits you." Yumi looks at my cheek, but not into my eyes.

I wipe my cheek with my hand in case something is on it. It feels strange not to tell them about Jonathan Rasmussen now. But where would I even start? "It's just that I had to leave Toronto, Yumi. To be myself. To be fully myself."

"Great."

"You know what I mean, right? I feel like I'm growing there. I can breathe."

"I know exactly what you mean."

"Tell me about you, though. How are you doing? How is *your* business?"

"I've scheduled my surgery," Yumi says. "It's happening May sixth."

I turn my head. "What surgery?"

"Double mastectomy."

"Oh, Yumi!" I put my teacup down. "You're really going to do it?"

"I am," Yumi says. "My GP sent in my assessment. The province pays for the surgery."

"May sixth," I say, thinking out loud. "That's Ascendency graduation."

"I had hoped that we . . . that you might . . . well. I can't believe you're not coming back." Yumi stands up. "Excuse me for a minute." They walk to the back of the bar, where the restrooms are.

My stomach flutters and warps. What just happened? What did they mean? I try to breathe, but my throat feels constricted. There isn't enough light in this place. The only window is the glass door, way up at the front of the restaurant. It's streaked with wet sleet. These wooden walls and floors make me claustrophobic, like I'm going to roll off the top of Niagara Falls. *Listen to the messages from your body.* A steel cage clamps shut around my chest. I have to get out of here. The energy in this place is all wrong. I feel around in my tote bag and dig under the bundle of wool for my wallet. Yumi will understand that I have to leave. This place is energetically taxing for me. Yumi would want me to take care of myself. I'm glad I thought to pick up Canadian cash at the airport ATM! I'll pay for both of us. I take out a shiny green twenty-dollar bill, leave it under my teacup, and shove my coat on. I leave before Yumi returns.

Me

I'm so sorry I had to leave! I started to feel very strange in the restaurant

Me

claustrophobia maybe, or toxic energy at a table nearby?

Me

I'm so proud of you for taking this big step with surgery

Me

This is HUGE!!!

Me

May 6 is so soon!
I'll be thinking of you

Me

ps thank you so much for
my new leg warmers!

That was a sincere apology. I feel terrible leaving them like that, but I just couldn't be in that space anymore. I wait, but they don't text me back.

Me

Juliette, where are you?

Me

I know you're busy just
type K if you're ok

Me

can I come over?

Me

I'm leaving on Sunday and
I'm afraid I won't see you

Juliette
(...)

Me

I won't stay long just a hug and hello

Juliette
K

When Juliette greets me at the door her face is smiling but her energy is heavy. She's wearing an olive-green sweater dress that I haven't seen on her before, and a thin yellow belt that brings attention to her waist. When I hug her, I feel as though I'm hugging her through a blanket.

"Welcome!" she says as I embrace her. "I'm so glad you could come over!" That Juliette gloss. She's been like this since she's had the girls. Even before that, really. I'm used to trying to cut through the layers of polish to find her, but tonight there are some thick layers. Maybe she's pregnant again. That would explain why she's been hard to reach lately.

"How have you been?" I ask. "You're renovating your coach house? The Sacred Solitude project? What else am I missing?"

She looks pained. "There's a lot going on right now," she says. "Come in, I'll show you."

Her house smells sweet and mossy, like strawberries gone bad. The girls' toy baskets are in the middle of the living room, overturned, and a glittering pile of Lego pieces spills out of a plastic cube. Picture books are spread out on the floor. Beside the couch, a collection of multicoloured, fist-sized stuffed toys are lined up in two rows. Every toy is facing the same way, and the large plastic sewn-on eyes stare in the direction of the fireplace. Siebel likes to put her toys in rows; she's done that since she was a baby.

"Where are the girls?"

"Out back," Juliette says.

We walk through her narrow townhouse kitchen, and she opens the back door to show me a small construction site at the foot of the yard against the fence, where the bike shed used to be. The new building looks like a miniature house, with two windows on either side of a red door. The exterior is covered in white plastic sheeting. A blue light flickers from inside—a movie is projected on the wall.

"They're playing video games," she says. "The girls are testing a new game for Knigel."

"You're building a games room?" I ask.

"We're getting a divorce," she says. "That will be Knigel's apartment. He'll be separate from the house."

She closes the door and we sit in the kitchen. A triangle of parsley is stuck to the side of the sink. Juliette prepares us two cups of peppermint-fennel tea and sets out a dish of chocolate-covered almonds. The Teleritual is starting soon, but I can't leave Juliette now. She takes a handful of almonds from the dish and eats them.

"He's had mistresses for years. Girlfriends? Women. It's terrible to say this, I know, but for a long time I just accepted it, because when he stayed out at night, and the girls were asleep, it meant I could be alone. I'm never alone. I never get to be alone." She puts another almond in her mouth and chews.

"How long have you known?" The tea is too hot to drink.

"I finally just told him that I want a monogamous marriage," she says.

I nod. "Let yourself want what you want," I say. I blow on my tea.

"Our marriage is over now. But with the coach house, we can still co-parent without disrupting the girls. They can still live with their father, and our family is kept together."

"Does Knigel bring his girlfriend here?"

She shrugs. "I don't pay attention," she says. "Honestly, I just love having the house to myself. I feel more like myself than I have in years. I can listen to whatever music I want. My whole bed is *covered* with design books. I *sleep* with them!" She smiles.

There's a sore-looking crack in the centre of her bottom lip. "You're bleeding," I say. I get up and tear a piece of paper towel off the roll.

"Ugh, sorry," she says. She presses the paper to her lip and disappears from the kitchen. Outside in the backyard, lit-up shapes move across the inside wall of the coach house.

"Are you okay?" I ask Juliette when she gets back. She has a layer of cream on her lips that is not quite worked in. "Sort of," she says. "Getting there. I'll be happy when the coach house is finished and I don't have to look at that Tyvek anymore! And when Knigel sells this video game. I hope that will pay off the line of credit I opened to build that place."

"I wish you'd told me this was going on."

Juliette picks up her mug, takes a sip, and puts it down again. "You've been in New York," she says.

"Which reminds me, I have a gift for you," I say. I pull another grey Lunar Devotional box out of my bag. "You know I'm always here for you, Juliette. You're my best friend. You can always call me. You can call me at three o'clock in the morning."

"I know," she says. "Okay, I'll call you next time something happens."

There are two almonds left in the dish, like two tiny eggs in a nest. What time is it? I have to go soon.

"Open it," I say. "I have a Teleritual tonight, so I have to go, unfortunately."

"It's not like my life is breaking apart!" she says, suddenly. "That's the weird thing about the divorce—I feel my life is coming *together* now."

She didn't even hear me say anything about the Teleritual. She's barely noticed the box in front of her. Poor Juliette is so disconnected, and not at all present! She could really benefit from Ascendency. I can see her struggling. I can feel her denial coming off her, in waves. I am grateful that I took the day off social media, so I could restore my attention and be here for her now, undistracted.

"One of the things Eleven teaches us is that love is a verb, not a noun," I say. "Love is *active*. So it makes sense that you're feeling things coming together now—you're actively giving yourself what you need, you're doing what you love, you're setting boundaries, you're giving yourself a lot of self-care."

Rose quartz, come to think of it, is *perfect* for her. It's all about self-care and self-love. It's like my subconscious knew the right beads to pick for her, and I just went on instinct! I wish she'd open the box. Juliette just looks out the kitchen window. Shadowy shapes crouch here and there in the backyard. They look like German shepherds, or wolves. I'm startled at first, but they have no auras, and they don't move. Ah! They're shrubs! Juliette has covered her shrubs in burlap and tied them with jute, to protect them over the winter. They're lit by the light from the video game. I hadn't noticed them before.

"For a minute I thought there were wolves in your backyard!" I say. "Isn't that hilarious?"

"What's a Teleritual?" Juliette asks. "Is this something for your Eleven cult?"

"It's not a cult," I say. "It's a program. I'm taking a course."

"Isn't Eleven a trained actor? She could be manipulating you. She has that charisma."

"She's not *acting*," I say. "She's sincere. She's amazing onstage, and she's a good leader."

"Don't get drawn into a game, Lily. Don't start selling any-thing," she says. She's still worried about me selling things? Like she doesn't sell things on her blog *all the time*. Like she doesn't have a whole line of products for sale at the Bay.

"Ascendency has been pretty profound, actually," I say. "I don't have time to go into it tonight, but I've been experiencing some pretty big life changes."

Her phone tings from the living room. She doesn't move to check it. "So what's happening in your life?" she asks. She drinks her tea, staring out the kitchen window.

Where do I start? She doesn't even know about Jonathan Rasmussen! "I wrote an article for an online magazine called *WhaleMind*," I say. "Maybe you saw it?"

Juliette shakes her head. "What's *WhaleMind*?"

"I'll send you the link," I say. "The thing is, I met someone. I—"

At that moment, the back door pops open and Siebel bursts in.

"Mabel's dog lost all the candy!" she screams. "Mabel lost all her candy and when there was a fish she couldn't stop dancing!"

"Take your boots off, honey," says Juliette. "Stop! Stay there. Boots off, please."

Siebel digs at one heel with the toe of a boot and stumbles. Then she pulls it off with her hands and kicks the other one off after multi-ple tries. One foot is bare—the sock stayed in the boot—and the other foot has a sock half-attached, hanging on by her toes. She laughs and screeches, "Mabel's dog was jumping all over the grass where the fish was. Mabel—" she sees me. Siebel stops talking and stares.

"Hi, Siebel!" I say. Her cheeks are rosy and her nose is crusty with dried snot. She looks at me and says nothing. "Was it a fun game?" I try again. Her eyes are wide, taking me in. No response.

"Say hi to Auntie Lily," says Juliette. Siebel does not smile or blink or give me any other sign that she understands me, or that I am a person she can communicate with. She barely breathes. Is she afraid of me? I'm not going to take this personally.

"It's okay," I say to Juliette. "She doesn't have to say anything! Anyway, the Teleritual is a live call, a ceremony that Ascendants do together on the phone." I stand up and put my coat on. "Are you really okay? I can do the Teleritual here, if you need me to stay."

"No, you should go," she says. "Thank you for coming to see me."

"The other thing in the Ascendency Prayer I wanted to tell you is do no more than three things a day," I say gently to Juliette, before I leave.

"What three things?" she asks.

"No, just three things. Only three things. So you don't over-load yourself." I hug her goodbye and open the front door. "Maybe you're trying to do too much in a day."

She exhales and her breath plumes. "That's completely unrealis-tic for my life right now," she says.

I wish I had more time to talk to her, to explain! "That's just it," I say. "Maybe you're doing an unrealistic amount of things."

"I have two little girls," she says. "You don't understand."

Outside, the temperature has dropped. The slush is turning to ice.

"I know I don't," I say. "One thing I've always had is a lot of time alone." My feet slide when I step out onto the porch.

"You're more lucky than you know," Juliette says.

"Remember to call me, okay? I always have time for you." I hold the banister to keep my balance as I walk down to the sidewalk.

ELEVEN: Welcome, everyone, to our first Teleritual. I am honored to share this special time and space with you. Some of us are in North America, some of us in Europe, some as far away as Korea and Australia. Whatever time zone you are in, thank you for being here. Please remain present with us now, and turn off all your devices. If you are calling from your computer, as I know many of you are, I ask you now to close all the background windows or programs that are running. Dim your screen using the brightness buttons on your keyboard. Close the door if you are in a room with a door. Do whatever you need to so you can focus and be here, and only here.

I am lighting four candles, one for each of the elemental forces that shape our life. Everyone on this call has been assigned an element. Element Leaders, when I light the candle that corresponds to you, please unmute yourself by pressing star two.

There is one Element Leader for each of the elements, and she will start each incantation for the group. Follow her, and recite the incantations you received by email last week. Even though you'll be on mute while you're repeating the incantations, we are all going to speak together, which will form our morphogenetic field.

Anna-Mackenzie, can you see that everyone is on the call with us? Do we have a full circle?

A-M: Yes, it looks like we're all here.

ELEVEN: Wonderful. Okay, my darlings, let us begin. Water. I light a candle for water. Please unmute yourself if you are the Water Element Leader.

A-M: Remember to press star two to unmute yourself.

GLORIA: Hello. Water is here.

ELEVEN: Welcome, Water. Please go ahead.

GLORIA: We are connected to water, the element of
    refreshment and renewal. It moves and flows
    around us, showing us our depths and our foun-
    tains, and it holds the truth of our emotions.

ELEVEN: Lovely. The candle is lit. Now, Fire.
    I light a candle for Fire.

A-M: Please unmute yourself, if you are the Fire Element
    Leader. Press star two to unmute yourself.

HALEY: Fire is here.

ELEVEN: Welcome, Fire. Please go ahead.

HALEY: We are connected to fire, the element of creativ-
    ity and enterprise. It burns with intensity within us,
    providing energy and heat, and shows us our courage
    and imagination. It holds the truth of our passion.
ELEVEN: Thank you. The candle is lit. Now, Air.
    I light a candle for Air.

ZOE: Air!

ELEVEN: Welcome, Air. Please go ahead.

ZOE: We are connected to air! The element of thought and
    consequence. Oops! I mean, consciousness. Thought
    and consciousness. It moves like the wild. Sorry. It

moves like the wind. And birds of flight. Ah! Sorry!
I'm so nervous, speaking in front of everyone!

ELEVEN: That's okay, sweetie. Take a breath and continue.

ZOE: (*Deep breath*) Okay. It moves like the wind and
birds of flight! Providing constant movement and
new perspectives. It shows us the power of our
mind! And holds the truth of constant change!

ELEVEN: Wonderful. Thank you. The candle is lit.
Now, Earth. I light a candle for Earth.

A-M: Press star two.

(*Pause*)

ELEVEN: Earth, are you here?

A-M: We might be having technical difficulties. One moment
please. I can see her here. It looks like she's here.

(*Pause*)

ELEVEN: Please unmute yourself, Earth.

A-M: There. Can you hear us? Say something.

(*Pause*)

A-M: Have you pressed star two? Press star two.

LILIAN: I'm here! I'm here! Can you hear me? Hello?

ELEVEN: Yes, we can hear you.

LILIAN: Oh my Goddess! I could hear you perfectly
the whole time, but you couldn't hear me!

ELEVEN: This is electromagnetic energy we're using.
Sometimes it can be frustrating, I know.

LILIAN: Okay, do you want me to—should I start?

ELEVEN: Please start. I light a candle for Earth.

LILIAN: We are connected to earth. The element of stability and
growth. It roots us, and reminds us to stay grounded. It
shows us how to be present in our five senses, the power
of stillness, and the truth of our physical body. That's it.

ELEVEN: Beautiful. The candle is lit. Now that we have set the
elements in motion to support our work here together,
I'd like to start. You've been designing your online presence beautifully. Remember that your website is a system,
a reflection of you. It can be organic. You don't need to
make it perfect and then leave it that way forever. Expect it
to grow with you.

When you're designing your brand with intention and love,
you want to pay attention to how you feel. Grinding begets
grinding—creative joy begets creative joy. So watch your
mind as you are working. You should never feel a sense of
dread or heaviness around your brand. If you do, you'll be
building your brand with heaviness and dread. And you
don't want to attract those feelings.

Find your design elements this way: Ask yourself, if you
were a color, what color would you be? Do you feel like
deep navy blue, or warm, rich brick red? Are you fresh yellow? Every color has an energy, and that energy will vibrate

differently for every one of you, because you have your own energy vibration, too. Know yourself inside and out, and know yourself using metaphor. Metaphors are not just ways to play with language. Metaphors can express the true nature of reality, by connecting and collapsing boundaries.

If you were a hot beverage, what hot beverage would you be? Warm and natural green tea? Clarifying hot water and lemon? Or rich, indulgent cocoa? Let yourself blur the distinctions between your inner truth and the concreteness of the outer world.

Share your story with your followers. Write to them as though you are writing to a dear friend. Let them in; let them trust you. Your stories of personal struggle will inspire them. And when you are writing about my products, have fun! Don't be an affiliate for anything that you don't believe in. So if you don't have one of the Lunar Devotional malas yet, don't advocate for them on your site. Start with something simple, like the body oil or the nail polish.

This is not about the money. This is about the power of connection and positive change.

Let your followers know that intention is everything. Their intention fills these beautiful objects with divine energy. The products are pretty, and they're made with the finest ingredients that I could possibly source. Your clients can be assured that these purchases are not harming the earth. But beyond that, their power is all in the intention with which they are used.

Benevolent marketing is not the same as advertising. Advertising is tricking someone into buying something you want them to buy. Ethical marketing is telling stories and connecting to each other through storytelling. Know who you are, and then share who you are. You aren't trying to trick anyone—you want them to be their best. The whole world is a better place when people are at their best. So show them what you have and teach them how to live fully. Give them permission. When someone learns from your experience, they're empowered to change their own life.

The Lunar Devotional malas go for three hundred and seventy-five dollars. For every one you sell, you'll get seventy-five dollars. You can find beautiful badges for all the Ascendency products in your affiliate account: the exclusive Manifested Denim line, the amber and rose face and body oil from Plant & Kin, the sheer ivory nail polish from Finch UK. I add new products to my Soul Boutique all year long—stay tuned for that. And for every new student you bring to Ascendency, you'll receive three thousand dollars.

Let's breathe together. That was a lot to take in.

(*Pause*)

Thank you, my divine darlings. Are there any questions? Anna-Mackenzie, could you open the lines for questions?

A-M: The line is open! If you have a question for Eleven, press star six to raise your hand.

FLEURJE'S SELLING A house tonight. She's at the real estate office now, negotiating the deal. We have plans to meet for a drink afterward. It will be good to see her. I'm glad that she can make it work. I haven't seen Fleurje in so long—a year? Two years, maybe? But it's funny, even though it's been that long, I feel as if we can connect more than ever right now, because we're both in similar but different situations, with good money coming in and success to celebrate. The Universe works like that—we see who we need to see, at the precise moment that it helps us. For the past couple years, I've been feeling broke and aimless. It would have been hard to really connect with Fleurje without feeling as if I was doing something wrong. I was unsuccessful, floundering, getting in my own way. But now that we're in alignment, the Universe is putting me and Fleurje together again. I probably *needed* that time away from her, to get on my own true path. It will be so good to see her! I can feel the truth inside myself: as much as I love being with Eleven and the women at the Temple every day, I also want to relate to a friend, an old friend who has known me deeply, who can understand me right now *and* in the context of my history.

Of course, Eleven understands me. She knows my history. She's known me longer than anyone else.

I sit on Fleurje's Sedge sofa to wait for her text. Her living room smells like honey, and there's a vase of white tulips on the coffee table. The Sedge is beautiful, but it's filled with down, which makes me uncomfortable. You don't need to be protected from the elements when you're sitting on a couch. Filling this entire sofa with feathers is a huge waste of life, and the cause of so much needless suffering. *Love is a verb, not a noun.* I lie back on the couch, close my eyes, and concentrate on sending compassion to the birds who were harmed for this luxury sofa, and all the birds who are living in captivity for the down trade.

Fleurje has acquired an interesting piece of art. A large piece, wood and encaustic, hangs over the mantel. It looks like a Paterson Ewen— but that's impossible, because that would have cost thousands of dollars. It's a piece of plywood that's been tackled by a router. The cuts are tangled and organic, as if they were made by giant termites. The wood is painted with patches of smooth blue and red and pink melted wax. It reminds me of something.

The Teleritual was so motivating tonight! I feel alive and uplifted. It's incredible how close I feel to the other Ascendants on the call, even though we were just on the phone and couldn't see each other's faces. Audio is very intimate. And I'm glad I decided to unplug for the day and preserve my attention. I felt so much clarity and focus while I was on the call.

I check my phone in case I have it on silent by mistake. It's almost nine o'clock. No message from Fleurje. Sometimes the meetings go late. She's negotiating with the buyers, which can take time.

Fleurje has a packaged pizza in her freezer. It's made with non-dairy cheese and a gluten-free crust! I can eat it! I guess Fleurje is on a special diet. I've missed dinner—only chocolate almonds are in my stomach right now. I unwrap the pizza and turn the oven on. I'll just have one slice, and then I'll wrap up the rest and save it in the fridge for when Fleurje comes home.

I check Instagram. The Teleritual is over, so I can break my mini-detox. My golden latte shot this morning has 1,498 likes! @Tunameltsmyheart is posing on a wooden chair, wearing a little T-shirt that reads, *I'm Psychic*. @MysticDumpling is making slow roasted cherry tomatoes and posted a pic of her blackened baking sheet: a wooden spoon resting next to soft, wrinkled tomatoes on parchment paper. How does she make greasy parchment paper look so pretty? @FifiTorre posted a pic of her #tarotspread on her yoga mat, with candles lining the floor under the windows of her yoga studio. Why do I still follow her? I don't feel good when I look at her pictures. She's using the Radiant Mystery tarot deck, which has hand-drawn images by Saira Jefferson that I can't decide about.

If I had been inspired and creative enough, I could have made a deck with my own paintings. I just made packs of greeting cards, which is so unimaginative. Saira Jefferson has changed *consciousness* with her art. What have I done?

I guess Jonathan is watching the baby, if Fifi is teaching tonight. It's only six o'clock on the west coast. They probably ate dinner together before her class. Grounding rice bowls, with nori and avocado. Or fish. I know Jonathan eats fish—he's talked about it before. I certainly hope Fifi didn't eat a lot of wild salmon during her pregnancy. The heavy metals are dangerous. Who knows? Not my problem.

I hold my phone up in camera mode and scan Fleurje's kitchen to find something to share. But there's only the box and plastic wrapper from the frozen pizza, and the Food Network show in the background. Her kitchen is nice, but uninspiring to photograph. I go to her living room. The piece over the fireplace is compelling. I take a pic, then try a Cooper filter. Too dark. I try Anderson to lighten it up. The red and pink turns hot in the filter—magenta.

This reminds me of Sophia and the warmth of the colour her aura brought to the studio. She had such a calming energy—but vivid, too. Stimulating, yet relaxed. What a colour. I should get in touch with Nana Boondahl. I should really finish that piece for her.

I post the pic with no filter and no comment. I'll ask Fleurje who the artist is, and update the pic when I know who made it. It looks pretty in my feed—a nice colour block, with such appealing texture! I should be posting more art. I should be making more art. I refresh my feed. @FleurjeZubrov posted a picture of a cocktail: *Peach brandy Manhattan*.

Me

Saw your cocktail!

Fleurje

:) it's so good!

Me

How did the sale go?

Fleurje

celebrating w sellers now

Me

Want me to make you some dinner?

Fleurje

no thanks I'll b late

Me

Should I stay up? I'd love to see you.

Fleurje

I'll b late, sorry :(

When the pizza is hot and the fake cheese looks melted enough, I sit on a barstool and eat a slice while I watch an episode of *Cooked! Canada*. At the commercial break, I get up and take a second slice. The pizza was actually pretty small when I took it out of the box— two small slices of this pizza are equal to one large slice of a normal pizza. The gluten-free crust tastes sweet, like biscotti. The soy cheese is soft and gooey, and when mixed with tomato sauce, reminds me of what mozzarella used to taste like. The host of *Cooked! Canada* introduces five new chefs. Fleurje has a wrought-iron wine rack under the counter, with several bottles lying sideways. Some of them have white tags tied to the bottlenecks. I get up to see: the tags have dates written on them.

It's hard to believe that only a few months ago I was broke, subletting a cold grubby apartment in Parkdale, completely disconnected from myself. I had spent years looking for external approval. I didn't know *how* to listen to my inner wisdom. I mean, that's why I used to have a drinking problem! I cut myself another small piece of pizza.

The texts from Fleurje look flat, blue on white, just like everything else in my messages. Like my automated AT&T messages. Like the texts Air Canada sent me about my flight. There's nothing that feels warm or real or true in her texts. Who is Fleurje? Are we even real to each other? I can't remember the last time we were in the same place at the same time. I hate texting. It turns us all into automated robots.

A chef steals a jar of capers from a neighbouring chef's table when she isn't looking. The soy cheese has cooled and solidified.

I've heard about an experiment they've done with rats, to understand addiction. When rats are alone in a cage, and have a choice between clean water and drugged water, they'll drink the drugged water until they overdose and die. But when they're living in a community, with plenty of good food and lots of other rats, they avoid the drugged water and drink the clean water. We're animals, too. We need to feel *safe and connected*. Before Ascendency, I was struggling, because I didn't feel safe. I needed to be part of a community. Now I've finally found my people. We might live all over the world, but we're still a community. I take another bite. The crust has a chewy texture, like a yoga mat.

I think I need to Compost Heave about Fleurje missing our date. I open the mobile version of the Ascendency classroom.

[Lilian Quick] Hello my dear Ascendants! I'm spinning out a little tonight. Is there anyone out there who can do a quick Compost Heave with me now-ish?

The judges look at the dish that one chef has prepared: a seared scallop served on mango salsa. The chef looks young. The judge in the black suit takes a bite of the scallop and looks perturbed. She nods, and the freckled boy smiles.

[Shona Silverman] Hi Lilian! I can Compost Heave with you now if you like. :)

It's Shona from my Potency Circle! What are the chances she'd be online right at this moment?

I meet Shona on Skype. I Heave everything that I have right now about my friendship with Fleurje. I go way back, and tell her about the year Fleurje and I were roommates. She worked in a juice bar on Bathurst Street and at the end of the day she'd pour the juice down the drain instead of bringing it home to share with the house. She said it was because the juice had oxidized so much by then, the nutritional value was all gone. I tell Shona that when my dog Friday died, Fleurje bought us both tickets to Vancouver Island, rented us a cabin by the ocean, and spent a week with me there, and that I cried in her lap every day. I tell Shona that I think Fleurje has a Paterson Ewen in her living room, but how that's impossible, because Paterson Ewen didn't work with beeswax, and this painting is definitely encaustic. And that her place feels like it's been staged, to photograph or to sell. There's nothing personal anywhere, like photos or notebooks or handbags or unopened mail or anything. Except the pizza in the freezer, and the wine rack. I Heave about eating basically the whole pizza. Shona is a really good listener. She lives in Seattle, and she's never been to Canada before.

After my Heave, I feel less spinny and more grounded. I describe the snow outside Fleurje's apartment, and Shona describes the cherry blossoms on her street. She asks me how long I've known Fleurje. It's been almost twenty years, but I haven't seen her in two. I catch her online on Facebook sometimes, we message each other. Mostly, I keep up with her life on Instagram.

"Remember the Elevator Syndrome," Shona says.

"Is that from Ascendency?" I ask.

"No, it's from an interview Eleven did with someone. I'll send you the link. Basically it goes like this: You're at a party with everyone you know. There are bowls of pretzels and chips around, and there's a nice view of the city. It's a fun party, but you start telling people, 'I want to go up.'"

"I want to go up," I say.

"Yeah, I want to go up. When you say that, people look at you funny."

"Right."

"They're like, why would you want that? Look, there's such a nice view here! And all these great snacks. Why would you want to leave?"

"I want to go to the next floor."

"Right? 'I want to go up.' So they look at you like you're crazy, and you feel afraid to want what you want. But still, you want to go up. You press the button and wait for the elevator and when it comes, you step on. And they look at you, upset. They're mad at you for leaving."

Juliette said it so frankly: *You've been in New York.*

"Then the elevator doors close. And you're in this little place all alone. And you think, What have I done? Why did I leave? Maybe you're mad at your friends, because they didn't come with you. But you have to wait through it. That part of Elevator Syndrome is natural. Everyone goes through it. You might be alone in that shaft for a while, but eventually the doors will open and you'll be on a totally new floor."

"I think I might be coming close to a new floor," I say.

"I know you are!" Shona says. "Listen. When I was drawing my first manifestation mandalas for *Color Your Soulmate Volume One,* I felt abandoned by everyone. My ex-wife had left me. She'd taken both of our cats."

"No!" I cry. "Why both of them?"

"They were littermates. We couldn't separate them," Shona says. "I had to leave our condo, because no way could I pay the rent on my own anymore. I moved to a room in this big house that had been divided into apartments. My neighbors were twenty-year-olds, all U-Dub students. I was in *completely* unfamiliar territory. It was the loneliest time in my life."

"I'm so sad about your cats," I say. "That's just the saddest thing."

"But I was *called* by the mandalas. I kept making them. I didn't even know I was making a book, at first. They were just these drawings."

"So were you *in* the elevator at this point?" I ask. "I'm trying to understand the elevator part."

"Yes. And here's my point. Even though I was completely alone and in a strange place—both literally and figuratively speaking—I felt at *home.* The work showed me what I needed to do. I was going up, to a more evolved place. When the doors opened, I was on a higher floor."

Shona's colouring books are Amazon bestsellers. She now offers in-person Soulmate Color Consultations to help clients focus and maximize their experience with the books, and she's hired to speak at events about colour symbolism and how it relates to manifesting true love. Maybe we could collaborate one day!

"You're going up, too," she says. "What's happening for you right now, with your new website? That's part of it. You're just in the elevator shaft. When the doors open for you, everything will look totally unfamiliar, but you'll feel right at home. That's how you'll know that you've found your higher floor."

I thank Shona for answering my call, and say goodnight. I am so grateful for this community! Shona is a friend from the higher floor. She listens, and she really sees me. She wants me to be my best self. That's what true friendships are for.

Should I check my phone? No. I want to savour this feeling of warmth and connection.

I wrap the two inches of pizza that's left in a piece of foil, and stick it in the fridge. I wish I hadn't eaten so much of that pizza. I wish there was a SoulCore class in Toronto. I tap the switch and turn off the lights. I pick up my phone to do my web check-in for my flight to PDX tomorrow morning. Goodbye, Toronto.

I check my latte pic: it now has more than two thousand likes. I double-tap a few pictures in my feed, and then go upstairs to pack my things. Before I go to bed, I place the malachite and carnelian mala I bought for Fleurje, still in its Lunar Devotional box, on her dresser. I'll be well on my way to Portland before she wakes up.

Wait! I forgot to do my web check-in! I turn on my phone again, and my finger goes to Instagram again, right away. Why is this happening to me? I force myself to close Instagram. With a deep breath and with great focus, I open the airline app and check myself in.

◊ ◊ ◊

In Portland, giant rhododendron bushes lean into the houses, and moss carpets the rooftops and oozes up through cracks in the sidewalk. Eleven and I have been here for three days already. We're spending all our time together, true quality time, in a way we haven't done since we were kids. We've gone to Willow Spa for mud treatments and manicures, visited Forest Park to find the right place for Saturday's Forest Sanctuary ceremony, and gone on a sunset cruise along the Willamette River. On the cruise, we drank mint-tea citrus spritzers as the light from the setting sun turned our faces pink-orange. We went through all our most important desired feeling-states one by one, because before you can do what makes you happy, you first have to understand that the way you want to feel drives the things that you do. We went deep. We really got to the heart of how we want to feel in everything we do (me: magical, creative; Eleven: powerful, free).

Yolanda and the others don't arrive until tomorrow. Eleven trusts Monicke's event planning, and besides, they've done this event enough to know it will roll out smoothly.

Today, we have a date with Winnie Prudhomme for lunch. The three of us are sitting at a booth at Bento Guru, one of the spots I found for our Ascendants to try this weekend. Winnie has bright green eyes and cool, ashy-olive skin. What look like silver baby spoons are curled around each of her thumbs.

"So this is the magical Lilian Quick," she says. "Eleven has told me so much about you."

"She has?" I look at Eleven, who opens and closes her menu. I feel strangely untethered now that someone else is sitting with us. I forget how to have a conversation.

"She says you see auras," she says. "Can you see mine right now?"

"I've never seen human auras," I explain. "Only animals."

"But human beings *are* animals," Winnie says.

"Yes, but we're a different kind, I guess."

"She's holding herself back," says Eleven. "I've tried to get her to tap on it."

The server brings us kombucha in stemless flutes. Winnie orders zucchini noodles. Eleven and I both order the kelp. There are heavy metals in kelp, but I hope the iodine neutralizes them. We all choose the spicy peanut sauce.

"Well." Winnie raises her glass. "Here's to our successful partnership."

"And to all the enlightened women who are raising the collective consciousness right now," says Eleven.

"To finding each other again," I say to Eleven. "And to meeting you!" I clink Winnie's flute. The kombucha is the colour of weak tea, and it fizzes on my tongue.

We make plans. We discuss Winnie's Sacred Eating workshop on Sunday. Eleven tells her the chocolate truffles are selling fast. As they talk about the orders, I look out at everyone in the restaurant. I study them, try to get a sense of their human energy as colour. I don't feel or see anything unusual. Am I holding myself back from a higher level? Our noodles arrive.

Winnie chews and swallows. "Zucchini doesn't really have flavor, does it?" she says.

"Lilian has more than twenty thousand subscribers," Eleven says proudly. "She built her list in just a few weeks. Did you read her piece in *WhaleMind*?"

"You've got to sell the truffles," says Winnie. "I haven't read your piece yet, but I shared it."

"She's right. You can just put one of the badges up," Eleven says. "The picture is gorgeous on its own. You don't even have to write anything about it. I know ads don't work the way they used to—but you're getting so much traffic."

My kelp noodles feel rubbery in my mouth. "Okay!" I say. It does seem like a good thing to do. "I haven't tasted them yet, though."

"We'll fix that today!" Winnie says.

"Winnie love, you're a *priestess*," says Eleven. "I meant to thank you for connecting me to Dr. Leopold. She's going to design a hybrid."

"Who's Dr. Leopold?" I ask.

"A horticulturist here in Portland," Eleven twirls her noodles on a fork.

"Wiccan," says Winnie.

"She's helping me design a new kind of rose. It's going to be named Eleven Novak."

Winnie takes a deep breath, and her face goes sacred. "What color?" she asks.

"White, with tips of bright green."

Winnie presses her hands together. "You're a phenomenon," she says.

I don't know if it's the jet lag or what, but I want a sandwich. I could eat three more bowls of these noodles. They weren't even spicy. I want a basket of fries, with salt and malt vinegar. My phone rings. I pause and listen to my full A tone. The sound has a golden quality I hadn't noticed before.

"That might be Yolanda," says Eleven. "She's meeting with the flower essence people today."

"It's Jonathan Rasmussen," I say. Eleven exchanges a glance with Winnie. "Do you mind if I do this now?" I ask, feeling clear for once. "It would help to have you here." I've been avoiding his calls since the article came out two weeks ago.

Eleven nods. "Please do," she says.

I answer it. I shouldn't hold my phone to my ear—I know this causes brain tumours—but this call won't last long.

"Lilian. I've been calling and calling."

"I've been busy."

"I can see that."

I push my bowl away. Winnie looks at me with her big green eyes. She gives me two thumbs up. The two silver spoons curl away from each other. My stomach feels sick and prickly, and my skin feels heavy.

"How's the west coast?" I ask.

"Challenging, honestly. Since your piece came out."

"How's Fifi?" I ask.

"I thought you were a balanced person. I thought we understood each other."

"Yeah, me too," I say. "I thought that, too."

"Why are you doing this to me?"

"Congratulations on Espluma," I say.

"Espuma. This isn't what I taught you," Jonathan Rasmussen says. "This isn't about presence. This is about something else."

"You're not my teacher anymore," I say.

"My livelihood depends on my ethical integrity. I haven't done anything wrong. They're calling me abusive now. My whole reputation is at stake, Lilian. I never meant to hurt you. You aren't even hurt! Why would you do this? What am I supposed to do, now?"

"Be present with it?" I say. "Let the experience crash into you, like a wave?"

"I have a family," he says. "You have to write an apology."

"I didn't even write your name. Why did people assume it was about you?"

"You have to fix this."

"I'm not responsible for your integrity," I tell Jonathan Rasmussen. "You are."

I hang up. My ears feel hot. My throat feels full of tears that won't come. Did I do the right thing? I can't speak.

The cooks bang pots in the open kitchen, swirl vegetable noodles with long stainless steel tongs in big stainless steel bowls and slide them down a large stainless steel countertop. Running under the noise of the kitchen there's a sound like gravel being dumped into the bed of a flatbed truck—the music. And on top of all this, the people are yelling at each other. They shout across the tables and the sound hits the steel surfaces and plate glass windows and polished concrete floors. Panicked, with no softness or way to escape, the noise bounces around and around like a bird in a house.

"It's an honor to witness your clarity," says Winnie.

"Respect, my darling," says Eleven.

A leggy woman in a coral tank top is beside our table. She crouches down and looks up at me. "Are you Lilian Quick?" she says.

I nod at her, still swallowing my tears. Is this how it's supposed to feel, when you're in your power?

"I wanted to say thank you. My name is Chloe. I'm sorry to disturb your lunch." She smiles apologetically at Eleven and Winnie.

"It wasn't the wine—it was *gluten*!" The man beside me shouts to his lunch date, two feet away.

Winnie smiles at the woman kneeling in front of me. "I *love* the color of your top," she says.

"Your piece in *WhaleMind* was really important for me to read," the woman tells me. "I had an experience like that too. With my yoga teacher. It was very intense. It broke up my marriage. I had to leave Connecticut, my community, my work. It was bad."

The man beside me keeps shouting. "I started to drink kombucha—fermented foods help a lot!"

"I'm so sorry," I squeeze out the words.

"Thank you." She twists a few wispy strands of hair around her forehead and attempts to stick them to the crown of her head. "I was so ashamed about it, I never told anyone. Then I read your story. You're very brave."

"Well," I say, "I just felt that I should share my story." Is that even true? Eleven told me to do it, that's why I did it.

She gives me a wide-eyed nod. "I connect to you so much! I do. I feel like you're just like me. I feel like I know you, or that I could be you."

I take Chloe's extended hand and touch metal. "Can I just hug you," she says, and gripping my hand, she rises from her crouched position to mantle me with her arms. "Thank you," she murmurs in my ear as she squeezes.

"You're welcome," I tell her. I can't see Eleven from inside Chloe's grasp, but I can see Winnie. She sips her kombucha and watches.

Chloe lets me out of the embrace and presses both of her hands meaningfully on my shoulders. Then she turns to Eleven and tells her how much she loves her work. Eventually, she leaves our table. I feel drained and anxious.

My phone looks quiet on the table, face down, pretending to rest. Inside that shiny gold exterior, it's teeming with digital activity. I can feel them out there, signing up for my newsletters. My chest feels like a nest of live electrical cords. What is my own anxiety, and how much of this is the noise of Bento Guru? If I don't pick up my phone to look, is anything really happening to me?

"If you steam them before grilling," the man shouts, "the glycemic index is lower!"

I feel a deep and irrational sadness. Something isn't right. I have so many followers, so many subscribers. I should be happy, but I am so lonely. But everything is connected! I shouldn't feel lonely, because everything is connected.

"Let's go have chocolate," says Winnie.

I can't stop thinking about loneliness. Was I lonely before? Yes. But this is different. Either I'm changing, or I'm finally starting to discover who I really am. I'm learning how to set boundaries, and not trying to make everyone happy anymore. This is an important part of self-actualization. But the way I spoke to Jonathan Rasmussen: Who was that? Was that me? And the way I just left Yumi at the bar, after they told me about their surgery. They were about to ask me something important, and I flipped out. Right at the point when I should have listened. Now they aren't responding to my texts. I betrayed their trust! How could I do that? I'm Lilian Quick! I'm a people person. I like making people happy. I don't even recognize myself. Am I in the elevator shaft?

"I feel strange," I tell Eleven, as we drive to the Conscious Cupcakery.

"What part?" Eleven is wearing a white minidress with long bell sleeves, and the sleeves flap wildly in the wind as she shifts into third. She rented a Mustang for the week. White. She said she wanted a Mustang "for old times' sake." I don't know what she meant by that. I assume she meant her years in Hawaii with Bea, because for as long as I remember, Uncle Jimmy drove a Chevy.

"It's like my mind hasn't caught up with my new life. Ascendency. I still feel like the old Lilian Quick, but I also feel different."

We drive over a bridge, and the Willamette River sparkles underneath us. The old Lilian would have wanted to paint that, with washes of cobalt blue and Payne's grey. She'd apply masking fluid with a tiny brush to make the white diamonds scatter over the water. With watercolour you have to think backward, and keep white as raw paper under all the layers of colour.

"Who is the old Lilian Quick, though?" Eleven asks.

"I feel so uncomfortable," I say.

"Look in the mirror," Eleven says.

I think about that. I *am* nothing but mirrors, really. Aren't we all supposed to be infinite reflections of one another? "Ah," I say. "I see what you mean."

"No." Eleven reaches over and pulls down the visor on my side of the car. The traffic slows down, and she shifts again. The engine makes a softer sound as we brake and come to a stop. "Look at your eyes," she says.

I have splotchy pigmentation. I need some more Luze! I'm falling apart!

"Look deep into your eyes. Be honest. Who do you see there?"

My eyes are blue-green. My pupils are lamp-black. In a painting, I'd use a spot of white on my pupils to give the appearance of light and focus—that's how I built expressions into pet portraits. Dogs are easier to give expression to than cats. I've heard that cats are like autistic humans, in terms of facial expression. That's why some people don't think cats have warm personalities—their faces don't express emotion like dogs. You have to watch a cat's tail to understand what it's thinking.

"So? Do you see Lilian there?"

My eyelashes are mascaraed in MAC Gigablack. I am growing a silver streak at my hairline.

"I have grey hair now," I say. "Do you have grey?"

"I'm trying to help you," says Eleven. "Try to focus. You haven't seen your own power yet."

"I'm so confused," I say.

"Self-discovery includes confusion," she says.

"Where did you learn all this?" I ask. "Why did you name yourself Eleven?"

"I listened to the voices in my head," Eleven says. "I thought I was crazy. I fought it for a long time. I went to some doctors, who prescribed things for it. Then I just accepted it." The traffic starts moving again, and we are whizzing through a neighbourhood full of trees and flowers. "They named me Eleven," she says. "The voices."

"You know you sound delusional," I say.

"Delusion is the only reasonable response to reality."

The shingled houses on either side of the street are painted in fun colours: sage green and dusky purple, pale blue with dark blue trim. I squint at them like Monet would have, and I make the light refract into speckled flecks of colour. "Do you really think I can see human auras?" I ask.

"You can see all vibrational energy, sweetheart," she says. "You're just an HSP, a highly sensitive person, which makes it hard for you to assess sometimes."

I look in the mirror again. "I can't really see myself," I say. "I just see my face."

"I know," Eleven says.

Our conversation makes no sense. I feel a tingling sensation above my head. Eleven makes a left turn at a light, hand-over-hands the steering wheel, and pulls into an industrial area marked by a clump of low red-brick buildings. I push the visor up.

"This is it," says Eleven. She pulls her own visor down and fluffs her hair, making it bigger than it was before. Eleven made a Temple for herself. Now she's making a rose of herself. It occurs to me that my cousin might be a narcissist.

We get out of the Mustang. The air smells like chocolate. "Where's your phone?" Eleven says. "Take a picture of us!" I do what she says.

> @LilianQuick> Getting ready for Ascendency Portland with the divine @ElevenNovak!

I get seventy-five likes right away. How do they find it so quickly? An algorithm?

We enter the chocolate meditation pod wearing white coats and silver hairnets. The guttural non-melody of chanting Tibetan monks grinds out of the speakers embedded in the ceiling, and the sound is neatly absorbed into the white, foam-covered walls. The Cupcakery is stark and spotless, with stainless steel counters and mysterious-looking silver cylinders stacked on the glass shelves. It smells like spice, cream, dark fruit, and sweet musk. Workers make notes on clipboards tethered to oven-sized boxes. They twist dials gently, changing the red LED numbers on the face of each box.

Winnie gives us samples—tiny pieces of each chocolate in Eleven's Conscious Truffle Collection—and we eat them one by one. She instructs us on how to eat consciously: eyes closed, following a special breathing exercise that attunes us to the contraction and expansion of our lungs and heart. This connects us to our ultradian rhythms, the patterns that direct our hormonal systems, hunger and thirst, body temperature, sleepiness and wakefulness. After a few weeks of this eating practice, you feel more connected to the earth, as well as the ocean. When you really work up to it, she says, conscious eating will eventually connect you to the rhythms of the moon and planetary systems.

I do everything she says. I feel calm and more connected. It works. It really works! I will definitely sell these on my site.

I meet Eleven's eyes as we walk from the rose pistachio truffle station to the chipotle truffle station. Her eyes are alive, with flames inside. Winnie's thumbs flash at me, those two fat silver rings. My eye traces the path they make in the air, as if I'm a cat hunting a reflection.

I've felt this way before. As a girl, running through the golf course with Florence at dusk. Playing invisible at the church social. Florence could make the world into a fairy tale—where nothing felt real, but everything felt more vibrant than the real. I used to feel this way when I was painting. When I could become the line of the drawing, the boundaries between myself and my subjects dissolved, just like this. I recognize this feeling. I know this is how I am supposed to feel. Everything around me vibrates and glitters. It feels dangerous, because it's so intense and true.

April 2016

Dear Lilian,

I'm dreaming about my flower beds, and looking at my online garden template builder to see where these double narcissus in peach, cream, butter, and apricot are going to come up this year. I started collecting these special bulb varieties a few years ago, adding to the bed every fall, and I realized I've never written about them before now! I just love the frills of double narcissus—they almost look like peonies, but they come up in the spring, so you don't have to wait as long. Every day I peer out to the garden to see if any green is poking up. The crocuses have just started.

Sorrel is the first green that comes up in my herb garden, and I love to blend it with peas and shallots in this easy spring green soup. I'm having it for lunch today, in fact. Even the girls love it—it's zesty, and the peas make it naturally sweet.

Speaking of the girls—they're getting ready for Easter next weekend, and on my site today I show you some cute ways to freshen up your Easter baskets with things you already have at home! It's amazing what you can do with silk flowers, a nip of floral tape, and spray glitter.

We discovered that Mabel is allergic to eggs, which made Easter a challenge this year. Luckily, the Easter Bunny is one creative rabbit! This year, instead of eggs, he's hiding these orange and yellow crepe-paper carrots all over the house. Each one is filled with small toys and treats. The girls will have so much fun unrolling each carrot to find what's hidden inside . . . and the process of unwrapping creates festive streamers! Go to my site today to get a full tutorial on how to make the carrots.

Knigel's been hard at work on a demanding project this month, with not a lot of downtime. So I made these Spring Cocktail

Infusions to cheer him up and make the end of every workday a little celebration: <u>Lemongrass Blood Orange Vodka, Cucumber Lime Gin</u>, and <u>Pineapple Ginger Tequila</u>. I share the recipes on my site today—you'll need a big Mason jar with a tight lid for each infusion. I included some delicious cocktail suggestions for each one, too, just because.

One more thing: I'm coming to New York! I'm speaking at the <u>Lifestyle Design and Inspo-preneurship Conference</u> on Friday, April 22. I'll be onstage speaking about how I created PureJuliette.com. If you live in the area, I'd love it if you came to say hello.

Here's to spring,
xoxo, Juliette

ON THURSDAY, WHEN the rest of the temple team arrives in Portland, we get to work, and the hustle is real. Eleven asks us to make two hundred and thirty-three special welcome baskets, one for every Ascendant, to identify each one with their personalized flower essence, and drop them off at their hotel rooms before they get there. The flower essences complicate the process, but we make it happen. When I return to our hotel, Eleven tells me I'm off duty. I am to participate in all the weekend events as an Ascendant, like I did in New York in March.

On Friday, the opening night of Ascendency Portland, I do the DjeDje workshop, which is a kind of movement practice meant to connect you to primal rhythms. I am given a dried gourd to shake like a rattle, and a silk dress with a fringe under the sleeves so I can fly around the room as my given animal totem—a dragonfly. We all paint our faces with glow paint and stick-on Swarovski crystals and dance to the drums and flutes that Ziad plays with her DjeDje band. When I return to my hotel room I look at myself in the mirror and try to see Lilian Quick. I think I might recognize myself. I feel different. My eyes have tiny twinkling specks deep inside them. But as soon as I think about who I am, I feel confused again.

Don't think about it! *Rest until you want to play; play until you want to rest.* This is the magic. Let it happen.

I take a quick shower, get dressed in jeans and a flowered blouse, and take a PickUp to Lotus Blossom to meet my Potency Circle. When I arrive, the other three women are already there, debriefing over a shared tapas platter. Shona and Matilde brought gifts: *Color Your Soulmate Vol. II* from Shona, and a thumb drive from Matilde loaded with her new album, *More Than Enough*. Matilde, who flies in from Paris for every Ascendency event, is a party and event planner by day, DJ by night. She's also a singer-songwriter. How she makes time for that, I don't know! She's a time master—she bends and shapes it so it works for her. *More Than Enough* is an album written and produced to help women manifest prosperity. I would have *loved* this when I was broke in Toronto.

I did what Eleven suggested, and put an affiliate link up on my site for the Conscious Truffle Collection. My website traffic isn't slowing down at all—it's increasing as the *WhaleMind* article spreads through yoga and meditation circles around the world. I'm getting requests for interviews and more guest posts. I tell Anoosh, Shona, and Matilde about it over dinner. They all advise me to take it slow, and to focus on Ascendency while I'm here in Portland.

"It's the weekend," says Anoosh. "You don't answer email on weekends."

Anoosh smells like black pepper and tuberose, and her thick hair hangs to her chin in a sleek, shiny bob. Her eyes are thickly lined with kohl. She says she doesn't even carry her phone with her all the time anymore. She only uses it at certain times of the day.

"I believe what will happen is that as consciousness evolves, we will spend less time on our devices," she assures us. "It will be a sign of prestige: the elite will no longer have to carry phones in their pockets."

"Do you think elevated consciousness depends on privilege?" asks Matilde.

"Perhaps it does," murmurs Anoosh.

"It's available to everyone," Shona says. "How can consciousness be a privilege? It makes no sense. It's a human right."

"Ascendency is expensive," I say.

Shona nods. "Yes. But *you* manifested it, didn't you, Lilian? You made it here, even though you didn't have *any* money when you signed up."

"Look at you now!" says Anoosh. "Flourishing."

"I didn't have to pay for it though," I say. "It's part of my job, which is why I get to do it."

"But you *manifested* it. When opportunities come to you, they don't always look the way you'd expect."

"Lilian has a point," says Matilde. "If my husband didn't work for Air France, could I be an Ascendant? I don't know."

"But the music you make is a celebration of this work," says Shona. "And it opens doors for so many people, brings them to a higher vibration, so they can bring abundance to *their* lives."

"*Oui*," says Matilde. "Maybe I have been given this opportunity so I may help others."

I try to focus on what they're saying, but I'm so tired, their manicures make tracers in the air as they move their hands. The light is doing something to their faces—it's blurry and glowing, like my eyes are smeared with Vaseline. "I have to go to sleep," I tell the women. "I'm starting to see things. DjeDje messed with my head."

"Good night, little Dragonfly," says Shona. Shona was Bear tonight—I remember her lumbering around the dance floor on all fours.

"The Forest Sanctuary Ceremony starts right after breakfast," I say. "I'll see you then."

Before I leave, I ask the server to take a picture of the four of us. Matilde, dressed all in black, takes both of my hands in hers when she poses beside me. Her hands are soft and strong. "I'm so pleased to know you, Lilian," she says. "You are a very special woman."

I return to my hotel feeling nourished in every way. I do not feel like checking my phone at all.

◊ ◊ ◊

The trails in Forest Park are green upon green—lush and jungle-like, with trees like skyscrapers. There is a hum in the forest, of life and action and chlorophyll and breath. The air feels alive and vivid.

Eleven wears a white cape and flower crown for the ceremony. "We acknowledge and thank the Multnomah, Kathlamet, Clackamas, Chinook, Tualatin Kalapuya, and Molalla tribes for this land," she says. "They used this area for summer encampments for thousands of years, before they were forcibly removed by white settlers." We pause in silence, and I have that lonely, hollowed-out, sick sensation that I always have whenever I think about what was done to the indigenous people of this continent. Then she sends us off in small groups, staggering our departures so we don't overrun each other in the forest.

"Find yourself a space in solitude, where you can sit comfortably," she tells my group. "You will create the entrance to your Sanctuary. Picture it, and you'll make way for your ancestors to come and visit you. Sit, and wait for them. Invite them to come. When they arrive, tell them everything you need to tell them before you die. What happens in your Forest Sanctuary is your own private magic. It is your own experience of healing communication, and I cannot tell you what to expect beyond that. Call upon your element for support. Know that we are all here in the same forest with you." Behind me, someone starts crying.

"Don't be afraid. Nothing will come that you aren't prepared for, my divine darlings. You are as powerful as these trees. You are made of stars, of leaves, of oceans." Yolanda opens the van door, notes the mileage, and writes it down on her clipboard. Anna-Mackenzie and Monicke are back at the theatre, running the Sound Bath ceremony with Marie. The Ascendants are divided into four groups today, alternating between downtime and ceremonies.

"Earth element, go ahead. Water is right behind you. We'll follow you in, after giving you time to find your spot. There is enough forest for all of us this morning, my petals. The forest will expand and hold us all in her arms."

As she speaks, I feel my energy vibrate, and the energy of all the women around me, shaky and strong at once. The forest plays me like a cello, and my body feels like a warm sound. The path is soft, the earth dark as chocolate cake. I go off the trail and tread carefully between pointed green ferns and baby cedar trees, flimsy and delicate, shorter than my knees.

The forest is dripping with living green. I pass stumps exploding with ferns and leaves and cedar logs that have turned themselves in, softly decaying into a carpet of moss. I walk until I can't hear any of the other Ascendants rustling around me. I find a quiet place, with a flat rock embedded in the ground. I can sit on the rock without getting too damp or dirty. I imagine I am in a little woodshed with a door in front of me. Is that what Eleven meant by imagine an entrance? Maybe she meant more of a tent? I try to picture a canvas tent, but the woodshed image sticks. I'll take it.

I sit. "Welcome," I whisper to the trees. "Welcome to my Sanctuary."

The air shimmers, prismatic. There is so much animal life in this forest, it's hard to filter their auras into single colours. A sparrow sings in the branches somewhere above me, and I look up to catch a stroke of its aquamarine light before it flies away to another tree. The branches above me are alive with colour and motion. Nature!

"I'm ready to see you now," I say quietly, to nothing.

Nothing but invisible colour and silent music. It's everywhere. It's inside of me and outside of me. I'm breathing it, and it's breathing *me*.

My father visits me first. I recognize him right away, lit with periwinkle light. He looks tired but happy, as if he's spent the whole day writing and discussing the Stoics with his friends from university. I don't know what I'm supposed to say to him. I just stare, and watch the purple aura pulse around his body. He won't speak unless I talk to him first, just like when he was alive. Tentatively, I say to him, "I'm here with Florence. She's called Eleven now. Did you know?"

I remember when you were eleven, he says, without speaking. Of course! That's how he can be here. He's a vision from inside my own head. What do I want to say to him?

I have something to ask you, I say. It's about Uncle Jimmy. I want you to be honest.

He listens, looking up at my forehead instead of my eyes, the way he used to.

Florence was afraid of Uncle Jimmy, I say. Do you know why?

We can easily forgive a child who is afraid of the dark, he says. *The real tragedy of life is when men are afraid of the light.*

I don't understand what this means. I ask, Did you ever talk to him?

You can discover more about a person in an hour of play than in a year of conversation.

Can you respond in your own words? I ask. Do you have words?

He looks up at my eyebrows. What about your responsibility? I ask. You were the adult. You were supposed to be in charge.

I tried not to cause any harm, he says. His periwinkle light flares to a hot white point, and he's gone.

A finger of sunlight burns a bar of cold heat into my heart. My father was too afraid to do anything about anything. I will not be like him.

Minutes or hours pass, and then violet light swirls beside me, and it's Friday! Her tail is made of feathery heat. She sits beside me and lifts her paw in greeting, the way she always did.

I miss you, I tell her. Thank you for finding me. You were my best friend. You saved my life.

You saved my life.

I try to think of what I can say to her, to resolve things.

We have nothing to resolve. Friday nuzzles my thigh with her warm nose. She's made of amethyst light. *I heard you call. I wanted to see you again. Hello, friend! It's always good with you.*

She sits in her sphinx position, paws straight out in front. *This is good because we are here together.*

I love you, Friday, I say. She jumps up, frisky and important. *Best friend!* she says, and with a white-hot flash, she leaves, and her lavender-pink aura vanishes behind a thin curtain sliced through the air.

My heart is light now. There's no time in here—the forest operates without time. When I think about real life, and the other Ascendants waiting in the parking lot, and Eleven in her flower crown, it's like remembering a confusing dream.

A swath of dark green curls around me. I smell tomatoes and something else, spicy sweet, like sage.

Hello dear, says Grandma Bertolucci. I think it's Grandma. But she looks my age.

I'm Theresa. Your grandmother's sister. We've never met.

She looks so much like Grandma.

You look like me! It's clear in the eyes. Look at your upper lip! Your nose looks like Rosie's nose. But then Rosie's a beauty, so you're lucky.

What do I need to resolve with Great-Aunt Theresa? I'm sorry we never met, I say.

I'm here to tell you something. Sisters try their best, but they don't always see the same path. I didn't understand your grandmother until she died. It takes a long time, but it doesn't feel like any time has passed at all.

I don't understand what she's talking about. Her Italian accent is thick.

Accent? This is Italian. You can understand me. Stop thinking, it doesn't help. Her dark-green light emanates from her in powerful whorls, like clouds.

Florence's mother and your mother, they're both sad. Their sadness is like mine was. It's deep and runs through their hearts. It's dug holes through everything. Your mother was right to leave Rosie be. The unfortunate thing is seeing how it's dripped down to you girls.

You mean me and Eleven, I say.

You're doing everything right, Lilian. Don't take everything so seriously. You don't have to understand what's happening. Look at me!

She kisses my forehead and I smell aromatic leaves and then she's gone, in a rich drop of hot-white light. I feel a roundness in my chest, like a juicy grapefruit, and clarity. As though I've been underwater and broke the surface to sip fresh air.

The sparrows sing above me. The forest is empty and overflowing.

My phone says 11:11. I've been out here for more than an hour. I don't want this to end! I push myself off the rock and stretch. I'm exhausted and thirsty. My body feels as if I've been hiking for hours. All around me, I notice the bodies of my fellow Ascendants, crouched under trees and leaning back on soft mossy stumps. We are everywhere.

I head back to the parking lot, walking as softly as I can so I don't disturb anyone. Are they having visions too? Are they seeing colours, or is it just me?

◊ ◊ ◊

I'm in my hotel room, ready for bed, catching up on my Instagram feed, when I hear women talking in the hallway. Ascendants are everywhere in this hotel! I recognize Ziad's voice, throaty and louder than the other two.

"They filmed it in Jackson, but it's supposed to be a small town in Indiana," she says.

"Her small town?" This voice has a thick southern accent.

"I don't think it's a real place. They made it up."

A higher voice squeaks, "It's based on *her* story?"

"No, no, no. It's sci-fi. They just named the character after her."

"Ugh," says the woman with the accent. "I hate sci-fi."

"They couldn't really tell me anything, it's all top secret until the release this summer," says Ziad.

"Her father was a *monster*. In real life."

"Do you believe that all happened?"

"Are you saying she made it up?"

"Her childhood was like a prison. Her mother was brainwashed."

"I heard Jonathan Rasmussen is making a doc about *himself* for Netflix."

"He was supposed to be at grad in Oahu, but he cancelled." A breathy sound. Laughter?

"He didn't cancel. Eleven cut him out of everything."

"Have you talked to Fifi?"

"She's doing amazing. She loves being a mother," says the southern voice.

"Eleven and Lilian are family. She's protecting Lilian, that's why she cut him out." That was Ziad.

The ding of the elevator. The voices go quiet. My heart pounds— I realize I am holding my breath.

"Hello, magnificent ones!" Fabric rustles outside my door as the women embrace and greet each other. I hear people shuffle down the hall, and two doors click shut. I exhale and feel a flat stone in my stomach. She must know that people talk about her, but still. It would feel awful to overhear it.

There is a tap at the door.

"Are you okay, sweetie?" Eleven's voice is quiet and raspy from her closing ceremony speech and incantation.

In the Closing Circle tonight, people shared conversations they had with old friends and family members who had passed to the other side. They also described a sense of losing time, and intense emotions that were brought up by the dreamtime conversations. But nobody—not one other Ascendant—mentioned anything about colour flares and shimmering light. So I kept my story to myself. I didn't even tell Anoosh, Matilde, and Shona. There aren't really words to describe it. I wish I'd packed my watercolour set. I keep thinking about how to get those colours on paper. Aunt Theresa's dark green, my father's light purple. Friday's brilliant, warm violet-pink, and the way it broke open the air and burned white hot as she disappeared. I want to use thick, wet dots of purple on a wet wash of crimson lake and let the colour bloom to create that dreamy effect.

Eleven's wearing white cashmere leggings and gold slide-on slippers with pointy toes. Her white cape is swept up on one shoulder, making a cowl. Her skin is free of any powder or radiance cream. I see Florence in her face tonight. I look at her nose and remember what Theresa told me.

Eleven hugs me, and I breathe in. "You smell delicious," I say. Her hair is damp, and her curls are tamed with a leave-in styling cream.

"Are you exhausted, darling? I won't stay long—you need to get some rest." She closes the door behind her, slides her gold slippers off, and sits on my bed with her legs crossed. She pats the space beside her. "Sit," she says.

I climb back into bed. "Your closing ceremony was wonderful," I say. "The part about seeing yourself as a child, and the poem? Powerful."

She presses her hands together in namaste. "You don't have to share with me if it feels too personal," she says. "But when you came out of the forest yesterday, I saw your face." She looks into my eyes. Her pupils are dark, gleaming pools. I have the sensation of falling.

"I saw some things," I say. As soon as I say it, I feel shy. I'm not ready to tell her what happened. "I felt like I was on drugs," I say.

"That's often how people describe the first time," she says. "As you keep returning to Sanctuary, you'll enter that space more readily, and you'll feel more control. The veils between the worlds are thin, and passable. You'll learn how to master the skill of slipping between them."

I should have said I was too tired for a visit. I feel foggy, and I want to go back to my Instagram feed. I just posted a pic of the Keep Portland Weird mural, and there are a few more hashtags I could add. A photographer from Singapore sent me a direct message. It could be spam, but it might be something interesting. I have so many comments and activity to look at from the past week.

"Would you like a cup of tea?" The hotel supplies a capsule brewing machine and a tray of tea and coffee pods. "There might be an herbal," I say.

Eleven shakes her head. "Tell me what you saw," she says, eyes sparkling. Does she already know? "If you feel like sharing, that is."

My voice slips and catches in my throat. I stare at her, unable to speak. Why don't I want to tell her?

"Of course," she says. "Say no more—it's private, and that's how it should be. I just wanted you to know that I'm here, if you want to Compost Heave about any part of the experience this weekend."

"Thank you," I say quietly.

Why is Eleven here? Does she want something from me? What's real about what happened today, and what am I making up? I remember eating ice cream on the porch swing with Florence when we were six years old, peeling back the paper wrapper and biting into crunchy frozen chocolate and peanuts. Did we both feel safe with Uncle Jimmy that day, or am I just remembering it that way?

"Do your parents still call you Florence?" I ask. "Remember your dad used to call you Flossy?"

"They call me Eleven," she says. "I don't feel like Florence at all anymore." She looks over her shoulder and out the window. A pink, blue, and green neon arrow blinks on and off across the street.

"That's too bad," I say lightly. "Because I loved Florence. Florence was one of a kind."

Eleven turns back to look at me. "How so?"

"She understood things that other people didn't. For instance, when I told Florence that the tiny aura around mosquitoes was pretty, she could have laughed at me like the kids at school did. But she didn't."

"What did I do?"

"You stopped killing them."

Eleven blinks. "I don't remember," she says. "Where were we?"

"In Sudbury."

"What color did you see?"

"The mosquitoes? This pearly, minty blue."

She looks down at her white nails, scanning for chips in the polish. "Monicke is at the bar downstairs with Anna-Mackenzie," she says. "And Yolanda went to bed early." I wait for her to finish, but she doesn't say anything else.

"Do you want to go down to the bar?"

"I don't want to see anyone else," she says. "Just you."

"Are you okay?"

Her eyes plunge into mine. "Sometimes, there's a black wave that crashes down over my consciousness." Her voice is low and scratchy. "I feel like I can't breathe. Like I'm trapped."

"Oh, Eleven!" I say. "Is that how you feel now?"

She shakes her head. "It creeps around the sides of my mind. I've felt it before. It used to come more often. It's like this dark, dangerous water is stored in my memories, and I can't let it leak out."

"I'm sorry," I say. "I won't talk about memories anymore."

"No, it's okay. You can. I'm smarter about it now," she says. "I trained myself to rise up out of the darkness. Now that I'm Eleven, it doesn't come most of the time. Hardly ever, anymore."

"Have you—do you have a therapist? Someone to talk to?"

"I'm supposed to be the one teaching people how to rise." She wraps the white cape around her body and hugs herself. "There's no one who I can really explain this to. Nobody would understand. I'm supposed to *be* the guidance."

"But that's ridiculous," I say. "Everyone needs guidance! You're a human being. You're not a—" I stumble. I was going to say *goddess*.

Her wide-set eyes are naked and blue, and her face is pure Florence: focused and intent. Her forehead is deeply creased from years of intense thought. "I'm just so grateful that you're here, Lilian. I trust you more than anyone else I know." She releases her arms from around her body and puts her head in my lap. I can read her wrist tattoos: *this too / shall pass.*

I stroke her curls. "I've had depression too," I say. "I got close to rock bottom once." I'd had a disagreement with Juliette, and I felt lonely and friendless. "Then this strange black dog came to me, out of nowhere. I don't mean the metaphorical black dog.

I mean an actual dog. A stray. That was Friday, from Quick+Friday. Friday was the dog that saved me from myself." Oh, Friday! Her purple light, her little raised hello paw. *This is good because we are here together.*

I'm doing it again! Talking about myself when I should just be listening.

"I'm not depressed," Eleven says.

"Maybe you could get a little dog, or a cat," I say. "Animals are healers in furry bodies."

"Thank you, sweetheart." She pulls herself back up, combs her fingers through her hair, and massages her temples. "Time for bed. Early day tomorrow."

"The car picks us up at seven thirty?"

"Oh honey, I don't know. Yolanda will call me when it's time to get up. Do you want her to give you a wake-up call too?"

"No," I say. "I'll get up myself."

Eleven sighs. "You look like Aunt Marie," she says. "I know, nobody wants to hear they look like their mother. It's just so striking tonight."

"It's the Bertolucci nose. You have it, too. Look." We both turn and look at ourselves in the mirror on the opposite wall, assessing our profiles. "Too bad they don't talk anymore," I say.

"There's a lot of history there," she says. "They're doing the best they can."

Seriously? Our mothers have been stonewalling each other for over twenty years! "Have you ever offered Ascendency to your mom?" I ask. It would be good for Aunt Rosie to take this program. She'd learn self-care and have the opportunity to do some real reflection. And she'd make friends with other women—I don't think she's ever had any female friends.

"She's not interested," Eleven says. "It's too far from her comfort zone."

"It would be way out there for my mom too," I say. "But my mom's doing okay. She has a community. She drinks a lot of frozen blender drinks, but at least she has friends."

"Your mom is more connected to her feminine spirit," Eleven says. "She's not afraid of her own pleasure."

"Your mom loves luxury," I say.

"My mother felt she had to choose," says Eleven evenly. "Her husband or her sister. She chose her husband."

"I know," I say. "But my mom was trying to help her out of a bad situation."

Eleven raises her arms and leans back, stretching. "Look, of course I wish they'd talk again. My father is a bully. I wish my mom would leave him, too. But it's their path, Lilian. Their own karma. It's none of our business." When she sees my face, she asks, "Why is this so important to you?"

What did my father say today? *The tragedy of life is being afraid of the light?* I don't want to be afraid. I always want to look honestly at myself!

"If I had a sister," I say to Eleven, "I would listen to her advice. I would trust that she wants what's best for me."

Eleven doesn't blink. "Not if you don't know what you want for yourself. Her advice is only ever going to be what *she* wants for you."

I remember Aunt Rosie crying in the kitchen. This was just before a Fourth of July picnic at the church—my dad had come back from the library with his briefcase in his hand, because it was closed for the holiday weekend. I carried a big cling-wrapped platter of watermelon slices out to the car. When I came back inside, the pitcher of iced tea had spilled. Aunt Rosie's T-shirt was wet and sticking to her chest.

"You threw that at me," she cried. "Why would you do that?"

Uncle Jimmy was very calm. "I did not throw it at you," he said. "It was a simple accident."

"Why would you do that?" Her face was red and blotchy. "Why would you do that? What did I do?" She threw her shaking hands up to her face and down her body.

My mom came in and said, "Here, Rosie. Dry off." She had a towel in her hand.

Uncle Jimmy watched my mom pat down Rosie's shirt. Then he said, "Didn't take your pills today, did you, Rosie?"

My body feels heavy. The dim light from the hotel nightstand makes shadows on Eleven's cheekbones, making her face look sunken. The lines around her mouth look deeper than they are in real life.

"I'm sorry," I say. "I'll stop talking about our childhood now."

Eleven touches my knee. She keeps her hand there, and I feel her energy root down through my leg, through the mattress, and into the floor. "We are not responsible for our mothers," she says. "We bring a higher vibration to our ancestral stories now. You understand this is what Ascendency is, right? It's changing our DNA. It's a karmic adjustment. It's an energetic course correction. So we don't continue walking the same toxic paths that our parents and grandparents did. We can change the habits of the Universe and create a new level of consciousness."

"I can see that," I say. Maybe I do want to tell Eleven about what I saw in the Forest Sanctuary. One day, I'll tell her. When we're not both so tired.

"We're special," says Eleven. "You and I are special, Lilian. We've *always* had this deep connection to spirit. I know you know what I'm talking about. In the past, we would have been priestesses. Medicine women. That's why I invited you here. We are both called to this work."

I hear a buzz. "Who's phoning me at this hour?" I say.

"You're feeling some of the consequences of your calling," Eleven says. "It's a lot to take in, at first—I know. I've done this too, remember."

"My calling?" I ask. "What is my calling?"

My phone buzzes again, and whistles. Someone left *voicemail*? Who leaves voicemail?

"The work we are doing together, sweetheart," Eleven looks blurry and soft-focused. I'm so sleepy.

"I miss painting," I say out loud.

Eleven removes her hand from my knee. "Then paint," she says. My body feels light, like it might float to the ceiling. "You're falling asleep," she says.

This is the last thing I remember. I wake up the next morning, and she's gone.

◊ ◊ ◊

You know who leaves voicemail? Nana Boondahl, that's who. It was Nana Boondahl who called when I was in Portland. She's coming to New York this month, for the Flourish Women and Business Summit and wants to see me. She wants to pick up her portrait of Sophia. I haven't finished it yet, of course. The Temple and Ascendency have taken over my life.

And yet.

I'm starting to understand something I've never understood before. It feels familiar and unfamiliar at once, as if I'm remembering something I knew when I was very little. I'm seeing how energy moves through all of us—it moves through every single thing on this planet. We are made of energy. During Ascendency Portland, I became so involved in the energetic field, I could almost see *atoms dancing inside matter*. I know I can't actually see atoms, but I can feel them. I can feel the energy all around us. It's not separate for me. And now I can see energetic colour. Right? That has to be what's happening.

The colours I saw in Portland didn't stay in the Forest Sanctuary. I can now see auras around everything and everyone. It's as if I'm looking through a lens or a filter that creates colour wherever there's light. Even the ugly buildings on Avenue B have a fuzz of colour around them. The deli at the corner of First and Tenth is purple moving to green, and the Pret a Manger by Astor Place is bubblegum pink moving to buttery yellow. I say *moving* because aura colour doesn't bleed, the way watercolour blends—the auras I see are constantly in motion, making streaks that move in the way northern lights do in the sky. They don't stand still and glow: they are alive and breathing, and their breathing paints the atmosphere. Central Park is my favourite place in the city: it's a glowing, pulsing centre of energy.

To get to work each day, I take the green subway line from Astor Place to the Upper East Side. It's a direct trip. I get off at Eighty-Sixth Street and walk through the park to get to the West Side, where the Temple is. It's easy to just take the one train. Then the walk allows me to stare at the trees, the rollerbladers, the rocks. And the water! The fountain aura makes a prism, and the water vibrates in so many colours as it pours. It shatters into rainbows as it hits the pool. I could watch the fountain forever. The dogs in the park still have the purest auras—it's like they've found their one strong colour, and they're comfortable there. But I can see auras around people now, too. People are more prismatic; their colours shift throughout the day. People's auras look like mood rings!

If there's something wrong with my eyes, I don't want it fixed.

The energy in the Temple is harsh and jagged, and the auras are intense. Yolanda wears a white blouse with severe collar points. Her aura is green-yellow-peach. "Anna-Mackenzie has an appointment," she tells me. "Portia is yours today." She hands me the pink leash. Portia looks up at me with her round brown eyes, and her shoelace of a tail whips at the carpet when we make eye contact.

"Chocolate orders are through the roof," Yolanda continues. "Get in touch with Winnie in Portland. And keep a close eye on the numbers. Put up a back-order notice on the site as soon as they sell out."

"Morning, Canada!" Monicke shouts.

"If Winnie can't keep up with our sales," Yolanda says, "then you'll have to write an email to explain to everyone on our list. Say there's a six-week delay for current orders."

"How long will it take her to make more?" I ask. Portia whines at my feet.

"Ask Winnie," Yolanda says. "Just do whatever you can to keep things under control." She turns around. Her heels click down the hall. She knocks once on Eleven's door, and then opens it and disappears inside.

Portia leads me to Anna-Mackenzie's desk and promptly lies down underneath it, on a pink, doughnut-shaped cushion with embroidered sprinkles. I unfasten the metal clasp that attaches to Portia's collar and drape the leash over the back of the chair.

"Just under fifty boxes left," Monicke calls to me from the front desk. She's put her laptop on the seat of her desk chair, and she kneels in front of it. She has a green-violet aura that feels good to be around this morning. "You want to take over from here, watch all these orders come in?"

"How fast are they selling?"

"Hey! There are only thirty-four left now!"

I look at the clock on the wall above us. A lime-green card is sticking out of my porcelain pocket mailbox.

"Are these affiliate sales or direct?" I'm just curious.

"They're everything sales," she says. "I'm not filtering."

I leave Portia on her doughnut and grab the lime-green note.

Come see me. XO E

I log in to my Affiliate Center. As it loads, I click back to check my email. A subject line stands out: *Some Feedback*. I don't recognize the sender. I read it, and my stomach goes cold.

I quickly click back to my Affiliate Center page, and scroll down to the line that reads Conscious Chocolate Collection. My breath catches in my throat, and I feel light-headed.

"Monicke," I say.

She must hear something in my voice, because she comes over to check out my screen herself.

"That was *you*, Canada!" she says. "That was all you!"

While I was asleep last night, I made an enemy. I also made ten thousand dollars in affiliate sales for chocolate.

"This is *lit*," Monicke says. She hops on her phone and thumbs it for music. "Hey, ladies," she shouts. "Canada just sold more than two thousand boxes of chocolates!"

She picks "Feed Me Diamonds" by MNDR. The music pillows in and moves all the space out until the room is full of its pulse. We dance. Portia jumps up, trying to reach the centre of the action, so

I pick up her little body and hold her in my arms. She barks, and I dance. Yolanda shoots me a tight, approving nod from the opposite side of the Temple. Eleven comes out of her office to join us, and she illuminates the room with her pink-white-lime aura, dancing with her arms in the air.

I meet Eleven in her office and bring the email to show her.

> Lilian. Im surprised you would exploit your experience not to mention the traumatic experiences of so many Good People for the sole purpose of giving yourself a platform and making money. Your starting to sound too American for my liking. I am disappointed in you and what you stand for and I have unsubscribed from your newsletters. I have been a follower for some time and was saving up to order a picture of my cat from you but there is something phoney and wrong about what you are doing now. its really too bad.

The email came from angelfyre@gmail.com and it was not signed.

"That's what the delete button is for," says Eleven. The late-morning light is golden, and I can feel the radiance of her office energy like a clear bell ringing through my body. What does she *do* in her office to make it feel so clear? Eleven's aura pulses. "You're not here to make everyone happy."

Portia whines from between my ankles. She's been staying close to me all day. "So you think I just delete it, and don't respond?"

"Just delete them all, honey," she says. "That's just the first of many. Do you know how much hate mail I receive every day?" She beams. "Delete them, and every time you press delete, treat it as a meditation bell. Take a breath and celebrate how far you've come. Delete—and think of what you've accomplished. Good things come to those who give light to the world. Truth is always light. You sharing your story the way you did—with so much transparency and openness—that integrity gives you payback. It's not always literally in cash, but hey! This time you got literal payback! You got dollars! You do not need to feel guilt about this. You deserve this."

My phone bleeps in my pocket. I thought I'd turned it to silent. "My phone has been acting up lately," I say. "Buzzing for no reason. Or beeping when it's not supposed to. Or not ringing, even when I turn the ringer on."

She nods. "We need upgrades," she says. "The whole team needs an upgrade. Yolanda will put in an order."

"But didn't we just get these?"

"They're two models old already. We just caught the tail end of this model, unfortunately. The new new model has a phenomenal camera."

Eleven looks utterly at peace, sitting at her white desk. The crystal in her window makes rainbow minnows sprint up the wall. My heart quickens.

"I feel confused," I tell Eleven, "about what to do next. I would like to feel more calm, more connected."

"I know. That's why I asked to see you today." Eleven says. She is quiet for a moment, and closes her eyes. "Okay, there's a lot going on for you," she says. "Tell me more. How does it feel when you say that? 'I feel confused.' How does that feel?"

I feel confused. There's a hardness in my chest. My skin feels woozy. "It doesn't feel good," I say. In Eleven's paper recycling basket, there's one of Jonathan Rasmussen's Active Meditation Institute postcards. "I feel kind of—heavy and breakable. Also, like my skin is dizzy."

"Good, good." Eleven opens her eyes. "Okay sweetie," she says. "If you feel heavy and breakable, if your skin feels dizzy when you say those words, then I'd like you to consider that the statement itself isn't coming from a place of truth and wholeness."

I nod. Portia whines. "Okay," I tell Portia. "In a minute."

"If you want to feel calm and connected," Eleven continues, "what is one thing you can do now to feel that way? Is there some way you could connect right now?" My phone buzzes again. Portia whines.

"I have no time to connect!" I say. "I have to take care of the five hundred emails from people who were felt up by their yoga teachers!

I have to plan the Ascendency Oahu retreat! I have to take care of the chocolate back orders! I have to edit the audio for your podcasts! I have to finish painting my commission for Nana Boondahl! I have to write my newsletters every week! I have to do my laundry!" I begin to hyperventilate. Everything in the room feels thin and transparent. Portia puts a paw up on my shin, and her paw is warm. She is an orange glow. "I have to take Portia for a walk," I say. "She has to pee."

"Breathe," Eleven says. "Okay, sweetheart. Breathe. You're overwhelmed. You need white space. Here's how to take care of your inbox. Write a letter to everyone, answering the FAQs. Just write one letter that can respond to everyone. You can be specific in the letter. Just send something out so you feel you have some space."

I take a deep breath and try to let it out evenly. My heart is still beating too fast. I haven't told Eleven about the auras I'm seeing around people, because there hasn't been any time since Portland. I want her to help me understand what's happening to me. It must *mean* something. I keep thinking I'm going to tell her, but whenever we have a chance to speak privately, she only wants to talk about work.

"Invite your followers to next year's Ascendency," she adds. "Schedule the email to go out soon, so they have time to plan to come to graduation. Use your affiliate link."

"I should invite them to Oahu?"

"They can come to Oahu for free if they register for the next Ascendency through you," she says. "It's a gift."

"Got it."

"What's the first thing you're going to do, love?"

"Delete the hatey email," I say.

Eleven puts her hands together in prayer position. "Always stay gracious," she says. "When in doubt, ask yourself, What would Beyoncé do?"

Arman smiles at me as we pass each other in the hallway. His aura is a glowing paprika red mixed with blush. He's carrying a bucket of wilted purple lilacs under his arm.

"Hey, Lilian," he says. "They found a new species of tarantula and named it after Johnny Cash!"

"Hey," I say, startled to see him. "Isn't it Thursday?" Arman always comes on Mondays.

"I switched to Thursdays last month," he says.

He did? Why didn't I notice? When were there lilacs? Were they here all week? They're my favourite! The Buddha has a fat bouquet of yellow tulips in his lap now. I missed the lilacs? I missed lilac week? Where have I been?

Dearest Lilian,

My darling, this poem is in honor of the wild space in your heart.

I wrote it to call for simple magic.

It recognizes, in you, the stillness at the center of a storm.

Love,
Eleven

P.S. To hear me reading this poem out loud to you, <u>click here for the audio version</u>.

You Don't Have to Hold It
(A poem for when life is too much)

There are days that I feel
Like everything I am to everyone I know
One hundred million points of reference
Crammed into my skin
Like the seeds of a pomegranate

I am a grenade
And with too much time spent
Holding it all
(My skin can't hold it)
(My heart can't hold it)
I will witness
A rupturing.
I am
So
Close.

But there is wild open space
The field of presence
The whiteness of this page:
I am whild.

It all comes back to this
The whiteness
The spaciousness, the intake
Of each breath

The sanctity that is openness

There are meadows of space
Every seed has an acre
I am full, I am full
Of gratitude.

IT's NOT JUST angelfyre, though. I read through the comments on the *WhaleMind* piece and feel sick. People love Jonathan Rasmussen so much! He has a loyal family of supporters, and they're all mad at me now. It's so true: one negative remark can overpower ten positive ones.

I can't stop thinking about angelfyre's email. This could be someone I met before, at a craft show. It's definitely someone from Canada. I read the note again and feel a wash of shame. Is angelfyre right about me? If I could take the piece down, I would. But I can't—the discussion threads are still active on *WhaleMind*. Did I overshare? Ugh, I overshared.

My bank balance is steadily rising. It's not all affiliate sales: my Temple paycheques go in there, too. Whenever I look at my bank account, the back of my neck tingles.

I ask my Potency Circle what to do, during our new moon video call. They all agree with Eleven: that it was right to have written the piece about my experience, and that I should ignore any negative feedback. This new moon is a supermoon in Aries, which marks the start of a new astrological cycle. It's time for a fresh start: Aries asks us to go forth and break old patterns, to envision new ways of doing things, both personally and in a greater sense.

"But I want to listen to *everyone*," I say to everyone on my screen.

"Lilian is so Canadian!" says Shona. She's sitting in front of her bedroom window, and the pine trees behind her blow in the wind. "She's so *nice*."

"You've given other women permission to name their own experiences," says Matilde. There's a slight delay in the video connection from France: her lips aren't moving with the sound of her voice.

Anoosh tells us that she took evening yoga classes when she was in high school. Yoga was still counterculture back then, she says, and the class was filled with women her mother's age. She was the youngest person in the class. It was held at the community centre in her small suburban town.

"Whenever I was in downward dog, the teacher liked to put his hand on my ass," she says. "I thought it was part of the class, what he called 'an adjustment.' But it never felt right to me. I didn't tell him to stop, and I should have."

"You were only a girrrlll—" says Matilde. Her face freezes, the video turning to a still of her blurred face, eyes half-closed.

"It's a boundary issue," says Shona. "Anoosh didn't speak up because there aren't always words for it. In that case, the pressure for her to stay quiet must have been immense."

There's a droopy beep, and Matilde's image disappears from the screen. "Oh no! We lost Matilde!" I say.

"What Lilian's done is start an important conversation," Shona continues. "Feathers are getting ruffled, which is understandable."

"She's breaking apart a very old paradigm," says Anoosh. Her face stops moving and then starts again.

"Sorry, everyone," I say. "I'm having connection problems. Something's using all my bandwidth." My Wi-Fi is password-protected, but maybe someone in this apartment building knows how to hack password-protected networks? I've heard of that happening.

"Lilian has exposed something real," says Shona, "and when truth reveals itself, it's going to feel uncomfortable."

"Shona, can you hear me?" I ask. "Can you see me?"

"I think we lost Lilian," says Anoosh. "Her face is frozen. Lilian? Are you there?"

◊ ◊ ◊

I'll just whip it off quickly tonight—write a newsletter to let people know they're invited to the graduation ceremony in Oahu, grab my affiliate code for the Ascendency, put in the link, and that's it. But it takes me two hours to get the wording right in the letter. And then another forty-five minutes to set up the link and schedule it in MailFix.

I open a box of spelt graham crackers and a container of fermented cashew cream spread. I use a bit of the cream like putty, stick two pieces of cracker together like a sandwich, and eat it. I do the whole thing again with another cracker. I sit on my bed, watching the pink-red glow of light rise up from the lower half of my building, where the sushi bar is hopping. Again, I think about how much Yumi would love it there. Oh, Yumi! I eat half the sleeve of graham crackers.

I'm doing it again! Eating unconsciously! I must stop! So soon after Portland, and already I slip into my old pattern. What can I do in this moment to connect?

On my kitchen counter, still wrapped in gold-flecked paper with a lime-green ribbon, is my box of Conscious Chocolate Truffles from Winnie. After our Sacred Eating workshop, she gave every Ascendant a box of her own to take home. I've been saving mine.

I read the instructions and get set up. For conscious chocolate eating it's best to create a clear space and a ritual. For tonight, that clear space is my bed. I pack up the remaining graham crackers and snap the lid back on the cashew spread. I wash my hands. How disgusting that was! Time to get sacred. I light a candle and place it on the shelf beside my mattress. I unfold the tissue paper, lay it on my bedspread, and place the box of chocolates on top of it. Then I crawl back up onto my platform bed, sit with my legs crossed, and close my eyes.

How do I want to feel? Magical. Creative. I want to feel *connected to my creativity*.

I wish Eleven were here right now. I wish we could go back to Portland and go on that sunset cruise again. I should have told her about what happened to me in the Forest Sanctuary when she asked. And I should tell her that I can see auras around people now. She's been believing in me since we were too young to talk! Why am I keeping secrets from her?

I picture Florence standing in front of me. The air around her stills and thrums from her presence. Her eyes are clear. She knows who I really am. Not my flat hair, my bulky thighs, my awkwardness. She sees past everything that's on the surface. When she looks at me, I feel true connection, as if we are one and the same, in the way trees are connected in a forest.

I state my intention: "I want to feel connected."

The lid of the box slides off with thick elegance, like it does when you open a brand-new iPad. The chocolates are nestled in rosy-coloured corrugated paper, separated into their individual compartments. They emit a pink, pearlescent glow and a coral-peach light. Sparkles flutter in my chest and stomach. I choose one of the coral ones to eat.

The chocolate is round and heavy, with a piece of crystallized orange rind resting on top. I put it in my mouth and close my eyes again.

"I want to feel creative," I mumble. My mouth is full with the chocolate: I keep it whole, rest it on my tongue.

Then I bite into it. The chocolate explodes, pure and cool in my mouth, a liquid of rich intensity. It tastes like mango, like spice, like earth, like rum. It folds over my tongue, blanketing it in dark sweetness. My heart beats faster.

I eat another one. This one has a pink aura, and crystallized rose petal on top. I have the sensation of a fizz against my skin—the aura feels like champagne! "I want to feel creatively connected," I say. "I want to paint."

I bite it. The centre is creamy, the consistency of coconut butter. It tastes like a garden of sugared flowers. The oils coat my mouth with delicate roses. I feel dizzy. It's so sweet! I can feel the ritual working. My arms and legs are buzzing. I see sparkles behind my eyes, and my body vibrates with coloured light.

"I want to be my highest self," I say. And then I eat another.

Dear Lilian,

I am sitting in a geodesic dome as I write this letter. A massive storm system passes overhead. The cedar trees are thrashing all around me, as if to say, You will not rest until you say what you need to say.

This is not an easy email to write. There is something I need to share with you, my students, colleagues and friends, that I've never shared with anyone before.

I've kept this secret to myself for so many years, I didn't know if I'd even have words to tell it. Until now—it's become clear, in light of recent events, that I need to let this out, that I cannot stay silent any longer.

I hesitated even this morning, before I sat down to write this letter. I was worried about my reputation. I was afraid that if I revealed the truth, you wouldn't like me anymore. I was afraid that no one would love me—that people would hate me.

I was afraid that people would think I was doing this as some kind of self-promotion, to get media attention.

But when I became very still, I knew that I had to do it anyway. Because if I can help even one or two people by being honest about what happened to me, it would be worth it.

I've never spoken about this in public, though I have written about my uncle Robert before, in previous newsletters. This is a very different kind of story that I'm telling about my uncle Robert.

Because of the nature of my story, I asked a trusted teacher, Roshi Kyle Bird from the Alive Institute in Minneapolis, if he'd lead the conversation, because he is trusted in so many overlapping spiritual and secular circles. I needed to be vulnerable—perhaps the most vulnerable I've ever been—and I needed his help, so I could tell my story honestly. We recorded our conversation, made this podcast, and released it today. To download the audio file, right-click (or press ctrl-click if you're on a Mac).

Note: This podcast contains a story that concerns physical and sexual abuse, and may be a trigger for some listeners.

Blessings,
Jonathan

I WAKE UP with heavy hands pressing on my chest. My mouth is full of flour and water. I can't breathe. She is pushing me underwater but the water is made of glue. My neck hurts. I'm wearing an emerald necklace, with diamonds set all around it. Get it off my neck! I pull at it and pull at it until something snaps. Diamonds and emeralds fall down my chest. Her hands don't let up. My body burns. My skin is angry. What's on my legs? I'm kicking something hot and it stings—it's a reef made of fibreglass. Stones are rolling into my eyes. Everywhere they touch me, they sting. I can't move my arms. My legs are in poison water, acid burns. I can't breathe. Get off! Get off me!

In the morning I find a string of texts from Juliette on my phone.

> Juliette
> I'm coming to New York on April 22.
> Want to have brunch?

> Juliette
> I'm staying at Smithany in SoHo

> Juliette
> LDIC conference—look it up

> Juliette
> Hey YOU should come! It's for lifestyle bloggers

> Juliette
> Txt me xx!

It's Friday. A siren screams on the street, under my window. The sound is a strange, broken blooping. The morning light comes in without asking. My body is itchy. There are little red dots all over my calves—like pimples, but hard and itchy. A rash! I run my fingers up one leg, from ankle to knee, and this sets my skin on fire. I must be having a reaction. Did I brush up against something? Is there a spider in my bed? It's so itchy!

A shower doesn't help. The hot water makes the bumps angrier. I put on grey leggings and cover up with my ombré forest-green-to-turquoise kimono and pour myself warm water with the juice of half a lemon. Need to get alkaline. This is major inflammation.

I check the comments on my *WhaleMind* piece. Now people are arguing about Jonathan Rasmussen's latest podcast. I close the screen—I can't even read the conversation anymore. Angelfyre's email is still in my inbox. I know Eleven is probably right about deleting it, so why am I keeping it? It's not as if I'm going to reply: any response I come up with feels defensive and pathetic. Thank you for reaching out? You're wrong about me? I'm sorry, I'm sorry? So I just hang on to the email and feel sick about it.

More sirens outside, and now the smell of smoke, woody and dangerous. The sun shines brightly in a clear blue sky as if there is no problem whatsoever. As if this is a beautiful day, and there are no pressures.

My legs are so itchy. I should drink rooibos today. It would be soothing. There's a box in the cupboard above the sink. I look up the LDIC while the tea steeps.

LIFESTYLE DESIGN AND INSPO-PRENEURSHIP CONFERENCE

A conference for bloggers, storytellers, lifestyle designers, and brand artists. Be inspired. Tell your story!

Keynote speakers
Friday: Juliette Lafromboise,
CEO of Pure Juliette
Saturday: Don Joseph of The Daily Design
Sunday: Grafton Hope Davies of
Alive + Smithing

April 22–24
New York, NY

Maybe it would be good for me to take a break from the Temple, see how other bloggers are doing it. Juliette is headlining! She could introduce me to the other artists there, and I could do some networking. Yes, it would be good for me to get a new perspective.

Me

Just looked at LDIC!
Congrats, keynote!

Me

I'd love to come. I'll get a ticket!

When I get to the Temple, Monicke, Anna-Mackenzie, and Yolanda are in leggings, rolling up yoga mats in the lobby.

"Did I miss yoga?" I ask. "Sorry I'm late. I had a bad sleep last night."

"Spring cleansing poses," Monicke says. "Not yoga. Rich Movement, to help us transition with the season."

Yolanda points. "What happened to your neck?"

"Can you take Portia for me, please?" Anna-Mackenzie says. "This just in: Eleven wants a new website." Her eyes go to my neck and then up to my face again.

"What is it?" I ask. Is something wrong with my neck?

"New design," says Yolanda. "Everything has to be updated in time for summer." Her phone rings in C tone.

It's so weird—it's just the single note, and it should sound like a bell, like any of our other bells, but Yolanda's tone always sounds relaxing to me. We close our eyes and stand in mountain pose, breathe in and out. Monicke exhales with a loud "haaa" breath. I open my eyes. The colours around all three women swirl, like smoke. Anna-Mackenzie's eyes are still closed, but she holds her hand out gently to me, palm up. The pink leash is looped around her hand. She emanates pink and periwinkle light. Yolanda's lavish eyelashes are magnified through the lenses of her glasses. How long does it take Yolanda to get ready in the morning? Where does she get her hair done in twists like that? How does she keep her skin so clear? I mean, why doesn't she ever break out? Does she use SPF in her moisturizer? Her eyes flash open as if she can hear my thoughts.

Anna-Mackenzie hands me the leash and presses the elevator call button.

"A new website? But we aren't even finished prepping for Oahu," I say.

Yolanda looks at me. "You want to tell her to wait for that?" she says. "Go ahead."

Monicke tries to laugh quietly, which is impossible for her. She makes a hissing sound like an espresso machine.

"I've ordered our new Temple phones," Yolanda tells Monicke. "Keep an eye out for the courier today."

"And install Eleven's new app in the phones as soon as they arrive," Anna-Mackenzie says.

"Last night's new moon was a supermoon in Aries," Monicke says. "So there's a lot more energy to harness right now."

"I had intense dreams," I say. "Did either of you have dreams last night? I mean, I dreamt someone was trying to kill me. Her hands were pressing all the air out of my chest and I couldn't breathe, and something was choking me, something around my neck." I touch my neck, and the skin is sensitive. I can still feel the dream in my body.

Are they staring at me, or just waiting for me to finish? I keep talking. "I woke up with this rash all over my legs. Hives. I've never had hives before—I wonder if I ate something? If I have an allergy? I'm so, so itchy!" Portia's ears go up, and she looks at the elevator. "Do you think the moon has anything to do with my dreams?" I ask.

The elevator dings and the doors split apart. "Could be," says Anna-Mackenzie. She and Yolanda walk into the elevator. Their light mingles together—purple and yellow-pink, with flickers of bright fuchsia. Portia moves to follow them, but I hold the leash to keep her back.

When they're gone, Monicke says, "I'll look up what Louise Hay says hives mean, emotionally."

Portia smiles at me. Her teeth are white pegs, her pink tongue a wad of chewing gum. Her black nose is wet and alive. Black and white whiskers sprout out of her fleshy snout. Her ears, like shells my mom would sell in her co-op, are set wide on her fist-shaped head.

Coarse white fur grows in the place where each ear meets skull. She blinks, licks her lips, and rests her head on her paws, delicately bringing her ears back the way a beetle folds its wings. Oh, I want to paint her! I wish I had time to think about painting again.

Hives, apparently, are an expression of anger in the body. Monicke asks me if I'm angry.

"I don't think so," I say. "I don't *feel* angry."

"That's why the hives," she says. "If you could feel your anger, then you might not need hives to show you you're angry."

Our new phones arrive. I spend the rest of the morning syncing my old phone to the new one, fixing the settings to make sure my email account and social media accounts are connected. I transfer my contacts, calendar, apps, and podcasts. I ring my desk meditation bell, record the sound of A, and upload it as my ring tone. Beside me, Portia bites and licks her toes obsessively. I open TewDew and look over my list of tasks for the day, and my spine becomes ice-cold liquid metal.

The list is infinite, specific, detailed, crucial, and unfinishable. I cannot do the things on my list. I will never finish all these things. My phone makes a new sound, a soft, wooden-sounding bell I've never heard before.

Stop what you're doing.
Remember, the Universe is energy!

Who sent that? My neck itches again—are the hives spreading? I turn on my phone camera so I can take a look.

There's a red line of dots around my collar. I lift my kimono to see it better. It looks like a red cord, a necklace of irritation. It's shaped like a *V* and goes down between my breasts. Wait! Where is my mala?

"Good morning, petals! I'm not really here, you don't see me! I'm just here to pick up my new phone." Eleven's bracelets make a tinkling sound as she walks down the hall, toward my desk. She gestures to her throat. "Ooh, sweetie, you're having a nasty reaction to something."

Portia stops licking and stands up. Ears up. Her orange light rises in the air around her, glinting like cellophane, crinkling and full of movement.

Eleven looks at me carefully. She wants something from me. Or is this connection? I smile. I feel like I'm wearing a scarf made of razor blades. "Let me see," she says.

When I stand up, I tuck my new phone into my kimono pocket, and the weight pulls me down on one side. It's bigger than our last phone—the screen is wider, and even though the body is thinner, the new phone feels awkward. It buzzes every minute, because the default settings on all my apps are set to send me push notifications again.

I let Eleven look at my neck. "Are you feeling okay, darling?" She puts her arm around my waist, and her bracelets tap against the phone in my pocket.

"I think I'm overwhelmed," I answer.

"Why don't you take Portia out for a walk," she says. "Go to the park. Breathe in the fresh air, let yourself feel grounded in nature."

Dear FIRST NAME,

A SPECIAL INVITATION FOR YOU!

When you pre-register through me for the next Ascendency, you're welcome to join me in Oahu this May FOR FREE, to take part in our graduation ceremony and find out more about the program first-hand!

At graduation, you will be treated with special care as a brand-new Ascendant. I will share my experience with you, and usher you into the community by introducing you to the **Sacred Ascendency Prayer** so you can see how it works in practice. You'll also learn powerful Ascendant meditation and clearing techniques, like **Compost Heaving** and **Mirroring**.

I would love to meet you in person, celebrate your essential self in Hawaii, and welcome you to Ascendency!

Click here to register for next year's Ascendency program, and come to the FREE graduation ceremony experience.

Thank you for being a friend to me, for your support and encouragement, and for being with me on this journey.

With love,
Lilian

THE AIR IS vibrating—it's edgy, warmer than I thought it would be. I'm sweating in my leggings, and my inflamed thighs and calves prickle in the heat. My phone dings and dings in my pocket. Portia sniffs the trunk of a spindly sidewalk tree and lifts one paw up, tentatively, over a patch of ground. Her hind legs quiver and her eyes stare off into the distance of Central Park. "Let's cross the street here," I tell her. "Sit, and wait for the light."

I take my phone out and find Settings. A black car passes us closely—my body feels the air waver from the speed. How do I turn off push notifications? Portia's leash goes tight—she's crossing the street—and I follow her.

I slide my finger up and down the screens, looking for clues. *Push notifications*: I touch the screen. *On.* I touch it again and the nubby bar turns from green to grey. *Off.* A red circle notifies me of 3,204 new emails. What are those red circles called? Badges? How do I turn them off? I slide my finger through Settings, looking for anything that mentions badges. Turn them off. How do I turn them off? I'm on the other side of the street now. The park shines ahead of me. The leash slackens and tightens and slackens as Portia pulls me to sniff the rocks and hedges in the park. I can't read three thousand new emails!

The ground on one side of us is carpeted in old crocuses, past their best days, leaning on each other and starting to look sleepy, but still bright purple and yellow and white. On the other side, the sun glitters the rocks, dusting them with gold. Sheep Meadow is alive in this sunshine. The grass looks wet and glazed in honey. Is it brighter than normal? I can't stop looking at the grass. I feel funny. My phone dings twice in a row, two sharp bleats. Portia pulls my arm out and up. I feel the leash going up, like I'm holding a kite. Everything hums around me. A cardinal makes a sound like a tight pirouette. His red feathers and green aura make a contrast that dizzies me, and my stomach makes a turbulent flip. I feel too many colours all at once. The oak trees radiate. The sky is full of the hot sun. Prisms shoot out of the branches and hover over my skin. The colours of everything crash and collide in my body. When I try to understand where one colour starts and stops, I feel black spots in the air, like rotten places where the light is missing. I lean against a rock and close my eyes to make the colours stop.

"Are you okay?" someone is saying.

I squint my eyes open. It's all navy blue, threaded with violet.

"Can you hear me?" The blue light surrounds a man's face.

"I'm fine," I say. "I just had a head rush. Low blood pressure." The leash hangs from my hand. Friday sniffs my shoe with curiosity. I mean Portia, not Friday. I can't keep the colours separate. Everything feels blended. Time and space are bleeding into each other. What is happening to me?

"Are you sure?" the man says. "Why don't I wait with you for a minute." He is wearing a trench coat, a bow tie, and a fedora. His aura is golden-green with pale blue. He looks like a gentleman from another era. Is he part of the past? An angel? Have I tripped through a tesseract?

"I'm here now," I say. "Thank you for your kindness." I hug him, and feel his bright energy flow through me. He feels true.

I power down my phone, pressing the button until I'm sure it's lifeless. Portia and I walk back to the Temple. Her orange aura looks the way it always does: cheerful and snug. The air is opalescent, filled with translucent hues from everything. The colours shift like curtains moving in the wind. I feel woozy. I get on the elevator and press the button to go up. I give Portia to Monicke and say I'm feeling sick, and I need some time off.

◊ ◊ ◊

The floor of my apartment is cold, smooth, and gritty. Two of the rudrakasha seeds from my broken mala have rolled under the stove. They lie there with glowing green auras, like forgotten frozen peas. I would never have seen them if I hadn't crawled down on the floor like this. My phone is eerily silent. It's still in my jacket pocket, hanging from the hook beside the door. Since I've turned it off, I've been hearing phantom dings, just in my head. I am so conditioned to respond to my phone, I jolt even when I hear imaginary beeps. Cold air is coming down from somewhere. The window is open to the street below—just a crack. The air sneaks in, drops to the floor, and rolls to where I am lying on my stomach.

My cheek is pressed to the floor. The floor has a silvery white light touched with mint green. I smell cigarette smoke from outside. A siren calls from far away, at least a few blocks. A little piece of indirect sunlight floats in the window, cold and flimsy, reflected by the windows across the street. I hear another ding in my head, and I feel a buzz, like a shock in my chest. Those two beads under the stove. The crystals are faceted. They're standing on a patch of white, powdery dust. The dust has a blue aura.

When I slow way down, I can focus on the auras of everything. Now I just have to practise turning it on and off so I don't make myself sick again.

The floor is a cool, walnut brown. I am lying parallel to the strips of flooring. I am lying with the grain of the wood. I open up my peripheral vision and let the silver-green colour hover there, in the wings of my eyes, so I can see the wood without feeling the coloured light.

My hives must be a sign of stress. It's this Aries supermoon—new moons are all about inner work, visioning, and personal reflection. I don't know how long it will take me to feel better. Eleven will understand why I need time away, but I'm not sure Yolanda will like it—it's a bad time to be away from the Temple. Anna-Mackenzie was gone last month, but she was having a family crisis, which is different from this. What *is* this?

I hear the sound of a wooden bell—the sound of the Universe texting me through Eleven's new app. But my phone is off.

When I picture my phone, I feel nauseous. There's a force field that won't let me even go near it. I can't go back to the Temple yet.

The two rudrakasha seeds stand like tiny monuments. I won't touch them. They will stay under the stove for the next tenant to find. Maybe they'll stay there forever. *Listen to the messages from your body. Do no more than three things a day. Rest until you want to play; play until you want to rest. Let yourself want what you want.*

Okay. My box of coloured pencils is under the coffee table. And my sketchbook. I can reach them from here on the floor.

I push the pencils under the metal blade and twist. The smell of sharpened colouring pencils is wood and berries. Waxy shreds of orange and lemon and emerald green crumble under my fingers.

I work tentatively, at first.

I draw what I can see from where I sit on the floor—the seeds from my broken mala, my coffee table, the front door. I use my pencils, some ink, and a dab of watercolour. While I'm drawing, all the auras harmonize and make more sense. The goldenrod yellow from the table is coherent with the mint green of the floor, the way the flavour of basil supports the flavour of tomatoes. I experiment with opening my peripheral vision as I draw, and gradually I let more and more in, until I feel the colours I'm painting. It's satisfying to work this way, becoming the lines, becoming the colours. I draw until the day goes out. Then I go to sleep.

I do this for several days. It feels so good. My hives stop itching and begin to disappear, my appetite surges, and I feel strong enough to turn my phone back on to order food. I left the cord at my desk at the Temple, but this new phone has a longer-lasting battery than my old one. How long will it live without power? I clear my notifications without reading them, and ignore everything.

My guy comes twice a day: he delivers me Skyscraper Black Bean Burgers from Café Blossom, squash and spinach tofu quiche from Peacefood, Dragon Bowls from Quintessence, and fresh cashew milk from Organic Avenue. I eat chia seed and almond milk pudding all day, because for some reason, I have two full bags of chia seeds in my cupboard. I never have to leave my apartment.

My drawings turn into paintings. I'm glad I brought my Fabriano pads from Toronto. I use a butter knife to slice the pages free from their seal as I go through them.

After a week, my phone battery is at 10 percent.

Me

hello my phone is doing

Me

Sorry! Doing

Me

not doing Doing!

Me

AGH DYING

Me

also I might need more tie

Me

*time

Eleven

(...)

Me

Is everything ok at the Temple?

Eleven

(...)

Me

Is it ok that I take a few more days?

Eleven

I want to see you.

Me

Of course! Me too!

Eleven

When?

Me

please give me a week

Eleven

I'll see you first thing on Thursday

Me

k!

Me

Can you please bring my phone cord?

Me

Tx!

In my mind and body, I can feel the pink shimmer all around Sophia's head. I try it with white mixed with red, and drop in the tiniest speck of blue. I use my finger and a piece of tissue to mush the water in and absorb it in the same instant. I haven't used my fingers like this before—it's messy—but the shape of the blob I just made, there behind her eye, feels true. I keep it. I have no choice but to keep it; this is watercolour.

I feel ink spreading out by her paws before I see it. I have to be careful, to keep the white of her paws white. The ink is a confident black. Too dark for Sophia herself, but just right to show the form of the pillow she's sitting on. I push my brush around the bottom of the page and move the ink like shadow through my fingers. Her paws will be white. When it dries, I will see the contrast. Wait for the next phase. Patience. Let it dry.

While it dries, I go to the other piece. I dip a rigger brush into the bottle of pale-yellow masking fluid and drag it lightly in several quick strokes near the inside of Portia's ear. Portia has pink shell ears. The scarlet is transparent pink on the watercolour paper. I layer scarlet in broad strokes and paint right over the masking fluid. The hairs on the inside of her ears are white. I dip in the masking fluid again and repeat for her other ear. The lines are pale and barely visible but they protect the paper. When they dry, I'll rub them off and they'll show the white paper underneath. Again, for her whiskers. Three on each side. I'll add more in dark brown in the final phase.

Let it dry. Can't speed the process. The paint takes the time that it takes. The other piece is ready for me now. I work on Sophia while Portia dries.

I work like this for hours, moving back and forth between the two portraits of these dogs, suffusing myself first in Portia's sweet orange, then Sophia's hot pink. At some point, I start crying. I become the coloured light as I paint it. My tears pucker the pigment and make little whitefish asterisks on the wash of tangerine, because tears are salty and salt absorbs water. The pigment ripples, and it is true. Everywhere a tear falls on the page, it is true. I am so happy. I am grateful. I am in awe of creation. I paint slowly, using thin, barely perceptible washes of transparent colour. While I wait for the paper to dry between layers, I lie on the floor and stare at the ceiling.

I find elegance and hope in Sophia's pose. Her restfulness brings me calm—the way her four silver paws collect in a bundle underneath her on the picture plane, anchoring the portrait. Her paws are a bouquet placed at the feet of an opera singer. The pink aura around her brings me hopeful energy, familiar and warm. It's the best portrait I've ever done.

Nana Boondahl will be pleased.

When I'm painting, I'm connected to everything around me. I become the colour, I become the lines, I become the subjects that I'm painting. This is who I really am! I don't even feel like "Lilian Quick" right now. There is no "Lilian."

I laugh out loud. *This* is connection. I don't need a name! I don't even know what day it is.

I love this. I love, love, love, love, love, love, love it.

◊ ◊ ◊

After two weeks of this, Eleven visits. She brings me strawberry rooibos and an armful of branches dotted with pink cherry blossoms. "Are you really sick?" she asks. "Talk to me."

Where do I start? Seeing her stand in my doorway in her white moto jacket and those tall microsuede boots and her pink and green light makes my heart beat faster. Why am I nervous to see her? I wasn't lying about being sick. But how can I explain this?

"I needed a chance to recover before Oahu," I say. I go into my recycling bucket and dig through all the takeout containers until I find the glass cashew milk bottles from Organic Avenue. I rinse them out and fill them with water, for the cherry branches.

"If you need a rest, please come to me first," Eleven says. "Before leaving everyone like that." She gives me the branches and I unwrap them on my counter. I put one branch in each bottle and place the bottles in a line on my coffee table. They look nice.

"We were all concerned, sweetheart."

I feel a lump like putty in my throat. I let her down. I'm sabotaging myself again. Why do I always have to ruin every good thing that happens to me?

"I'm sorry," I say. "I've been so stressed out, and I've been afraid to tell you." That doesn't feel entirely true. "Ascendency has been bringing a lot up for me. I don't know how to talk about the things I'm feeling. I'm processing." That's true enough.

Eleven pulls my phone cord out of her pocket and hands it to me. "You can't just disappear on us," she says.

"I've been painting," I say. I plug my phone into the cord and set it on the counter.

"I can see that." She looks around my apartment. The floor is strewn with my watercolour sketches, balled-up tissue, and several glass jars. Each is full of water in a different colour, from murky grey-blue to clear pinky-orange.

"What day is it today?" I ask.

The room is quiet. Even the traffic goes still. Eleven looks deep into my eyes. Her pupils are black pools ringed with bright blue. Her aura is as blue as the sky, it's beyond blue, it's suffused with violet and green and gold. I feel my breathing go quiet.

"Lilian, is this working for you?" she asks. "Is this what you really *want*?"

Sadness plunges into my abdomen, bleak and cold. This was all too good to be true, wasn't it? It's finally happening. I've ruined everything.

"Because I can help you," she continues. "Wherever you want to be, whatever your heart most desires—I can help you get there. I see your potential. You're luminous. I can support you, strengthen you, and show you how to find your own highest self. But unless you *want* to see it, I can't help you. If you aren't ready to rise, just say so."

"I'm so sorry," I say. "I'm really *trying* to find my highest self."

She looks at me. "Maybe this just isn't the right path for you."

"No!" I say. "I love the Temple! I love being an Ascendant!" All the new colours, the way I'm painting, this connection I'm feeling— it's all because of the Temple! I *can't* leave. What would happen to me? Where would I go, if I had to leave New York? Toronto? I can't go to my old apartment. I can't call Yumi. They haven't responded to any of my texts, and I don't blame them. I've destroyed our friendship. The only person in the world who maybe loved me. I can't go back. What would I do? Live with my mother in Florida?

"I'm on the right path," I say.

"I didn't think it through," Eleven says. "Knowing you the way I do."

"I'm rising," I say. "This is me rising."

"You're very sensitive. I may have asked too much."

"I was in a zone, I was painting, and I just forgot about time and space." A wind blows through the open window and pushes some of the papers around the floor. "But I'm here now," I say. "I'm here."

"We live in a world that worships linearity, structure, productivity, and commerce," Eleven says. "It's a patriarchal system, so it makes sense that as you tap into your feminine power, you feel alienated from it. As you mature as an Ascendant, you have to practice using your power *without* disrupting life for others."

"I'm sorry I left you for so long," I say. "Can I show you what I've been working on?"

"Everyone on the team has been hustling double-time to cover your tasks," Eleven says. "And I've started coming in on Fridays. So we're in okay shape. We're working with Flight Co. on the design for the new site. Yolanda is managing the whole redesign process, so all you have to do is coordinate with Monicke and Anna-Mack on Oahu communication. They can get you up to speed tomorrow."

I look at my phone. The apple symbol disappears and my home screen rises. Immediately, it begins buzzing and dinging and popping again. What is that new sound? My screen loads with new texts and notifications.

"When Bea taught me how to swim in the ocean, she told me that sometimes you're going to be pulled by a strong undertow. When that happens, you *think* you have to swim closer to shore, to where the waves are breaking, because it feels closer to safety. It's counterintuitive, she said, but you want to actually follow the water's energy. You have to hold your breath and go under, and let yourself be pulled far away from shore, if you want to live."

I want to say, *But wasn't that how Bea was killed?* But I know death is a metaphor for transformation. "Yes, I get it," I say.

"These last weeks leading up to graduation are very rich," Eleven says to me. "I know they're intense—I designed them to feel like this. Give yourself whatever you need so you can let the metamorphosis occur."

"But that's what I was trying to do this whole time!" I cry.

"Oh, sweetheart," she says. "Good. Let out your anger."

"Sorry," I say. "That came out wrong. I meant to say thank you. Because it's so important to rest, and integrate all these changes to my mind and body. It really has been an adjustment."

Eleven takes in the paintings around me. "These are really something," she says. I can't tell if she likes them or not. "You've been working on these all week?"

"I've finished a commission for Nana Boondahl," I say. "I was so behind on it, and I finally got inspired."

"*The* Nana Boondahl?" she looks shocked. "How do you know her?"

"She's coming to New York, and asked me to have it ready for her."

"You'll be meeting her here?"

"Next weekend," I say.

Eleven touches the cherry branches and twists one of them so the flowers face the window instead of the bed. "Can you come to work tomorrow," she says, but it's not a question. "Harness all that creative energy. You're starting to wake up. It's uncomfortable, but you are alight. Bring that light to the Temple tomorrow. I want you to *use* it."

I am using it, I want to say. But something in her eyes stops me. She's coming on strong, like she does when she's onstage. Her aura has turned grey-blue and green. I feel opaque places in her colour, like thick puffs of cloud, that make it hard for my eyes to breathe. Does she even see me, or am I just an audience right now?

Maybe she's right: I should put my energy into something bigger, more transcendent, something that connects to the whole Universe. If my true gift is seeing the energy of the Universe through auras, then *this* is obviously what I need to be doing. I need to share my special power with the world.

Then again, maybe there's something else that she wants from me.

She opens the door. Her hair is a golden cloud, her face is soft, and her eyes are piercing blue. Her energy has cleared, and it's golden-green. "Remember to breathe," she says. "Tomorrow, bring your integrated, connected self." Before she leaves, she adds, "And prepare to slay. We have a kick-ass graduation ceremony to pull off in two weeks, and a groundbreaking new website to launch this summer." She closes the door behind her.

Dear Lilian,

As you get ready for our Ascendency graduation ceremony in Oahu—this is our two-week countdown!—you may find yourself questioning things you used to believe to be true.

You may find yourself unable to tolerate the same things you used to tolerate from the people you love. Behaviors that were once common in your life may now start to feel wrong. Keeping a secret may now feel like harboring a poison dart in your body. Energy-sucking people—even your family and friends—may repel you now.

You are growing, my darling sparrow. And it is a beautiful thing to behold. You are becoming light. And light cannot tolerate the dark.

What were you enduring in your old life? What was normal for you to tolerate?

This is your lovingly curated, cultivated, nourished life. This is not the time to tolerate anything. Endurance is for a marathon runner, not an awakened woman.

What did you put up with before Ascendency changed you? What have you discovered about yourself and the people you know?

What will you put up with now, with all your uncovered light? **We meet for our final Teleritual next Saturday. For full instructions on how to dial in and for your Element Incantation, <u>click here</u>.**

In this Teleritual, we will be working on conscious reversal through Mirroring. If you have already experienced Mirroring,

you know a little bit about what to expect. It is important
that you integrate Mirroring into your practice now, before we
meet in Hawaii, so you can bring your fully elevated self to our
graduation ceremony.

As you will see, there is no hiding in Mirroring. It will lift the veil
from your eyes, and show you that you have the courage to see
reality. Your work as an Ascendant will give you the strength to
bear it, so you may always remain awake.

I cannot wait to Ascend with you.

With love,
Eleven

P.S. Due to a scheduling change, Jonathan Rasmussen won't
be presenting at Ascendency Oahu next month, but I'm thrilled
to announce that Zaphira Patel will be leading us in sacred
rhythmic dance on all three days. Zaphira is the founder of
Priestess Movement™, and she has certified thousands of
PM teachers in her teaching centers, located all over North
America as well as in Costa Rica and Bali. I know you will have
a powerful experience. Click here to meet Zaphira and learn
more about the profound work that she's doing at her Miami-
based Priestess Movement™ studio. An updated schedule for
Ascendency Oahu can be found here.

IN THE TEMPLE on Friday morning, Eleven's scent permeates the air with caramel and flowers. There's something else, too—a woody sweetness. The windows are open, letting in the spring breeze. Hyacinth? Freesia? The energy in the Temple is clean and muted, the way the atmosphere feels after a Compost Heave. Someone has been crying. My body can sense it: a field of wavering brightness surrounds me.

"We've been calling you," Yolanda says.

"My phone has been off," I tell Yolanda.

"Have you not received our calls?" she asks. The tips of her blouse collar are edged in brassy metal points, like arrowheads. Her necklace hangs just under the collar, a fan of long white stones. Her aura is vivid purple-blue, electric.

"I've been setting digital boundaries," I say. "Now I'm focused, and ready to work."

"Did you see the news this morning?"

"I haven't looked at my phone," I say.

"Prince died." Monicke speaks these words with unusual quiet. She is obviously shaken. Her aura is clear, sapphire blue.

"We had a moment for him together in yoga this morning," says Anna-Mackenzie.

"It's a Rich Movement class," Monicke murmurs. "I don't teach yoga anymore."

"You missed it," Yolanda says to me.

Aside from "When Doves Cry," which I rewound and replayed on my Walkman until I warped the tape, I never really connected with Prince's music. He lived in Toronto, didn't he? At least some of the time?

"First David Bowie, now Prince," I say. "I can't believe it."

"He was my king," Monicke says.

"I understand you needed to process some personal issues," Yolanda says. "Is there anything we should know about?"

"I'm sorry I wasn't here," I say. "I'm really, really sorry. But I'm feeling integrated and strong now."

"The Ascendency can be confronting," Yolanda says.

"I'm here," I say. "I'm ready for Oahu prep. I promise I'm ready."

There are letters tucked into my envelope on the wall. I don't read them right away, but I put them in my bag. I brought my water-colour of Portia today, in a frame that I found in a store on Twelfth. It's made from different kinds of tropical wood, with an inlaid her-ringbone pattern. Portia comes over to greet me when I go to my desk, and gives me an ankle sniff and a low-to-the-ground stretch, like a formal bow.

"Look what I made!" I say to her, and I pull out the portrait. "That's you!"

"Wow, Canada, that looks just like Portia," says Monicke. "You did that?"

"I love it!" says Anna-Mackenzie.

Yolanda surprises me when I turn around from the altar. "Did you paint that?" she says. "Eleven wants to talk to you."

I sit at the meeting table across from Eleven and Yolanda. The fibre-optic daylight lamp spits a circle of sunshine on the floor.

"Tell us what's up with your phone," Yolanda says.

The light in this room confuses me. Where is the window, if there is this spot of warm light? I've never noticed how off-putting it is to sit with ghost sunshine. Is it even real?

"When I turn it on, it buzzes too much," I say. I look in my tote, and push aside the mail I picked up earlier. There's a letter from Nana Boondahl! A real letter, with a Canadian stamp! It's a Year of the Monkey stamp, cherry red. I pull out my phone. It gleams in my hand, powerless. "I turned it off. I'm starting to hate it."

"This *is* a full Scorpio moon," Eleven says. "We are all touching the shadow side right now, in one way or another. What we need to do is try to recognize the darkness without naming it." She makes a mudra with her hands—index fingers touching thumbs, two little circles. "If you name the darkness, you will be tempted to separate it from light and joy. But everything is whole, together. Death and life are inseparable. Everything is complete in energetic form." Is she still talking about my phone? Or is this about Prince?

"I'm really, really sorry I didn't call last week," I say.

Yolanda's eyebrows tighten and release. "Thank you for acknowledging that," she says.

"The Temple is not a productivity factory," says Eleven. "We don't run our business by the masculine ideals of progress."

"But I know the new website is happening," I say, "and all the communication for Ascendency graduation needs to be scheduled to go out."

Yolanda nods sharply. "There was a problem with chocolate orders. Winnie Prudhomme wasn't notified about the high demand, so we are on emergency back order. We've collected all the payments, but clients don't know the chocolates won't be available until summer."

"In the Temple, we make room for feeling and process," Eleven says. "We are human beings, not machines."

"You want me to call all the people," I say.

"I want you to know that you don't have to be afraid to ask for time off when you need personal time."

"We make time for personal work," adds Yolanda. "Like Anna-Mackenzie last month. We all help each other."

"If we don't work together, the model breaks down," says Eleven. "We are all integral parts of a whole. Mental, spiritual, physical, and emotional health is all interrelated. Health and work cannot be compartmentalized. This is why feminine leadership is the change that the whole world needs to see."

Yolanda nods again. "Also, Lupin Thorne has sent her head shot for the Oahu print program, but it's low-res, and the shot is too . . ." Yolanda looks at Eleven.

"It's a little too corporate for us," Eleven says.

"We need you to Photoshop it, maybe make it black and white. Or see if she has another one for us."

"She's Money in the Morphogenetic Field, right?" I can't put this into TewDew, because my phone is off. I have to remember this.

"Right," says Yolanda. "She does a lot of corporate consulting, which is why her photo looks the way it does."

"You just have to tell us," Eleven says. "If you need time off to process some of the stuff coming up for you as an Ascendant, we can help you."

"I promise, it won't happen again."

"We need you to be strong," Eleven says. "The whole team is under a lot of stress right now."

"I'll figure out how to fix my phone," I say. *"Courage is action in the presence of fear."*

In the afternoon, the energy in the Temple is quiet and focused. Monicke stands at her desk in bare feet, stretching out her foot muscles on her Rich Movement pad of stones. She's wearing her purple crystal headphones and her whole body is in subtle motion as she types. She's moving her head side to side, her shoulders are weaving in and out, her calves move up and down as she steps over the rocks and stones underfoot. She's dance-typing, and her aura is a muted blend of powder blue and cadet blue.

Anna-Mackenzie's red hair sunsets around her face in waves. She wears a chunky bracelet made of rose gold and pressed newspaper. The rose gold looks lovely against her skin and compliments her freckles. She sips tea out of a white mug and types something into her phone. Her aura is clear pink and yellow. When she senses me watching her, she looks up from her tiny screen and motions for me to come closer.

"Check your affiliate account," she whispers.

I go back to my desk and do what she said.

My followers have not only bought hundreds and hundreds of Eleven's malas, cosmetics, jeans from Manifested Denim, and Conscious Chocolates, they've also been registering for the next Ascendency, through me. I receive three thousand dollars for each new Ascendant I bring to the program, and my recommendations have convinced sixty-eight women to come to the Ascendency graduation ceremony in Hawaii next week! Sixty-eight women signed up because they read my newsletter and blog post, and used my link. I don't recognize any of their names.

I have over three hundred thousand dollars in my affiliate account! How much tax will I have to pay on that? What happens when I turn this into Canadian money? Do I have to get an American bank account now?

I take a breath and plug my phone in. It sucks in the power and wakes up. A roll of notifications cascades down the screen. Juliette's name repeats and repeats. There are a lot of messages from Juliette. I don't have to read them to know something is wrong.

Eleven shouts, "How did *he* make it, then?" Her voice charges through the meeting room walls, even though the door is closed. "I don't care if she says it's not possible. It's all just electromagnetic energy! The code *is* possible. Everything is possible! Who made his? Find out who made it, and then get them."

Anna-Mackenzie is quietly typing away in front of me, working on the post-Oahu sales funnel letters that we'll be sending to all the brand-new Ascendants. Her shoulders curve and twitch as Eleven hollers.

"What's going on?" I ask her. "What did I miss?"

She swivels around to face me. Her little gold cross is off-centre on its chain, snagged by a thread on her light-grey cardigan. "What did you miss," she repeats. Her eyes are lined with metallic emerald-green liner, which looks a little harsh with her pale skin. Oh, Anna-Mackenzie. She's so nice to me, all the time. Are we even real friends, or is she just like this with everyone?

"I think it's about—you know—his new website and campaign," she says.

"Who?" But I know already.

"Jonathan Rasmussen has a new website," Anna-Mackenzie whispers. "You should see it! It's beautiful. Now Eleven thinks her site is outdated."

"She told us she wanted a brand-new site," I say. When was that? The day I woke up with hives. Two weeks ago?

"Jonathan Rasmussen has these layers that sort of move when you scroll down the screen, and these waves that kind of pulse and flutter as you move down the page. It's not like Flash or video, it's different. Look it up, it's hard to explain. Same URL. He launched it, like, overnight. Without telling anyone it was coming. He beat her to it."

I don't even want to look, but I pick up my phone and begin to type in activemeditation.com, just to see. Another text from Juliette comes through just as the site is loading. Synchronicity!

Juliette
I'm staying at Smithany in SoHo.
Please come see me tonight. SOS

I text Juliette to let her know I'll be coming right after work.
Then I call the clients who ordered chocolates and leave messages
with all of them. I call and call and leave messages all afternoon.
Nobody answers their phone anymore. I email Lupin Thorne about
sending another head shot. It's six-thirty by the time I finish. When
I look up from my desk, the piece of sky I can see between the buildings outside is pale violet and twinkling.

◊ ◊ ◊

Smithany is a boutique hotel that just opened this year. The walls are
clean, white-painted brick and the chandeliers are wrought-iron models
of atoms, with Edison bulb protons, electrons, and neutrons. The tables
and chairs are all made of wrought iron, with reclaimed wood seats and
tabletops. Everyone wears chambray. Is chambray the uniform for the
people who work at the hotel? I can't tell who works here and who's
visiting. I ask a man standing behind a bar-height wood and iron table
if he's the concierge. He is! He calls up to let Juliette know I'm here.

"She calls herself *Pure Rosa*." Juliette spits out the name like a grapefruit
seed. "Look at her *font*! Look at her *ribbon graphics*!" I peer at her iPad
screen. It's another lifestyle blogger, clearly trying to be like Juliette. A
photo of a dark-haired woman with pomegranate-red lips. Two small
white dogs on her lap, tongues out. They look suspiciously clean, freshly
brushed, and happy. Their auras are mint green and periwinkle blue.

"Obviously, she was inspired by you," I say. "But she's nothing—"

"Her yellow is only seven numbers away from my signature hex
colour code!"

"You started this whole thing, though. You're a first-generation
online lifestyle blogger. You're original. You're Pure Juliette. No one
can ever be Pure Juliette."

"Look! F3FF07," she says. "I'm F3FF01. This is *not* a coincidence."

I pause to count. "Wait, that's actually six numbers."

"It's my *brand*," she says. "She's stealing from me."

"You are so much more than F3FF01," I say.

Juliette's aura is wine-coloured, flickering with green. Her hotel room is untidy. Four or five pairs of shoes—grass-green suede ankle boots with tassels, shiny black pumps, Tory Burch flats with the gold amulets on the toes—are strewn over the floor by the foot of the bed. Styrofoam boxes are stacked on top of the bar, and the garbage can is loaded with coffee cups, all stamped with the Smithany logo and circled with stiff brown cardboard holders. It smells soupy in the room, like garlic, onions, and grease.

Juliette's hands are shaking as she punches the iPad with her finger.

"A vegan crab cake recipe? *I invented vegan crab cakes!*"

I try to open the window. She has a corner room, and the glass stretches generously across half of both walls. I can see the Hudson River from here, and the World Trade Center. The glass is completely sealed.

"It's not fair," I say. "I'm not saying it's *fair*. But it makes her look pathetic, if it's any consolation."

"What infuriates me," she goes on without hearing me, "what makes me *so angry*, is that she hasn't had to work at all for her image. She's just pretending to be me! She hasn't taken any time to find her own voice, her own brand, her own style. Look at her perfect stupid life! Look at her two stupid dogs!"

"Hey," I say. "It's not their fault."

"I didn't even know she existed until the conference. I'm the keynote speaker. I'm the so-called *expert*. I'm the one in *Lovely*, I'm the one with an exclusive line at the Bay. I'm the one who was invited to this *conference*, to share all my *skills*. I basically went up there and told everyone how to copy me!"

Her phone dings, but I can't see it anywhere in the room. She jumps when she hears the noise, but doesn't move to find it.

"And I tell people to enjoy the little things in life." Her voice quavers. "I tell people to find joy."

"You show people how to find beauty," I say. "That is what you do."

She starts to cry. "I can't do this anymore," she says. "I'm so tired."

Her white blouse is wrinkled, and the frayed cotton threads of her ripped boyfriend jeans are knotted. This outfit has seen fresher days. In her closet, there's a navy blue poplin dress with white polka dots and a keyhole neckline. Cute. I bend down and sort through her shoes, pair them up, and place the green suede booties under where the dress hangs.

"Look," I say. "Let's go out and get our nails done." I feel useless even as I say the words, but I keep talking. "We can go get almond milk and turmeric lattes and pick out polishes." I pull tissues out of the dispenser built into the bathroom counter and hand them to her. She takes them in her fist and crumples them as she cries. I sit beside her on the bed and stroke her frizzy hair.

"I took out a home equity line of credit for the carriage-house reno for Knigel," she says. "I can't *stand* him living there. I can't stand him in pyjamas all day on his computer. I can't stand seeing all the delivery boxes that come to his door, and seeing his garbage out on the sidewalk in front of the house every week. He's bringing Celine there too, now. Of course. Why did I think that would be okay?" She blows her nose. "We're getting a divorce. Separating our finances was a nightmare, but we did it. I have to pay him child support!" she cries. "His backers stopped funding his game development. Pure Juliette has to support all of us now. I worked so hard for all this, but I have to give him my money. He cheated on me, but he still gets my money! That's the law. It's like another mortgage payment every month. I have to pay him."

Her phone dings again. "I came to the Inspo-preneurship conference to make enough money from this speaking gig to pay my lawyer. What am I doing? I'm a fraud. Nothing is real. My life is a hot mess, and I go onstage and tell everyone how beautiful it is."

I watch her cry and feel strangely relaxed. As she cries into a pillow, her aura turns green. I touch her back and rest my hand on her shoulder blades as she cries.

Tentatively, I say, "Thank you. What else is there to say about Knigel, your divorce, and money?" This is a Compost Heave move. I've never tried it in the wild.

"I have to sell the house!" she cries. "I can't afford the payments. I have to move to a"—she takes a jagged breath—"a *condo*."

A helicopter lands on the roof of a building across the city. I have an idea.

"Pure Rosa is in *Martha Stewart* magazine," she says with acid. "I'm over. I'm a fake. What will I say? What will I tell everyone?"

"Good," I say. "Is there anything else you want to say?"

She looks at me with red eyes. Her lashes are dark and wet, and her green aura calms to a beautiful teal blue. She sighs. She shakes her head no, there's nothing else.

It's working! I feel clear and focused. "Here's what you're going to do," I say. I text Fleurje, copy Juliette on the text, and set up a meeting for them next week. "You're going to sell your house." I find her phone on the floor on the other side of her bed, make sure the text went through, and slide it into the little phone pocket on the inside of her purse. "Fleurje is the best real estate agent in the city," I say. "She works constantly. I haven't seen her in two years." Juliette stops crying, and watches me move around her hotel room.

"You know the Toronto market is insane," I say. I open the bar fridge and find four glass jars of water with the Smithany label stuck on them. Mason jars for water! Innovative, low overhead—and much more sustainable than plastic. "Houses are going up fifteen percent every six months." I twist open the lid of the wide-mouthed jar and place it on the wood plank beside her bed. "Your house has a *yard*. It has *parking*. You're right downtown. You work online—you don't have to live there. You're going to sell it for at least two million dollars." She doesn't move—she just watches me. Poor Juliette. She looks so tired.

"You'll have lots of money, and freedom, and then your whole perspective will change."

"What am I going to do, Lily?"

I point to the jar. *Love is a verb, not a noun.* "You're going to get dressed, and drink this water," I tell her. "Get rehydrated." I stand up. "We're going for a walk. Put on your navy blue dress."

We spend the evening walking through lower Manhattan. Juliette points out a butterfly mobile in a shop window display, and I buy it for Siebel. I also find an iron-on patch of a blue-green mermaid for Mabel. We get a packet of chocolate-dipped orange rinds from a fancy candy store and eat them as we walk. Juliette tells me she doesn't want to be alone, so I spend the night in her room. We watch *Jane the Virgin* until we both fall asleep. On Saturday morning, we have breakfast at the hotel, and I stay with her until the car picks her up to take her to the airport.

◊ ◊ ◊

Eleven opens the Mirroring Teleritual with the same grounding ritual as before, with the lighting of candles. This time the conference call technology works, and as Element Leader, I smoothly introduce earth with my incantation. We go through all the elements, and I hear the voices of Gloria, Haley, and Zoe.

Then Eleven says, "Yesterday was the full Scorpio moon. You may have been feeling the psychological effects of this. Just before the culmination of this full moon, we lost the earthly presence of Prince. We wish him swift passage on his journey into the ultimate unknown. My darlings, this is a time of inner discovery—the full moon brings to light things that have been previously hidden. Scorpio is the wizard of the zodiac, the king of extremes, the secret-keeper herself, ruling both our spiritual depths and peaks of awakening. This marks a time of spiritual intensity for all of us. Expect this intensity. Prepare for it, and make room for it."

No wonder Juliette was having a meltdown. And that Pure Rosa was revealed from the shadowy corners of the Internet where she'd been lurking before this full moon. The timing makes sense.

Then Eleven teaches us conscious reversal, or Mirroring. The key to Mirroring practice is to recognize that you are constantly projecting your thoughts, beliefs, and feelings about yourself onto other people, even the people you love the most. Once you recognize that, you can slow down, pause, and consciously reverse your reactions, so you can rise above everything and become a better individual.

Eleven coaches Haley during the Teleritual, so we can all witness it and learn. "He's unmotivated," says Haley. "He never initiates anything. If I didn't plan everything for us, we'd never do *anything*."

"Now turn it around, sweetheart."

"He always initiates?" says Haley. "But that's not true!"

"Try turning it around differently," Eleven coaxes.

"I'm unmotivated?" Haley tries. "I never initiate anything?"

"What about that sounds right, honey?"

There's a long pause on the line. We listen to Haley breathing and thinking.

Then she says, "Oh my God. It's *true*."

"What part is true, love?"

"I take care of everything else in the household, except my own dreams. I never initiate my own dreams."

"Like what, sweetie?" says Eleven. "What would you do, if you were to initiate something important for yourself?"

"I want to learn how to speak Italian," Haley says. "I've always wanted that."

"Have you ever tried? Even just a start?"

"No! Never!" Haley sounds teary.

"What could you do right now, one tiny step, that could bring you closer to that dream?"

"I could find a class," Haley says.

"Good," says Eleven. "And what would you say to your husband, if he were listening tonight?"

"That I'm really the one who has to initiate. That I was just projecting all that onto him."

"Yes, sweetheart," says Eleven. "Beautiful."

It's incredible to watch Mirroring happen in real life. Eleven *is* a gifted teacher.

"I'd like each of you to open your journals now," Eleven tells us, "and write about a person you admire. Make a list of everything that you love about them. Everything that you know is good about them. Be very specific."

I write in my notebook: *Powerful. Smart. Unafraid to be peculiar. Does whatever she wants. Generous. Honest. Ageless.*

I think about her poetry, and the way I understand it without understanding it. Her amazing turquoise-and-white hair, and how she puts it up in twists the way a teenager would—and totally gets away with it. The ridiculous way she makes her voice go up when she speaks through her dog's consciousness. I write: *Magician. Artist. Visionary.* My wrist tingles when I write this, as though I just received a gentle shock from the paper.

"The beauty of conscious reversal is that it works both ways," Eleven says. "So when you see someone who impresses you, someone you think is really elegant, smart, beautiful, or strong—guess what, my loves? To reveal the truth, you just *turn it around!*"

I look at the words I've written down. I don't understand what she means.

"Everything you see that sparkles is a reflection of yourself. You'd never see it, otherwise. You simply would not recognize it. This is the art of Mirroring practice, my dear flowers. Now, please write your name at the top of the list you just wrote. We're going to pause as you read your list back to yourself."

At the top of the page, I write: *Lilian.*

"As you read," Eleven intones, "know that with every word, you are describing yourself."

I read my list out loud, and I have the weirdest sensation: my head lifts off my neck, my skin disappears, and I dissolve into molecules. My heart floats out of my chest and up to the ceiling. And there's this beautiful container around me, like a crystal vase made of white light, that's holding me together.

Dear Lilian,

I just got back from New York City, and I am feeling the great élan of spring in Manhattan. The good people at <u>The Lifestyle Design and Inspo-preneurship Conference</u> invited me to speak this year, and it was such an energizing event. I was able to meet many of my readers in person, which was a thrill. And I made new friends, too!

Here is a round-up of some of the presentations that inspired me the most:

Hearts and Moons
Constantine Freddo is a jewellery designer living on beautiful Edisto Island, South Carolina. Her designs are breathtaking—she works with druzy, which is the centre of geodes, and creates pendants, studs, and rings that feel utterly enchanted. Her talk was all about how she's inspired by nature, and how it nourishes her business. I loved it—it made me wish I could take a walk on the beach every day.

The Sunshine Box
Christy Ng's talk was about nutrition—she's an Integrative Dietary Consultant and private chef. She delivers healthy boxed lunches to people who work and live in food deserts, mainly in the southern United States. Her talk inspired me to check out her website, which is packed with amazing recipes and healthy lunch options, including meals that kids will love! She also has a whole six-week kids' lunch menu and shopping plan that you can download for free when you subscribe to her list.

Rafi Baumgartner
Rafi spoke about learning how to use your voice, how it heals the body, improves your immune system, and activates your intuition. I don't sing, but since her talk, I've been belting it out in the car and in the shower! Go to her site to read more about

her work as a voice coach and the hospital choir she started in Binghamton, New York.

The conference left me feeling replenished, energized, and full of ideas for the coming year.

Because, guess what? Pure Juliette is evolving again! It's too early for me to share the details yet, but I can tell you that I've been working with <u>Fleurje Zubrov</u> on an exciting new project. Fleurje is an award-winning real estate agent, and she's sold homes to some of Toronto's most well-known artists and interior designers. We are collaborating on something very special that I'll announce later this year. I can't wait to let you in on everything—stay tuned.

I'll be back next month with more recipes and craft projects for you to do at home. For now, I hope you're enjoying these warmer days of true spring. Remember to take some time for yourself this month. A hot bath, an early morning coffee date with yourself, a delicious novel to read before bed. Whatever makes you feel special and loved.

xoxo, Juliette

THE UPPER WEST SIDE is so nice on a Saturday morning. It reminds me of Toronto—the sidewalks are bigger, the traffic is slower. And there are so many cute dogs! I've only seen this part of New York during the week, when I'm working at the Temple. Today, the streets bristle with the last push of April. I notice the beauty in the ordinary: corner stores stuffed with flowers and buckets of blossoming branches, people walking in the sunshine, eating croissants out of paper bags. The auras are bright and simple today. Some brave restaurants have removed their boxy plastic fronts to expose patio seating to the air. It's still too cold for that, but I like that they're optimistic and getting ready for it.

A sign on the sidewalk presents itself to me like a high-five: "Style Your Crown Chakra. Theodora Ove, Hair Shaman." Why not? We fly to Oahu tomorrow night, and it would be fun to have a new look for the last weekend of Ascendency. I have lots of time before I meet Eleven for the Flourish Summit.

> **Fleurje**
> Thank u for connecting me w your friend!

> **Fleurje**
> Her house is perfect. Don't have 2 do a thing 2 it

> **Fleurje**
> Where r u? R u in TO? Want 2 have a drink?

> **Me**
> (...)

Theodora Ove is amazing. She gives me a scalp massage using a wide-toothed comb made out of rose quartz, does fifteen minutes of reiki over the top of my head, and then puts pastel-rainbow-and-silver tinsel extensions in my hair. I look like a unicorn! I take a selfie and pick a filter that makes my skin look more smooth, but keeps my eyes bright blue. I post it to Instagram super quick.

@LilianQuick> Thank you @TheoOve! I feel tingly all over! #hairshaman #crownchakra #sparkle

I walk to the Temple on sidewalks that are buzzing with energy. A man in a blue suit is standing in front of a coffee and juice shop. He's got a headset. Security? I catch his eye as I walk past him. His aura is warm and golden yellow-orange. He holds my gaze and smiles.

"With the radicchio, that makes five ingredients," he says.

Not security! He was just talking on the phone. I give him a wink. A breeze picks up, catches my big portfolio like a sail, and blows it into my face.

The man laughs. Is he laughing at me? "Sterilize them first," he says. "Don't let them touch anything."

Me

I'm in NYC!

Me

I moved here.

Fleurje

OMG! U did??

Fleurje

When r u coming back 2 TO?

Me

(...)

I start to type a reply but erase it. Seriously, Fleurje?

"You look like you just came from a tween dance class!" Eleven cries. "What's that?"

"Thank you," I say, and flip a chunk of my new blue-green-pink sparkly hair over my shoulder. "This is my portfolio. I have a painting to deliver to Nana Boondahl."

"Are you cold?" She eyes the thigh warmers Yumi gave me last month.

"It's so nice outside, I might have to take them off," I say. "You won't need more than your jacket." I quickly take a toe selfie, making sure to catch some of my thighs. "Hold on," I say. "I just have to post something."

@LilianQuick> Loving my blues, **@ReKnits!**
Thank you thank you <3 #cashmere #OOTD

Eleven pulls on her white moto jacket and a wave of amber and rose passes through the air.

"Nana Boondahl is speaking at two," I say. "Did you call Abdul?"

"Abdul can't work today," she says. "Call a PickUp."

"I actually can't do that."

"Use the Temple credit account." She pushes the elevator down button.

"Try a new LMS plugin," Yolanda says from the front desk. Yolanda is working on Saturday because tomorrow we go to Oahu, and she's in hustle mode. She says she'll rest next month, after Ascendency graduation—Eleven booked us all three days in Maui at the Kea Lani.

"My new phone didn't sync properly," I say. "I don't have the updated PickUp app."

Eleven looks at me. "Download the app," she says.

"I did," I tell her. The elevator dings.

"No, that's an LMS *theme*," Yolanda says. "You don't need that—you have that already with Page ExpressVerse. You need a plug-in that works with your forum plug-in."

"Who are you advising?" Eleven calls to Yolanda.

Yolanda puts up one finger. "Sorry, Ginger," she says. "One moment please?"

Eleven holds the elevator open with one hand. "Is everything okay with the site?"

"It's an Ascendency grad," Yolanda says. "She called for a consult. She's licensing the pilot."

"Oh, good." Eleven nods. "Let's go," she says to me.

The elevator hums. "Nice shoes," she says. These are my new pink glittered ballet flats. With the turquoise and royal blue thigh warmers and my new hair, I feel downright giddy.

"You've got quite a look going on," she adds.

"What's the pilot?" I say. "Is this a new program?"

"It's a development," she says. "We're licensing Ascendant grads so they can lead Ascendency programs themselves."

"That sounds like it could be lucrative," I say.

"It's more scaling, yes. But it's also about giving a more multi-faceted experience of the Ascendency presence. It's not all about me. These are my ideas, but I don't own them. Every woman brings her own divine wisdom to Ascendency."

"What's the pilot called?"

"It's still called Ascendency. It's the Ascendency licensing program."

"Thank goodness you could trademark 'Ascendency,'" I say.

"Did you know that someone in the U.K. bought the domain name in three countries? We had to buy the addresses back from them for fifteen thousand dollars each."

"So worth it," I say.

Eleven sighs. "I'm proud of you, Lilian. You've come so far since you moved here. You've challenged yourself, transformed yourself. And you've really made a difference to the team." The light goes on at *L* and the door opens. Eleven calls a PickUp by touching her own phone, and we wait outside, watching for the car.

"Ascendency is powerful, isn't it?" she says. "I love this program. Congratulations, Lilian. It fills my heart with light to see you reaching for your highest self."

The car pulls over, and we get in. The seats are black leather. The driver, inexplicably, wears a cravat. I slide my portfolio in the space between my knees and the back of the seat. "One Universe Foundation," Eleven tells him. "711 Greenwich Street."

"It's Grandma's birthday today," I say. "April thirtieth."

"How old would she be?"

I subtract 1913 from 2016 on my phone. "A hundred and three," I say.

"Happy birthday, Grandma Bertolucci," Eleven says.

My phone makes a soft wooden sound, and a notification appears on the screen.

Stop what you're doing.
Remember, the Universe is energy!

We get to the rooftop patio at One Universe just in time for Nana Boondahl's beautiful presentation. She reads highlights from her new memoir, *The Words Are Light Written on My Face*, in front of the koi pond, amidst a jungle of tropical plants arranged in poured concrete containers. Everyone at Flourish receives a copy of the book in her swag bag, which we're given at the entrance. I wish they would give us the bag when we leave, instead. It's awkward enough moving through the crowd of women and finding a seat with my portfolio. I feel as if I'm carrying a big black shield, and I know it's blocking some of the authentic connections I could be making here.

I spot Raquel Rocco and take in the clarity of her red aura from across the patio—we've booked her to present her Soul of a Goddess Sensuality Ceremony at Oahu next weekend. I didn't even know she was part of the Flourish Women and Business crowd, which I thought was mainly product-based businesses. She does have her own line of products—she sells jade and quartz eggs to activate stronger orgasms—but I didn't think it was a big part of her business model. Maybe jade eggs are big business now, since Gwyneth made them more mainstream. I look in my swag bag just to see. Yes! We each get our own jade egg! This is a very generous event. There's also a bottle of Edith Saguaro perfume, and a cosmos-print scarf by Amy T. Won.

"I'm just going to see if I can catch Nana Boondahl before she leaves," I say to Eleven.

She raises her eyebrows. "Good luck," she says. She doesn't stand up. I have to pull my portfolio up and over the heads of the women in front of me as I sidestep my way out of the row of seats. When I turn back, Eleven is hugging a woman in a blue pantsuit.

Nana Boondahl is beside the bar, signing books. She sits at a thick wooden table with a bowl full of white lotus flowers, a living wall of ferns and mosses behind her. Sophia sits right next to her on a folded blanket. When she senses me, the greyhound looks up. She glows with her pink, radiant light. I know that light so well—it feels like it's part of me.

A line of people waits to get books signed. Nana Boondahl takes them on one by one, scrawls a tangle of a signature on the inside page, closes the book, and hands it back with a nod. Her turquoise-and-white hair is curled stiffly upon her head like meringue, and her skin looks plump and dewy. There's something wrong with her eyes. I watch her carefully as she signs a few more books, and then I see that she's wearing false eyelashes. But they don't look like lashes. There's something stuck to her eyes. What is it?

"I'd like to know how to reach Nana Boondahl when she's finished signing," I say to her assistant, who stands a few feet away from her table. "She told me there would be a small gathering after this event?"

"I'm afraid not," he says. "She has a flight directly back to Canada after this."

I'm puzzled. I pull out my invitation and show him the note she sent me. It's in her big, messy handwriting: *meet me at the hotel for a thing after.*

He reads it, looks at me, and then smiles. "Oh, you're *Lilian Quick!*" he says. "I'm sorry! I didn't realize you were Lilian. Yes, she told me you're her friend, and to expect you. We're gathering at the Gansevoort after the signing. Just give your name at the door; you're on the list."

I walk over to the other side of the rooftop without Nana Boondahl even seeing me, and I find Eleven posing in front of the waterfall installation for a photograph with Crystal Hewitt, the famous astrologist. They look like they could be sisters: Crystal's hair is the same colour as Eleven's, but it's straight and glossy. Their auras match—olive green, greyish-yellow. The camera flashes, and I pull

Eleven aside. "We're meeting Nana Boondahl at Hotel Gansevoort," I say. "Come with me."

She looks surprised, but she picks up her swag bag and follows me out.

A bass beat thumps, and from the top floor of the hotel, the whole city glows in afternoon light as if it's caught in a jar of apricot jelly. Two women in short chiffon dresses and heels are posing for each other's phones, setting their smiles perfectly, turning their shoulders for the right angle. A young woman levitates out of the pool, squeezes water from her rope of long dark hair, and struts down the poolside catwalk to rinse her leggy body in the pool shower. Are these Nana Boondahl's Luze models? Or guests of the hotel?

"The press is here," Eleven says, smiling at the cameras as they flash around us. "Is that Jane Pratt? Hello, gorgeous!"

I feel the deep pink light of Sophia's aura as soon as she arrives. Nana Boondahl sees me right away, and opens her arms for a public hug. We haven't hugged before. Perhaps she is performing for the crowd? She looks me up and down. Her eyelashes are made of laser paper cut-outs shaped like tiny keys. How do they not get tangled when she blinks? "You look well," she says. "No more stabbing incidents, I trust."

"I loved your presentation," I tell her honestly. "Congratulations on your book."

"It's like cutting hair," she says, and moves her hand in front as if pushing away a spiderweb. "It was alive until I wrote it, and then it falls onto the floor to be swept."

Eleven is standing beside me. Her energy slices the air. "Eleven Novak," she says, and extends her hand.

Nana Boondahl accepts her hand and shakes it.

"Hello, Sophia!" I say.

"Sophia feels at home in New York," Nana Boondahl says. "I had our driver bring her down to meet me here. She loves road trips, but she will not fly. *I cannot be contained in a cage*, she says."

"I brought you this," I say. "It's very late. I'm ashamed to give it to you now, because it's been so long since you commissioned it. But it belongs to you." I hand her the portfolio. Nana Boondahl sets it down and unzips it brazenly, so one side falls open and to the floor.

Sophia glows, a magenta cloud of pigment rising around her. Her eyes look mischievous, like she's about to break into an unexpected song. In French. And play an accordion. It's really one of my best pieces! She floats off the page.

People gather around to see the painting. It's on a piece of eighteen-by-twenty-four Fabriano acid-free rag paper with a raw edge. I feel Eleven watching me. "It's unframed, as you requested," I say. "Please accept this as a gift."

Nana Boondahl is quiet at first. Then she opens her mouth and sings. "Aaaah!" she cries. "Aaaaaah!"

I think she likes it! "It's a bright aura," I say. "But there's depth to it, too. It's like watermelon, just kissed with magenta."

"It's magnificent! You have captured her essence, and brought it to life! Your gift is illuminating this paper! You have accepted her spirit and you have touched it with your paints!"

"I'm pleased you like it," I say. "I think it's special, too. Sophia will always be with me. When I paint their auras, my subjects become part of me."

"Thank you," Nana Boondahl says. Then she looks at me, and turns her head to the side. "You look good," she tells me. "Your skin has good fat."

I give her a big smile. It's so nice of her to notice! I feel her striking blue aura coming off her like heat. I suddenly want to tell her what I can see. "Your aura is exceptional," I blurt out. I want to tell Nana Boondahl everything. "It's a deep, royal blue," I say. The blue is actually lit with sharp petals of orange, like smouldering tips of something that is burning slowly. Eleven stands beside me, listening.

She considers this. "So you are now like my Greek friend," she says. "Seeing auras of people. Not just dogs anymore! How are you managing all of it?"

"It's not easy," I admit. "I know the colours must have been there all the time, but I just couldn't see them before. Now I see them, and it's . . . a lot to take in. I feel like an alien sometimes, just walking down the street. Because nobody *knows* how much colour they're giving off. Even the buildings and the trees. I get dizzy sometimes. But I love it. When I'm painting, it helps me."

"And what are you doing in New York?" she asks.

"I work here," I say. I step back, and gesture to Eleven. "I work with Eleven Novak now," I add.

"Aha," Nana Boondahl says to her. "You're the guru."

Eleven takes a deep breath. Her aura dances around her, phthalo blue now, mixed with the hot pink of dragonfruit. "I'm just a teacher," she says.

"And how is it?" Nana Boondahl asks me.

"I'm making a lot of money," I say.

Nana Boondahl nods approvingly. "Oh, that's *very* good," she says.

"She's lost something, hasn't she?" Eleven says. She looks out the car window, so I can't see her eyes. "It was bound to happen. Even to Nana Boondahl." Our driver puts on a jazz station.

"What? I thought her reading was amazing," I say.

"It makes me sad to say it, sweetheart, but she's on her way out," she says. "She's just not going to be here much longer."

"What are you talking about? She was on fire today. Did you not see the crowd?"

"Oh, she'll keep her loyals," Eleven says. "But Nana B. doesn't have any digital reach, and there's no storytelling in her brand. She's still using an outmoded model, based on the old system. Print advertising? Broadcasting? It doesn't work anymore. Consciousness is changing."

"Everyone uses Luze though," I say.

"Millennials don't even know what Luze is," she says. "Glimyr has the market on skin care now, because they've tapped into the higher consciousness. They're resonating with it, and women can *feel* that resonance."

"Even if Luze goes under, which is impossible, Nana Boondahl is still *Nana Boondahl*. Everyone studies her poems in high school."

Eleven nods. "She's smart to try a memoir this year. I wonder what her full strategy is there, beyond the speaking tour. Maybe she's going to rebrand Luze, try to relaunch it as vintage."

The car stereo has an LED light effect, and it cycles through the colours slowly, going all the way through the spectrum and back again. Our driver takes us back up to the Upper West Side, and we drive along the Hudson, past the High Line. The rusty rail path makes me think me of Elgin Street in downtown Sudbury, and the lines of railroad tracks where the freight trains park. I haven't been back there in so long. What is it like there now? What colour aura would the Canadian Shield have? Birch tree forests? Blueberry bushes? And—oh!—all the lakes! The auras are probably calm and steady, because there aren't so many people. What would it be like to live close to nature again? Luminous and pure.

"Water?" Our driver dangles two bottles over the back of the front passenger seat. I take one, even though it's plastic. I'm so thirsty! I should have brought a Mason jar of water from home.

"No, thank you," says Eleven.

"Are you hungry?" I ask. "Want to stop, get dinner at Eataly?"

"We fly to Oahu tomorrow morning," Eleven says.

"All the more reason to get dinner now," I say. The water bottle is icy cold. Does our PickUp driver have a little cooler up there? What great service! I open my bottle and take a sip. "Give this guy five stars!" I tell Eleven. "This water is *delicious*."

"How long have you been seeing auras around people?" she asks me.

I swallow too fast and freeze my teeth. A cold knife of pain slices from my jaw to my temples. "Oh," I say, "I'm not sure when it started."

"Lilian Quick," she says. "Keeping it mysterious."

She won't look at me. I open up my peripheral vision to take in her whole aura, lit-up phthalo blue clouded with dark yellow. "What's interesting," she says, "is that Nana Boondahl knew this about you before I did."

"You know I've always seen colours," I say. "This isn't that different."

Eleven carefully moves a blond curl away from her face and behind her ear. On the speakers behind us, Macy Gray starts singing a Bob Marley cover. "Let's stop and get something to eat," I suggest again.

"Stop here?" the driver says.

Eleven turns to look at me. Her eyes look cavey and tired. She hasn't had her brows groomed in a few weeks: several errant hairs are growing through her eye shadow. "Can you see my aura right now?" she asks.

"Yes," I say. The driver slows down. "No," I tell him. "Don't stop here please, keep driving."

"Describe it," Eleven says.

"It's bright blue, with yellow in it. The yellow is kind of . . . swirling with the blue." I don't say it, but it looks like a bruise. She pauses, and takes this in.

"This is amazing," she says. "I wish you'd told me sooner. You need to share your gifts, sweetheart. You're still hiding your light."

We drive through Chelsea and pass so many cool-looking restaurants. There wasn't any vegan food at the Nana Boondahl party. "Ooh look, there's Momoya," I say.

Eleven opens her lip gloss. "You'll definitely be a presenter at next year's Ascendency," she says. She slides her finger along her bottom lip to apply the gloss. "We can put something together for the first or second weekend." She presses her lips together, twists the lid back on the tiny glass jar, and drops it in her purse. "How many do you think you can paint in a weekend?"

"Dogs?" I say.

"Aura portraits," Eleven says. "Though we can send them to Ascendants after the weekend. No need to do them all at the time of the sessions."

The car turns a corner and we head up another avenue. Where are we? Seventh? Eighth? I can't get my bearings. I'm starting to feel carsick.

"I've never painted people's portraits before," I say.

"We'll factor the cost into Ascendency tuition," she says. "Don't worry, you'll be compensated fairly."

"It's not that," I say. "It's that I don't paint people."

She looks at me. "Sweetie, you have to remember that growth always feels like expansion, not contraction. You're playing down again, and trying to be smaller than you are."

The driver brakes abruptly, and two angry red taillights glare at us through his front window. Then the light turns green and he accelerates, but he speeds up too fast. My stomach lurches. I press the button to roll the window down and get some air. A man on the sidewalk shouts something at me I can't understand. Is he shouting at me? The traffic? Or is he just shouting at the night in general?

"I'm writing a book," Eleven tells me. "It's a memoir, and it's also about the methods I teach in Ascendency. It's written in poetic verse."

"A memoir about everything in your life? About what happened before you became Eleven?"

She nods.

"Are you writing about Uncle Jimmy?"

Her expression goes smooth. "Yes," she says. "I'm writing through all of it. My father was a bully, but the truth is, I also grew up with a lot of privilege. I'm going to be completely honest in this book."

"I can put you in touch with Nana Boondahl. She has literary connections."

"No!" Eleven cries. "I already have my own connections. I've been sharing my first drafts with CloudLet, a producer in Portland. He's setting the poems to music and recording a companion album."

"It's a concept album?"

"I'm releasing the music along with the book, and CloudLet and I are going to tour it as a concert series. My publisher is working with the record company. I'm going to monetize it across both industries."

I let this sink in. "Meanwhile, I'd like you to come with me to Arizona in May," Eleven says.

"What's in Arizona?"

"I'm shooting video for Blisslab Beauty and Wellness. They're building Rest Pods in shopping malls across the country. I'm going to be leading customers through a guided meditation."

"You're filming it?"

"Shopping malls are an energetic cacophony. This will provide a grounding rest for Blisslab customers. It will also bring mall shoppers into their stores—it's genius."

"Why do you want me there?"

"It's a VR shoot, so people will put on glasses, and the video will transport them to the desert where they'll experience the meditation with me."

"So it's live, or not live?"

"We use morphic resonance to connect people through space and time."

"That sounds like something Monicke would want to do with you."

Eleven checks something on her phone. "Monicke is taking a break to see her family after Oahu," she says. "Her brother is on leave. Besides, I want you to assist me for this project."

"Aren't you a little worried that you're taking on too much at once? You're still rebranding the website and licensing Ascendency. When do you *sleep*?"

Her eyes turn plastic, and she turns her head away from me.

"Sixty-fourth?" says the driver.

"Sixty-fourth," says Eleven.

"I'll just get out there too," I tell him. To Eleven, I say, "I'm going to order a bowl from Blossom. You want something? Come over and eat with me."

"I'm going to meditate and prepare for tomorrow's flight," Eleven says.

"You have to eat something," I say.

"I have food at home."

We drive a little while in silence. Eleven takes out her phone and types quickly with her thumbs. I take out my phone. If I order food now, it might be ready as soon as I get home, and then I won't have to wait for food. But if it comes quickly and we hit any more traffic, then I risk missing the delivery.

This app requires updates to open. Please update this app, my phone says.

Eleven looks up from her phone. "So the shoot starts May twenty-first, and I'm booked there for a week."

Reading my screen while we drive, even just those two sentences, makes me feel sick. "A week?"

"It's a six-part series," she says. "And we're shooting on location." She types into her phone again. "I just put it in your calendar," she says. "We'll plan more post-Oahu."

The car slows down and stops. "Sixty-fourth," the driver says.

"See you tomorrow," I say. I wish she would look me in the eyes.

She kisses me on the cheek, and her hair crunches against my skin. "See you tomorrow," she says. She opens her door. By the time I get out of my side of the car and walk around the other side to the sidewalk, she's already started walking away.

May 2016

My dearest Lilian,

This is it, my darling. This is your Ascendency graduation.
You have come so far! Do you remember where you were
when you started this journey?

You came to Ascendency as a closed bud, your petals
wrapped tightly around themselves, protected and delicate.
You stretched yourself and peeled back your layers every
day, working in a sacred circle of divine feminine power.
Together, you and your sisters helped each other recognize
the limits you've placed on yourselves for decades, limits
that you've culturally assimilated, limits that have been
passed down through generations. You've stretched yourself
away from these old stories and painful memories, and
you've risked everything in your spirit.

You said, I am worth more.

You said, I am radiant beauty.

You said, I am more powerful than any story.

You moved into your flourishing zone.

Now, it's time for us to come together in the garden.

Here's what you need to know about this weekend:

Ascendency Oahu begins on Friday evening, the night of the
new moon in Taurus.

This is the third of six supermoons we will have this year.
Taurus is all about mother earth. Taurus is feminine

energy, grounded and rooted in peace. This new moon is an appropriate time for us to graduate. It is a pause we will take together, to touch the earth before we rise.

You'll find the Temple Headquarters at the Royal Hawaiian Hotel on Waikiki Beach. If you need anything to prepare for your celebration this weekend, find Yolanda, Monicke, Anna-Mackenzie, and Lilian there. You can email us at ascendencygraduation@elevennovak.com for help with logistics, directions, or any last-minute challenges. I hope they don't come up, but you know, life happens. We're here for you.

If you're the type who likes to plan ahead, check out the online **Ascendency Concierge** to find helpful PDFs, like a map of Honolulu, a list of our recommended restaurants for lunch and dinner, our favorite cocktail bars, a shopping map (you'll want to get a pair of Hawaiian slippahs while you're here), and all the information about how and where you can get surf lessons, bike rentals, and stand-up paddleboard rentals.

All of the above has been printed for you, as well, and you'll find your welcome packet waiting for you in your room after you check in. You'll find a little surprise from me in there, too.

Our Ascendency journey culminates in Hawaii because Hawaii holds the energy of Pele, the goddess of the volcano. She is the earth itself, renewing itself. She is dangerous because she's so powerful. She is mesmerizing because she is so creative. You, my love, are also Pele.

You can feel her, can't you? Your souls recognize each other. Here in the jungle, in the new mountain of earth, where the lava and the ocean swell and mingle together in the fiery and watery breath of creation, you will know your own true essence.

I cannot wait to celebrate your emergence, together, on Friday night. We kick off the weekend with Sacred Dance with Zaphira Patel and Priestess Movement™.

Dress like you are a goddess, whatever that means to you.

With love and fire,
Eleven

THE WHOLE TEMPLE team has been here for five days to prep for Ascendency graduation, and I've seen a rainbow every single day that we've been here. The guide at the Dole pineapple plantation tells us that the Hawaiian islands are so sunny and showery, rainbows happen several times a day. That's why they're on the license plates. At the gift shop, I buy matching pineapple keychains for Mabel and Siebel. There's nothing in the shop that Juliette would like—it's all way too tacky—but you can order flower leis at the desk and have them shipped anywhere in the world. I pick a classic one, all-white orchids, to congratulate her on putting her house on the market.

At the top of the Diamond Head crater, I look out at the water and see a large orange-pink aura out in the ocean. A whale aura! The blue light of the ocean superimposed by the peachy-pink light from the whale makes my eyes feel like they are humming.

The auras I see here in the ocean and the lush mountains are beautiful, wild, and more dramatic than anything I've seen before. Being out of the city means I am almost always close to the coloured light of nature. It's like walking through Central Park, but exponentially. It feels energizing and peaceful at the same time. In the city, the constantly shifting auras from millions of people make me uneasy. Being here has confirmed something for me: my strange nature requires nature.

Fleurje told me that with the money I've saved from working at the Temple, I probably have enough money to buy a small house and piece of land in northern Ontario, maybe even on a lake. I'm considering it. It would be good for me to have a little getaway like that.

There's a lot of work to do while we're here, of course, but we've been good about taking time out every day to explore Oahu. *Rest until you want to play; play until you want to rest.* Eleven isn't driving us so hard, either: she's quieter than usual this week. I'm a little concerned about her. Anna-Mackenzie says Eleven calms down every May because she knows Ascendency is almost over. But I think it might be something else. Being back on Oahu must remind her of Bea—this is the island that took her away.

It's Friday, the first scheduled day of graduation. Today is the day of Yumi's surgery. I texted them this morning to send love and strength, but there's still no response.

Monicke and I spend the morning delivering two hundred and thirty-three welcome packages to all the hotel rooms. Zaphira Patel hasn't arrived yet, because her flight from Miami was delayed due to weather somewhere, and she missed her connecting flight. We're waiting to hear from her now. The Ascendants are starting to arrive: the energy in the Royal Hawaiian starts to lift as the women greet each other and check in to their rooms. The clicking and smacking of high heels and flip-flops reverberates in the grand entrance. I retreat to my hotel room and change into my Friday-night outfit: a sleek white Birch + Glass maxi-dress.

My room smells like amber and rose. Two towels are folded into swans on my bed, and a white lei made of tuberose and green ti leaves is laid out for me on the dresser. I put it on. The leaves and petals are cool on my neck, and the scent is heavenly. The flowers have a fresh green aura that's fun to wear so close to my body.

My very own Ascendency package is resting on my bed, along with the welcome card we placed in all the Ascendants' rooms. But mine has an extra, personal note on top of it, in Eleven's handwriting, on the creamy card stock with her name embossed in gold at the top:

This weekend you're an Ascendant. No Temple team duties for you. xo E

My package includes a gold-flecked box of Conscious Chocolate Truffles wrapped in a lime-green ribbon, an Eleven-scented soy candle (that explains the smell in the room), and a journal—blank white pages with gold leaf edging, a photo of a white rose on the cover. That must be the Eleven Novak rose. It's a beautiful, surreal-looking flower: the petals are a clear lime green at the top, and they fade to pure white at the bottom, where flower meets stem. The cover of the journal is embossed with gold text: *Want What You Want.*

There's also a reusable glass water bottle from PureSilver, the Newfoundland/Iceland blend. The label says, *You Are Love.* I read the tag: *The PureSilver team was so inspired by the work of Dr. Masaru Emoto and his team in Japan, they began labeling their water to positively impact the vibration of the water crystals before you drink them. This is a photograph of water observed under a microscope after it was shown the word "love."* There's a picture of a pretty snowflake.

I twist off the silver cap and drink the whole bottle quickly. I'm more thirsty than I thought! I imagine the water crystals flowing through my body, vibrating and dancing like glitter. I will keep this water bottle forever. I will never use another plastic one.

My room is all white, with a big mirror mounted on the wall opposite the sliding doors to the lanai. The mirror reflects the pool and a large grassy lawn beyond it. Yellow-and-white umbrellas sprout over the hotel grounds like daisies. I turn off the air conditioning and pull open the heavy sliding door. The sound of electronic beats pours in, and the screechy sing-song of women laughing. Ascendency grads swarm the edges of the pool in filmy cover-ups and cork wedge heels, wearing big hoop earrings and shiny enamel bracelets to accessorize their bathing suits. I guess they're dressing like goddesses. Everyone gets to decide what that means for herself! Their auras are a haze of swirling, flickering light. I turn around and face the mirror, scrunch my hair to fluff it at the roots, and flip it forward on either side of my head so I can see my sparkles. My dress is long and draped, and it has a simple elastic at the waist, which I thought made it look goddessy and sculptural. It's a bit shapeless, though. It just hangs on my body. Did I spend two hundred dollars on a tent dress? Maybe it's better when I move around, or when the breeze catches it.

In the mirror, I watch the reflection of a woman in an emerald-green bikini fiddle with the straw in her drink. She looks far away—I'm on the second floor, so she's in the distance on the lawn—but the sound bounces off the water in the pool and I hear her voice clearly, as if she's right under my window. Her aura is a strange mix of neon pink and blue-red. "Airbnb started with an air mattress on the floor," she says. "Why can't you just start with one horse?"

"I know I have to do it," another voice answers. This woman is out of view—I can't see her in my mirror. "I just have to work on my communication plan, get the psychology right." Her voice feels dark purple, if I had to guess at an aura for her.

"Did you read Jonathan Rasmussen's latest post?" the first woman asks.

"I hate to say it, but I think he's trying too hard."

"It sounds like his marriage is in trouble."

"I know. I thought the same thing. How she must be feeling about him right now."

"He has a *child*. He shouldn't be processing his private life so publicly like this—it's hard to watch. Right? It's like, we're all watching this happen, and I just feel for the *child*."

"I think she's still teaching yoga, though, old-school, with the Sanskrit."

"It's hard, because there's so much good to be found in yoga. But it's inappropriate."

"What about the Forest Sanctuary?"

"I'm sure Eleven had permission. She thanked the tribes."

"I've been reading about Rich Movement. Do you follow Jane Bastet?"

"Yes! Love her. I've stopped sleeping on my mattress. It feels amazing. I don't even use a pillow anymore."

I slip on my pink Converse, grab my phone and the plastic hotel key card, and tuck them both into the pocket of my dress. Before I leave the room, I read the poem printed on the welcome card:

Inflorescence
to Ascendants, for your graduation ceremony

With fire
With intensity
With pleasure
She rises
Her dance is a chrysanthemum

Of love
She meets you in your center
Platinum hot
Your collapse
Is your own depth
Meeting itself
She is what your soul
Already knows
She is
Your
Divine
Nature

xo Eleven

I should probably go out there and mingle with the Ascendants, make some connections before the events begin. I should find Anoosh, Shona, and Matilde. Maybe I can meet some of the women who signed up through my website. I grab my sunglasses and put them on for a bit of energetic protection. There are *hundreds* of women out there, and their auras are *chaotic* right now. It's a mess for me to see it all.

"Hi, Lilian!" a group of women lounging on pool chairs wave to me. Do I know them? I do not know them. I smile and wave.

"You're so gorgeous!" one of them says.

"I love your dress!" another shouts.

"You're a goddess!"

I meander over the lawn, looking for a place where I can be myself and feel relaxed. I'm recognized by many of the Ascendants, and they wave at me, but it's hard for me to just walk up and say hello. Even with my sunglasses on, the auras are so strong. I want a break from the noise, just for a few minutes. I find a spot between a palm tree and a hedge with waxy green leaves, and I can't help but hear another conversation.

"It wasn't the picture of her baby, it was the comment she wrote that made me unfollow her," someone says. "'Having a baby is a rite of passage to truly understand womanhood.'"

"That's not even a sentence!"

"You know how people are writing their blogs on Instagram now?"

"I like that," the first person says. "It's more personal."

"Whatever happened to Vandela Christie?"

"She stopped posting on her blog last year."

"What do you think she's doing now?"

"Maybe she died."

"Joy!" The women laugh. "That's a terrible thing to say!"

"Well, it's possible," Joy says. "People die."

"What if she just took a break from social media?"

"No, you have to say something publicly if you're going to do that."

"What I was trying to say is, I'm just not into it. Like, don't equate womanhood with motherhood."

Their voices swarm in my head like cluster flies. My back scrapes against the bark of the palm tree. I feel like an intruder here. My body feels bloated and heavy, as if my insides are expanding out of my skin. I can feel myself crushing the grass, which is giving off such a sweet purple glow. The tiny blades are crying under my shoes. There's nowhere to walk without stepping on grass. I wish I could hover above it and be weightless and invisible. Everywhere I turn there's a clash of colour and noise.

I walk quickly down to the beach, where there's a horizon, and space. As soon as I get there, I can breathe. The waves shrug and suck themselves up and back and then release their bodies, exhaling on the shore. The breeze lifts my lei off my chest lightly, and I smell salt mixed with tuberose. The wind whips my dress around my legs. The sand is soothing to look at. It's prismatic, and the colourful auras of the tiny crabs and whatever other sand creatures are all beautifully muted by the silver aura of the sand itself. I look out at the ocean, hoping for a whale. It's a sparkling plate of cobalt blue, and the light it gives off is ultramarine. I close my eyes, breathe in the clean, salt-and-flower-scented air, and exhale the chaos of Ascendency. I take more deep breaths, and with each breath I feel more like myself.

I could paint this ocean, use a wet wash of greens and blues. Definitely would use phthalo here. And get some texture with a sponge, to create that white crush of surf.

My phone interrupts me. It dings and dings and vibrates in my pocket like an alarm.

Yolanda
Zaphira's flight is delayed

Yolanda
We have to cancelling sacred dance

Anna-Mackenzie
Oh no!

Monicke
I'll DJ tonight

Yolanda
Meet me at 6pom in the air train

Anna-Mackenzie
I'll write something up for them at reception

Yolanda
atrium

Monicke
atrium = HQ?

Yolanda
HQ yes

Me
(...)

Yolanda
We've gothic Lilian, Ill call if I need ouzo

I turn around, and wave to the bands of goddesses all the way back to the pink arches of the hotel. My nerves are shot. What's happening to me today? Why can't I relax and enjoy myself? I wouldn't even know what to Compost Heave right now, even if I felt like Heaving, which I don't.

I go back up to my hotel room on the second floor. I close the door to the lanai, and the noise from the pool retreats. I pull my drapes closed and sit in the white chair in my white room. I could open my box of Conscious Chocolate Truffles. That might be nice. No, I should probably avoid sugar and caffeine, even the kind that's in good chocolate. Besides, I'm not even hungry.

Create before you consume. Should I paint something? I brought my watercolours with me, and a small pad of paper. What can I do to feel better?

I get up to refill my You Are Love bottle with tap water. Should I let it sit for a while, so the message can infuse itself into the water crystals before I drink it? I take a sip.

A voice inside my head says, *You don't need anything right now. You just need to sit and breathe.*

I sit in the white chair. I breathe. The tuberose petals at my neck flutter when I exhale.

The last thing I should do right now is check my email.

Dear Lilian,

I am writing you this letter from the Coast Mountain Range in Whistler, British Columbia. The air is cool and the late-season snow feels impossibly pristine. The pink light of the setting sun casts a luminous glow over the snowy mountains ahead of me, making them look like magic castles.

I'm in Whistler with filmmaker Sol Epstein, shooting a documentary. This is a film about masculinity and vulnerability, about family, friendship, and loyalty. It's about loss, grief, and personal transformation.

It's my story. It's not easy for me to be so transparent on camera. This film is telling the whole truth about where I came from, and how I became the man I am now.

The path I am on branched from a place I've tried to keep hidden. From myself, and from the people I love. Sol and I are sharing this story in the hopes that it will inspire others.

Sol Epstein has written and directed six revolutionary films in his career already. I've always admired his work, especially *Song Doctor* (2007) and the moving *My Father, Osho* (2001). Most recently he won the St. Louis Gateway Film Critics Association Award for Best Non-Feature Documentary for his film *Trixie* (2014), a film that explored the rich fantasy life of a girl who believes she is a doll. I am blessed to be working with him.

As a young man, I first came to Canada from New Zealand to work on the ski hills here in Whistler. As I ride the gondola up the mountain and swing precariously over the trails below, I can peer out the window and see myself as I was then, in the bodies of the young skiers and snowboarders racing below. Time is not what it seems. More than ever, I am experiencing the simultaneous vertigo and groundedness that comes with this revelation: we are all one.

It is hard work. I am away from my family, sometimes for weeks at a time. Fifi is at home with Espuma, and this time apart has been heartbreaking for all of us. But the project is important. Telling this story is important.

I invite you to <u>watch a sneak peak of the film here</u>. You can support our project and <u>donate here</u>. All who donate five hundred dollars or more will receive an exclusive Sol Epstein DVD collection. His work is evocative, raw, and delves deep into the marrow of the ethical questions about family, intimacy, and identity—questions we all face today.

Thank you so much for your continued support. I would not be here if it weren't for you. We are all on this journey together.

Blessings,
Jonathan

AT THE BOTTOM of his newsletter there's a tiny line of text that says Unsubscribe. I click it. My finger touches the MailDharma logo by mistake instead, and I'm brought to that company's email marketing page. A pink lotus flower blooms out of a stylized brown envelope. I go back to the previous page, zoom in with my thumb and forefinger to get a better target, and try again.

We're sorry to see you go.
Are you sure you want to unsubscribe?

I touch Yes.

You are unsubscribed from this thread, but don't worry.
You will remain on Jonathan Rasmussen's mailing list.

My throat tightens. My eyes shoot to all four corners of the tiny phone screen, looking for a sign showing me another way out. At the bottom of the screen, there's a tiny empty checkbox beside the words *Unsubscribe from all mailings.*

I touch that checkbox, but my finger hits the logo again and it takes me directly back to MailDharma's pink lotus.

No! No! I go back again, zoom in again, and do the whole thing again.

We're sorry to see you go. Are you sure you want to unsubscribe from all mailings?

I touch Yes.

Please let us know why you're saying goodbye.

I skip all the provided excuses and fill in the text box labelled *Other reason:*

P.S. You misspelled sneak p-e-e-k. (A peak is that thing at the top of a mountain.) Easy mistake.

I press Submit. I'm free! I drink the bottle of You Are Love and sit in the white chair and I feel all the happy, beautiful water crystals dancing in my body.

◊ ◊ ◊

I wake up at 6:30 on Saturday morning. I want to catch breakfast before most of the other Ascendants wake up and come downstairs. I pull open my patio door and hear the ocean. A few women are jogging on the beach, chugging up and down the shore. All three of them wear black capris and neon tank tops. The air smells like flowers and rain.

At the buffet, I fix myself a bowl of coconut yoghurt and granola with fresh pineapple and a generous sprinkle of raw cacao nibs. I eat at a corner table and listen to the waves. It's so nice and quiet this morning! There's no one around, other than two men from the hotel: one rakes the sand and the other pulls out cushions for the lounge chairs. They both do their work in bare feet. The pool makes a humming, trickling sound. Little grey-and-red birds peck at the lawn in small groups here and there.

"Can I rent a bike?" I ask at the front desk.

"Of course." The man smiles. "What room are you in?"

"Two-twenty," I say. He punches this into the computer.

"Lilian Quick?" he says. "I'll get you set up with a bicycle right away." He taps something else into the keyboard, slides a plastic card into a slot, and when it pops out, he hands it to me. There's a picture of a bicycle on it. "This is your bike rental card. Give it to them at the bike shed around the south side of the hotel. When you return the bike, you'll get it back. Don't forget to bring the card back."

"Got it," I say. "What's your name?"

"Derek." He grins. "I try to remember everyone's name, too!"

"Thank you, Derek!" I feel unexpectedly light. His face is wide and his smile is very straight, except one front tooth that comes down at an angle. It's cute. His eyes are dark brown and shining, and his aura is sky blue and rich purple.

My bike has fat white tires and a straw basket. I head south along the boardwalk, past palm trees and short needles of grass. What a weird grass variety—it looks tough and spiky, like Astroturf, and it grows in sand. A group of sumo wrestlers are sunning themselves together, and their large mass creates a noticeable, fleshy, human-shaped bump in the beachscape. Children wade in the shallow water by the shore. I bike past surfing schools and parking lots and a large, shaded, treed area with a tennis court. Joggers share the trail with me, sweaty and puffing.

I keep on biking. The farther I go, the more impossible it feels to go back. Lupin Thorne will be presenting on Money and the Morphogenetic Field at 9 a.m. What does that even mean? That our relationship to money changes with our genetics? That we carry wealth and poverty in our DNA? Where does Eleven *find* these people?

Eventually, the bike path ends and I find myself on a road, with real traffic. The ocean is ever-present on Oahu—the highway is a ring around the island, a belt of asphalt that separates the shore from the jungle. As I bike, the ocean is always there, on my right. I keep pedalling. I want to find a quiet beach. I want to be away from all the Ascendants and the tourists and the stores. Is there anywhere on this whole island where there are no crowds, no stores, no restaurants?

I find a place. The beach is a small, flat pan of sand flanked by black rock. It's perfect. There are only two cars pulled into the parking strip. I push my bike through the sand and the wheels disagree with the action. The ocean makes a loud sigh with every wave. There's a figure on a stand-up paddleboard in the distance, and a fishing boat to the left of him. I watch for a whale. The water is blue, with a sapphire-blue aura. I'm skipping Lupin Thorne's presentation. I just need to be here.

The sand shines with silver and coloured light, like a dark opal. The tide is out, and the sand is wet and packed. It feels like clay under my feet. There are small holes where creatures have crawled out, or maybe the holes are made when they're still buried and breathing. I see the colours of everything together, and I feel dizzy. But I'm not afraid. I know how to handle this now. I just have to make something with the colours and let myself be present, without trying to understand where they all end and begin. It's not scary, because it's not something that's happening *to* me. I can be *part* of it.

I put my hands into the wet sand and swirl the auras up. The sand is sticky but grainy, so the mounds I make are rough at first. I'll smooth them out later. It smells like damp and salt. I make small piles and pack them together. My eyes relax as I work and I feel colour shimmering easily all around me. It's so much easier to take in the colours when I'm making something with them. It's like it doesn't even matter what the colour is; I don't have to name it or see it to understand it. I'm just in the auras, interacting with them. I have to squat down to get the curves on the sand right, and I must be squatting for some time, because my quads are burning. Finally I just sit right in the sand. It feels like sugar. Like glitter.

I use the sides of my palms to make lines and I centre my body over the whole piece to create symmetry. The palm of my hand makes a true shape. I can feel that it's a true shape by the way my hand feels in the sand—as if there's no sand or skin to separate, as if my hand has dissolved into sand, as if we are the same stuff. When I step back, I can see where the ears need to go, and how they should flip. I add some shells to her neck, but then I take them away and re-fluff it with new sand. The shells don't feel true. The sand feels true, in all the places where my hand touches it and my body leans into it.

I sit back, stretch out my legs, and look up. I made a sand-Friday! And—I swear this is really happening—it's glowing with lavender-rose light. My sculpture of Friday is so true, it has the same aura as Friday herself! I brought Friday back! The figure of my old dog stands tall, much bigger than she was in life. My blue skirt is damp and crusted with sand. My legs and arms are coated with salty grit. The sky is bright blue and the breeze sounds like bells ringing. When the waves crash onto bits of rock and shell, I hear the tinkling of miniature piano keys.

"Can I take a picture?" A young girl is standing beside me. How long has she been there? Her hair is in a messy French braid and her legs are sprinkled with fine golden hair. She wears pink flip-flops and a pink dress, and holds up a phone in a pink case. "That's cool."

"Thank you," I say.

She points her phone at the sand-Friday and touches her screen a few times. "I can see your underwear," she tells me.

"Aloha," says a man with blond dreadlocks and board shorts. I pull my legs back together and awkwardly stand up. He's with a woman in a wide-brimmed straw hat. Her arms are full of beach towels, and a canvas tote bag hangs from each of her elbows.

"Aha!" I say. I brush sand off my skirt. "So funny! I thought I was alone here."

"What are you doing?" the woman asks me.

"It's sand art," I say.

"What's it for?"

"I just felt like making it."

"Is there going to be a sand art show?" the little girl says.

"I just thought it would be fun to make something, to play in the sand."

As they walk away, the woman says, "That woman wasn't quite right."

"Totally," laughs the man. "But that dog was amazing."

"She might be some kind of savant."

"Maybe English wasn't her first language."

"I liked her sparkly hair," the little girl says. "I want to do that."

I rinse my legs off in the surf. They don't get it. That's okay. I don't care. Right now the thing that amazes me is that the sculpture of Friday literally *has Friday's aura.* When I'm painting, my subjects become a part of me—that part I knew already. But when I'm making a true piece, can it bring the subject through space and time? *This* is why Nana Boondahl was so delighted by Sophia's portrait! That's what she was singing about! She could feel the real Sophia on the paper!

The ocean laps and crashes, licks the shore, and recedes. I can't tell if the tide is going out or coming in. Eventually the waves will crash back up to this part of the beach. I leave Friday, knowing her rosy-purple aura will dissolve into the silver aura of sand again, knowing I can bring her back at any time. This is what I do. This is who I am.

◊ ◊ ◊

Back at the Royal Hawaiian, I shower and get dressed for cocktails and dinner. I skipped the entire Ascendency program today, and it's a free night tonight, with an optional evening activity planned at a dance club in Honolulu. I'm exhausted after my day on the beach, though, and I think I'll skip the outing. I put on my royal-blue romper and silver sandals and run a comb through my damp hair before going downstairs. I am so going to have a piña colada!

I return the bike key to the front desk—Derek's not there anymore, too bad—and follow the sound of women's voices outside. "I love your work," an Ascendant named Claudia says to me at the pool. She bites a skewered chunk of pineapple and chews it with pleasure. Her aura is maroon-grey. "I'm actually a certified dog psychologist." She hands me her card. "Let's stay in touch. I'd love to collaborate and heartstorm some cross-promotional ideas together."

Claudia's phone and my phone begin to wail at the same time.

Everyone's phone is wailing. A sound like a siren howls through the hotel pool and atrium area. The music has stopped. The alarm goes through the speakers at the same time as it rings through my phone. The chilling beep echoes against the marble floors and walls, and attaches itself to my spine. Across the lawn, hundreds of heads dip as the Ascendants look down at their phones.

Claudia picks her phone out of her straw handbag. "Amber Alert," she says.

The sky is deep purple. The yellow-and-white umbrellas fade and then come into focus again.

"What's happening?" I ask.

"Amber Alert," she repeats.

"What is that? What does it mean?" My phone beeps and

vibrates. A garden of noises pop and ring and bleat around me—everyone's getting texts. "Are we in trouble?" I ask.

If we are in trouble, everyone looks pretty calm. The music is playing again. The beats are mellow and languid. The Ascendants sip their drinks and laughter flutters around the pool.

"A child has gone missing," Claudia explains. "They send an alert to everyone's phone."

"Apple sends it out?"

"It's broadcast statewide. You don't have Amber Alerts in New York?"

"I thought we'd just been bombed."

"I know, it's a scary sound," she says. "Anyway, it's nice to meet you. Congratulations on your graduation!"

I check my phone. A girl is missing, age twenty-one months, last seen in a beige Toyota Sierra van. There are no children here at the Royal Hawaiian. Should I do something? Can I help? Should we start looking for the van? The auras around me are clashing, and I close my eyes so I don't see the colours of everyone around me. I picture myself sitting on soft pine needles, by a lake, surrounded by birch trees. My phone beeps again.

Yolanda
meet us in HQ

I leave my drink at the pool and then feel bad, because that means someone else has to pick it up. The Temple team is sitting around a small table in the atrium, in a quiet area surrounded by potted palms.

"Eleven wanted us to make sure to include you in tomorrow's ceremony," Yolanda says.

"Sorry to interrupt your dinner," says Monicke.

"Eleven wanted you to be included!" Anna-Mackenzie squeezes my arm. "She's giving you a special role!"

"Remember, it's a Taurus new moon," Yolanda continues. "So we'll all be in greens and browns."

"I brought a green dress," I say.

"What color green?" asks Yolanda.

"Olive green." I hope there's an iron in my room. The dress is linen, and probably wrinkled.

"That's perfect."

"Ascendant grads are going to receive a package onstage," Monicke says. Then she squints and says, "Wait, aren't we spoiling the surprise for Lilian if we tell her? She's a grad, too!"

"Are we spoiling the surprise for Lilian?" Anna-Mackenzie asks Yolanda.

"Where's Eleven right now?" I ask. My phone vibrates in the pocket of my romper. The pockets are so deep, I feel it go off on my thigh. "Did you all hear the Amber Alert just now?"

"I'm going to tell you about the surprise now instead of tomorrow," Yolanda says. She straightens her glasses. "It's a certificate, signed by Eleven. Also a gold bracelet."

"It's engraved," says Anna-Mackenzie. "We gave grads necklaces last year, but this year we're giving bracelets."

"Maybe keep what the engraving says a secret," says Monicke.

My phone vibrates down my leg again. "Did your phones all ring at once? Did you hear the alarm?"

"I turned government notifications off on my phone," Yolanda says.

"It's a scary sound," says Monicke.

Anna-Mackenzie nods. "The alerts create fear, and fear-based action."

Eleven

come meet me in my room!

"Are you okay, Canada?" asks Monicke. "Did you have enough water today? You look frazzled."

"It's been an intense day," I tell her, which isn't a lie. I don't want to say that I skipped Ascendency. These women are all taking graduation so seriously! Like what colour dress we wear onstage is a matter of life or death.

"If you want," she says, "I can help you get realigned tonight with some cranial." Her aura is light purple and a gentle aqua, swirling together in a pale dance, like drops of dye in water.

Monicke could maybe be a real friend, one day. The Temple made it seem like we were instant friends, but I don't know much about her at all, really. What do I know? Her parents are from South India, she has a brother in the Navy, she's allergic to walnuts. That's not enough. We haven't earned a friendship, yet.

"Thanks, but this is what I look like when I *am* aligned," I say to her, lamely.

Yolanda hands me a plastic hotel key card. "This is for Eleven's room. When you're in the elevator, put it in the slot and press PH."

When the elevator doors close I send Eleven a text to let her know I'm on my way. She lets me in—rather, the elevator doors open into her room. The light in the penthouse is gorgeous, and the sky is pouring in the windows. The carpet is plush and white. My feet sink into the floor with each step. The sofa is slipcovered in white linen, and two mustard-yellow pillows are poised upon it. The coffee table, a glass circle, hovers on top of thin gold legs in the shape of metal triangles. It looks like a crown.

Eleven's been burning palo santo, and the air smells like sweet woody smoke. She sits cross-legged on the carpet, wearing a white slip and a lime-green silk robe. Her aura is lighter and airier than it was in New York: it's a blend of lemon and pale blue.

"I'm so glad you're here," she says. "I want to talk to you privately before you graduate."

"I already know about the bracelets," I say. "Yolanda told me."

"Oh, Yolanda," she sighs. "She has no sense of mystery."

There are orchids everywhere. A centrepiece of white orchids, the petals spotted with deep purple as if spattered with ink, sits in a pot on the glass table. A line of purple orchids grows in an arch on top of the credenza, their petals fat and leathery. A stem of delicate pink ones, each flower no bigger than a jellybean, sits in a ceramic dish beside the sofa. A breeze comes in from an open door: there are more orchids, lime-green, standing in a white planter on the lanai. I soften my gaze and take a few deep breaths, and let their colourful auras recede just behind my field of vision, like I've been practising. I'm much better at doing this now.

A plastic card with a picture of a surfboard on it lies on a side table. "Are you going surfing?" I ask Eleven.

"I rented an SUP. I'm going on a sunrise paddle tomorrow."

I sit down on the carpet. "I missed Soul of a Goddess," I confess. "I went to the beach instead."

Eleven lifts a white porcelain carafe from a tray beside her. "Coconut water?" She pours us two glasses of cloudy liquid.

"Your aura is nice tonight," I tell her.

"*Mahalo*." She smiles.

I take a sip. It tastes sweet, but it's at room temperature, and there's a sweaty aftertaste. Coconut water is best served ice cold. "I skipped Lupin Thorne this morning, too."

"Sweetheart, the work we've been doing together *is* money and the morphogenetic field. You don't need to learn about it, you're already living it." Her aura swirls around her hair, a hovering halo of lustrous blue and yellow. "Actually, that's what I want to share with you. I've been meditating on a disturbance I've been feeling in my nervous system. Something is stirring. I believe I might be entering a new energy field."

"What does that mean?"

"I don't know," she says. "I wanted to talk to you about my ideas."

"Your aura looks great to me," I say. "Serene."

She shakes her head and puts her glass down. "You've really transformed, Lilian. I can see that you're connecting to your deep self now. You're radiating."

I want to tell her what it feels like to see auras around everything. I want to explain how I dissolved while I was making my sand-Friday, and how the silver aura of the sand turned lavender-pink when I put intention into it. If only I could put into words what I think it might mean, that I've found a way to connect to life that goes beyond death, or maybe even time itself! I want to at least *try* to start talking about these things with her, because more than anyone else on earth, I know my cousin would believe me, and understand why I need to leave the Temple.

"Some unexpected things came up for me this weekend," I start.

"I know, honey," Eleven says. "It's happening to me, too."

"This is about the auras."

"Let me just say something before you continue."

"No, let me finish. I've decided not to come to Arizona with you, because I have to work on a project of my own."

She stops me by closing her hands in namaste. "May I please say something? Before you make any big decisions?" Her voice gets low and husky. "Right now, you're at a crucial point of breakthrough. Your inner and outer worlds are expanding and colliding. There's a limitless feeling, isn't there? Like you're dissolving. Like you have no boundaries, and you're part of divine creation itself."

Her aura opens up, like sun coming out of clouds. Lemon yellow and aquamarine with a pearlescent sheen. The air above my head tingles as she speaks. What she's saying feels true.

"It's magical," she says, "but there's an edge. You're in awe, but there's also part of you that resists it, or gets frustrated when you try to understand it or explain it to anyone else. The power of creation is showing itself to be of you and inside of you. You are a part of it. It is out of your control, and that's part of its exquisite beauty. It's also what frightens you."

Her eyes are so open and clear. If I could paint her right now, her essence could become part of mine. I'd paint the shape of her face with the barest hint of transparent peach and drop brushstrokes of cadmium lemon and cobalt turquoise around her, letting them bleed out to show her light swirling. But human auras are changeable: would her colours remain stable within the piece, or would it be alive and shifting?

"And yet, here we are, living in a world that has borders," she continues. "Countries, identities, relationships, currency. The reality is, there are no limits and there *are* limits. The challenge is to hold both realities at once."

"That's what I want to tell you," I say. "I've discovered a way to see beyond those borders. The auras are limitless. Literally. Auras can exist in two places at once. When I painted Sophia's aura, it became

Sophia." I take another sip of coconut water, and shake my head. "This is warm. Do you have any ice?"

"I've known you as long as I've been alive," Eleven says. "It's rare to have a family connection that is so evolved. I mean, we can *choose* our families, because our souls know each other, and that transcends space and time. But you're my soul family *and* my real family."

Is she even listening to me? "Let me show you what I'm trying to explain," I say. "I'll paint a portrait of you. I can show you your own aura."

A small bird with grey-and-red feathers and a crisp, lettuce-green aura swoops down from nowhere, pecks at the concrete floor of the lanai, and flies away.

"What color did you see on that bird?" Eleven asks me.

"Green. Light green."

"And on me?"

"Lemon yellow. Turquoise."

"Darling, it sounds like you're cresting into a powerful shift of consciousness. You have to be careful. Remember where you were last winter? You've come so far. It could be dangerous if you leave Ascendency now, without proper support."

"I've been training myself," I say. "Practising how to be with the auras. I'm paying attention. But I'm an artist. I can't work at the Temple anymore. I have to pursue what the colours are telling me."

"Are the colors telling you where you will go?" she asks. As she speaks, her pale-aqua light turns a deeper shade of turquoise, as though more pigment has been dropped into it. "Are they telling you how you're going to make a living?"

"I want to live close to nature," I say. "I've been thinking about returning to Sudbury. To the woods." It makes sense once I say it out loud.

"You're going to be a hermit," she says.

"An artist."

"A starving artist." She sighs. "Sweetheart, I understand. I used to wish we lived in a world that operated without economics, too. But I was naive. I was fighting reality. Once I surrendered, I could see it. The reality is, money is a form of energy."

The purple orchids on the credenza face me, six of them in a line. Their aura is deep red. They remind me of Yumi. I know that sounds strange. But they do, they have expressions just like theirs. Orchids aren't just flowers—they're living beings that defy categorization. Their petal-faces look out with intelligence. These orchids see me the way Yumi did: no judgment. They used to look at me so openly, just looking, with quiet interest and mutual respect.

"When you are immersed in flow the way you are now," she continues, "your ego will step in, because it's afraid of dissolving. It's important for you to keep going. Don't quit before culmination. The moment you feel like dropping out is the moment the magic happens. I'm talking about true transformation and power. Follow the energy where it is leading you. It will feel dangerous. It will feel like you're going too far. But it's the way." Her cheeks are pink, and her eyes are sparkling. "Please trust me on this," she says.

"I've always trusted you," I say. "Now you have to trust me."

"What you're experiencing right now is a beautiful part of what the Ascendency offers. The auras you're seeing? You're accessing the beauty of divine source. Don't underestimate your role in the evolution of consciousness. Can't you feel it? Keep working with me. I have a proposal."

The breeze picks up again. From up here, the wind sounds just like the ocean. Haven't I always wanted this? Haven't I always waited for my cousin to invite me into her next impossible, beautiful plan?

"This afternoon, at the beach, I created an aura from memory," I tell her. "It came out of the sand. I'm telling you, it's like magic. The things I'm creating aren't separate from me anymore."

"I would never ask you to stop making art," Eleven says. "I only want you to share your gift with the people who need to learn from you."

I take another sip, and make a face. "How can you drink this without ice?" I say.

"Coconut water is full of electrolytes."

"And more potassium than bananas, I know. Do you have ice?"

"If you examine the thought that is telling you that coconut water has to be ice cold to be enjoyable, you'll see that it's just a thought, and you can change it," she says.

I stand up. "I'll get some," I say. There's no freezer in her bar fridge, just plastic bottles of water. I refuse to put more garbage into the Pacific Gyre! I empty my glass in the sink and get tap water instead.

"I'm sure you've noticed, I've been consumed by creativity in recent months," she says. "As long as I keep making things, I feel connected. I know you feel that way too."

I hear Yumi's voice in my mind, telling me to come back to the studio. I would love to paint a portrait of Yumi. Their aura is probably magnificent, a combination of colours that doesn't exist anywhere else. An aura that breaks the spectrum. Oh, Yumi! I don't even know what hospital you're in. Will you ever talk to me again?

"But I know that I can't follow this track of constant creation forever. Energy needs to restore itself for the cycle to regenerate."

"*Do no more than three things a day,*" I say.

"I've been asking my intuition for help, and it's been sending me significant dreams. It's becoming more clear."

The breeze from the lanai blows Eleven's curls across her face. She tucks her hair behind her ears, and the curl, swollen from the humidity, pops out again. Her eyes are dark and glassy. Is she crying?

I kneel down beside her. "Are you okay?" I ask.

"There's more that we have to do together," she says.

"I'm not disappearing from your life," I say. "I'm just not going to be an Ascendant anymore."

"You're the only one I trust with this idea," she says.

"You can trust Yolanda," I say. "She's smart. And Anna-Mackenzie, and Monicke."

"But you understand *everything*, Lilian. You and I are connected to source." She reaches over and puts her hands on my shoulders. Her aura turns from turquoise to teal, with drops of dark orange. The breeze blows through the penthouse, making the orchids flutter and shake. Their auras become more vivid, and move closer, more aggressively, into my field of vision. Eleven's hands feel dry and feverish on my skin.

The last time I saw Florence, we were twenty years old, at Grandma Bertolucci's funeral. Uncle Jimmy looked the same—tall, tanned, and bear-like. Aunt Rosie had let her hair turn silver and cut it into a severe bob. Florence wore black jeans to the funeral, a pair of scuffed-up combat boots, and an unusual black blouse. It was flouncy, with ruffles on the cuffs, gathers at the shoulders, and a Victorian collar that buttoned all the way up and covered half her neck. Her face looked as if it were carved from stone, polished, and mounted on her body. We exchanged hugs politely, paid our respects to Grandma lying in the casket with the blue-beaded rosary in her hands, and said nothing to each other.

What had happened to Florence in those lost years? And in the years after that?

All the colours in the room are brightening again, clashing with each other and starting to cloud my vision. A wave of dizzy fatigue hits my chest. Something doesn't feel true. I breathe deeply and move all the auras back into place behind my vision, where I can feel them more indirectly. Eleven adjusts her position on the floor, unfolds her legs, and tucks her feet under the opposite knees. Her toenails are painted glossy white, matching her fingernails, but her heels are dry and cracked. The base of her big toe juts out at an angle. Under the toe, a calloused pad of whitish skin has built up over the bone. Eleven's pale yellow and aqua light is gone now. A deep peacock blue oscillates around her body. The orange edges of her aura flicker in agitated little motions, like a strobe light.

"I used to be so angry at Bea for dying," Eleven says, out of nowhere. "She'd been surfing since she was thirteen. She knew the ocean so well. I couldn't understand why she'd let herself get taken by the waves."

"The ocean is unpredictable."

"I used to be angry at you, too," she says.

I look at her, startled.

"You never came back to Evansville. You never called, you never even wrote. It was like one day, you didn't exist anymore."

"Oh, Florence," I say. I think of Aunt Theresa in the forest telling me that our family's sadness has dug holes through everything, and is dripping down into us now. "You're right. I should have called you. I'm sorry."

"I'm not angry anymore," she says. "Conscious reversal: I was angry at myself. I should have come looking for you, long before now." She takes a breath. "Keep painting, Lilian. You need to make beautiful things. I misunderstood my dreams. I need to enter this new energetic field by myself."

I tell her I'm looking forward to the graduation ceremony tomorrow. We say goodnight. When I leave the penthouse suite and press the button for my floor, the elevator says, "Going down."

◊ ◊ ◊

It's Sunday morning. Graduation day. After giving it a light press with the hotel iron, I slip into my green dress. It's beaded around the neckline in a Moroccan style. It's quite short, actually. Am I too old to wear a minidress? I look in the mirror. My legs are good. My phone buzzes on the dresser.

I slept uneasily last night. From my window, the fabric of the Green Pavilion is a wedge of lime floating above the ocean. I give my hair a fluff, pull out the sparkle strands to make them stand out, and put my hotel key card in my pocket. I stand in front of the big mirror to see how short it really is. It's not *that* short. As long as I'm standing up, it's okay.

I carefully apply my bright coral lip colour, the one Yolanda picked for me to wear today. I try to do it the way she showed me. I draw an *X* on the centre of my upper lip with the tip of the lipstick, and then a small swipe on the bottom lip. It's bright! Yolanda's intense red lips always look flawless. Can I pull this off? I blot it with a tissue. The orange pigment makes my eyes look more blue. Yumi always noticed the colour of my eyes.

Finally, I put on my graduation ceremony lei, a string of green and white orchids that was delivered to all Ascendants last night. The petals look fresh and alive, and glow with an aura that's the same colour as the green flowers. Apparently, unlike other cut flowers, orchid petals can absorb moisture and nutrients from the air. For such a delicate-looking plant, orchids are pretty smart and tough. My phone buzzes again.

Yolanda
30 mins. Meet backstage at the Grim pavlova.

Me
got it!

I look up #orchid on Instagram. A grid of blooms appears. I scroll through them until I find a pic of speckled purple ones that also remind me of Yumi. These have spots, as well as fine stripes. The mouth of the orchid looks like a beetle. The more I stare at it, the more I feel a craving to draw it. I can make time.

I start in the centre and pencil out the wings of the beetle, the mouth of the flower. The line traces the tongue and I follow it up to the nose, or beak—what is that?—the very centre of the orchid, where it's completely white. I draw the circle of it, the nib, and see that there is colour there. A faint green tinge. Like it's the place in the flower that gets energy from the stem and the leaves. My pencil lines feel true. I trace out from there and follow the lines that radiate out. The orchids around my neck rise and fall with my breath as I draw. My phone buzzes and a message pops up.

Yolanda
15 minutes

Me
K!

Do I have time to use a bit of paint? I open my travel paint kit and use the hotel water glass to wet my brush. I make careful drops of purple on the edges of the petals—and draw them in with the very tip of my brush. I tease the colour into the beetle-like centre and leave lots of white space around it. I darken just the edge of that centre, go over it again to show the sharp fangs of the orchid through contrast. The edges of my body crystallize and dissolve into white specks. I dip my brush in the water so the colour is diluted and then lightly brush a lavender wash over parts of the fan-like petals. Finally, I place three spots over top of the wash. They bleed and soar into each other. Each petal is as deep as a galaxy. Yumi!

My heart is beating. The painting has the pale-blue aura of the flower itself. I snap a picture of it and post it on Twitter.

@LilianQuick> this is for you, @ReKnits.
#orchids #watercolour #watercolor #friendship #love

I try to send Yumi a private message on Instagram, but I can't find their account. They've disappeared from Facebook, too. They have unfriended me.

◊ ◊ ◊

The Green Pavilion is shaped like a huge shell, the mouth of which faces the ocean. It stands on steel legs, crisscrossed with steel rein-forcements. It's capped with a shining bright green awning, stretched tight over steel rods like a big umbrella. Breakfast concluded half an hour ago, and the women are now gathered in front of the stage.

As I approach, I hear the Ascendants singing. Rashira Metha is leading them in her Ritual of Voice workshop to open our gradua-tion ceremony. Hundreds of women are standing with their backs to the ocean, their hands on their hearts, eyes closed, mouths open.

"Sing into your third eye," calls Rashira. "Now slide up, up, up. Slide up, and sing into the space above your forehead."

The voices come together in a sweet and buzzing way, an *aaaaaaaahhhhh* made of hundreds of different threads twisting into one thick rope of sound.

"Imagine that you are singing in a sacred temple. The walls of the temple are silvery with moonlight. You are singing the silver light. It comes out of your mouth. When you open your mouth to sing, you coat the walls with silver."

"Aaaaaaaaaahhhhhh!" the women sing.

"Are you Lilian Quick?" A large woman in a fluttery yellow dress puts her hand on my arm. She's barefoot and wears a gold *E* necklace wrapped around one ankle. Her aura is a soft yellow-pink mixed with a warm brick red.

"Yes," I say.

She pulls out her phone. "I love your blog. I have a shel-tie at home—his name is Toast—and I've always wanted to get a Quick+Friday aura portrait done. And now you aren't painting any-more!" Her dress blows in the wind, sticking itself to her curvy shape. Triangular ruffles drape over her breasts like bunting, and the way they drift together gently in the breeze reminds me of dahlia petals. "I knew I shouldn't have waited. Now it's too late."

"I'd love to paint Toast," I say.

"You would?"

"I'm painting again," I say. "We can do a sitting on Skype."

"Oh, thank you!" she beams. "Can I please take a selfie of us? Would you mind? My name is Jessamyn." She moves beside me and puts an arm over my shoulder. Her arm is warm and loafy, sunbaked. Her skin smells like coconut and pineapple. "Where are you from?" I ask her.

"Jonestown, North Dakota," she says.

"Do you like it there?"

"Of course! It's my home," she says. She snaps several pictures of us. Where is my home? I see snow-covered rocks, pine trees, and spindly white birch trees. My phone buzzes in my pocket.

Yolanda

is Eleven with you

Me

No!

An icicle slides down my spine and lands with a nauseous ache in my stomach.

"I'm so glad I met you, Jessamyn," I say. "Tag me in that so I can see it." She smiles, and the light of her aura flares from brick to poppy red.

"Happy graduation!" she says, but I'm already running to the Green Pavilion.

◊ ◊ ◊

Yolanda, Monicke, and Anna-Mackenzie circle around a clothing rack backstage. Yolanda is looking at the floor, breathing as she paces. The pendants on Monicke's long necklaces clink together on her chest as she follows Yolanda around the small space, arms out, trying to reiki her. Yolanda exhales noisily. Anna-Mackenzie stands still, smiling without rest. They barely notice me when I arrive.

"Where is she?" I ask. They look at me.

"We thought with you," says Monicke.

"She's not in her room?"

"No," says Anna-Mackenzie. "She's not in her room."

The floor is made of a spongy material that bounces a little when you step on it. I check my phone just to see if there's anything from her, even though I know there isn't. Nothing since her last text: *Come meet me in my room!*

There's applause and shrieking from the stage as the Ascendants finish Ritual of Voice. Rashira parts the green curtains and joins us backstage. She has short dark hair in a bowlish cut, and wears small round glasses. Strands of tinkling gold coins are looped around her waist, and her aura is hot purple with bright blue. She brings the energy of the crowd with her, and I feel a rush, as though a jet has taken off from my chest.

"She's not coming," I say.

"What?" Yolanda looks up.

"She tried to tell me last night. I didn't get it." I grab a headset from the caddy and slip it over my head. "Can you do my mic?" I turn around so she can clip the battery to my dress.

"She has to be here," Yolanda says.

"There's no time—do me up."

"You need a belt," Anna-Mackenzie says. "It's too flimsy, it won't hold otherwise."

"What are you going to do?" Yolanda asks me. "Eleven usually gives the lighthouse talk to graduates."

Anna-Mackenzie starts twisting strands of my hair around her fingers and spraying them with something. "Do you know it?" she asks. "*You've become a beacon of light. In this storm, you lead the way with your stillness.*" She dusts powder on my cheeks. "I like the bright lips. You're not wearing mascara?"

Eleven's belt is too big for me. It's a wide, metallic gold elastic band.

"That's too big for her," says Monicke. I feel her hands pulling my shoulder blades back, so I stand up straight. "Open up your chest," she says. I breathe.

"I'm clipping it," says Yolanda.

"You can sling it over her hips."

"The mic pack will slide."

"Breathe into your feet. Breathe into the ground. Feel your roots growing through the floor, into the center of the earth."

One of the hotel workers carries a tall stack of cardboard boxes backstage. Several paper shopping bags hang from his elbows. "Where should I put these?" he asks.

Yolanda tests the belt by cinching her hands over my waist and wiggling it lightly. "Did you find Winnie?" she asks Anna-Mackenzie.

"I found her!" she says. "We have cupcakes!"

"These are the cupcakes," the man says.

Yolanda looks at me. "Do you *know* where she is?"

Her forest-green aura is contrasting loudly with Anna-Mackenzie's white-pink and Monicke's purple-green. All their colours, together with what's emanating from the stage and the mic and everything else, clamour in my eyes like flashing lights. I do not know where Eleven is. I do not know the lighthouse talk. I do not have mascara.

I close my eyes. What did Eleven say last night? Think. Were there clues that I missed? The palo santo in the air. Her silk robe. A new energy field. The orchids surrounded her like guardians, facing me with those silent stares. I knew something wasn't right when I felt her colours change frequency and turn vivid and flickering. What was she trying to tell me?

I pull the auras back, and centre my eyes on what's under all the coloured light. Anna-Mackenzie hands me a heavy cedar box carved with hummingbirds. It's the size of a shoebox. Yolanda pats me on my lower back. It could be a supportive pat, or just a mic-pack test.

"The first fifty are in there," Anna-Mackenzie says. "I'll come out with the next fifty when you're ready."

Monicke puts one hand on my heart and one hand on top of my head. "You've got this, Canada."

I step through the green curtains. When I look out at the women, a wave of colours crashes up to my face. They're all staring at me. I'm flooded with their clashing auras, and the light slams into my chest, threatening to knock the wind out of me. Ascendants from previous years are here, too. There's Violet, front row, wearing a sheer, iridescent bathing suit cover-up. There's Jessamyn, unmissable in bright yellow. Shona and Matilde and Anoosh are all standing together. When they see me, they raise their hands and cheer. The sound catches on, and the whole crowd joins in. The women's mouths open, and sound comes out like a chorus of beautiful, howling-singing birds. They're all in dresses and flowy clothes, and the breeze blows the fabric around, turning them all into petals.

I take off my flip-flops and stand on the spongy surface of the stage in bare feet, to steady myself. I look out at the hundreds of women. They look back at me, and their colours smash together. The colour waves fractal out infinitely, the way clouds form in the sky, the way soy milk curdles in coffee.

Behind them, the ocean is also moving. The waves are bright blue inside and outside, above and below, both water and light. It's all moving colour, and my body receives it by vibrating.

"Hello. My name is Lilian Quick," I say. The mic takes my voice and shakes it before throwing my words out from the stage. It's loud! It echoes through my muscles. The Ascendants are an ocean before the ocean—the first a kaleidoscope of chaotic colour, the other a glimmering field of blue.

"You've become a beacon of light. In this storm, you lead the way with your stillness," I say. I breathe in the dizzying colours and try to steady myself. I exhale the blue of the ocean's aura. There's a prickling sensation as I exhale. There's so much more than blue in that blue. What else can I say about a lighthouse? "A lighthouse shows others the way to safety in an uncertain world."

Flecks of silver and pink light glitter in the ocean waves. The colours open and bloom and then disintegrate into the surf. A swath of burnt orange specks blink on and off like fireflies. A purple glow emanates and fades, emanates and fades. Crabs! Clams! All the creatures in the sand and water! What is the pink light? It must be fish. The ocean is blue and breaking apart into filaments. There is no pattern, but the colour moves together like a symphony. All the blinking and fading is happening at once, with a layer of bright sea-blue, the water and the light together.

Oh! All of you women have become a field of fragmented colour lights! I wish you could see it!

"Keep going—every woman has a beacon within herself," Yolanda says from behind the curtain.

"It's stage fright," says Monicke. "Breathe in and out, Canada."

"She's just nervous," says Anna-Mackenzie.

"Open the box and start calling names," says Yolanda. "Do you want me to do it?"

"She's fine," says Anna-Mackenzie. "Just open the box, Lilian. You're doing great."

I still the auras of the women and the ocean and everything around me again, moving them back behind my vision so I can focus. "Every woman has a beacon within herself," I repeat Yolanda's words, but I don't know what's supposed to come after that.

The wooden box is quivering with beautiful light: rose, mint, plum, sunset yellow and orange, multiple glowing blues and purples. I let my eyes linger over the colours and feel them tickle my chest, my throat, my cheeks. This lets the auras from the crowd come forward again and dance around my vision, lighting up everything. The podium, the floor, the box, my hands—it's all becoming coloured light.

I part the colours again, and send the light away. "When we were growing up, my cousin was my lighthouse," I say. I've said "lighthouse" so many times already. The word starts to sound funny. Lighthouse. Lighthouse. Lighthouse. Lighthouse. What does that even mean? It's just a collection of sounds. Language! It doesn't even work!

There's something on the horizon, in the darker blue of the ocean, way beyond the people, far beyond the shore. A puff of white—there and then gone. A thumbprint of orange light hovers over the faraway line between ocean and sky. It's a whale! It must be huge, if I can see its aura from here. The rhythm of the waves reaches me through the humming colours of the Ascendants' auras, all the way to the back of my eyes, where I have contained them.

It's become very quiet. All I can hear is the sound of the ocean. Everyone is listening to me, waiting for me to continue. The force of the women in front of me is benevolent. Their bodies and eyes are plugged-in, happy, and electric. I'm safe. I can do this.

I soften my gaze, open my peripheral vision, and release all the auras.

I awaken to a full symphony of coloured light in front of me: magenta, gold, olive, sapphire, ivory, leafy green and coffee brown, violet, peach, and straw. The infinite variants of coloured light swirl out as far as my vision reaches. The waves continue their blue journey forever. The women's arms are by their sides, spinning pinwheels of coloured auras that rise above their bodies and swirl into the air. *Lighthouse, lighthouse, lighthouse.* I start to giggle. There's no escape from the auras. They're always here, they've always been here. All my life, I've been holding them back.

"I want to tell you my favourite poem." I smile at the crowd. "This is by the Canadian poet Nana Boondahl." How does it go again?

May you taste the V-shape of your life
May you know why it is held that way:
In the paws of the wolf, the tongue of the snake,
The closed eyes of the tiniest rodent.
It is in your nature—
The rising and falling and rising—
It is yours. Use it
even when you think you know god.
You don't know
the first thing about god!

The Ascendants move from side to side as a bundle as though they're all on a raft, floating in the waves. The colours of everything fluctuate peacefully. There's no more chaos. I relax in the flickering, glowing light. Did I actually remember the poem out loud? Nice!

"Let me go out there," I hear Yolanda say. "She doesn't know what she's doing."

"She's okay," says Monicke. "Don't worry, she's going to ground herself."

"Please protect Lilian with light and love," Anna-Mackenzie prays out loud.

"Where is Eleven?" Yolanda says.

"Monicke," I call, and turn to look through the dark opening in the green curtain behind me. "Can you give me some music? Something slow and alive. Something that sounds . . . violet and blue, please."

"Whatever you say, Canada." Monicke laughs.

I wait a moment for the sound to start. It does. It's good. Solid, smooth beats. The auras are surrounding me. I let myself be present, and trust that the right words will come in the moment.

"When you're doing the stuff we've all been doing, as Ascendants, you begin to vibrate differently. I know you've all felt this, being here together this weekend. Maybe it's because we're all drinking more water, and water is what . . . the ocean is made of. Right? Where I come from, the Great Lakes area, I mean, the water is so big, there's so much when you look out at one of these big lakes, it's *like* looking at an ocean. Lakes, oceans. *Water* is what I'm talking about, here."

I'm okay, just a bit awkward. The colours are still slow-spinning and calm.

Then the ocean gives me a signal. It crashes me a wave. There are millions of sea creatures in the waves. I feel them winking at me. The music huffs and caramels around the stage. A saxophone riffs and repeats, a textured sound like houndstooth. I'm fine! The words are coming to me!

"Those are just my thoughts on why we should all drink more water. That should be in the Prayer! Because think about *Dance about it*. See, when we dance about it, we are connecting to . . . life force. You ever see a field of grass in the wind? It's dancing. When we dance about something, I think we are connecting to the same force that moves *everything*. Like, we are the blades of grass and the wind is our *life*."

"That's enough," says Yolanda. "They aren't following you. Stop there."

"Calm down," says Monicke. "She's doing great. Look, they're loving it."

There's a burn in my throat telling me I should keep going. I don't know where Eleven is right now, but I'm going to do right by her. I feel the radiant blues and greens and oranges and pinks of the people and the stage and the ocean and the land, and I let all the colour curl around me so it supports my body. The women are silently staring at me. They're feeling my pause. I'm holding their energy by *being* their energy!

"You know what part of the Ascendency Prayer has been hard for me, though?" I continue. "*Create before you consume.* Anybody with me on this? I wake up wanting to consume, you know? But when I think about it—"

There's another white puff on the horizon. White against blue. The afterimage of orange light. It hovers over the ocean and disappears.

"When I think about creating, I mean. When I think about making art . . ." This box is starting to get heavy. Someone carved this box by hand. The hummingbirds have jewels for eyes—small bright crystals glued into little divots in the wood.

"What I mean is, we all have art to make." That makes sense, right?

I open the box. There are rows and rows of names printed on thick white cards. Each card is actually a small envelope. Small prismatic auras hover over each of the envelopes. Pretty!

"Ascendants, we've graduated," I say. "And now, our life becomes our art! Please come up when I call your name."

"Thank God," says Yolanda.

"Amen," says Anna-Mackenzie.

"Alisha!" I say.

I've never met Alisha. Who is she? I scan the crowd. A wide-brimmed hat rises from a middle row. The woman approaches the steps at the foot of the stage and grins at me. Her lips are stained the matte hot pink of dyed pistachios. Her aura is cornflower blue and golden-green. I hand this woman the envelope with her name on it. "Congratulations on graduating Ascendency," I say. I push my cheek to her cheek and she squeezes my shoulders.

"You're far out," she says to me.

"Angie!" I call out next. Two women approach the stage. There are two Angies in the box! How will I know which is which? It doesn't matter. "Okay, one at a time," I say, and I give each one an envelope.

Eventually, Anna-Mackenzie comes out with the next box, and a little stool appears, so I can rest the box down. I call out all the names of all the graduates. It takes a long time. When I get to L, there's only one Lillian there—Lillian with two l's. It's my friend from seat F11! I give her the envelope.

"You're *so inspiring*!" she yells at me, with a wide smile. I can see her aura—chartreuse and grass green.

After I call Yasmin and Zara, the last box is almost empty. The remaining envelope is heavier than the others. In Eleven's handwriting, it reads, *For Lilian Quick*. I slip this envelope into the pocket of my green dress and look out at the crowd.

"Monicke, can you turn the music off?" The beat fades out until there's nothing coming out of the speakers. The waves won't stop. The ocean is breathing blue light, and prisms of colour are exploding within each wave. How can I be the only one seeing this beauty?

"Turn around," I tell the women. I move my hand in a circle to show them. "Turn around. That's right. Look!"

A few women look over their shoulders and then back to the stage. I move my hand, point my finger out at the horizon. "Look," I say. "Look!"

Why won't they take their eyes off me? Why do they refuse to *look*?

Anoosh, Shona, and Matilde move together as one unit. Friend-groups begin to move together, and then entire rows. They turn around in clumps. More and more women turn their backs to me until finally, they're all looking away.

"Can you see it? Let your eyes relax, and take it in."

My hand feels for the envelope in my pocket. The envelope is the size of a credit card but heavier. There's something inside. I pull it out, slide my thumb under the seal, and open it. The contents slide into my palm, and my eyes sting with hot tears.

The crowd bubbles and gasps with shock. Right in front of the stage, not one but *two* humpback whales ease up out of the water and dive down again. The air is saturated with their potent orange auras. They're so close! We're all bathing in marmalade light. It covers the crowd. Impossibly, the two whales flip their tails at the same time, like they're waving goodbye.

The back of the brooch is cut in half by the line of its pin, fastened with a safety clasp. My throat throbs when I turn it over. The pear is shining just as I remember it, set with pink and green iridescent rhinestones. I'm lying next to Florence on the floor of the abandoned house, telling her I believe her. Time folds in half: it's as if I'm holding pieces that fell out of a dream. The walls of my stomach cave in.

I wipe my tears away with one hand. Florence has always seen what's true about me. She kept this for me, all these years? The rhinestone pin has a glistening, hot-pink aura. It almost hurts to look at it. It hits my eyes like an electric shock.

I'm looking at my own aura.

The colour is so shiny. It's velvety and warm. Looking at it feels like eating ripe raspberries. I melt into my hot-pink light and watch it surround me like an iridescent bubble. My disbelief braids into joy. I am surrounded by pink light. It's always been here! I've just never seen it before!

"Separateness is an illusion!" I cry out to the backs of the Ascendants, all of them looking out toward the ocean now. "You are a part of everything you see!"

The Ascendants raise their beautiful arms, make flags out of the sleeves of their dresses. They are clapping and singing to the whales. Their hands are waves crashing. The light of my own aura is harmonious with the auras of the women, which are superimposed on the aura of the ocean, pure blue, sparkling and glistening from the throbbing multicoloured lights of life it carries inside itself. My eyes can't make sense of it, and I finally stop trying to control it. I float up through my own light, the rosy bubble lifting me up to the green skin of the pavilion, and then the pavilion is gone. Eleven will come back one day. Or not. *Lighthouse, lighthouse, lighthouse, lighthouse.* There's nothing else I have to do here. I've always belonged to the auras. I give myself to making, and I become what I make. The colours of the Universe run together. All the edges dissolve.

Acknowledgements

THANK YOU THANK YOU THANK YOU

Samantha Haywood, my agent and my compass, for seeing this book from the very start and nurturing it when it was just barely even a thing. Because you believed I could write it, I did.

Jennifer Lambert and Lea Beresford, my smart and gifted editors—for pushing me in all the right ways, and for illuminating so much of what was hidden. Sarah Wight, my extraordinary copy-editor, and Natalie Meditsky, my patient production editor—your attention to detail is superb.

Hannah Williams, my earliest reader and beacon, who read the roughest, weirdest first draft of this story and pretended it was a really good book. Because of your spirit, I found the courage to finish it.

Sarah Henstra, Miranda Hill, Heather Jessup, Ronit Jinich, Carrie Klassen, Jill Margo, Jessica Moore, Trish Osuch, Lana Pesch, Frances Phillips, Erin Robinsong, Jennifer Schramm, Ainsleigh Spencer, Margaux Weisman, and Wendy Woods, my generous early readers, writing companions, and guides. You made this book better, and writing it would have been lonely and difficult without your help.

Jayson Biggins, Natalie Foley, Frances Phillips, Carrie Schiffler, Kate Golding, Johnny Lam, and Warren Sheffer, who offered me space to write in their homes. Krista Dalby and Small Pond Arts in Picton, Ontario, The Banff Centre Leighton Studios, Vito Zingarelli, Jessika Auerbach and Hedgebrook in Tuscany, for giving writers sanctuary. You all took such good care of me.

All of the writers who are part of the Sarah Selecky Writing School community, also known as Story Is a State of Mind, especially my school's phenomenal teachers, who guide our students through the Story Intensive each year—I'm inspired by your bravery, creativity, and openheartedness every single day.

Francesca Lia Block, Zsuzsi Gartner, Ruth Ozeki, Ann Patchett, George Saunders, and Neil Smith, for their wisdom and encouragement, and for speaking so honestly with me in their Master Classes.

Al Watt, who teaches humanely about the mystery and structure of story and shares his insight generously in his books and on his website. Kelly Diels, who coined the term "Female Lifestyle Empowerment Brand" and confronts this subject deftly on her website.

Karen Joy Fowler, who gave me invaluable feedback on the first chapter of this book, and revolutionary writing advice that I will live by now and forever.

Special thanks to Margaret Atwood for giving me an unforgettable year of generous mentorship and the place to write the first draft of this novel.

To Satva Hall, for planting the seed that grew into the idea for this book.

Mary Jane Selecky, for supporting my writing, always.

Ryan Henderson, with love, for *everything*.